SISTER *of the* LIONHEART

A NOVEL IN THE TIME OF THE CRUSADES

SISTER *of the* LIONHEART

A NOVEL IN THE TIME OF THE CRUSADES

Hilary Benford

Hilary Benford

WordFire Press
Colorado Springs, Colorado

SISTER OF THE LIONHEART
Copyright © 2016 Hilary Benford

ISBN: 978-1-61475-420-6

Cover painting, "God Speed" by Richard Leighton (1900)

Cover design by Duong Covers

Art Director Kevin J. Anderson

Book Design by RuneWright, LLC
www.RuneWright.com

Published by
WordFire Press, an imprint of
WordFire, Inc.
PO Box 1840
Monument CO 80132

Kevin J. Anderson & Rebecca Moesta, Publishers

WordFire Press Trade Paperback Edition June 2016
Printed in the USA
wordfirepress.com

MAP OF FRANCE IN THE TWELFTH CENTURY

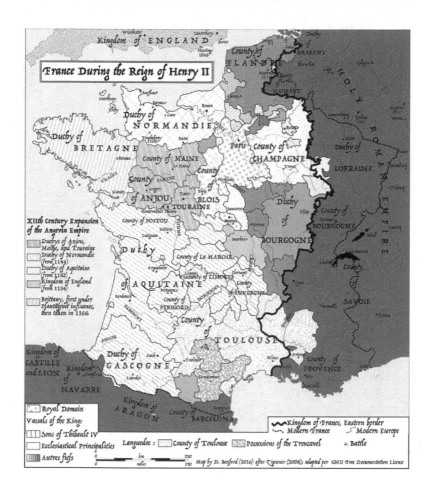

ROYAL FAMILIES OF
ENGLAND & FRANCE IN 1170

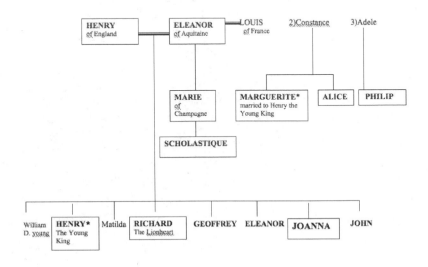

- Personages in bold appear in this book.
- Eleanor of Aquitaine married twice; first to King Louis of France (two daughters), second to King Henry of England (8 children)

List of Characters

In Poitiers

Joanna: princess of England, daughter of King Henry and Eleanor of Aquitaine

Queen Eleanor: in her own right, Duchess of Aquitaine, married to Henry of England, previously married to King Louis of France

Eleanor: Joanna's older sister, later married to King Alfonso of Castile

Young Henry: oldest son of Henry and Eleanor, heir to the throne of England

Marguerite: married to young Henry, daughter of Louis of France by his second wife

Richard: son of Henry and Eleanor, heir to the Duchy of Aquitaine

Alice: betrothed to Richard, daughter of Louis of France, younger sister of Marguerite

Geoffrey: son of Henry and Eleanor

Constance: daughter of the Count of Brittany, betrothed to Geoffrey

Nounou: Joanna's nurse, a Norman woman whose given name is Jeanne

Sir William Marshal: champion of tournaments, made Master of Young Henry's household

Marie: Countess of Champagne, daughter of Louis of France and Eleanor of Aquitaine, half-sister to Joanna

Scholastique: daughter of Marie of Champagne

Master Hubert: a pastry cook

Chrétien de Troyes: a poet in Marie of Champagne's train

Sir Ralph: the seneschal (steward) at Poitiers

André: chaplain to Marie of Champagne, tutor to the royal children, author of the Code of Love

In other parts of France

Henry: Joanna's father, King of England, Duke of Normandy, Count of Anjou, married to Eleanor of Aquitaine, based in Winchester, England, but moving all over his French possessions

Raymond de Saint-Gilles: son and heir to Count Raymond of Toulouse and a friend of Richard's in Toulouse

King Louis: of France, in Paris

Philip: son and heir to King Louis, in Paris, born the same year as Joanna

Mother Audeburge: Abbess of Fontevrault

In Winchester

John: youngest child of King Henry and Queen Eleanor

Adèle: daughter of the Baron de Laigle, a lady-in-waiting to Joanna

In Palermo (Panorme to the Normans)

William: King of Sicily (which included Naples and the southern part of Italy), of the house of Hauteville in Normandy

Queen Margaret: mother of King William, formerly a princess of Navarre

Constance: aunt of William and his heir, later Holy Roman Empress

Count Tancred of Lecce, bastard cousin of William

Sybilla: wife of Tancred

Walter: Archbishop of Panorme, a Norman

Nicholas of Athens, Chamberlain of Joanna's household

Matthew: William's Chancellor, originally a notary from Salerno, thus a Sicilian

Caid Richard: William's Great Chamberlain, a Saracen and a eunuch

Richard Palmer: Bishop of Syracuse, an Englishman

Count Roger of Andria: a Norman

Ahmed: William's physician, an Arab

Part One
France 1168

CHAPTER ONE

February, a cold cloudy day with no wind. In the royal apartment of the great Abbey of Fontevrault, Joanna and her older sister Eleanor watched from an upper window as their mother, Queen Eleanor, left for Poitiers. The stone sill was slippery from the mist and Joanna's nurse held onto her to keep her from falling out. Below them, the horses and men of the escort churned the Abbey bailey into a mud pond. Smells of horse dung came up to the girls at the open window and the sounds of jingling harnesses and snorting horses mingled with murmured conversations below. Joanna took her hands from the cold sill and rubbed them together to warm them. She wiped her nose on her sleeve. Everything felt clammy and dank.

Joanna saw her father, King Henry, mounted already and riding up and down impatiently. As usual, it looked as if he had tossed his clothes on in a hurry. His cloak was slipping off one shoulder and his tunic looked all crumpled. He never cared about such things. Yet, despite the fact that the men around him were richly dressed, a stranger would have known which was the King.

As he wheeled his horse around, the knights fell back, allowing him room. He was clearly in a bad mood and nobody wanted to get in his way. He sat hunched forward in the saddle, his bull neck sunk into his heavy shoulders. His complexion was always ruddy, but he looked more than usually high-colored today, either from anger or the cold air.

"In God's name, where is the Queen?" he bellowed suddenly, catching sight of Queen Eleanor's maid who had emerged from the Abbey with a leather box in her hands. The King rode straight at her and for a moment, it looked as though he would run her down. Joanna gasped, but Amaria had known him for years and, although she sank into a curtsey, she held her ground. The King swung by inches from her and reined in. His horse snorted and shook its head and he automatically calmed it, laying a hand in its heavy leather gauntlet on the horse's mane.

"She's coming immediately, my Lord King," Amaria said, rising.

"Immediately? Sweet Lord, I know her idea of immediately. Tell your mistress I'll wait no longer for her. If she's not here in a cock's crow, I'll leave without her, by God I will."

"Sire." Amaria inclined her head and turned back.

At that moment, silence fell upon the bailey. The blacksmith stopped hammering, the knights and men stopped talking and laughing. It was as though they had been frozen in place, one with a mug of ale halfway to his mouth, another with one foot in the stirrup about to mount. All eyes turned to the entrance of the royal apartments. Joanna almost fell from the window, craning to see what they were looking at. Then Queen Eleanor rode into view.

She was in her late forties, but she sat her horse with an ease and grace that few women half her age could muster. She should have been an old woman, but somehow she was not. People sometimes speculated whether she had indeed renewed her grandmother's pact with the devil. She was still beautiful. If she had gray in her hair or lines on her neck, her wimple hid them. For the rest, her face was as gay and her back as erect as a young woman's. She was riding astride her horse, a fine black mare, and wearing a skirt that was not a skirt, but divided in two. It outlined her thighs and hung loosely to her ankles. Over this, she wore a man's knee length divided tunic and a jeweled belt low on her hips. The whole extraordinary costume was of fine white wool heavily embroidered with gold thread and over it a crimson ermine-lined mantle held in place by a huge ruby brooch.

The King straightened up and opened his mouth as though to speak, then closed it again. She stopped perhaps six feet from him and they stared at each other. The girls could not see her expression as her back was toward them, but they could see their father's and it frightened them. The Queen turned her horse's head and for a terrible moment Joanna thought she was going to lead the way out through the gate, but even she was not as bold as that. She walked her horse around in a circle as though challenging everyone to see and admire her. Some of the younger knights seemed to admire, but the older men were plainly scandalized.

Without a word or a signal, King Henry set spurs to his horse and galloped through the gates. His bodyguard raced to catch up with him and the vanguard crashed into each other trying to get out in front. The Queen's guard assembled around her and with much clanking of arms and jingling of spurs, the rest of the men fell in behind them and they all moved off. As she reached the gate, the Queen turned back and Joanna saw her face for a moment. She was laughing like a girl.

It was not to see the children that she turned. She had forgotten to say goodbye to them.

"Well!" Nurse exclaimed, letting out a long breath.

Joanna came suddenly back to her present surroundings. In imagination, she had been riding high and proud beside her mother on the muddy road south to Poitiers. Beyond the Abbey walls, she could see the Queen's red mantle hanging down over the mare's black tail, the only spot of color in the gray-green, mist-shrouded landscape.

"I have *never* seen anything so scandalous! Sitting astride a horse like a man, it's not right, it's—downright sinful! And that costume—in all my born days—if I had known, I would never have let you watch. Well, great ladies have their whims, but that's beyond all. Dress it up how she will with gold thread and all, those were *breeches* and it's against God's law for a woman to dress as a man."

"I thought she looked splendid," Joanna asserted boldly.

Nurse shook her soundly. "Splendid, you little ninny! Shameless, more like. She's your mother and she's the Queen, but I'm bound to say it, though don't you ever tell her I said so. Someone must care for your immortal soul to keep it from the fiery pits ..."

Eleanor and Joanna started to giggle as they usually did when Nurse started on the fiery pits.

"Come to the fire, come away from the window, you'll catch your deaths." She sat heavily on a bench by the fire and held out her hands to the glow. "Page, it needs more logs! What, are you dreaming? Come on, come on, children, warm yourselves. Your hands are quite red with cold, Joanna."

She took Joanna's hands and rubbed them vigorously between her own. The numbness in them gave way to stabbing needles of pain.

"Ouch! That hurts, Nounou," Joanna protested.

Nurse took no notice. "It's a sorry business, the whole thing. I don't know what the world is coming to, a wife leaving her husband and setting up court on her own, it's unheard-of. That's what it is, for all that the Earl of Salisbury is there to keep an eye on her, she's off to rule on her own, and why King Henry allows it, I can't imagine. A whistling woman and a crowing hen ..."

"Aquitaine is her own fief," Eleanor pointed out. "She is King Louis' vassal for Aquitaine and Poitou."

"She's a married woman. Vassals and fiefs notwithstanding, it's her husband's place to rule them. Who ever heard of a woman ruling anything? It's not natural. Look at the trouble it caused in England when your grandmother Matilda tried to set herself up as Queen. War and fighting and suffering and it never did *her* any good, they put Stephen on the throne anyway." Nurse wagged her head dolefully and Eleanor went off into giggles again.

Joanna stared solemnly at them. "But *why* is it bad for Mother to ride astride?" she said, reverting to the original issue, which was not yet satisfactorily clear in her head. "Would God *really* make her go to Hell for that?"

Nurse seemed to recollect herself. "It's not my place to criticize my superiors," she said primly and pursed her lips.

"But you just did!" Joanna pointed out. Grown-ups could be very confusing at times. "*I've* ridden astride, behind the soldiers. Is that bad? No one told me not to."

"You're only a child, that's different. You'd fall off if you tried to ride sidesaddle, as like as not."

"You mean," said Joanna, pouncing on this, "that it's easier and safer to ride astride?"

"Of course."

"Then why do women have to ride the difficult way? That's not fair."

"Fair! Easy! It's not a question of that. It's a question of what's modest and seemly. *And*," she added, as Joanna opened her mouth to argue further, "the worst fault a woman can have is to be argumentative and obstinate, as you show every sign of becoming. No, not another word!"

Joanna closed her mouth and frowned. Her mother was Queen of England and Duchess of Aquitaine. She was tall and beautiful and imperious and Joanna could not imagine that anything she did was wrong. She admired her mother more than anyone in the world.

Yet she loved Nounou. Nounou had loved her and cared for her since she was born, had sat up at night with her when she was sick, had fed her and dressed her and played with her, had prayed for her and with her every night that she could remember. Nounou would never lie to her. If Nounou said that women should be modest and quiet and submissive, it must be right. And yet her mother was none of these things. Was there a special dispensation for Queens? Joanna looked thoughtfully across the hearth at her nurse. Nounou sat with her knees apart, her pudgy hands held out to the blaze. She was not even noble, after all, let alone royal. How could she know what was right or wrong for a Queen? Painfully, Joanna struggled to sacrifice Nounou's omniscience for her mother's impeccability. She hunched her shoulders and wrapped her arms around her knees and stared into the fire.

CR ❀ ℬ

Eleanor and Joanna left Fontevrault some weeks later with their households to join the Queen in Poitiers. It was early March and a glittery, bright, rain-washed morning. The girls had furs tucked around them in the litter they shared. They laughed together about the poor horses that were to bear the weight of Nurse's litter and laughed again when they moved off and the rocking motion of the litter tumbled them together.

For the first part of the way, Joanna was alert and excited. It was still early, not long after Prime, and they had twenty miles or more to go before they reached the royal castle of Mirebeau, where they were to sleep that night. Joanna had never been on such a long journey except when, as a baby, she had gone from Angers, the city of her birth, to Fontevrault and, of course, she did not remember that. So now she looked around her eagerly and plied Eleanor with questions that the older girl tried patiently to answer.

The sun was not yet far above the horizon. Its angled rays struck light off the windows of the Abbey church and its great gilt cross. Joanna craned behind her to watch it recede.

"See how little it looks, Eleanor? And the houses—just like little toys."

"Don't lean over so far, you'll tip us out. And you're letting all the cold air in under the furs," Eleanor said.

"Look over there, see that man pushing his wife in a wheelbarrow? No, *there*! Yes, isn't that funny? He's pushing her to work in a wheelbarrow!"

Peasants fanned out across the fields around them, their bent heads wrapped in dark hoods, their arms folded against the cold. The ploughs turned over heavy clods of earth and magpies followed them, skimming the furrows in search of worms. In the fallow fields, sheep were grazing and at the fields' edges, up against the hedgerows, wild flowers grew among the ragged grasses, daisies and anemones and pale primroses. Fresh green leaves showed on the hedges and spiders' webs, glittering with raindrops, spanned the thorny branches.

Joanna could hardly bear to sit there in the litter. In all this exuberant landscape, only the peasants moved stolidly, silently to their work. She watched two of them who had stopped at the top of the furrow. The ploughman was binding his hand with something, rags perhaps or strips of leather. His beasts stood waiting, their breath steaming in the cold air. Presently he took up the handles and the oxen moved slowly forward. A hare, its ears laid back, raced for shelter, raising a trail of glittering drops behind it. The sower settled his pouch on one shoulder and followed the plough, his arm swinging rhythmically as he scattered seed that was invisible to Joanna at that distance. They seemed unreal, tiny, in that wide landscape.

Soon they entered the forest and the sucking noise of the horses' hoofs in mud gave way to a soft thudding. At first this too was interesting to her, the herds of swine rooting among the dead leaves for acorns and beech nuts, the woodcutters leaning on their axes to watch them go by, the squirrels chattering high above them in the oak trees. The sun dazzled Joanna as it alternately hid behind the slender trunks of the beeches or shone through their pale new leaves. As they went deeper into the forest, it grew quieter. The rocking of the litter, the continual jingling of the horses' bridles, lulled Joanna and she slept.

⌒ ✻ ⌓

She was sleeping again the next day when they emerged onto the broad plain below Poitiers. Eleanor woke her and Joanna struggled up from under the furs, rubbing her eyes.

"Eleanor, it's so *big*!" she gasped.

The city spilled down the hillside, houses, churches, inns, shops clustered within walls that were within walls as the city had spread and enclosed more and more parishes, all the way down to its encircling rivers. Everywhere the pale stone of new buildings caught the late sun's rays. Beyond the rivers, valleys fanned out into the distance, with here and there a priory near a stream or a hamlet or a mill. Joanna saw vineyards and orchards and a neat checkerboard of fields where peasants were still working at the spring planting.

The sun was already going down, and as they crossed the bridge of Moutierneuf, the Angelus rang out from St. Hilaire. The horses' hoofs clattered on the cobblestones as they went up through the town to the palace. Everywhere people stopped putting up their shutters for the night to crowd along the sides of the narrow streets and watch them pass. A barber and his last customer came out to see, the customer with a white cloth still tucked around his neck. Furriers stood with their arms full of pelts and a pastry cook with a tray of tarts. Joanna saw one little girl of her own age peering from behind her mother's skirts and staring round-eyed at the royal children in their fur-lined litter.

Ahead of them, the men-at-arms shouted, "Clear the streets!" The town seemed noisy after the day's ride through the forest. Joanna heard sheep bleating, people calling to one another, the banging of shutters and clanking of utensils, dogs barking, the horses' hoofs drumming on the stones, and, above everything, the bells of the churches of Poitiers.

It seemed to take forever to push through the narrow, stinking streets. At last they came through the gatehouse and into the bailey before the Maubergeonne Tower. The litters were set down. Poor Nurse was so stiff that the soldiers had to help her out. Bewildered by the strangeness of the place and the confusion around them, Joanna clung to Eleanor's hand. Knots of men stood arguing in the bailey and steaming horses were tied by the door, as though messengers had just arrived on urgent business and would leave again immediately.

Nurse came bustling up. "Now then, here we are at last. Oh my poor bones! I'll be glad to sit by a good fire on something that isn't jogging up and down. I swear those beasts hated each other or me. They could *not* get into step. All the way, it was up at one end and down at the other until I felt I was being pounded into jelly. Where is the seneschal, I wonder? The place seems very poorly organized. I wonder the Queen permits such disarray. We must pay our respects to your mother and then it's straight to bed for you children. Oh, that must be Sir Ralph over there. Come along!"

She pulled them over to where the seneschal, Sir Ralph, was talking agitatedly to the captain of their escort.

"Sir Ralph? Here are the royal children. We would like to greet the Queen. Be so good as to lead us to her, if you please."

"The Queen is not here, mistress."

Joanna felt cold suddenly. The man looked drawn, as if he had not slept for a night or two. There was a day's growth of beard on his cheeks and chin.

Instinctively, Joanna clutched at Eleanor's hand and the two sisters drew close together.

"An attack? On the palace? Heaven preserve us!" Nurse's hand flew to her throat.

"No, an ambush. She was on her way here, to receive the children."

"And the Queen is kidnapped? Merciful Lord! In her own domain?"

"We don't know yet what has happened to her. Come in, all of you, into the Hall."

In a daze, Joanna let herself be led inside. Images of her mother floated before her eyes. She saw her on her black mare as she had last seen her, confident, gay, elegant in her crimson mantle, turning back and laughing. Her face was vivid in Joanna's memory, the arched brows, the high cheekbones touched with color on that raw February morning, the even teeth—she had kept them all, which was remarkable, all but one on the far left and that gap was only revealed when she smiled widely, as she had done that day. Joanna felt a heavy lump of misery had settled in her chest, impeding her breathing. The seneschal's words reverberated in her ears. "Disappeared, an ambush, we don't know what has happened...." Her mother kidnapped, imprisoned, held to ransom, dead ... Joanna pushed the thought down before it could fully formulate itself.

It was dark in the Great Hall and the servants had let the fire die down. Now they heaped logs on it and soon it was blazing up again. They lit candles and the torches on the walls, and the graceful arcades running the length of the vast room sprang into relief against the flaring light. The servants went round closing the shutters over the many long windows.

The girls sat on a bench near the fire. Joanna was trembling, from fear or cold, and Eleanor put her arm around her. A servant brought wine and she took a cup. It was warm and spiced and she curled her numb fingers round it gratefully.

"I have sent for William Marshal. He was there and can tell you the whole story better than I," Sir Ralph said.

"When did this happen?" the captain asked. His cloak fell back from his arm as he tossed his wine down and held out his cup for more.

"Yesterday, Sir Gilbert. They were riding from Lusignan. The Earl of Salisbury was the Queen's escort."

"Where is the Earl now? Has he disappeared, too?"

"Lord Patrick is slain, sir."

"Salisbury dead? That is grave news indeed."

The men were silent. Sir Gilbert stood staring into the fire. To herself, Joanna said over and over again, "Please God, please God, please God." She twined her fingers tightly together.

Just then the men crowding into the Hall made way for a tall, slim young man who strode up to the fire.

"This is William FitzJohn, Sir Gilbert. The Earl of Salisbury's nephew."

"Yes, I know your father, Sir William. It is *Sir* William, isn't it?"

"Yes, sir. I was knighted just before the battle of Drincourt."

Joanna noticed that his left arm was in a sling.

"What happened yesterday?" Sir Gilbert sat down and unpinned his cloak. It fell in heavy folds around him on the bench. Eleanor and Joanna huddled together. Beyond them, beyond the circle of firelight, the soldiers and servants and household officials crowded in to listen.

"Sir, we were riding from the castle at Lusignan on our way north to Poitiers. It was a small escort, twenty men or so, under my uncle Patrick, and we weren't expecting any trouble, so we weren't wearing armor. The King had put down that rebellion after Christmas very thoroughly, as far as we knew. Most of the ringleaders escaped, the Count of Angoulême and the Count of La Marche and the Lusignans, but we thought they'd fled to the Île-de-France. King Louis is offering asylum to the rebels, you know.

"Well, anyway, we were riding along through the woods south of here …"

"Did you have no scouts going ahead?" Sir Gilbert interrupted.

"Er, no, sir. We had outriders, but what with one thing and another … We'd stopped for a meal, in open land, and after that, well, we were not far from Poitiers and the wine we'd had and the Queen was in high spirits and the men telling jokes and the outriders were more *of* the group than not.

"We should have been more careful. I see that now, of course. We were ambushed in a small clearing, a perfect place for it. They rode out in front of us and behind us at the same time, yelling and shouting, and just came right at us. No warning, no challenge. I heard my uncle call for his hauberk but he never had time to put it on. We had nothing but our swords.

"My uncle shouted to me, 'Guard the Queen.' We had been riding one on either side of her. I turned my horse to cover her left flank and three of them were coming at me. I was kept so busy for a while I couldn't tell who was where or anything."

"Who were the leaders?" Sir Gilbert asked. "Did you recognize them?"

"Yes, sir. Geoffrey and Guy de Lusignan. I recognized Guy de Lusignan myself and their wounded have been put to the question and named Sir Guy and his brother Geoffrey."

"Ransom, that's their game," Sir Ralph said. "A reckless bid, but I suppose they feel they have nothing more to lose, their castle captured, their walls razed. Tell them the rest, William."

"As I said, I was kept busy. I killed some ten of them, I know that. My sword arm is still stiff." He grinned suddenly and looked very young. "It was a real mess. Most of the horses were not destriers, as we were not expecting a fight, but only palfreys, and they were rearing up and terrifying the others and trampling men trying to flee, and the wounded were screaming…. When I had a moment to take stock of the situation, I could no longer see the Queen, or my uncle, either. I supposed he had managed to draw her out of the scrimmage somehow and was hiding her in a safe place until it should be over. Then they were on me again and I had no more time to think."

It was the kind of story Joanna loved to hear sung by a minstrel, a gallant knight defending his Queen in a forest glade, but this account horrified her. She could imagine the whole scene, the terrified horses trampling on the wounded, the trodden blood-reddened grass, the *thunk* of sword on flesh. She felt sick. Her mother in the midst of it all … Where was she now?

"And the Queen?" Sir Gilbert asked, echoing her thoughts. "They got her?"

"I don't know, sir. It all seemed to happen so quickly, and yet I suppose we must have fought for an hour. We were completely outnumbered. Some of our men were put to flight and I think some were captured. I fought on until there were none left to fight. Then I saw some of them riding off, going like bats out of hell. I thought of pursuing them, but they were too many for me and had a good start. I couldn't see that they had any prisoners with them.

"I expected my uncle Patrick to return with the Queen at any moment, so I stayed there taking stock of the dead and wounded. I did what I could for our wounded but it was little enough."

"You were wounded yourself, sir, I see," Nurse said.

"Yes, mistress, but it's a clean cut through the flesh and will heal well. My uncle never reappeared, so after I had laid our dead out straight, I circled the area looking for them. I found him face down, some distance from the clearing. He had been killed by a sword thrust from behind. The Queen was nowhere to be seen."

A sigh went up from the crowd, then there was silence except for the crackling of the fire. Joanna held her breath and looked from face to face.

"It sounds to me as though she is taken," Sir Ralph said heavily.

"I am afraid so. What a ransom they could ask for the Queen of England! But there has been no demand for ransom yet?" Sir Gilbert asked.

"None. No news. I have sent a messenger to the King, of course."

"Ah."

There was a silence. Joanna knew they were all imagining her father in a rage.

"Could her horse have bolted?" Nurse asked.

"Easily. But she would have brought it under control and then where would she go?"

"Perhaps she was thrown and is lying out there somewhere with a broken leg," Nurse suggested.

William laughed scornfully. "I'd like to see the horse that could throw the Queen. She has a better seat than most men. Still, we did think of it. The whole area was searched today but we found nothing."

Her mother lying all night alone in the damp forest, unable to walk, with boars and wolves sniffing her out … No, Joanna could not picture her helpless. She was with these Lusignans, whoever they were, and probably ordering them to provide her with more comforts. Captive or not, she would never be less than a Queen.

The fire and the spiced wine were having their effect on Joanna. Her head drooped and she leaned heavily on Eleanor.

Nurse bestirred herself. "Sir Ralph, some refreshment for the children, if you please. And I trust our chambers are ready, despite all this?"

"Yes, mistress. I am sorry. We have been all at sixes and sevens since this happened, but a chamber has been prepared for you." He snapped his fingers at a servant who jumped to attention and ran off. The servant came back presently with slices of cold smoked herring on a silver tray and little quince tarts. Usually Joanna loved them, but she had no appetite. Eleanor was not hungry either.

"Come, child, eat something. You must keep your strength up," Nurse urged.

To please her, Joanna took a bite of each.

"Do I have to eat any more?"

"One more piece of herring and then I'll take you off to bed."

Joanna could hardly get it down though she chewed and chewed.

She thought she would not be able to sleep, in a strange room and afraid for her mother, or that if she did, she would have nightmares. In fact, she slipped almost immediately into a dreamless sleep.

CHAPTER TWO

When Joanna awoke in the morning, she could not think where she was at first. The sunlight coming round the edges of the shutters was on the wrong side and the wall opposite too far away. Then she remembered. Poitiers! And at once she remembered too that her mother had been kidnapped and the Earl of Salisbury killed. Apprehension settled clammily on her again.

Eleanor was still sleeping beside her. She sat up in bed, hugging the fur coverlet round her, and looked for Nurse. She was nowhere to be seen. In a panic, Joanna thought she had somehow been kidnapped, too. She opened her mouth and bawled like a baby.

"I want Nounou! Where's my Nounou?"

A chambermaid came in at once.

"Hush now, hush. Your Nurse is at Mass in the chapel. You were sleeping so soundly you didn't hear the bells ring for Prime. She said we should let you sleep on, as you were tired from the journey. She'll be back soon. Let me dress you now, then you'll be ready for breakfast when she comes back."

By this time Eleanor was awake, too, stretching in the warm bed. Joanna stood on the bed and two maids slipped her chemise over her head. Then they brought a basin of cold water and she washed her hands and face and rubbed her teeth as Nurse had taught her. They brought her bliaut and helped her wriggle her arms into the long tight sleeves and, lastly, a surcoat, fur lined because the days were still cold, and hose and slippers. They were brushing her hair when Nurse came back.

"Awake at last, lambkin? You must say your prayers before we go down. It *is* Lent, you know."

So Eleanor and Joanna knelt on the wood floor and folded their hands while the servants opened the shutters and let in the cold morning air. Eleanor began murmuring from the Easter office for Prime. Joanna mumbled along with her, not remembering the words until they reached the familiar bits at the end.

"Gloria patri et filio et spiritu sancto. Sicut erat in principio et nunc et semper et in secula seculorum. Amen."

In her head, Joanna was praying, "Please God, let Mother come back safely."

☙ ❀ ❧

It was late morning of the same day and Joanna was sitting with her sister in one of the deep recessed windows of the Maubergeonne Tower. Eleanor was patiently rethreading Joanna's needle every time she pulled it too far and the thread slipped from the eye. At the best of times, Joanna hated needlework and today she was too nervous to watch what she was doing. She wished she could be over at the gatehouse and listen to the news brought in by the soldiers returning from forays, but Nurse was adamant that idleness was playing into the Devil's hands and, kidnapping or no, Joanna should fill her time constructively. "Go to the ant, thou sluggard," she declaimed in the stern tones she reserved for biblical quotations, "Consider her ways and be wise."

Nurse had at least consented to let them sit in the window where Joanna could keep an eye on the gatehouse. It was cold in the unglazed window and they were wearing their mantles. As Joanna was looking at the gatehouse and not her needlework, she noticed at once the sudden activity there. The guards rushed to line up and she heard shouts and then the creak of the portcullis being winched up.

Joanna dropped her work and, leaning out of the window, curled her fingers round the cold iron grille. A small body of men in full armor clattered into the bailey and there in the center of them was the Queen. Her face, framed by the marten fur lining her hood, was flushed from the ride and she was laughing.

Someone started to cheer and they all took it up. The cooks came out from the kitchens and the smith from his forge, with his hammer still in his hand. The grooms and falconers pressed in behind the knights and men-at-arms and, behind them, the laundresses, waving their red roughened hands. Over on the left, Joanna saw Sir Ralph emerge onto the steps of the porch leading to the Hall and with him were the chamberlain and the chancellor and a group of ladies-in-waiting. They came down into the bailey as the captain of the bodyguard held out his hand to assist the Queen to dismount. Then they passed into the palace and Joanna could no longer see them.

Joanna was out of the room and flying down the stone staircase round and round with one hand on the central column before Nurse could say a word. Her mother was in the Great Hall, surrounded by officials. She stood, tall and slender in green and gold and marten fur, by the fireplace. Joanna hesitated in the doorway, her mouth open, her hands pressed over her pounding heart.

"Yes, of course, I am *perfectly* all right. Don't I look it? Don't *fuss* so, Ralph. God's teeth, give me some room here. My legs are frozen. I want to walk up and down."

Her gown swirled around her ankles as she turned. She saw Joanna in the doorway.

"Joanna! Come here, child." She bent to offer her cheek to kiss. Close up, she smelled of lavender. "That's enough, you're pinching my arms, child. Jesu, you all stare at me as though I were a vision! I'm real enough and *famished*, too. I can't wait until dinner. Bring me something light now. A little warm almond milk, that would be good. No, not a word until then, Sir Ralph. Stop bothering me. That's better, I'm warm now."

She looked behind her for a chair and two servants ran forward with one. She sank into it without another backward glance. By this time, Nurse and Eleanor had come down and Nurse pulled Joanna to one side.

"Where's William? He was magnificent. Not hurt or taken, I hope?"

"No, my lady, I'm here." William came forward and dropped on one knee before her.

"Your arm?" She gestured to him to rise.

"It's nothing, my lady."

"I was sorry to hear of your uncle's death. He died bravely."

Joanna thought, looking at her mother's face, that she was not all that sorry about Earl Patrick's death. The almond milk was brought and the Queen sipped it luxuriously, enjoying the suspense.

"Ah, that's good. Very well, Sir Ralph, you want to know what happened to me. You all, I could see it in your faces, thought I had been taken prisoner by those Lusignan bandits. I'm surprised you had so little confidence in your Queen. From *them*, it didn't surprise me. The oafs were laying about them, yelling and shouting, and paying no attention to their prize. I suppose they thought they would find me patiently waiting to be taken when the fighting ended." She laughed scornfully. "Not a bit of it. Did I tell you that William was splendid? He fought like a wild boar against the hounds. I want him to be given new armor and a horse and gold, 100 livres of gold. Yes, and some rich garments, an embroidered mantle. Sir Ralph, did you make note of that? Gervase, write it up for me and tomorrow I'll put my seal to it."

"Thank you, my lady," William murmured, and Sir Ralph stirred impatiently.

"It's very simple really. They were so busy fighting that I just rode off and nobody noticed. No, that's not quite true. Earl Patrick saw me leave and he came behind me, to protect me. One man came after him and cut him down as he rode. He died in my defense, you see, but to tell you the truth, I think it was unnecessary. They hadn't noticed me. His death gave me the time to get away as his killer was unhorsed. I rode like the wind, keeping out of sight as far as possible, and didn't draw rein until I had put several miles between myself and them. Then when I stopped to look about me, I saw that I had ridden away from Poitiers. I thought perhaps it was just as well, as they would more likely look for me on the road to Poitiers, so I kept on going, all the way back to Lusignan."

"Lusignan, my lady?" Sir Ralph burst out. "You were at Lusignan?"

"Yes, ironic, isn't it? The garrison was much surprised to see me return and alone, too, I can tell you."

A buzz of conversation broke out in the Hall. Watching her mother, Joanna could not imagine how she had ever feared for her. She was invincible.

She was laughing again. "Sir Ralph, you are such an old fusspot! Of course I rode alone! Do you think I was going to go back to that mêlée and say, 'Excuse me please, but would someone act as my escort?' No, I galloped all the way. It was glorious."

Joanna was ashamed that she had been so poor-spirited. *One day*, she vowed to herself, *one day I will be like her. I want to be a Queen! One day I will be a Queen, like Mother, and my life will be one long, glorious adventure.*

CHAPTER THREE

The first two days were a bleak enough introduction to Poitiers, but after that Joanna began to explore her new surroundings with her normal curiosity. First the women's apartments, then the Great Hall with its arcades, and beyond its long windows, the pleasance where the chestnut trees were decked for Lent with white wax lights. She ventured beyond the palace itself to the kitchens, and even one day as far as the mews where the falconer chased her off because a young seeled falcon was being walked about in the darkened interior.

Curiosity, according to Nurse, was another trait best suppressed in girls and women, and Joanna had a healthy enough respect for the birch rods that Nurse kept behind the door to do her exploring in secret. She was still too young to be expected to go daily to Mass and this was the time she chose. It was easy enough to escape the maids set to watch her; she always needed to retrieve her needlework from some other room or to visit the garderobe, and they never questioned her excuses, being happy enough to sit together and discuss their love lives. Eleanor knew of some of her escapades and remonstrated with her in private, but Joanna knew she was too softhearted ever to betray her to Nurse.

Sometimes even, at night, if she could stay awake after Nurse fell asleep, she crept to the gallery of the Great Hall to watch the Easter feasts: the processions of pages with steaming dishes, the minstrels and musicians, the knights and the young squires, but especially she watched the ladies. After the ever-present black robes of Fontevrault, the palace at Poitiers seemed to run wild with color, green and purple and yellow, deep blues and glowing reds, the colors of rowan berries and robins' breasts, of sea spray and cinnamon, of peacocks and aubergines and saffron, of Malaga wine and violets and poppies, and everything was laced and embroidered and fretted with silver and gold, and flashing with sapphires and rubies and amethysts.

Between Ascension and Pentecost, Joanna's brothers came to Poitiers. Henry came first, with his French wife, Marguerite. Henry was thirteen and an adult now, so he had no time to spare for a sister he considered still a baby. Marguerite was a different matter. She would sit in the solar working at her embroidery and prattle endlessly. The embroidery itself was a sore point with Joanna who was clumsy, being young, and had anyway no patience for it. Marguerite would hold up her frame for her ladies to admire and they would all exclaim over it.

"Ravishing, my lady."

"Exquisite!"

"Such talent and such care!"

Joanna despised them. She despised their tittering laughs and the mincing way they walked with their heads thrust forward and their refined Île-de-France accents. Most of all, she resented Marguerite's endless criticisms. Marguerite never missed an opportunity of pointing out that her father was King Henry's overlord or of insinuating that the Normans were barbarian newcomers compared with the long-established and civilized Franks.

"Though what she knows of it, I'd like to know," Nurse muttered to Joanna at bedtime one night, "seeing as she has been living at English courts since she was three. It's all those Frenchy ladies of hers. I say they should send the lot of them packing back to the French court, where they'd be only too happy to be from the way they talk, and give her some good sensible Norman or Angevin ladies to wait on her."

Joanna had another reason to dislike Marguerite which she could not tell Nurse for fear of hurting her feelings.

"Why do you permit that old peasant woman in here in the ladies' apartments?" Marguerite had asked her one day.

"Why, she's my Nurse, of course," Joanna answered, taken aback.

"Surely you're not a sucking babe any longer, though I suppose you're not long out of leading strings. Her usefulness is over. You should send her away, or at least she should live in the servants' quarters. And the way you let her talk to you! She even calls you 'Joanna' instead of 'my lady' and I've never once seen her curtsey to you."

"I don't want to send her away. Not ever! I *love* her," Joanna said vehemently.

"Love her?" Marguerite raised an eyebrow. "A fat peasant woman who doesn't even speak good French and you, a king's daughter, speak of loving …"

At this, Joanna flew at her in a fury, her face red and crumpled, her fists flailing. Marguerite's ladies rose like a flock of birds, their silk skirts hissing, and tried to seize Joanna. She kicked and struggled silently, tense with anger, seeing nothing. Through the chorus of scandalized exclamations, she heard Eleanor's voice, calm and clear.

"Joanna, let go. *Let* go!"

She sensed that the restraining hands on her arms were her sister's and allowed herself to be pulled back. Chest heaving, hair awry, she faced Marguerite and her ladies.

"A scandalous display!"

"She will be whipped, of course."

"The Queen must hear of this."

Eleanor's voice cut across their sibilant protests.

"I think not. If you tell my mother, then *I* will tell her what I have heard here, the criticisms of England, of the Normans, of the Poitevins, and even of my mother herself, the way Marguerite complains about my brother Henry, and all the letters to and from the French court. Don't think I don't hear and understand, just because I'm young. I know the French are sheltering my mother's enemies, and some might call your correspondence treason."

Joanna's anger had left her as suddenly as it had come. She stood quietly now between Eleanor's hands and watched Marguerite, pale and tightlipped, and her ladies, sullen and silent. She felt how tense Eleanor, standing close behind her, had become.

"How *dare* you speak like that to the future Queen of England?" Marguerite burst out.

"You should remember that," Eleanor answered. "You are a younger daughter of a king, just as Joanna is, and your importance comes from being the future Queen of England. The more you belittle England, the more you belittle your own position."

Marguerite's eyes narrowed. She searched for an answer but could find none. No one spoke or moved. In the fireplace, a log suddenly broke and fell, sending a shower of sparks up the chimney. Eleanor turned Joanna round.

"Come, Joanna."

With her arm still around her, she led her to their chamber.

"Oh, Joanna, that was terrible," Eleanor wailed, flopping down on the bed. "I *hate* scenes. You were very naughty."

"But," Joanna protested, amazed at this sudden change, "you were on my side. Besides, I *love* Nounou and I won't let *anyone* say bad things about her."

"Yes, you're very loyal and that's good, but you were wrong to fly at Marguerite like that. Of course she was wrong to be unkind to you. You *must* learn to control yourself, Joanna. Who knows, you may be a Queen some day and you can't go flying into these awful rages then."

"I don't see why not," Joanna said stubbornly. "If I were Queen, I could do *anything* I wanted. Father's a king and *he* gets angry."

"It's different for a man."

CR ❁ ℘

To Joanna, her sister Eleanor was all that was virtuous and clever and admirable. Where she gave her devotion, she gave it fiercely. It never occurred to her to be jealous of Eleanor because she was more beautiful or intelligent. It seemed natural rather than unfair that Eleanor, who was the beauty of the family, should also be the good one. It was not because Eleanor was patient and kind and did not fly into rages that Joanna knew she was good. Privately, although she loved Eleanor, she thought this rather poor-spirited behavior. She knew Eleanor was truly good because, peering through her fingers when they were at prayer in the chapel, she would see Eleanor staring rapt at the altar, her lips moving in silent repetition of the chaplain's droned prayers. Then Joanna would feel guilty that she found it boring and that her knees ached and her nose itched. For a few minutes she would try to stay still, in imitation of Eleanor, but her attention would wander again.

Eleanor, then, had no faults, but there were times when Joanna wished she had a companion who was livelier, who would share her love of adventure and exploring, preferably someone her own age. Eleanor was four years older and would never accompany her on a raid of the kitchen or a visit to the forge.

She was on her way to the forge one morning that summer, a still and hazy morning that promised a hot day. Already her chemise was sticking to her skinny shoulder blades as she crossed the sunny corner of the bailey. Nurse and Eleanor were at Mass. She could hear the rumble of voices chanting in unison, then a pause when presumably the priest spoke, then again the antiphonal response. As if in mockery, a pack of dogs barked, a cock crowed, the dogs barked again.

Intent on her goal, eyes squinted against the sun, she ran across the bailey and was startled to hear suddenly a whinnying quite close to her and a thudding of hoofs. She looked around to see a white palfrey canter by, wheel round and stop facing her. The rider's back was to the sun. She put up a hand to shield her eyes and then she saw it was not a man, but a boy, his shock of golden hair tousled, grinning down at her.

"Well, well! What are you doing out here so early? I wager your Nurse doesn't know of it."

"N-no, she doesn't," Joanna admitted. "But don't think you can make me go back. She won't miss me yet. I'm just going to watch the smith for a while and then I'll go in and Nurse will never know."

"Make you go back?" He raised his brows. "I wouldn't dream of it. What are Nurses for if not to run away from?"

She stared up, delighted, and her brother stared back, grinning jauntily.

"What do you think of Gracieuse?" He stroked the horse's neck affectionately. "She's a lady's horse really, but a beauty, isn't she? And you should see her go."

Joanna took her eyes off her brother and looked at the palfrey. From this angle, it looked enormous, all gleaming muscled flank and heavy feet and great white teeth. She felt afraid of it and at once determined to conquer her fear.

"Richard!" she said suddenly. "Teach me to ride. *Please!* Let me ride her, just for a minute"

"Ride? Whatever for? Girls don't ride."

"Yes, they do. Mother rides. So do all the ladies when they go falconing."

"Sidesaddle," he sniffed. "That doesn't count."

"I want to learn to ride properly. When I'm Queen—I mean, if I'm a Queen—I shall ride every day and as well as Mother."

He cocked his head on one side for a moment, considering her, then said suddenly, "All right. Here, give me your hands. No, that won't do. Turn around and stick your arms out. I'll lift you up in front of me."

Joanna felt him seize her under the arms and hoist her up. Her skirts impeded her and she hitched them up. The saddle was much wider than she expected. Off-balance, she grabbed behind her for Richard's arm and slithered sideways on the saddle.

"No, don't hold me. Hold the pommel, so. And straighten up. You can lean against me. Come on, Gracieuse, up, girl."

He flapped the reins and the mare bowed her head as if assenting and started forward at a walk. Joanna found herself bounced from side to side. She gripped the pommel and stared down at the horse's mane. Gradually she learnt to anticipate each sideways lurch and compensate for it. She dared to raise her head and look around. From high on her perch, she looked down at a cat slinking across the bailey. A scullion emerged from the kitchen door and threw some slops out on the ground.

Joanna laughed delightedly.

"This is fun, Richard! I love it!"

"Wait till you learn to gallop. That's *really* fun. I remember when I learned to ride. My groom walked my pony round and round in a circle on a long rein, while I just hung on for grim death. I was about your age. You should have seen Geoffrey, though. He was determined to keep up with Henry and me, and he kept kicking his pony into a canter and falling off. He'd climb back on and do the same thing again. Always foolhardy. Why, the last time we went hunting, he set his pony at a jump anyone could see was too high for it, just to prove he was as good as the men! Well, the pony wouldn't take it, of course, stopped short and Geoffrey went sailing over in fine style! Landed in a ditch on the other side. How we laughed!"

"Can I do it by myself? Can I, Richard?"

"I don't know. Your legs are too short to reach the stirrups. Well, why not? You have spirit. I like that, even in a girl. Just hang on, then."

The saddle tipped as he swung himself down. Then she was all alone up there. She settled herself in the centre of the saddle and smiled a little nervous sideways smile at Richard.

"Don't let go of the reins, will you?"

"No, don't worry. Off you go."

The horse took a step and Joanna slipped. Another step and she slipped a little more. She clung agonizingly to the pommel.

"Straighten up. Stay on top. You don't have to crouch like that. Sit with your back straight. You said you were going to be a Queen, remember? Queens don't ride all hunched up, they sit tall. That's it. Good girl. Now let go of the pommel. Hold the reins in your left hand. No, not so tight, you'll hurt her mouth. Yes, like that."

"Why don't I hold on with my right hand, Richard?"

"That's your sword hand, you have to keep it free. Or it would be if you were a boy. I don't know what girls do. Just put it on your thigh. Now, if you want her to go, kick her with your heels, and to stop, pull back on the reins and say 'Whoa!' All right?"

Tentatively, she nudged the horse with her heels and it started to walk. She was amazed; this huge beast, twice her height and who knows how many times her weight, obeyed her!

"Richard, I'm riding; I'm really riding!"

There was a sudden burst of talking from near the chapel. People began to pour out into the bailey and scatter to their various places of work. Faintly, Joanna caught the smell of incense. She pulled back on the reins and cried 'Whoa!' The horse stopped so promptly that she fell forward on its neck.

"Lean back when you stop," Richard advised her.

"I must go. Mass is over. Richard, can I do it again? Properly. I want to learn how to ride properly."

He lifted her down. "All right. If I have time. You're a game little thing, Joanna. You'll need a small pony so you can reach the stirrups."

"But keep it a secret, will you? It'll be *our* secret. I'm sure Nounou would say I'm too young."

"Nurses are like that." They smiled conspiratorially at each other. "I'll get my groom to fix something up for you. He's a good fellow and won't breathe a word."

CHAPTER FOUR

Joanna hardly dared hope that Richard meant it but he was there the next morning. He had brought her a pony himself and threw her up into the saddle.

"We can't ride in the bailey, you know. Any number of people will see you here. We'll have to go outside," he said.

"Outside?" she faltered. "But, Richard, I'm not allowed to go outside."

Richard laughed. "You're not allowed to be out here at all. As well be hanged for a sheep as a lamb. There's a path that runs below the walls. We'll go there. The watch will see us, of course, but I don't think they'll say anything if you're with me."

The path was little more than a sheep track on the grassy slope below the palace walls. Impatient to master the rudiments of horsemanship, Joanna did not look at the town of Poitiers that lay below them or the view that stretched beyond it, of plains and valleys and forest, to the blue horizon. She patted the pony's rough, sun-warmed mane happily. Richard rode before her, twisted sideways in his saddle so that he could watch her and advise her. She learned to pull the reins across to turn left or right and to kick the pony into a canter.

They pulled up from a canter on the far side of the palace. The smell of crushed thyme and sheep droppings hung in the air. Joanna felt flushed from the ride and triumphant: not only had she stayed on, but she had matched the pony's rhythm until it felt like a magical extension of her own body carrying her swiftly and effortlessly through the warm bright air.

"Well done!" Richard said, leaning on his pommel. "You learn fast. You'll be a good horsewoman."

Joanna basked in his praise. She smiled at him from sheer overflowing joy.

"We're all the way round behind the forge," he said. "Listen: you can hear the smiths."

"So you can." The clang of hammer on anvil carried clearly from the other side of the walls and the smiths were singing as they worked.

"Richard!" she shrieked. She pulled sharply at the reins and the pony stepped backwards. "They're *working*. That means Mass is over and I'm late and—oh Mother of God—we're as far as we could be from the gate."

"You're right," he said swiftly. "Come on. We'll go back at a canter."

He wheeled his horse, passed her, and was cantering back along the trail before Joanna had even turned. Agitated, she pulled back on the reins and the pony stepped backwards.

"No, no," she said aloud to it. "Turn!" She pulled again and the pony took another step back. "Richard!" she called but he was already out of earshot.

In a panic, she kicked the pony and he sprang forward. "Whoa!" she called. The pony stood still, but it tossed its head and flicked an impatient eye at her. How was she supposed to turn it? Richard had not taught her that. Her hands were sweating and the reins slipped. She wiped her left hand on her dress and took a firmer hold. She could have cried from frustration and impatience. She was desperately late and the wretched animal would not understand what she wanted it to do. She forced herself to think. Richard had taught her to turn left and right; if she kept turning until she had completed half a circle, that should do it. She pulled the reins across. The pony snorted and stamped. She pulled harder and kicked it. Reluctantly, the pony turned its head and kept turning. It worked. Now she had it facing the way she wanted to go. The pony put its head down and refused to budge.

Richard came cantering back down the path. It looked so easy when he did it. "Come on! What are you doing?"

"It won't go," she wailed.

"Hit him with the end of the reins. Here." He came up alongside her and slashed at the pony's hindquarters with his reins. The pony took a leap forward that almost unseated Joanna and then plunged off along the path. She clung to the pommel, bumped and bruised. There was no way of recapturing the fine, rhythmic ride of a little while before; it seemed that every time she came down, the pony's back was coming up. She dared not let go of the pommel. She wondered if she would escape a beating if the pony threw her and she broke an arm. Grimly, she hung on.

Richard came through the gatehouse right behind her. "Run," he said. "I'll take the pony back." He caught her bridle.

Joanna slipped to the ground. Her legs felt stretched into a permanent arch but she ran stiffly across the bailey. Perhaps Nurse had stopped to talk to someone, perhaps she had not yet noticed her absence. She slowed down outside her chamber, trying to look as though she were returning from some innocuous errand, though her heart was pounding and her sides ached.

Nurse was waiting for her, standing in the middle of the room, her face grim.

It was not the beating she minded so much, nor even Nurse's anger, though she was miserable when she and Nurse were at odds. The worst part was that Nurse insisted on her attending Mass every day from then on, so that she could keep an eye on her, as she said. There was to be no more riding, no more clandestine exploration, no more secret meetings with her brother Richard. She saw him only at a distance, sitting at the High Table at dinner while she sat with the children at the far end of the Hall, or riding off with his friends to morning sword practice while she watched from her window.

"It's so unfair," she said, throwing her work down on the window seat and watching Richard's fair head thrown back in laughter as he rode out at the gates. "Everything that's fun is forbidden, either because I'm too young or because I'm a girl."

"You have an obstinate character, my girl," Nurse said. "We'll have to stamp that out of you before you grow up."

ᙣ ❀ ᙟ

In the late autumn, not long after Joanna's natal day in October, Henry and Marguerite left. Joanna did not miss either of them. They were to go to England where they would hold their own Christmas Court. The other children, except for baby John and Joanna's married sister Matilda, spent Christmas with the Queen at Poitiers. Nurse was scandalized that they had not joined King Henry as usual at his Christmas Court in Normandy.

Christmas was the best time of the year. For all the twelve days of Christmas, everyday rules were relaxed and no one worked. On the Feast of the Holy Innocents, Richard was one of the boy bishops who presided over the service at the cathedral and on the Feast of the Fools, Joanna and the other children laughed to see the priests in masks censing the chapel with smoke from the soles of old shoes and eating sausages before the altar.

Richard and Geoffrey, each with his own mesnie, left a few days after Christmas. Joanna understood that they were going to an important meeting at Montmirail, to be held on Epiphany. From the women's gossip, she gathered that the Queen had been deliberately omitted and that she resented this. Joanna knew little about it until Marguerite, returning from England, enlightened her.

"*Your* father is to do homage to *my* father," she said, "for his Angevin provinces. Also he's going to ask my father's consent to Geoffrey's marriage to Constance of Brittany. Henry and Richard and Geoffrey are all there. King Henry plans to present them all to my father and confirm their inheritances. Henry, of course, gets Normandy and Anjou and Maine, Richard has Poitou and Aquitaine, and Geoffrey will get Brittany with Constance. I suppose King Henry thinks that will ratify his conquest of Brittany.

However, the *really* important thing is that Thomas Becket will be there. Let us hope that your father sees sense and is reconciled to him. In France *nobody* would treat an archbishop so. My father has always been the foremost defender of the Church's honor in *his* kingdom. And Becket is such a *good* man. I shall never forget how kind he was to me when I first arrived in England. And Henry, I know, is furious with his father for driving him into exile."

The news that really interested her, and took Marguerite by surprise, was that King Louis of France gave his daughter Alice to be betrothed to Richard, with the County of Berry as her dowry.

This was not, to Joanna, altogether good news. Alice was Marguerite's younger sister and Joanna imagined another Marguerite, always on her dignity, always concerned with proper procedure and ceremony, always criticizing and complaining. Alice turned out to be quite different. She was nine years old, rather small for her age, and very pretty, in a babyish way. She had a round face, big frightened eyes, a little button nose and full pouting lips. Her hair was long and fine and very fair.

Marguerite took her under her wing at once and tried to teach her proper pride in her position as daughter of King Louis. Poor Alice, who hated to displease anybody, was hard put to it to display tact all round, but she generally managed it. At first, Joanna admired her sudden about-faces, but she soon came to despise them as sly and hypocritical. Still, Alice was always kind to her, so she much preferred her to Marguerite.

It was the expression in her eyes that first made Joanna call her "mouse-face" in her mind, a shifty look as though she were about to scuttle nervously for cover. Marguerite never succeeded in teaching her dignity.

Richard laughed the first time Joanna slipped up and referred to Alice as "mouse-face" out loud.

"Mouse-face? Is that what you call Alice? What on earth for? She doesn't look a bit like a mouse!"

"It's not so much that she *looks* like one. She *acts* like one, twitching and quivering, and have you noticed how she holds her hands up, so?" Joanna imitated one of Alice's characteristic nervous gestures. "She looks as if she's sitting up and looking out for the cat."

Richard laughed all the more. "Oh, that's perfect, Jo! That's exactly Alice! Well, she's a Capet, you know. They don't have the courage of us Plantagenets. What about the others? Do Marguerite. What's she?"

"Marguerite?" Joanna considered. "Something sharp and sniffy ..."

"With its nose always in the air," he supplied. "A hen, perhaps, squawking and flapping."

"No, not dignified enough."

"A ferret? A weasel?"

"Too low to the ground. I think Marguerite's a ... camel."

Richard slapped his thighs. "Yes, a camel! And Geoffrey?"

"A fox," Joanna said quickly. "And Eleanor's a pussy cat and Henry's a horse."

"And you—I know what you are. A squirrel! A bright-eyed, quick, curious squirrel with tawny hair."

"It's *not* tawny!" Joanna said hotly. "My hair is fair." This was a sore point with her.

"Well, fair, of course. But a touch of auburn. Not unattractive at all, not *red* hair," he said and then teasingly, "well, perhaps just a *little* red."

Joanna gave him a great push and he rolled sideways off his chair, then came at her very fast. She dodged him but he caught and tickled her.

"Cry pax, little squirrel?"

"Never," she said breathlessly.

"Good. That's the spirit." He released her and sat back on his heels.

Joanna lay on the wooden floor of the solar, getting her breath back. Her ribs ached from laughing.

"And what's my animal?" Richard asked. His hair stood out, tousled, all round his head.

She answered unhesitatingly. "A lion, of course. A great roaring lion with a golden mane."

"A lion, eh?" He cocked his head on one side. "Yes, I like that."

He roared and made to jump at Joanna again and she twisted away, giggling. He got up and began to pace the floor.

36

"Richard the Lion! Sounds good, doesn't it? Trouble is, Matilda's husband is already called Henry the Lion. Can't have two in the family. But something with Lion in it. Richard the Glorious Lion! Richard the Brave Lion!"

"Richard the Mangy Lion?" Joanna suggested. He flung a cushion at her but she ducked and it missed.

"Richard the Great." He strode up and down, admiring himself. "History will find a name for me. I mean to make my mark, I can tell you, Joanna. Richard the Magnificent!"

"Richard the Rooster! Richard the Peacock!" she said, giggling but envious. What title could a woman earn? She would never be Joanna the Great. To be Queen Joanna was her ambition, but that meant no more than wife of a king. A woman could become a saint; that was perhaps the only independent fame she could win. Joanna felt a familiar stir of guilt and mentally thrust that path from her. She wanted to be like her mother, who was certainly famous and admired and powerful, even if she had no sobriquet.

"And Mother?" she asked. "What animal is she?"

Richard stopped pacing. "Mother isn't any kind of animal. Mother is a Queen." His mouth snapped shut and he strode out of the room.

CHAPTER FIVE

T he ladies were sitting and sewing one day in the solar when they heard about Marie. It was the summer season and they were talking of Richard's first joust which was to take place that summer.

"He should do well," Countess Isabel said. "What do you think I should use here, Ermengarde, green or red for the lady's sleeves?" She held her embroidery frame at arm's length, considering it.

"Oh green, definitely. Green and gold are my favorite colors. Red is so vulgar, except on cardinals. Yes, he has long arms and is strong for his age. How old is the boy now, anyway?"

"The young *Count* is thirteen. Well, I think I shall make them red. Green would not stand out from the background foliage."

"They'll let him win anyway," one of the Châtellerault cousins said. "Can you imagine unhorsing your overlord at his first joust?"

"Of course they won't. It's against the rules," Joanna said indignantly. "Anyway, he won't need them to *let* him win."

"Unless he comes up against William Marshal," the Countess of Flanders put in. "He's the champion. How many tournaments and undefeated? They say he's making a fortune from the ransom money."

"He's making up for his poor start. You know what happened? It was his first battle, at Drincourt, and that night at dinner the Earl of Essex asked William for a small present out of his spoils. 'Surely,' he said, 'you won forty or sixty horses today? You can spare me just a crupper or an old horse collar!' Poor William had to admit that not only had he failed to seize any booty, but he had lost his own horse into the bargain! And a few days later there was a tournament which he couldn't enter without a horse. At the last moment, his tutor lent him one and he won three combats! *That* time, you may be sure, he took care to exact horses and arms and ransom money."

"He won't be here unless young William Marshal comes, too. Do you forget he is made master of Henry's household now?"

"That Lusignan ambush was the making of him. A landless younger son and suddenly he's guardian and companion of the heir to the throne. He'll go far, that one."

At this point Joanna's aunt Emma of Anjou came hurrying in.

"News, ladies, news! What do you think?"

The ladies put down their sewing and gathered round her.

"The tournament is banned!" guessed one.

"Is it a marriage?"

"Or an excommunication?"

"You're all wrong! Give way. Let me sit down. No, there's a letter from King Louis. This concerns you, children, so listen. He is concerned for the moral welfare of his daughters the princesses Marguerite and Alice ..."

She was interrupted by laughter.

"Well he may be! To a monk like that, a little singing and dancing must seem like the devil's own work."

"And of course we have all the handsome young knights here! Why would they want to go to that gloomy old Cité palace?"

"Surely he has not decided to withdraw his daughters? Marguerite is already married and Alice is promised."

"No, on the contrary," Emma said and she rocked back, laughing. "He is sending us yet *another* daughter!"

"Another?"

"What do you mean?"

"Has he betrothed little Agnes to John?"

"Quiet, ladies, listen. His most Christian Majesty of France, having in mind, as I say, the welfare of his young daughters and knowing the Queen of England to be so encumbered with cares of state that she cannot properly be held to manage his daughters, has taken it upon him to send a chaperone and mistress for them—his oldest daughter the Countess Marie of Champagne. And she's on her way here now."

A torrent of questions and comments broke out.

"The Countess of Champagne. Why, she's Queen Eleanor's daughter!"

"What's she like?"

"That will give the Count some freedom!"

"And the Countess, too, if she cares to use it!"

Nurse hustled Joanna out of the room to her own apartments.

"Well, you'll have to behave yourself! The Countess was brought up in the French court and they're very strict and religious there, from what I hear."

"Is Marie Mother's daughter, too?" Joanna asked.

Nurse folded her lips primly. She did not approve of the way nobles allowed themselves divorces. Then she relented.

"Yes, she is. She's the oldest daughter of King Louis and Queen Eleanor. Very strictly raised. She's been the wife of Count Henry of Champagne for six years."

"Six years? She's young then."

"No, she was married late," Nurse said. "She must be twenty-four or twenty-five by now."

"Does she have any children?"

"Two sons and a daughter, I believe."

"Will they come here with her?"

"That I don't know. She'll be here soon and you must mend your ways, that's all I know."

Alone, Eleanor and Joanna speculated on Marie. They envisaged her as a grim-faced dragon of a woman, a strict disciplinarian, pious, humorless, and harsh. When Nurse finally told them that she was there and that they were to go down and be presented to her, they were quite nervous. Nurse had to push them over the threshold of the Great Hall.

The woman who sat next to their mother was young, radiant and beautiful. Joanna noticed that first and then immediately afterward her fashionable clothes. Her veil was so fine as to be almost transparent and under it her hair was artfully waved. Her gown was of blue silk embroidered in silver and she wore no surcoat over it, only a belt of silver links round her hips fastened with a sapphire-studded clasp.

"So you are my little sisters? Come and give me a kiss."

She held out her arms to them. Nurse gave them a push and, dazed, they went forward. Marie smelled of roses and lilies of the valley. She kissed them on both cheeks.

"Now let me look at you. Yes, you are pretty. This is delightful. So many new sisters all at once. Let me see if I remember your names. Marguerite, Alice, Eleanor, Joanna. You see? And best of all, my lady mother." She bowed her head to the Queen.

Around them, the knights in the Hall stood transfixed, as they did. Marie's movements were so graceful, her head held so high on her long slender neck that Joanna was reminded of someone striking poses for an artist. Joanna was startled to realize that Marie was speaking directly to her.

"... your niece Scholastique. She is the same age as you, I think." Marie was pushing forward the girl at her side who scowled and hung back.

Joanna took pity on her and, darting forward, grasped her hand.

"Scholastique? That's a pretty name. I'm your aunt. You will have to mind what I tell you," Joanna teased her but the girl only stared round-eyed. "Shall I take her to show her where's she to sleep?"

"Yes, that's a good idea. Run along now, children."

Scholastique took a step back. "I don't want to," she said.

Marie's gracious smile disappeared. "Scholastique, you will go with Joanna *at* once."

Outside the Great Hall, Eleanor and Joanna plied Scholastique with questions.

"How old are you?"

"Do you have any brothers?"

"What's your Nurse's name?"

"How many days did it take you to get here?"

"What's it like in the Île-de-France?"

They were hurtling her up the circular staircase, each one pulling a hand. In the women's solar, she stopped and looked from one to the other.

"You talk funny," she said.

"What do you mean, funny?" Joanna asked indignantly.

"We have a Norman accent, that's what she means," Eleanor explained.

"Oh. I thought perhaps you were speaking the langue d'oc."

"Langue d'oc, silly? That doesn't sound the same at all. Why, don't you speak it?"

"No."

"Oh. Well, you won't get on well with Master Hubert. He's the pastry cook, you know."

Scholastique's eyes widened. "A cook? I'm not allowed in the kitchens."

"Nor am I," said Joanna, "but I go anyway."

CHAPTER SIX

Joanna was awake before sunrise. She stretched out an arm and was surprised again by the empty space next to her. Since Eleanor's betrothal to the King of Castile, she had been promoted to a chamber of her own. Joanna had a moment's sadness when she remembered this, but it was still two months before Eleanor would leave, and two months were as long as two years to Joanna. Besides, it was at last the great day of the tournament and she could not be sad today.

It was still dark, but she could make out the darker mass of the chest against the wall and the bed where Nurse lay humped under the covers, her breath whistling through her nose. By the door, two maids slept on pallets. As Joanna strained her eyes, one of the maids stirred and turned, sighed deeply, and was silent again.

Outside a rooster crowed, then another, farther off. Joanna crept from her bed and went to the window. She peered through the crack of the heavy shutters. It was lighter outside, but she could not tell if it were daylight yet or not. The air coming round the edges of the shutters was cool and she shivered. She went back to the bed and felt in the dark for her chemise and wriggled into it. She used the chamber pot in the corner of the room, afraid to face the long dark corridor to the garderobe set into an angle of the palace walls. Even in daylight she was terrified of perching on that hole set above the long drop to the moat. Still no one stirred. Then her ears caught the sound of a chain rattling. She moved swiftly to the window again and listened. A creaking sound and a slight rattle. Someone was drawing water from the well. A clank as a bucket was set down on the stone rim of the well, then a rattling as another bucket was lowered. It was morning at last. Now she could smell smoke, too. The servants were up and lighting the kitchen fires.

"Nounou, Nounou, wake up!" she caroled. "It's daytime, it's the day of the tournament!"

Nurse snorted and groaned. "It's nighttime, you silly child. See how dark it is? Go back to sleep!" She turned over with her back to Joanna, yawned deeply, and grunted again.

Joanna sat on her bed, arms wrapped around her knees, in an agony of anticipation. She stared fiercely at the window willing the sun to rise and the day to begin. Slowly, the sounds intensified. She heard the stamping of mailed feet as the night watch on the walls and towers was relieved. She heard the lowing of the cows and knew the herdsmen were going in to milk them. From the meadows came the sound of hammering where some final preparations of stands and booths were set in hand. The dawn chorus of birds swelled, dogs barked, and horses neighed. There was a burst of talk and laughter as a group of men crossed the bailey and then their voices faded into the distance. The smiths and armorers were already at work. She could hear them banging and hammering at horseshoes and nails, lance heads and swords for the big day.

At last the bells rang, a little one first from a monastery way down by the river, then the sound was taken up by other churches across the town, the bells of St. Hilaire and St. Porchaire and the cathedral of St. Pierre and, finally, from the palace chapel itself.

Joanna stood unusually still while her maids dressed her. She had a new bliaut that she was to wear for the occasion. It was deep blue with silver embroidery round the hem and neckline and sleeves, and what made her even more sure she would look like Marie in it was that it had a train. Not, to be sure, a long train such as Marie and Mother and the other ladies wore, but undeniably a train. The wardrobe mistress had demurred and Nurse had been adamant.

"A *train* on a little girl's gown? Certainly not! You'd be sure to trip over it or tear it and what a waste of cloth. Why, the price of cloth has doubled these last years. When I was your age, even bishops and viscounts went about in sheepskins, but nowadays it's all precious stuffs and snipping it here and slashing it there to show the lining, and the young men with their long hair and pointed toes—it's all vanity, vanity." She mumbled something under her breath about "monkeys dragging their tails behind them."

However, Queen Eleanor, when appealed to, had decided in favor of a train, much to Joanna's joy. "By all means let it have a train, but only a small one. Joanna will be sitting with us in the royal stand and she must be dressed according to her rank."

So now she fingered the smooth silk, smiling to herself, as her maids brushed her hair. She would have liked her hair waved like Marie's, but knew better than to engage in an argument she would not win. However, Nurse allowed them to braid one central tress and weave blue ribbons and gold fillets through it.

The chapel was crowded for early Mass. Afterward, Joanna filed out with Eleanor, behind the Queen and Marie and their ladies. In the Great Hall the girls breakfasted at the children's table, near the buttery door, on slices of bread and cups of fresh milk, still warm and frothy. Released from the silence of the chapel, they chattered eagerly.

"It's going to be a beautiful day for it."

"Do you think Richard is nervous?"

"Of course not. He's longing for it. When does Poitou fight?"

"I think it's to be the last mêlée. The grand finale."

"What if he and Henry meet?"

"They won't. It's been carefully arranged. Anjou is to fight the North and Poitou the South."

"Then Richard won't meet William Marshal either," Joanna said in relief. "He'll be leading the Angevins, I suppose, with Henry."

"Shall I tell you a secret?" Alice asked with a sly smile.

"Tell me, too," Scholastique cried. She was wearing a purple gown that Joanna had decided did not suit her at all.

"No, you're just a baby."

"I'm the same age as Joanna," Scholastique said indignantly, "and I won't tell, cross my heart and hope to die."

"Well, all right," Alice leaned across the table. "Marguerite is in love with William Marshal." She giggled.

"I don't think that's an interesting secret," Scholastique said.

"That's because you're a baby. What do you say, Joanna?"

"Does he love her?"

"She thinks he does." Alice giggled again. "He pays her compliments all the time and she doesn't see it's just because she's Henry's wife. Anyway, she's got it set in her head that if he asks her for a favor to wear at the tournament, it will *prove* he loves her."

"But that's nonsense," Joanna objected.

"Of course it is," Alice said. "In fact, I think he's almost bound to ask her, but you can't reason with Marguerite." She sighed dramatically and added, "That's the way love is. Madness."

"Richard will wear your colors, I suppose," Joanna said.

"Richard? Oh, I doubt it." Alice put on a piteous face. She was very good at it. Her lower lip trembled and her eyes looked big and tearful. "I don't think he likes me very much."

"I'm sure he does, really," Eleanor said, leaning forward. She always hated to see anyone unhappy.

"He probably wouldn't like you if he could see you now," Joanna said cheerfully. "He likes people with spirit. Come on, let's go. I'm ready."

But Nurse was not to be hurried. Joanna sank back onto the bench, her fists clenched between her knees, trying to contain her impatience.

"I don't really like the mêlées," Eleanor confided. She pulled the soft center out of her bread and nibbled it. "I hate to see people get hurt. I like the acrobats and the storytellers."

Alice leaned forward. "Did you ever see anyone get killed in a tournament?" she asked.

"No, never. Did you?"

"No. But I'd like to." She licked milk from her upper lip.

"Like to?" Eleanor crossed herself. "Alice, that's terrible."

"It's not that I want anyone to die, but it would be so *exciting*. Don't you love it when all those men on horseback crash into each other in the middle of the field," she smacked her hands together and her eyes glittered, "and then all that heaving and struggling and shouting and the splintered lances and hacked shields? I *love* it."

Joanna saw Nurse lift her head and look at Alice disapprovingly. Alice was not her charge so she went back to dipping her bread in her milk, country style, and sucking the milk noisily through it.

"I don't hold with these tournaments," Nurse said. "I think the Pope should ban them. There's Lady Alice saying she hopes to see some poor fellow killed and the men are even worse, dash into the fray with never a thought for their wives and children or their parents' grief."

"But Nounou, you don't understand, to a knight honor is more important than life. Roland says so, you know, in the *Song of Roland*. *Mieux vaut mort que déshonneur*. 'Better death than dishonor.'"

"I understand enough to know that honor won't support his widow and orphans. But I suppose he didn't have any."

"He had a fiancée, beautiful Aude, who was waiting for him back in Aix."

"And she was overjoyed to hear of his honorable death, I suppose?" Nurse asked sarcastically.

"She died of grief. Oh Nounou, it's so beautiful. She kept her oath to Roland just as he kept his to *his* lord. Charlemagne had six countesses stand round her bier to honor her."

"Hm. Well, she was as big a fool as he was. Thought you were so impatient to get out there?"

"Oh yes! Come on, Nounou! Do I look all right?"

"Pretty as a picture, my lamb, though I don't want to encourage your vanity. Come on, then."

A wave of noise hit them as they left the palace. Around the edges of the flat meadow, stalls were set up and the hawkers were all crying their wares, haberdashers, saddlers, glovers, pastry cooks. The ale booths were doing a busy trade and the clang of hammer on anvil rang out from the armorers' forges. Jugglers and musicians strolled through the crowds and here and there groups of people had gathered to watch a mime perform or listen to a necromancer. In ringed-off areas at the field's edge, the common people were already cheering on their own champions in wrestling and dart shooting and stone throwing. The Jews hovered a little apart from the crowds in twos and threes, nervously fingering the heavy money pouches on their belts. They were there to lend money to defeated knights who could not afford to ransom themselves. Joanna stared, fascinated, at their dark beards and pointed yellow hats.

Joanna clung to Nurse's hand. Around them, her ladies trod delicately, lifting their long skirts to keep them from horse droppings, fruit rinds, and spilled ale. She tried hard to see everything at once, the banners unfurled to the slight breeze, the colorful tents where the knights were already arming, the stands and galleries raised above the lists and filling with chattering fluttering ladies, the heralds strutting importantly up and down within the lists. Constantly she was distracted by some new claim on her attention, a swarthy horse dealer from Lombardy or Spain bawling in heavily accented French the merits of his stallions, a trumpet fanfare which she thought announced the start but was only a young trumpeter practicing or just carried away by enthusiasm, a stall with a heaped pyramid of cold, spit-roasted songbirds and quails and pigeons.

Once in the stand, with an uninterrupted view over the wide flat green meadow and the knights' tents and the crowds all round, she could not bear to sit but remained standing, craning to see. The knights were gathering now, the young ones self-consciously nonchalant, the older ones sitting on benches and drinking the Gascony claret that their squires brought them. The chief herald eyed the ladies' stands, looked back toward the palace, then resumed his strutting. Impatience mounted. There was a flourish of drums and the sound of horses neighing. The smaller stalls were closing now and their owners pushing forward to get a view. Joanna scrutinized the arms on the knights' surcoats, the boars and hawks and dragons and eagles, but she could not see the golden lions of Anjou. Squires hovered nearby, holding shields blazoned with their masters' arms. Here and there, free lances mingled with the other knights, younger sons without land, whose shields carried no arms. They would fight in any mêlée and hope to win a large ransom.

There was a sudden stir in the crowd and Joanna spun around, almost losing her balance. The chief herald raised his trumpet to his lips and the others followed suit. There was a tremendous fanfare. The crowd fell silent and the echoes of the trumpets seemed to fly up into the sky. Queen Eleanor and Countess Marie came up into the stands, followed by their ladies. They stood for a moment, looking around them, then settled down. Over their heads, the pavilion flapped in a sudden breeze. With a rustle, the ladies sat. The drums rolled, the heralds lined up. Beyond the lists, grooms brought up horses and the squires helped their masters into the saddle and handed up their shields. A buzz of talk broke out among the crowd as last-minute wagers were exchanged.

There was a flourish from the herald. He stepped forward and stood below the royal pavilion. "My lady Queen," he bellowed, "my lords and ladies." His voice fell at the end of each phrase as though it were complete.

"The noble knights of Brittany." Ragged cheers greeted this. "Challenge the valiant knights of Gascony and Guienne." Prolonged cheers and applause. "To enter the lists here today. And meet them in combat. To prove their much-vaunted valor." More cheers and raucous laughter. "Or to concede victory to the Bretons."

"Never!" someone shouted. "A Gascon never yields!"

"He only strategically withdraws!" answered a knight sarcastically, from the stands opposite.

"Better than prematurely withdrawing, like a Breton!" shouted a third voice.

The crowd roared its approval of this exchange. Insults and cries of "Brittany!" "Gascony!" rose above the neighing and the drums.

The herald sounded his trumpet again. "My lady. I present to you: The knights of Brittany."

The lists at the far end of the meadow were opened and the standard bearers moved forward, followed by the buglers, then the knights. Their squires walked alongside. As they passed, the herald cried each man's name and honors. Joanna caught some of them, Rennes and Penthièvre, Dinan and Porhoët. Before the Queen, they bowed their heads, helmets under their arms. The horses' caparisons shook and glittered. The leading knight stopped below Constance.

"My lady Countess," he called and Constance rose in her place, blushing. Joanna could see she was clutching something in her hand. "I dedicate our victory to you! I crave the honor of a token to carry into battle and pledge …"

Before he finished speaking, Constance flung the sleeve she held bunched in her hand to him. The throw was short and it fell on the ladies below Constance who passed it forward and over the lists to the squire. The knight leaned down from his saddle and his squire knotted the sleeve around his right arm. He raised it in a salute to Constance and all the Bretons cheered.

Constance sat down abruptly, flushed. Joanna thought, *If I were her, I could have done better than that.* She should have said something to cheer him on. Nine is not grown up, but she is their Countess. Joanna fingered the handkerchief in her sleeve. No one would ask her for a favor but if they did, she thought she could do better than Constance.

Now Constance's Breton ladies were leaning over the lists as the knights rode forward and offering one a scarf and one a handkerchief, some freely thrown, others coyly granted. There were cheers, some catcalls, and a few bawdy comments from the knights who had gathered in the men's stands opposite. Tucking the tokens into their helmets or tying them on their arms, the Bretons trotted to the far end of the meadow, on Joanna's right, and lined up.

Then it was the turn of the knights of Gascony and Guienne. The crowd roared itself hoarse. Gascony and Guienne were part of Queen Eleanor's great fief that ran from Tours to the Pyrénées, and had not the Queen herself been born in Gascony? Besides, the Gascons were favorites with the tournament crowds; showy, brave to the point of rashness, always good for a spectacular mêlée. They came in jauntily enough, flashing the colors of Agen and Auch, Bergerac and Dax, and the Queen's own birthplace of Belin. Reacting to the crowd's approval, they capered and wheeled and approached the ladies with poems and snatches of songs.

"We can't hear you!" shouted someone in the crowd.

Obligingly, one of the Gascon knights trotted over to the crowd and sang for them. Joanna clapped delightedly.

"Oh I hope they win!" she cried and saw Constance shoot her an angry look.

The Gascons cantered off to the left, accompanied by the yells and whistles of the crowd, and formed their line. There was a sudden silence. People edged forward tensely now the preliminaries were over. Far apart, at opposite ends of the long meadow, the two lines waited. The herald was fussily ordering people to clear the areas at the ends and get back behind the lists. The drums rolled and the trumpets blared. In the distance, the Breton herald stood out in front of his line and issued a formal challenge. His Gascon counterpart accepted it and added an insult which brought a roar, immediately silenced. Now the chief herald ordered squires and heralds out of the lists.

The moment lengthened. The knights pulled their helmets down and lowered their lances into position. The sun flashed on mailed sleeves and burnished shields. A fly buzzed around Joanna's face but she could not bear to move. All eyes were fixed on the herald, waiting for the signal. A horse snorted and shook his head up. Just as the suspense was becoming unbearable, the herald raised his trumpet and the fanfare sounded.

A gasp went up from the crowd and the two lines of horsemen charged. The Gascons shouted as they came, the Bretons looked dour and grim. The horses' hoofs drummed on the turf, the sound growing into thunder as they reached a gallop and drew closer. Joanna held her breath. Then with a tremendous crash, the lines met. A shield went spinning far up into the air and fell back. Horses reared and neighed and someone began to scream, a shrill high scream that went on and on.

For a while, Joanna could not see what was happening. She stood up, trying to see over the heads in front of her, trying to see

53

the source of the screaming. There was a tight mass of men and horses and shields swirling in the center of the field. Then the line broke into knots and couples. A horse galloped off, riderless, another lay kicking on the field. She saw some men down, one rolling onto his knees, another lying still. Those who were still mounted were separating into couples fighting sword to sword. The field was littered with splintered lances.

The squires climbed under the lists, circled warily, then dashed forward to pull an unconscious man to safety. They rolled him onto his shield and carried him from the field. The fight rolled back and forth. A couple with locked shields tried to extricate themselves. A knight who had lost his sword tried to defend himself with the stub of his lance and was driven steadily back.

Through the noise of the crowd and the horses, Joanna could still hear the screaming. She watched as squires found the man now and carried him off, doubled up and writhing. The skirt of his surcoat was sodden and red, and blood spilled down his legs, darkening his leather gambesons. She saw that Constance had her face averted and her hands over her ears. Alice was sitting on the edge of her seat, staring avidly.

It was a relief for Joanna to laugh with the rest of the crowd as one knight hopped frantically after his horse, one foot in the stirrups, trying to remount. Some were down now, held at sword's point by their opponents and forced to yield. Sullenly, they mumbled their acceptance of the ransoms imposed, were released, and slouched from the field.

A Gascon burst from the mêlée, his left hand over his eye, blood running between his fingers. The crowd shouted its sympathy.

"I have another eye left," he shouted back, "and a one-eyed Gascon is better than a two-eyed Breton any day."

He wheeled his horse and, roaring like a bull, charged back into the fray. Joanna watched him, admiring his courage. His red and black blazon was easy to see. He rammed into a Breton with such momentum that the man was unhorsed and fell heavily on his sword arm. The Gascon leapt from the saddle and stood over the man before he could rise. He lifted his sword two-handed.

Blood spattered from his gouged eye and dripped on the Breton. Slowly, the Gascon knelt. Joanna thought it was to hear the other's surrender more clearly. Then she realized he was not kneeling but falling, toppling slowly like a felled tree, first to his knees then forward to lie full length on the Breton. Squires skipped around them, uncertain. The Breton rolled the other from him and rose to his feet, looked for his horse, and made to mount it. At a signal from the herald, the squires stepped forward. He argued with them. Joanna could not hear them but understood that the herald had ruled him defeated. As he left the field, he shook his fist at the herald and she saw Constance's sleeve flutter on his arm. The one-eyed Gascon was carried off on his shield and the crowd cheered him mightily, although he could not hear it.

The fight was breaking up. The Bretons were being driven back into a rout. The Gascons, eager to capture prisoners for ransom, chased the Bretons from the field. In the stand opposite, a young knight yelled "Stand and fight! Stand and fight!" Joanna looked across and recognized Richard's rufous mane. She waved but he did not notice.

In the distance, the Gascons pursued the Bretons with yells. The crowd was left looking at an empty field strewn with broken lances and hacked shields. Grooms were tending the fallen horses and squires were picking up the shields. As Joanna watched, a wounded horse was dispatched with a sword slash across the throat. An army of servants began to move across the field, clearing it of debris for the next mêlée.

Vendors were already crying out from their stalls, offering eel pasties and claret, spice cakes and salted pork tongues, and for those who could afford no better, bread and ale. Joanna was suddenly enormously hungry. Long trestle tables had been laid for the nobles in a field nearby. The sun was hot now and the ladies fanned themselves as they settled on the benches. Wasps buzzed eagerly over the food and the palace dogs had found their way there, following the scent of roast meat. The knights who had not fought that morning were eating hungrily.

The children seized what they could and sank onto the grass to eat. Joanna sat cross-legged, munching a flan filled with soft cheese and eggs. Crumbs dropped on her new silk bliaut but she paid no attention, intent on hearing all the gossip she could.

Constance had gone back to the palace in tears and would not eat. The one-eyed Gascon was not dead; he was unconscious but was expected to recover. Only one serious injury so far: a man caught by a lance thrust in the groin. He had received extreme unction. The leading Breton knight had ridden for home swearing he would not pay the ransom, though it was only his horse. The Gascons were holding five of his men as hostages. The conversation swelled around her and suddenly there was a cheer as the Gascons began to arrive. One was limping and another had splints on his arm, but all were smiling and flushed. The ladies offered to share their cups of wine and some of the bolder ones reclaimed their tokens in exchange for a kiss.

Alice sank onto the grass next to Joanna and Scholastique. She rested her elbows on her knees and chewed at a roast skylark, her little fingers daintily raised.

"Wasn't it marvellous?" she asked, through a mouthful of meat. "Poor Constance, she was as red as a coxcomb! Didn't you love the brave one-eyed Gascon?" Her hair swung forward and she tossed her head back.

"Where's Eleanor? Have you seen her?"

"I don't know. I think she felt sick. Didn't like all the blood." Alice ripped a strip of meat from the lark's wing and her tongue curled neatly round it and flicked it into her mouth. She leaned toward Joanna. "Look at Marguerite!"

Joanna looked up. Marguerite was staring at William Marshal who was walking beside the tables, serenading the ladies. He had tucked a flower behind his ear and was strumming a lute.

Can par la flor justal vert fuelh
E vai lo terns clar e sere.

Marguerite's mouth hung slightly open as she watched him. He had stopped and put a foot up on the bench now. Joanna knew the song well and sang it under her breath with him.

Dei ben chantar, car tug li met journal
Son joi e chan que no pens de ren als.

"I must sing, as all my days, Are full of joy and song and I can think of nothing else."

Alice giggled. "I don't think she'd notice if a wasp flew into her mouth."

"Does William fight today?" Joanna asked.

"No. It's Poitou after dinner, challenging the Southerners."

"Poitou! Why then, Richard will be fighting." She sat bolt upright, dropping the crust of her flan into her lap, and looked for him.

He was in the midst of a group of young men, laughing and talking noisily. She strained to hear. He was speaking langue d'oc, as usual, and telling an anecdote. There was a burst of laughter from the group around him. Now the boy next to him was speaking, a dark haired slender youth of Richard's height.

"Now there's a handsome one," Alice said. "Do you know who he is?"

Joanna shook her head.

"Well, he's only a boy. He looks about the same age as Richard."

"Richard's not a boy. He's thirteen."

"I call that a boy. Perhaps it's just because we're French, but Marguerite and I prefer men."

Joanna ignored this, to her, meaningless statement. The trumpets were sounding for the knights to arm.

"Whoever he is, he's fighting today. Look, he's going with Richard. Richard!" Joanna shouted, jumping to her feet.

He turned, his eyes scanning the throng until he saw her. Then he raised a hand and grinned.

"Good luck!" she called.

"I'm always lucky," he shouted back.

"He always swaggers," Alice said critically.

Joanna watched them go. They were talking about something, then they both turned and looked, whether at her or Alice she could not tell.

When they returned to the stands, William Marshal was in evidence again, rallying the heralds and singing topical songs. He had acquired a slapstick from a jester and was capering drolly before the stands.

"I would juggle for you, too," he called, "but I have no balls."

"More balls than the lot of them," someone shouted at once.

"I thank you, sir, whoever you are," William acknowledged.

The bench felt hot to Joanna through her thin skirts. She felt sorry for the knights who must be sweating in their quilted leather breeches and heavy ring-mail hauberks.

The crowd was singing too.

> *In the public house to die*
> *Is my resolution;*
> *Let wine to my lips be nigh*
> *At life's dissolution;*

With a sudden surge, everyone shouted the refrain:

> *Grant this toper, God on high,*
> *Grace and absolution.*

In the pause that followed, Joanna heard the bells ring. It must be Sexte, the sixth hour of day. Strange to think the monks were praying as always while everyone else was having a holiday.

The knights had assembled but it was too far for Joanna to recognize individuals now they were armed. The trumpets blared again. This time the crowd, relaxed and mellowed, was slow to quiet. At last the herald announced that the knights of Poitou … but here he was interrupted by such a loud and prolonged cheer that he had to give up and wait.

"Poi*tou*! Poi*tou*!" they shouted, banging their ale mugs together. "Poi*tou*! Poi*tou*!"

The drums rolled and the heralds called for silence. He began again. The knights of Poitou challenged the knights of the South, of Auvergne and Toulouse, of Narbonne and Périgord.

The Poitevins came trotting out. At their head rode Richard, his lance upright in his right hand. His left hand in its heavy bridle gauntlet gripped the reins. He wore a sleeveless scarlet surcoat over his hauberk, emblazoned in gold with the leopards of Poitou. His eyes were narrowed in the bright sunlight and he looked eager and excited. Beside him walked his squire, carrying his helmet topped with the gold circlet of the Counts of Poitou.

Joanna jumped to her feet, clapping and shouting. She shot a glance at Alice who was sitting forward on the edge of her seat. Richard looked neither to left nor right. He came forward steadily and stopped in front of the royal pavilion. There was a hush as everyone craned to see whose colors he would carry into his first tournament.

"My lady Countess of Champagne," he called.

"Marie!" Joanna breathed. Out of the corner of her eye, she saw Alice sink back into her seat, plucking at a fold in her skirt and looking unconcerned.

"Since you came here, you have been an inspiration to all of us, in song and poetry, in manners and courtesy. There is no one whose image could better inspire me to valor today. Let me wear your favor and I promise you a victory worthy of you."

Marie rose, smiling, and moved to the front of the stand.

"My lord, I think you are in no need of favors to inspire you. We all know how high your heart is. But by all means, take this as a token of my support and affection."

She pulled from the bosom of her gown a gauzy veil of pink and gold. Richard lowered his lance and she laid the veil on it. The crowd stamped and cheered. His squire tucked the veil into his helmet beside the sprig of broom, the *planta genista*, that he wore there. Marie stood for a moment longer, her head gracefully inclined, one hand holding up her long silk train.

Joanna stared at her, entranced. "Isn't she *beautiful*? 'An inspiration to all of us,' Richard said. What's an inspiration, Nounou?"

"'Favor is deceitful and beauty is vain,'" Nurse said dourly, "'but a woman that fears the Lord, she shall be praised.' And I'm thinking it's not to fear of the Lord that the Lady Marie is inspiring all those foolish young men."

"I don't know about that, but she's everything I want to be when I grow up."

"Don't say so!" Nurse said fiercely. Joanna was surprised into looking away from Marie, at Nurse. "Has nothing I've ever said to you sunk in at all? And here you are admiring someone who ..." Nurse started to mumble, but Joanna caught the words "every mortal sin."

Joanna squirmed uncomfortably on the hard bench and looked back at Marie, who had sat down again and was carefully arranging her train. If Marie were really as wicked as Nurse seemed to think she was, why did everyone admire her so?

Joanna turned her attention back to the field. The Poitevins, preceded by their standard-bearers and buglers, were wheeling off now. There was no doubt whose side the crowd here in Poitiers was on, but the Southerners made a brave display and the crowd cheered them anyway. Joanna clapped with all the rest. She paid no especial attention to the knight who had stopped before them. He was helmeted already and the nasal partly hid his face but there was something vaguely familiar about the blue eyes and the dimpled chin.

"My lady princess," he called.

Joanna hesitated. He seemed to be looking straight at her but she knew she must be mistaken. She looked at Alice beside her but Alice was looking at her.

"My lady Joanna," he called again.

Suddenly Joanna's heart began to pound. The blood drummed in her ears and she gripped the edge of the bench. She felt that all eyes were on her. Nearby, one of the ladies tittered.

"A child! What nonsense!"

"Not so foolish. The daughter of a king, after all. What a match it would be for him, if that's what he has in mind."

Their voices came to her as if from a great distance and the noises of the crowd ebbed and swelled like waves on the shore.

"I know that your heart is with the Poitevins, but I make bold to ask your magnanimity for this one knight who rides against them and would be greatly honored by a sign from you."

The voices behind her began again.

"He's wasting his time. That's one match the King would never allow."

"Good looking boy, though, isn't he?"

She swallowed to moisten her dry throat. Constance was not here to see her but she would not disgrace herself. She stood stiffly and looked down at him, praying that her voice would not squeak.

"Sir Knight," she said and was encouraged to hear how level her voice sounded though her heart was beating so hard it shook her whole frame, 'kings' daughters do not give their favors to nameless knights. Declare yourself."

He raised a hand to his helmet and pulled it off. She saw the dark hair and the straight nose and recognized him.

"Raymond de Saint-Gilles, at your service, my lady."

He was Richard's friend so it must be all right. She pulled the handkerchief from her sleeve.

"Then, Sir Raymond, wear this and I will pray for your victory." She threw the handkerchief and his squire caught it. "Unless you come up against my brother Richard," she added candidly.

He smiled then. "I will contrive not to, my lady."

The Southerners trotted off to the far left. Joanna sat down again, her eyes following the blue and white of Saint-Gilles.

"Well!" Alice exclaimed, seizing her arm. "You are a sly one. A *suitor* and you never said a word."

"He isn't a suitor and I've never seen him before today, and you're pinching my arm."

"Of *course* he's a suitor. Saint-Gilles. He's the Count of Toulouse's heir." Alice had a fund of information on all the noble families of France. "He's my cousin. His mother is my father King Louis' sister, you know. Oh *perfect*, Joanna." She clapped her hands. "It would end the feud between your family and Toulouse. Your mother is still claiming Toulouse as her inheritance, you know, which is nonsense because it's belonged to the Saint-Gilles family for years and *years* but this way her descendants would have it. You and Raymond!"

"Oh Alice!" Joanna protested. "Anyway, I'm going to marry a King, not a Count. Ssh! They're beginning the charge."

The two lines came pounding down the field, each knight fixing his gaze on a target shield in the opposing line. Joanna looked for the blue and white of Saint-Gilles and saw it near the end of the line, across the field from her. The lines met, crashed, broke. Horsemen galloped through, reined, and turned to fight. She could not see either Raymond or Richard. Then a group drew back and she saw the blue and white surcoat. Raymond was down. A Poitevin knight sat his horse above him and held his lance to his throat. Joanna clutched Alice's arm.

"Look! He's down."

"I know. I saw it happen. Knocked clean out of his saddle by the impact. But look *there*, Joanna."

Joanna looked where Alice was pointing. An unhorsed man was caught by his foot in the stirrup and his horse had bolted. It galloped across the field dragging the man behind it and then, shying away from the crowds, made for the open end of the meadow. The battle swirled before them. Raymond had disappeared but Richard was still mounted. Joanna saw his red and gold in the thickest part of the fray, saw him parry a blow with the shield on his left arm, saw his sword arm swing up. She cheered him on, thumping her fists on her knees.

The sun was at its zenith now. Over their heads, the awning hung motionless in the hot still air. Joanna's face felt hot and damp as she brushed her hair away from it and the silk bliaut stuck to her back like a wet rag. She felt tired and her head ached from all the shouting but for Richard's sake, she kept watching and cheering.

It was a long mêlée. Nones had rung out before the victorious Poitevins circled the field, waving to the cheering crowd. Joanna made no protest as Nurse led her off. Richard was surrounded by admirers, so she knew she could not congratulate him.

They trailed up across the meadows toward the palace. In the streets below, men were setting candles in the pear trees. The common people would feast at tables in the street that night while the nobles gathered for a banquet in the palace. There would be dancing on the greensward, with heralds and knights clapping the measure and calling the changes. She knew already it would be hard to sleep with the music and the forges ringing all night to repair the knights' gear and the brawls as bets were disputed.

Suddenly she found herself face to face with Raymond de Saint-Gilles. He stared at her bitterly and would have gone by without speaking.

"I am sorry, sir, that my token did not bring you better luck. Did you lose much?" she said.

"Enough. Here, take back your handkerchief. Much good it did me. It was a stupid idea from the start and none of mine."

"Then why …?" Joanna stammered, startled by his anger.

"Ask your precious brother," he snarled and pushed back into the throng.

"Does he blame *me* for his defeat?" Joanna asked, bewildered.

"Men will blame anything but themselves," Nurse said. "Don't fret about it, dearie. He's just angry because he lost."

"Besides," said Alice, picking her way beside them, "he's only the son of a Count and don't forget you want a King." She looked thoughtful for a moment and added, "Richard's only a Count, too. *I* would have preferred a King."

CHAPTER SEVEN

Joanna lay on her stomach in the warm, dry grass. She swung her feet lazily, up over her back and then down, scuffing her toes in the dirt. In front of the girls, an insect struggled across the ground between the grass stems. She put her head down on her arms and watched it. Close to the ground, she could hear all the clickings and murmurings and buzzings of myriad tiny lives. She held a blade of grass in front of the insect and laboriously it climbed over it, not to be diverted from its path.

Beside her, Eleanor was threading daisies into a chain. There was a pile of them next to her. She picked them up one at a time, slit the fat green stems with her thumbnail and carefully poked a daisy head through the stem. The chain hung down to her lap now and curled round her knee.

It was rare for Joanna to spend time with Eleanor these days. She always seemed to be busy with fittings for her trousseau or with Spanish lessons. Now that they were together, Joanna did not know what to talk about. She felt that Eleanor had grown away from her and seemed quiet and distant and much older.

She sat up suddenly, scratching her bare arms where the grass had tickled her, and looked at her sister.

"I wish you didn't have to go," she said for the hundredth time.

"I know." Eleanor slit one of the daisy stems too sharply and tore it. She pulled it out of the chain and threw it away. "I don't want to go, either."

"Why can't Alfonso come here instead and we could all live together?" Joanna asked.

"That's not the way it works, silly. Alfonso is King of Castile. He has to stay in his kingdom, of course."

"But it doesn't seem *fair*.... You have to leave me and Mother and your home and *he* doesn't have to leave anything."

Eleanor bowed her head further over the daisy chain, but Joanna could see how her lip trembled. "It could be worse," she said huskily. "Spain is not all *that* far ..." She hesitated momentarily, "... and you must come and visit me."

"At least," Alice observed, "Alfonso is young and not some doddering old widower of fifty." She was lying on her back, chewing a grass stem. "How old is he? Eleven?"

"He's fifteen," Eleanor answered, "and he's been King since he was three."

"Oh dear, that's not so good. He'll be used to having his own way. And watch out for his mother. People say mothers of young kings are always dragons."

"Well, it's better than my sister Matilda," Eleanor said. When she married Henry the Lion—the Duke of Saxony, you know— he was thirty-eight and she was eleven."

"Don't you think you're too young to be married?" Joanna asked hopefully. "I mean, if Matilda was eleven ... You will only be nine next month. Perhaps Father would let you wait two more years. Especially as he's so ill now with the tertian fever."

"Hmph!" Alice snorted. "Your father married Henry and Marguerite when she was only three. *My* father wasn't too pleased about that, so *I'm* not to marry Richard until I'm fifteen. Five more years! Of course, they weren't really married nor will you be, Eleanor, not for years. But don't you wonder about Henry and

Marguerite? *You* could ask her, Eleanor, find out if they're properly married yet. She won't tell me but it would come naturally from you since you're about to get married yourself. You know, ask her what it's like.... Actually, I don't think they are or I would have heard something of it from my ladies-in-waiting."

"What do you mean, properly married?" Joanna asked, confused. "Henry and Marguerite are really married, aren't they?"

"No, but I mean," Alice dropped her voice although they were alone in the wide field, "have they *lain* together? Henry's old enough, but I don't know about Marguerite. They say you go mad if you do it before your monthly courses start."

"I don't understand a word you're saying," Joanna said. "What's so special about lying together? Eleanor and I used to lie together every night until her betrothal."

"No, you silly, lying together in the way of men and women. Making love. Don't you know *anything*? How do you think babies are made?"

Joanna shook her head dumbly.

"Alice, she's still young," Eleanor protested. "Her nurse will tell her when the time comes. We're not supposed to talk of such things."

"Oh, nonsense! I've known for *years*! It's like ..." She searched for the right words. "Well, you've seen when a bull is led to the cows ... or when a dog mounts a bitch ..."

"Of course," Joanna said impatiently.

"That's how people breed, too."

There was a moment's silence while Joanna digested this in horror. "*People* do that? I don't believe you. Eleanor, she's making it up, isn't she?"

"No, it's true."

"Everyone who has children has done that?" Joanna was still turning over this information in amazement.

"Of course. Why else do you think the Virgin birth was such a miracle? Because the blessed Virgin *didn't* do it. You know how she says, 'How shall this be, seeing that I know not a man?' That's what it means by *know*, in the Bible."

Eleanor stirred uneasily. "Alice, I don't think you should talk about the Holy Virgin and all this at the same time."

"Why not? I'm only telling her the truth, aren't I?"

"You mean," Joanna asked slowly, "that Father and *Mother* have done that, too?" She counted on her fingers. "Mother has done it *eight* times?"

"Ten," Alice said triumphantly. "You've forgotten her marriage to my father and their daughters, the precious Countess Marie and her sister. In fact," she became confidential, "I think they do it more often. Lots of times."

"Why would anyone want to?" Joanna was bewildered. "I think it's disgusting."

"I don't know," Alice said vaguely. "I think they like it."

A bee, buzzing up from a thistle flower, droned lazily between them and startled them.

"*Marie*, too?"

Alice pouted. "There's nothing so special about Marie! And she's quite old, you know. She doesn't like anyone to know her age, but I heard some of her ladies talking the other day and they mentioned the year she was born and I worked it out."

"How old is she?" Joanna asked.

"She was born in 1145, so she must be twenty-five now. That's *twelve* years older than Richard, which makes it ridiculous for him to be mooning after her like a love-sick calf."

"Richard doesn't *moon* after her. He just admires her. She's his idea of a great lady. She and Mother, of course. Look, there are some of them coming back from falconing. It must be almost suppertime."

They sat and watched a group in the distance riding back to the palace. The sound of talk and laughter and jingling bridles carried clearly in the still air. The ladies' long skirts hung down over the horses' rumps. Men and women carried falcons, hooded now, on their gloved wrists. Greyhounds ran alongside them. The children watched in silence until the group had moved on out of earshot.

Eleanor stood up and brushed leaves and grass from her gown.

"I'm going in," she said. "It's hot out here. Are you coming?"

"I suppose so," Alice answered languidly. "Though there's nothing to do inside, either. I wish I were grown, so I could go hawking. Or dance. Or do *something* interesting, instead of just lessons and needlework."

Eleanor hung the daisy chain round Joanna's neck. "There you are, Joanna. That's for you."

Joanna fingered it, smiling. She slipped her hand into Eleanor's. "Couldn't you sleep with me again tonight? Please! Ask if you may. I hate being alone."

"I don't know. I'll ask."

Joanna swooped suddenly on something glittering in the grass. "Look, look here." She picked up a piece of metal and held it on her open palm.

"What is it?" Alice asked.

"I don't know."

"It's a ring," Eleanor said. "A piece of ring-mail. It's been straightened out a bit, but see, if you bend it again … it's a ring."

"Yes. Remember the tournament?"

They looked around them at the wide empty field, momentarily imagining the cheering crowds, the thundering horses, the flashing swords and bright pennons.

"Three men died here. Perhaps one of them died right here, on this very spot," Alice hissed, and Eleanor crossed herself. "Look harder, Joanna, perhaps you'll find the Gascon knight's eye!"

"Don't be *horrid*, Alice!" Eleanor exclaimed.

"Ugh!" Joanna said. "Suppose I step on it and it goes *squish*?"

She stared around her, holding up her skirts. "Let's get *out* of here. I'll race you back!"

"Too hot," Alice declined, but Eleanor took up the challenge.

They reached the palace breathless and dishevelled.

"Don't forget now, Eleanor, to ask about tonight."

That night she slept alone, though, listening to Nurse's snores and the sighing of the maids on their pallets.

CR ✤ ℰ

"Turn round. Slowly. Yes, that's good. Very good. You've done a good job, Jeanne," the Queen said, turning to the wardrobe mistress. "How many complete outfits does that make?"

"Four, my lady."

"Hm. And the jewels to go with each, of course?"

"Yes, my lady."

Eleanor stood still in the centre of the room, her arms away from her sides to avoid crushing her skirts. She looked utterly miserable.

"I hope you won't pull a long face like that in Castile. Do, for heaven's sake, try to look pleasant. Otherwise, I think you'll do me credit." The Queen sighed. "All right. You can take it off her now. Pack it with the others."

Eleanor moved toward the next room, accompanied by her maids. The Queen looked after her thoughtfully, then crossed the room to the window seat. She sat down and leaned her head against the wall.

The room was very quiet. Joanna uncurled herself from the low seat where she had been watching and crept across the room to her mother's side. The Queen's eyes were closed. Joanna stood near her and studied her face. Close up, her mother looked older. Usually, Joanna saw her at a distance, seated behind the High Table at dinner or enthroned in the Great Hall. Now Joanna could see the furrows between her brows, the faint line of hair along her upper lip, the pouchiness of the skin below her eyes.

"Will you miss her, Mother?"

The Queen's eyes opened, moved round to where Joanna stood beside her. Their heads were on a level.

"Miss her? I suppose so." She studied Joanna. "But I've always known she would go. It's a mistake to become too attached to one's daughters."

Joanna had always liked the way her mother never talked down to her. Queen Eleanor spoke to children as though they were adults, without caring whether they understood or not. This time, as so often, Joanna did not understand her words, but sensed the meaning from the tone of voice. She was filled with anguish, without quite knowing the cause, an almost physical pain that swelled in her throat and seemed to choke her.

"You don't love … her," she said. "Just because she's a girl. I don't want to be a girl. I *won't* be a girl. Girls have to go away and be married and Eleanor doesn't want to, I know she doesn't, but nobody cares about that, and it's all so unfair!" Tears stood in her eyes and she pouted in an effort to suppress them.

The Queen sighed and sat forward. "Fair? Of course it's not fair. Whoever told you life would be fair? Life is full of injustice and disappointment and pain. Parents die, children grow up and move away, husbands are tyrannical and lovers are faithless, women grow old and lose their power over men.... You always seem to ask the wrong questions, Joanna. Love ... fairness ... that's all irrelevant."

"I don't want to get married. Not ever."

"Of course you do. You complained about being a girl. I admit I'd rather have been a man, too, but it's a waste of energy rebelling against something you can't change. You have to assess your situation realistically, decide what its advantages are and how best to use them. A woman needs to marry if she's to do anything with her life. Would you want to be an old maid all your life, handed on from one relative to another, a hanger-on, a parasite, with no position, no influence, no household of your own, always dependent on a brother or nephew or cousin?"

"I could live with Richard," Joanna said defiantly. "Then I could stay here for ever. He'd let me."

"There's no point in even thinking about it. A king's daughter must marry. She's too useful in making alliances to be left single, so you may as well resign yourself to that and hope your father chooses well for you. Life is a battle, Joanna. Leaving home, going to a foreign country, coping with a strange husband, a hostile mother-in-law, whatever it may be, those are the bad parts of the battle, like being wounded or unhorsed. But the wounds heal in time and one fights on. With whatever weapons life provides. Sons, Joanna, are a woman's best weapons."

Joanna felt again that hot rush of distress and resentment. Sons, always sons! Daughters were of no account, to be married off and forgotten. Her mother was still speaking, but she seemed to be looking through Joanna, not at her. Joanna heard without listening, incomprehensible phrases, "extensions of ourselves into that male world of power," "husbands are, at the best of times, unreliable creatures, but a loving son ..."

Her mother got up to go.

"It *is* hard sometimes, being a woman, Joanna. Eleanor will be sad for a while and so will you, but it will pass and you'll both be stronger for it. It's another battle wound that life inflicts, that's all."

After her mother had left, Joanna sat in her place on the window seat. She felt confused and melancholy. All this talk of battles ... She and her mother always seemed to talk at cross-purposes. Joanna bit her lip. It must be because she, Joanna, was so stupid. She wanted to know that her mother loved her, wanted comfort because Eleanor was leaving, and hope that perhaps she herself would not have to go too one day, but her mother had not given her hope or comfort or love. Yet strangely, in spite of that, she felt less sorrowful. Her mother's words had inspired a kind of fierceness in her, to suffer bravely, to return to the charge like the Gascon at the tournament.... She slid from the seat and, straightening her shoulders, went to find Eleanor.

⅋ ❂ ⅌

On the eve of her departure, Eleanor came to Joanna and said, "Tonight I can share your chamber again. I asked if I could, this one time."

The day had seemed unreal to Joanna. Each moment of it had marked another small death, the last dinner she would share with Eleanor, the last time she would listen to music with her or hear the bells ring for Nones with her. She had even gone to chapel for Vespers because it was the last time she could do it with Eleanor and she had wept quietly all through it.

"You must not be so upset, lamb," Nurse chided her. "You take everything so much to heart."

"How can I not be upset when I love her and she's going away for ever?"

"Yes, you have a loving nature, child. I wish you could learn to love the Good Lord even as much as you love your friends on earth. Life is full of separations and deaths and trials. Learn to resign yourself to God's will."

"It isn't God's will, it's my father's," she sniffed, unconvinced and far from reconciled.

She willed the day to go slowly, but it moved inexorably forward. At last they were together in Joanna's chamber. Her ladies had helped to disrobe her and put her to bed. The shutters were closed and the room was warm and stuffy. It was late August and it had been a long day as the sun still went down late. They were tired but could not sleep. One by one, the others in the room dropped off to sleep. Now there was no sound but regular breathing and the distant sound of music from the Hall.

"Joanna! Are you still awake?" Eleanor whispered and reached out for her.

"Yes, I can't sleep."

They rolled toward each other and lay embraced.

"Joanna, I'm so afraid. I don't want to go," Eleanor breathed. Joanna lay silent but she held her tightly. "I don't want to leave you and Mother and France and everything."

"You'll come back. You'll come back as a Queen, very grand, for us all to admire."

"You know I won't. Matilda has never come back, has she? You don't even remember her, do you? She was married just three years ago; it was this time of year. You were only a little girl. You won't remember me either, you'll see."

"I will, I will! Eleanor, I'll never forget you!" Her throat ached and tears were forming behind her eyes. "No one's ever been as kind to me as you. Not even Nounou, she scolds me a lot. I can't bear you to go." She began to cry softly in the dark.

"Ssh! You'll wake them. Perhaps I'll come back. Mother travels, doesn't she?"

"Anyway, I'll come and see you," Joanna said, sniffing.

"Yes, and then I can show you the court. We'll have such fun, Joanna. They'll have to do as I say, if I'm the Queen, and I can tell the minstrels to play our favorite songs."

"And make the cooks bake special treats every day. *No* fish. And marzipan at every meal."

"And I can give you lovely presents, Spanish dolls. Do you think they're different from ours? And necklaces."

"And there'll be no lessons, we'll just play all day," Joanna said happily, forgetting to whisper.

"Ssh! You'll wake your Nurse."

73

"I won't bring Nounou. She wouldn't let me play all the time and eat lots of sweets." She added anxiously, "But I'd miss her. I've never been away from her."

They lay in silence for a while.

"Christmas, Eleanor. Perhaps Mother would let me come at Christmas. That's not too far off, is it? It will be warmer in the South."

"Yes, come at Christmas. We'll have a wonderful time together." Joanna knew from the sadness in Eleanor's voice that she did not believe it would happen.

"How do you say Eleanor in Spanish?"

"Eleanora. *Yo seré la reina Eleanora de Castilla.*"

"It sounds almost like French. 'I shall be Queen Eleanor of Castile.' Is that what you said?"

"Yes. It's not hard to learn. It's sort of in between French and Latin."

Joanna sighed. "You're so clever, Eleanor. I hope I don't have to learn a foreign language when I marry, English or German or something. Even Latin's bad enough."

"You speak langue d'oc as well as northern French."

Joanna widened her eyes in the dark. "That's not a foreign language. I've always spoken it."

They lay clasped in silence.

"I wish I could have been a nun. That's what I'd really like," Eleanor whispered suddenly.

"A nun?" Joanna was shocked that Eleanor, on the verge of becoming a Queen, should prefer any other destiny. "But—you'd never do *anything* that was fun. Just praying and reading and singing." She felt uneasy. Eleanor was so much more virtuous than she was.

"I like all those things. I don't like wars and politics and tournaments and noise and violence. Oh Joanna, I hope the court of Castile is not like Father's court, all dogs and shouting barons and drinking and swearing."

"If it is, then you must change it," Joanna said firmly. "You'll be Queen. Make it more like Poitiers, with music and poetry and ladies in beautiful gowns."

"Yes." She sighed. "But those are not the most important things in life, Joanna. We are put here to work out our salvation. That's all that matters. And I think it must be easier in a nunnery."

Joanna stirred uneasily. People had been saying things like that to her ever since her birth, it seemed, and she felt guilty that life on earth was more real to her than salvation. At least Richard understood her ambition and did not criticize it.

"I'd like to be the Preceptress at Fontevrault and spend my life teaching the little children there. I love children. It would be such a peaceful life and worthwhile."

"You'll have your own children, Eleanor."

"Yes, I hope I do. I will raise them to love God. That would be a worthwhile life too, wouldn't it?"

"Of course." Joanna sensed that she had found something that comforted her sister. "You'll be a wonderful mother, Eleanor, the best."

"You will too, Joanna, I'm sure, when your time comes."

"No, I don't think so. I'd rather spend my time with adults than with children. I can't wait to be grown up." She remembered what the next day would bring. "Except that I don't want to go away and marry a stranger and learn a foreign language and never come home again."

"No."

Joanna bit her tongue for reminding Eleanor.

"It's all right, Joanna," Eleanor said, sensing her discomfort. "I don't feel so badly now. I always knew this time would come. You cheered me up by saying that about my children. Perhaps in a small way I could help to make Christendom truly Christian. My sons and daughters can spread Christian virtues to every court of Europe."

Joanna giggled. "Perhaps some of them will even be saints." She was serious again. "Knowing you, Eleanor, I shouldn't be surprised."

CHAPTER EIGHT

That year the Christmas court was held in the castle of Bures. They had all traveled north to Normandy: Joanna, her mother, Alice, and all the courtiers from Poitiers. The castle here seemed stark and forbidding to Joanna after Poitiers. Dinner was served in the Great Hall. In a lull in the talk, Joanna heard the carolers' voices. The boys were singing now and the clear high sound rose to the smoke-blackened rafters of the Hall. They stood close together and Joanna saw how their eyes flicked sideways as each new dish was carried in. *"In dulce jubilo,"* they sang, their mouths round. Then the din rose again and drowned out their pure treble.

There was little jubilation in the Hall that day. The shutters were closed against the stormy weather. They rattled and shook as the wind buffeted them, and sometimes Joanna caught the sound of streaming rain. The chimney had been smoking all day; gray haze hung heavy among the beams and wreathed the flaring torches on the walls. The Hall was decorated with holly and ivy and crowded to overflowing with the nobility of Normandy and

Anjou, Brittany, Aquitaine and Poitou, there to attend King Henry's Christmas court. For all the finery and the music and the flashing jewels and sumptuous dishes, the faces of the diners were somber.

Even where Joanna sat with the children, the mood was subdued. Joanna ate silently. She had heaped her trencher with selected items from each course—glazed eggs and parsnip mousse, tansy cake and nut bread, gingered carp and roast lamprey, galantine pie and venison in frumenty, stuffed pheasant and swan neck pudding, squash flower fritters and dates in comfit. At the end of each course, with a flourish of trumpets, they had brought in a subtlety of marzipan or spun sugar, but to Joanna's disappointment, these had not been offered to the children. In Poitiers she could have counted on some of the leftovers from Master Hubert, but here in Bures, everything was different.

Thinking of Poitiers and last Christmas made her sad. This was her first Christmas without Eleanor. She wondered how she was doing, far away in Spain, and if she was thinking of her family. Strange to think that she was Queen Eleanor now. Joanna's eyes turned to her mother at the other end of the Hall. The Queen sat upright as ever, her lips tightly folded, her head slightly inclined as she listened to something that Archbishop Roger of York was saying to her. In the center of the High Table, King Henry slumped back in his chair, one hand clutching his gold cup on the table before him. His eyes darted angrily around the company. Near him, Joanna saw her brother Richard, splendidly dressed and eating ferociously. He had pulled in front of him the plate he shared with Alice and was leaning well over the table so that the sauces dripping from his meat would fall onto the plate. Beside him, Alice chewed daintily on a capon leg. She held it between her thumbs and forefingers and extended all her other fingers. Staring nervously over it, she reminded Joanna again of some small rodent. On her other side, Geoffrey sat, sullen and silent, glancing every now and then down the table at his father.

Joanna did not fully understand what had happened, but it was something important enough to have spoiled the Christmas festivities. She heard talk among the adults of the Constitutions of

Clarendon, the honor of God, the kiss of peace. Should the Young King have been crowned by York? Were the excommunications justified? Joanna understood only that it was a clash between her father and Archbishop Becket and that everyone was taking sides. On the one hand, Nurse praised Becket as a brave and holy man, and King Louis of France supported him, and if he stood for the Church and the honor of God, surely he must be in the right? On the other hand, her mother thought he was an ambitious and hypocritical man, and she had overheard some courtiers saying that Becket was trying to set himself above the saints themselves, and then of course, it was her own father he was opposing. Joanna was more than a little afraid of her father and knew he was not altogether a good man, but he was King and everyone had to obey him. Didn't they? She wished it were less confusing. If the grown-ups did not know what was right and what was wrong, then who did?

They had been in Normandy almost a week, at this hunting-lodge of Bures, a gloomy primitive place compared with Poitiers. It was icy cold. There was no snow, which she might have enjoyed playing in, but the ground froze hard every night. Today was a little warmer because of the rain.

The castle of Bures was dark and the atmosphere oppressive, and in the daytime Joanna was glad to escape and go out to slide with the other children on the frozen ponds. The grass, as they ran, crunched under their feet and their breath steamed in the cold air. The trees were leafless, like spiky witches' fingers against the leaden sky. A few red, worm-eaten leaves clung to the brambles close to the ground. Overhead, rooks glided and cawed.

The three prelates from England had arrived a few days before Christmas. Nurse, clicking her tongue and crossing herself, had supplied Joanna with what she knew. The Archbishop of York was suspended and the Bishops of London and Salisbury excommunicated by Archbishop Thomas of Canterbury because of the part they had played in the coronation of the Young King. No one quite knew how he had managed to get the notices into their hands without their realizing what was happening. Some said a boy had delivered them, others said it was a woman in disguise. King Henry received Roger of York, but had to refuse audience to the other two because they were under the ban.

Joanna, peering covertly round corners, watched them, fascinated. If they were to die now, they would go straight to hell. They were damned for eternity, yet they appeared more angry than afraid, striding up and down with their long cloaks swirling around them and rubbing their hands to warm them. She listened as the Norman nobles questioned them, amazed that anyone would dare talk to them, as even talking to them could endanger your own soul, too. No one was supposed to speak to them or come near them. A curse was on their food, on the cups they drank from, on their beds, even the air they breathed out.

King Henry remained closeted with his barons or the Archbishop. When she passed near that part of the castle, Joanna could hear his voice raised in anger and instinctively she tiptoed. At dinner he would either talk through the entertainments, ignoring them, or sit in sullen silence. He ate sparingly and drank a lot. Joanna hoped the presents would not be forgotten this year. She hoped, too, that there was a letter from Eleanor, but dared not ask. Her father paid no attention even to his sons Richard and Geoffrey, and her mother was icily regal and distant. She saw her only at dinner.

The adults were tense and irritable, arguing among themselves, and the children were pushed aside, ignored. They skulked in corners, looking longingly at the roaring log fires they dared not approach. They eavesdropped and speculated among themselves. Alice and Constance sat at the High Table with Richard and Geoffrey and they brought all the gossip they could.

Archbishop Thomas Becket had landed at Sandwich on December 1st. The Sheriff of Kent, Sir Randulf of Broc, who had been taking crops from Canterbury land, had sworn that Becket should not land. The King's men had attempted to seize him, but he had a letter of safe conduct from King Henry himself.

"The common people made a festival of his return," Alice recounted. "They drew his boat up on the beach, spread their coats on the road, and scattered branches in his path."

"Just like Palm Sunday," Joanna breathed.

"Joanna!" Constance said, shocked. "The Archbishop is only a man."

"He may be, but they treated him as an angel sent from God. It's only six miles from Sandwich to Canterbury, but it took him all day to get there because of the crowds thronging and pressing around him. Each foot of the way, they said, he was passing through kneeling throngs."

"I wish I could have seen it," Joanna said.

"And at Canterbury he was met by processions of chanting priests and weeping monks, and he entered barefoot into the city to the sound of trumpets and psalms."

"Barefoot? In December? He must be very holy," Constance said.

"What if your *father* is excommunicated next?" Alice said excitedly. "After all, he was *really* responsible for Henry's coronation last June and that's why the others were excommunicated, because only the Archbishop of Canterbury can crown the heir."

Joanna stared at her in horror. "But they can't 'escomominate'—what you said—*Father*. He's the King."

"Oh yes, they can," Alice said triumphantly. "Just think what it would mean. If he were under the ban, no one could speak to him, his barons couldn't take counsel with him, his servants couldn't wait on him, and he wouldn't have any girls to lie with him at night."

"Alice!" Constance warned.

"Well, *everybody* knows. My ladies say it was because of Rosamond Clifford that Queen Eleanor went off to Poitiers on her own."

"Who's Rosamond Clifford?" Joanna asked, sensing there was something here she was not supposed to know, but at that moment Nurse came bustling in.

"Now then, Joanna, it's high time you were getting off to bed. Excuse us, my ladies, but you must leave now. This child will be all done in with the late nights."

Alice and Constance left and alone with Nurse, as she lifted her arms for her gown to be taken off, she repeated her question.

"Who's Rosamond Clifford?"

Nurse gave a sharp tug on her gown. "None of your business. That's that Alice been talking to you again, I can tell. I don't want you talking to her alone, she has an unclean mind. Looks as though butter wouldn't melt in her mouth and the Queen says she's a taking little thing, but it's taking in she's good at, if you ask me."

"Is Father friendly with this Rosamond Clifford?" Joanna persisted.

Nurse snorted. "A deal *too* friendly. That's enough of that or you'll feel the back of my hand. Tomorrow is Christmas Eve and you'll be up late for Mass, so you must get some sleep now."

It took her a long time to get to sleep and when she did, she had bad dreams. She dreamed of her father. He was sitting in his place at the High Table and he looked angry. He must have been under the ban, as the servants were not waiting on him and no one would speak to him. Then, in some horrifying way, the floor of the Hall opened and, far below, she could see flames and boiling cauldrons and demons with pitchforks. Two great black grinning demons flew up and seized her father. He rose up, clutching the table and it all began to slide with him. Then the table, the nobles, her mother, slid down into the pulsing red horror below, and last of all she was falling, too. She woke up, trembling and whimpering. For the thousandth time, she wished Eleanor were there. Alice was good for gossip, but she could not confide in her. There was so much going on that she did not understand and she felt confused and frightened.

She was thinking of this now as she sat at the table. Christmas Day and it was raining outside, and her father the King sat sulking at the High Table. She clutched the doll on her knee. It was the only present she had received that she liked. Nurse had whisked away the other gifts—a brooch of gold and amethyst, a prayer book with an ivory binding, a pair of gloves embroidered with pearls, a polished silver mirror—saying she was too young for them. The doll was a wooden one with a painted face and hair, dressed in silk and fur. Joanna thought it beautiful. She held it tightly under the table with her left hand while she ate. Alice and Constance were sitting at the High Table with Richard and Geoffrey, and Scholastique had gone with her mother Marie to Champagne for Christmas. Surrounded by children as she was, Joanna felt lonely. Eleanor today would be sitting in the place of honor, next to King Alfonso in the palace at Burgos. Was she thinking of her younger sister now, just as Joanna was thinking of her?

Across the table, her little brother John caught her eye and stuck his tongue out at her. She ignored him. This Christmas was the first time she had seen him since leaving Fontevrault almost two years before. She had not liked him then and she liked him even less now. A fat, dark-haired, spiteful little boy who was always telling tales. She remembered the first time she had seen him without his bonnet on and how she had stared in astonishment at his dark curls. All of them, from Henry to her, had their father's coloring, ranging from fair to auburn, so her first thought was that his hair was not real. She put out a hand to touch it and John yelled. He was always crying anyway, but his nurse Biscuit thought she was pulling his hair and slapped her. Biscuit! That was what she and Eleanor called her, though her real name was something outlandish like Bricfrith. John had been born in England, in the same palace in Oxford where Richard was born, and his nurse was a Saxon woman, the first Joanna ever met. She spoke some French but with a heavy accent. Joanna remembered how she used to trick her into saying certain words she could never get her tongue around and then shriek with laughter at her pronunciation of them. She wondered where Biscuit was now. Probably could not stand John kicking and biting her any longer and went back to her own country.

The carolers had stopped singing now. They were filing out, the boys jostling each other in their eagerness to get to the kitchens where they would be fed. Their place was taken by a group of jugglers. There was a lull in the talk and noise of the Hall as people turned to watch. In the pause, the King's slurred voice sounded loud.

"By God's eyes, if all who shared the coronation of my son are to be excommunicated, I shall soon be counted one of their number."

On the other side of the Queen, the Archbishop of York leaned forward. "Have patience, my lord. By proper management we may yet turn the case to some advantage."

"How so?" asked the King.

A burst of applause for one of the jugglers covered their conversation. As it died down, Joanna heard the Archbishop speak again.

83

"My lord, it is not for us to say what should be done. Seek advice from your barons and your knights."

From somewhere just below the High Table, one of the barons called out, "My lord, as long as Thomas lives, you will never have a peaceful realm or see good days."

Joanna saw her father's brows draw sharply together and his chin thrust forward. She sat cringing into herself, her food forgotten, waiting for the fit of passion she knew was imminent. With one swift move, the King swept the plate and cup before him from the table. They clattered to the floor and a couple of dogs raced toward them. A page stepped forward and was restrained by an older servant.

"Who does this Thomas think he is?" the King roared. He thrust his chair back so violently that it tipped over and crashed to the floor. He stared down the Hall, hands on the table. "A nobody, a goddamn merchant's son, a great long skinny clerk. He owes it all to me. *I* made him chancellor and *I*, God curse the day, made him Archbishop. The ingratitude of the man! I thought he was my loyal servant, but now we see what a snake he really is. God's balls! The man would have my throne if he could!"

He moved suddenly back from the table, staggered and recovered himself. His voice rose to a scream and his fists beat the air. "God damn him! He defies me, and in my own realm! He dares to excommunicate my servants. Curse him and his treachery! And a curse on all of you, false lazy cowards that you are!" He paced the length of the Hall. His face was red and veins stood out on his neck. "I have fed you in my household all these years and not one of you will lift a finger to help me here, God damn it!" Head jutting, nostrils flared, he glowered around at the barons who avoided his eye and made no move that would attract his attention. "God, you make me puke. You are quick enough to fill your bellies at my expense, but you won't get off your fat arses to prevent this fellow's insolence." He was down at Joanna's end of the Hall now, and she saw how the spittle flew from his mouth as he spoke. He looked around, but no one answered him. There was silence in the Hall, just the crackle of the fire and the snuffling of the hounds. He smacked his hand down suddenly on the table and the plates and cups danced.

"Will no one rid me of this lowborn priest?" he screamed. He swung round and paced back.

"My lord," a baron shouted, "the only way to deal with such a traitor is to plait a few withes into a rope and hoist him up on a gallows with it."

"Damn right. A traitor he is." He swung round suddenly. "You're all traitors, the pack of you, to suffer me to be mocked so shamefully by this son of a she-mule." He was shouting still, but Joanna saw that his anger was fading. Around the tables, the nobles were beginning to relax again and a few, tentatively, murmured to their neighbors.

"By Christ's passion," the King muttered, moving back to the head of the Hall, "to be King and surrounded by a pack of damned cowardly disloyal varlets. Not a man among you. And you lot," he snarled at the jugglers who had stopped their act when he knocked his chair over, "are you paid to entertain us or to stand and gawp?"

Hurriedly, the jugglers rearranged themselves and began tossing their colored balls into the air. A page ran forward to pick up the fallen plate and cup, and talk broke out again around the Hall. The King sat heavily in his chair and stared before him. He gestured angrily at his empty cup and the cupbearer sprang forward to refill it.

Joanna saw men shrugging and smiling. They had heard similar outbursts on previous occasions and no longer paid much attention to them. At the High Table the Queen smiled as she said something to the Archbishop on her left. Joanna relaxed her hold on her doll. Perhaps it would be all right again now. Like a thunderstorm on a hot day or like throwing up when you felt nauseated, the King had purged himself of his anger and now they could all enjoy the twelve days of Christmas.

When she woke the next morning, a servant was opening the shutters. The sky outside seemed low and white and there was an unaccustomed quiet. Joanna lay, peering over the fur covers. Her breath condensed in the cold air of her bedchamber.

"The rain has turned to snow, my lady," the servant said.

"Snow?" Joanna bounded from the bed, trailing a coverlet with her that she tried to wrap around her. She leaned from the window.

The world had turned white overnight. Walls and battlements, trees and hedges were all heaped with a smooth layer of snow. The bailey was crisscrossed with footprints, from the kitchen to the well, from the barracks to the gatehouse. Her gaze went beyond the castle walls. If there were a small hill somewhere, they could slide down it. Behind her, another servant had set down the large basin of water for her to wash in. Ice floated on the top of it.

"It's too cold, I don't want to wash this morning," she announced.

Nurse came in just in time to hear this. "Of course you'll wash. What's a little ice? When I was your age, I often had to break the ice in the morning. I wasn't as lucky as you, having servants bring water to my room. We had to go out in the yard to wash. Come to that, I didn't have my own room. You don't know how lucky you are. Now come on and wash yourself."

"At least," said Joanna, moving swiftly through her washing ritual, "people will be a bit more cheerful now. It was so miserable until today."

"I wouldn't count on it. There's quite a froufra this morning," Nurse said.

"Oh dear. Whatever now?"

"It seems four nobles have left, I forget their names—no, wait—Sir Reginald FitzUrse is one of them, and I think they said Richard Le Breton."

"Well, never mind who. My father is angry because they left before he dismissed the court?"

"I gather he thinks they may be heading for Canterbury," Nurse said heavily.

"Canterbury? Oh," as this sank in, "to the Archbishop, you mean. Well, Father did say he wanted someone to do something. I suppose they will warn the Archbishop or arrest him?"

"It must be more than that. The Council had decided in any case to arrest him for stirring up dissension." Nurse lowered her voice. "I think they're afraid they will harm the Archbishop. The King has sent riders to all the ports of Normandy, I hear, to stop those four. The Constable of Normandy himself has gone. None of them is to be allowed to embark for England. Hotheaded fellows they are, all of them."

"But what can they do? The Archbishop's in his own city. He could always, if need be, take sanctuary in the cathedral," one of Joanna's women said.

"Ah but would they respect even that? That's one of the laws they've been trying to change, you see, the law of sanctuary. Here, slip this on, Joanna. You'll need your fur, too. It's cold this morning. He's a good man and he's in the right, I must say as I think. It's the King who made him Archbishop, but he's God's man now, not the King's. The laws of God must stand before the laws of men or where shall we all be? 'Saving our order,' that's what he said. 'Saving our order.' He's a good man and a brave man."

"But what does it mean?" Joanna asked dispiritedly.

"Mean? Why, it means, child, that he will obey the King in all things and uphold his laws except where it concerns the laws of the Church. He's a holy man. I've heard stories."

"Tell me the stories," Joanna begged.

"Well, one evening he was having supper with the King and Queen of France. Queen Adèle noticed that the cuffs of his tunic were tight around his wrists and that something seemed to be moving under them. She asked him about it and he didn't like to say that it was maggots. But she insisted that he open his sleeves and—hark! There's the chapel bell. We must go, lovey, or we'll be late for Mass."

"But the maggots, Nounou, what happened?"

They left the room and started to the head of the stairs.

"The maggots were miraculously changed into pearls which rolled onto the table and shone in the candlelight," Nurse hissed, bending down to Joanna as she walked.

"Did it really happen, Nounou?"

"Of course it did. Do you think God couldn't work a miracle for one who went into exile to defend the honor of God?"

The phrase rang in Joanna's head. It reminded her of something. Roland, dying, holding up his glove to God. God's vassal, faithful to the death. *"Sun destre gant a Deu en puroffrit. Seint Gabriel de sa main l'ad pris."* "He offered his right glove to God. Saint Gabriel took it from his hand." She remembered it clearly and she remembered, too. the words of the oath of fealty which every vassal swears to his lord, with its reservation of allegiance toward the King. "... from this time forward to be your liege man, to bear you faith of life and limb against all men who live, saving the faith of my lord King ..." She thought she understood the Archbishop. Roland preferred death to dishonor, and the Archbishop chose exile and disgrace to breaking faith with his supreme overlord. It seemed the Archbishop was in the right, after all. But then what did that make her father?

For two days the atmosphere remained heavy and oppressive. Her father went about in a grim silence that was even more frightening than his fits of rage. Her mother's lips were pursed and Richard and Geoffrey were sullen. Only John was unaffected by the tension and whined and tattled as much as ever. On the third day, the Constable and his men returned. He came directly to the royal apartments where the King was striding up and down before the fire while the Queen worked at her embroidery frame.

"Well, what news? Did you stop them?" The King had interrupted his pacing and stood with his hands on his hips.

"Sire, we scoured all the ports but could not find them."

The Constable looked anxiously up at the King as he knelt before him. "We heard they had already sailed."

The King flung his arms above his head and turned to the fireplace. He leaned his arm against it. Joanna, in the corner, kept very still, clutching in one hand the knucklebones she had been playing with. Presently, her father struck the chimney breast with his hand.

"Christ!" he swore softly. "Oh Christ!"

He turned back to the Constable. "Did you send men after them?"

"Yes, sire. They left this morning."

"It may yet be well. But they have two days' start. You are dismissed." He began to pace the room again.

Queen Eleanor had put her embroidery frame in her lap. She watched him coldly. "You brought it on yourself, Henry. You were disgustingly drunk."

"I was not drunk." He turned and paced back. "Shit! I must have been. I don't remember it, I swear I don't. What did I say to send them off like that?"

"Enough. What if they kill him?"

The King stared at her. "Kill Thomas? Jesus, what a disaster! They wouldn't do it. I couldn't have said that. Did I say it? Did I say kill?"

Joanna had been following their talk with painful intensity.

"No, you didn't," she said unthinkingly.

Her father whirled on her and she shrank back into the corner. "Come on, come on, I'm not angry with you. What did I say? Can you remember my exact words?"

"Yes, Father. You said, 'Will no one rid me of this lowborn priest?'"

"There! You see? Rid me of him, not kill him. Christ!" He kicked a log in the fireplace. "If they should kill him ..."

"You deny all blame and put the four of them to death, of course," the Queen said briskly.

King Henry looked at her sourly. "The responsibility is mine," he said slowly. "I could not, in all honor, have them put to death."

"Honor? I have no patience with you, Henry. There's more at stake here than mere honor."

The King interrupted her. "You're only a woman but I would have expected you, Eleanor, to understand. If everyone knows I told my men to get rid of him, what would they say if I executed them for following my orders? No, there's no way I can back down from it. And Thomas frightens me. He is stubborn enough to resist arrest. If they harm him ... Disaster, Eleanor, it would mean disaster. For me, of course. And for England, too. It would set the course of justice back in England for hundreds of years."

He stood motionless for a while, then he took a deep breath. "There is no point in prolonging this pretence of celebration. I know the twelve days of Christmas are not run, but I shall dismiss the court. I mean to leave for Argentan tomorrow."

"Yes. And we will return to Poitiers. And let us hope to God the Constable's men reach Canterbury before FitzUrse and de Tracey do something we shall all regret."

Joanna was beside her mother when Eleanor and her train came clattering into the palace bailey at Poitiers on New Year's Day. It was now the year of Our Lord 1171, a cold muffled day with a hazy sun locked in a heavy white sky. Riders from

Argentan were there ahead of them with the news. The Archbishop had been murdered on the altar steps of his own cathedral. Thomas Becket was dead and Joanna knew the world would blame her father for it.

CHAPTER NINE

There was no more celebration of Christmas that year. Even the Twelfth Night festivities were cancelled. It rained constantly, a steady depressing downpour. The rain pattered on the palace walls and sills, and sluiced against the mullioned windows of the Hall, and pocked the puddles that began to form in the pleasance beyond the Hall windows. The last leaves fell from the plane trees and Joanna marvelled that the sky could still hold more rain.

The King, they heard, had thrown off his royal robes and called for sackcloth strewn with ashes. He had dismissed even his own intimates and had gone into seclusion in a tower room at Argentan. He would see no one and refused food, until his courtiers feared for his very life. The aged archbishop of Rouen had been summoned to comfort him, but to no avail.

Over and over again they heard the story of Thomas' death, with added details as new messengers arrived, until Joanna almost felt she had been there. She could not bring herself to pray for her father; he was in the wrong, she felt it strongly. Yet she suffered for him, even as she suffered from the disgrace of being his daughter. Becket had died as a martyr, faithful to the higher allegiance.

"It's the most terrible thing to have happened since the Crucifixion," Nurse said. "The good Archbishop, that holy man ... no need to pray for him, my lamb. He's in Abraham's bosom, that's sure. To think of them killing him right there in the Lady Chapel!" She leaned toward Joanna. "There's a man called Aylward whose eyes were put out and he can see again now; he had a vision of the Archbishop at his bedside, telling him to pray to have his sight restored and now he can see again! There, that proves he is a holy martyr, doesn't it?"

Joanna was awed. In all the court, as more tales and rumors of miracles reached them, only her mother seemed unimpressed.

"Well, well," Queen Eleanor said, raising her eyebrows, "people will believe what they want. For my part—I say it now because I see it will soon be impossible to say anything against him—I never cared for Thomas Becket. A proud ambitious man. I always thought him cold. I remember Henry saying once, in later years of course, 'Becket mistakes his own will for that of Providence' and I think that summed him up. His death atones for much. He will become a saint, I see that already."

"A saint, my lady? Yes, I think he will. But the Archbishop of York declared in a sermon at St. Paul's that his death was an act of divine punishment. And some of the bishops even said he should not be buried in consecrated ground. Priests in England are not allowed to pray for his soul or mention his name in service, on pain of flogging."

"Henry is such a fool," the Queen said sharply. "He was always headstrong but this was his biggest error yet. How could he have forgotten himself so far?"

Normandy had been laid under an interdict. No bells were rung, no masses said. It could only be a matter of time before the ban was laid on King Henry himself. The King made what amends and concessions he could and then he left to invade Ireland.

Joanna's brothers, arriving one by one in Poitiers, agreed at least in condemning their father. Henry and Marguerite returned from England. Seeing him for the first time in months, Joanna noticed how handsome Henry had become, tall and golden haired with blue-grey eyes, yet she was annoyed when she overheard one of the ladies saying to another, "He is become the most handsome prince in all the world." Richard at this age was not as graceful as Henry. He seemed all arms and legs. Privately, Joanna thought him the most handsome of all, but even she had to admit that his hair veered toward red.

"Thank God none of my liege men were involved," Henry said of Becket's death. "*I* am in the clear, anyway."

"You were in England," Richard said quickly. "Why didn't you receive him? I thought you admired him so much."

"My dear brother, are you implying I could somehow have prevented it by receiving him? Yes, I admired him. But there are other considerations. When you are King, you cannot allow vassals, even archbishops, to take the law into their own hands. But of course you will never be a king so I suppose you don't realize that."

"Don't talk poppycock, Henry. You know as well as I there's little difference in ruling Aquitaine or ruling England. Except that I'd a good deal rather have Aquitaine, even without the title of King. If it comes to that, what would you know about the duties of a king? I haven't noticed you undertaking any."

"Through no fault of my own," Henry said angrily. "If Father were not so grasping ... you have Aquitaine and Geoffrey has Brittany but he won't relinquish any of the lands that are to be mine. That *are* mine. What was the point of crowning me?"

"Perhaps he's waiting to see you show as much interest in assizes and councils as in tournaments and feasts."

"Clerks' work! And no doubt that suits him, but it doesn't suit me."

So they wrangled and complained until Queen Eleanor sharply told them to leave the Hall.

"Your father's besetting sin is his violent temper and you bid fair to be as bad as he. Learn to control yourselves and until you do, stay out in the stables, where such behavior belongs.

"Strange," she said, looking reflective, "I used to despise Louis for his meekness. Henry's energy was so attractive by comparison. Now I hardly know which is the greater fool."

Joanna pricked up her ears. She had never heard her mother mention her former husband before.

"They say, my lady," said Countess Ermengard, "that he is become wonderfully mellow with age. He plays chess, dines with the monks, and sleeps a lot."

"Age? He is not so very old, I think, only a year or so older than I am. As for dining with the monks, he was always at least half a monk himself. Any more mellow and he will drop off the tree altogether."

"I had a letter from my husband today and he mentions the King my father," Marie said. "He repeats some remark of my father's, something he said to one Gerald of Wales ... 'your master the King of England lacks nothing. To him belong men, horses, gold, silk, gems, fruit, wild beasts, and all things else. As for us in France, all we have is bread, wine, and joy.'"

"All we have is bread, wine, and joy," the Queen repeated slowly. "There is the germ of a poem there, if Louis had phrased it better. Richard? No, of course, I sent them out, didn't I? Richard shows considerable promise as a poet, don't you think?"

"Indeed he does, my lady. You must be proud to have such fine sons, and Henry so good-looking."

"Yes, Henry is well enough. He favors his grandfather, Geoffrey the Fair. But I think Richard's looks will be more manly. Do you notice how tall and strong he is growing?"

Joanna crept away. In the schoolroom she found Alice and Constance and Scholastique. Alice was sitting at one of the tables they worked at, carving its surface with a sharp little knife. The other two sat on the bench below her.

"You'd better not let André catch you doing that," she said, indicating the heart Alice had carved on the table. André was Marie's chaplain and was teaching the children Latin.

Alice giggled. "I'll put his name next to it. *That* will really stir him up." She started to carve an A. "He's very bad-tempered these days, anyway. You know why?" She leaned toward them with a sly smile. "Your dear mother, Scholastique, has been setting him to write a Code of Love for the courtiers. It's true! *Tractus de Amore et de Amoris Remedia.* A chaplain writing a manual of love!"

Joanna thought of Thomas Becket. He would never have acted against his beliefs to keep his post. Or even to save his life. She felt contempt for Chaplain André. Better death than dishonor.

"Chrétien is going to read to the court tonight," Scholastique said, changing a subject that obviously made her uncomfortable. "I heard the Queen and Mother talking about it."

"Why do you always call her the Queen and not Grandmother?" Joanna asked curiously.

"She told me not to call her Grandmother. I don't know why."

"Is Marie in love with this Chrétien? She talks about him a lot," Alice said.

"Of course not! She's the daughter of a king and he's just a poet," Scholastique said indignantly.

"Hm. You're right. But perhaps he's in love with her?"

"Everyone's in love with Mother."

Scholastique had said the wrong thing.

"Oh Marie, Marie, Marie! Everyone's in love with Marie. It's just because of her position, it doesn't mean a thing," Alice snapped.

"Scholastique, let's try to listen tonight," Joanna urged. "Can you creep out without your nurse hearing, do you think?"

"I'll try."

Since Eleanor's departure, Joanna had become more friendly with Scholastique. They could not share forays to the kitchen or early morning riding adventures but they had in common a love of romances and poems, and Scholastique had an excellent memory. Perhaps partly because of Nurse's disapproval, the doings of the court were all the more fascinating to Joanna. She and Scholastique lingered unnoticed in corners or hid in the minstrels' gallery, their favorite place. From there, they had a view of the whole Hall. There were always guests and travelers who recounted tales of pilgrimages or news from France, and sometimes as many as two hundred sat down to dinner: soldiers, jousters, riding masters, troubadours, nobles, and chatelaines, and especially the young came in great numbers, squires and undubbed knights, debutantes and clerks and the princes' followers.

A new group had arrived this evening, five young knights from the Limousin. Joanna knew they had only just come because one of them rode on horseback into the Hall for dinner, with his friends around him, laughing and shouting. The seneschal, Sir Ralph, scandalized, went up to remonstrate. Joanna could not hear what he said but she heard the shouted reply.

"If it's good enough for her husband the King of England, I don't see why she should object."

His friends cheered him on. Sir Ralph looked for support to some of the knights who had been longer at court in Poitiers. They came over and argued with the boisterous young newcomer. Joanna and Scholastique watched, giggling, from behind the gallery rail. They had seen such scenes enacted over and over. In a month or a week, or even a few days, depending on how fast they learned, these new knights would be indistinguishable from the others, with elegant clothes and manners, perfumed, bowing, as proud of their wit or poetry as they now were of their horsemanship.

The horse was led from the Hall by a servant and its rider sat at one of the long tables and began to chew a piece of bread. They were arguing with him again when the trumpeters suddenly straightened their line and sounded a fanfare. Queen Eleanor entered the Hall, followed by her ladies. Joanna looked down on the tops of their heads, the flowing colored veils, the circlets of gold and silver. As they walked the length of the room, the courtiers bowed low, even the newcomers, who were nudged into it by their neighbors. The rider, abashed, held his hunk of bread behind him and made an effort to swallow what was in his mouth.

In the gallery, the musicians nodded to each other and their leader beat softly with his foot, one, two, three. Their bows slid across the vielle strings in unison. Down below, the ewerers moved among the courtiers. Flower petals floated on their bowls of water. The Queen took her seat beneath the baldaquin at the High Table and then the courtiers sat.

Joanna and Scholastique watched the newcomers who were now covertly observing their neighbors at table and making clumsy attempts to imitate their manners. As the meal progressed, they became more and more drunk. One of them pulled out a bag of dice and threw them on the table. Sir Ralph came over. Joanna saw him gesturing as he explained to him that other entertainments were customary here. The young man grimaced but he swept up his dice.

The servants moved quietly and efficiently down the Hall, clearing the tables and folding and putting away the trestles. The High Table on its dais was pushed back and the Queen and Marie and some of the higher ladies, King Henry's sister Emma, the Countesses of Flanders and Narbonne and others, sat in state before it. Around the walls, the courtiers sat on benches. The dogs were driven from the Hall and perfume sprinkled on the rushes. The smell of it came up to Joanna and Scholastique where they sat hunched behind the gallery rails. They heard, through the talk, the scrape of benches and the distant clatter of dishes, the sound of vielles being tuned, but tonight, they knew, instead of dancing or perhaps before dancing, Chrétien was to read to the assembled court.

Marie called him forward and he stepped into the cleared space in the center of the Hall. The buzz of chatter gradually died down as he bowed to the dais, his dark hair swinging forward. He wore his hair long, in the new style, and a sparse beard outlined his jaw. An expectant silence settled on the courtiers. Here and there someone nudged his neighbor, there was a giggle or the sound of feet disturbing the rushes.

"Your Majesty, my lady Countess," he began in his clear, rather high voice, "my lords, ladies, and gentlemen, tonight I crave your indulgence for a new work which my lady Countess did me the great honor of commissioning. I dedicate to her, in the hopes that her worth will make amends for my inadequacies, this new romance, the story of Sir Lancelot and Queen Guinevere."

A round of applause broke out and Chrétien bowed again. Marie leaned to say something to her mother and the Queen inclined her head, smiling.

"I have entitled it 'The Knight with the Cart'." He cleared his throat and lifted the book in both hands, standing with one foot forward.

Puisque ma dame de Champaigne
Vialt que romans a faire anpraigne ...

Joanna settled down happily, transported by his words and by the soft chords of the vielles into a magical world of chivalrous knights and fair ladies, noble kings and evil villains. Huddled in her fur-lined mantle, lulled by the music and by Chrétien's voice, she slid insensibly into dreams and from dreams into a deep sleep.

She was woken by a burst of clapping and talk. The music had stopped and Chrétien, his book closed, was bowing. Around the room, the courtiers rose to their feet, talking, smiling, applauding, moving out into the Hall. Joanna and Scholastique crept wearily from the darkened gallery.

CHAPTER TEN

Spring came early to Poitiers that year, 1173, and by May the roses in the Queen's arbor were in bloom. She had had it planted when they first moved there three years before. This summer the climbing roses had met overhead and made it a pleasant shady place to sit. It was a few days past Whitsunday and the roses were at their peak now, their creamy yellows and glowing reds springing out everywhere from the glossy new leaves. The air was heavy with their scent and with the languorous buzzing of bees.

Joanna was not paying attention to the roses or the bees. When a furry caterpillar fell from the trellis above and wriggled upside down in the folds of her skirt, she brushed it off almost without noticing it. She sat hunched forward, her thin arms thrust between her knees, fists clenched. She had not dared to join the ladies on the benches but stayed back in the shade, sitting on a stone step. There, behind a rose bush, she could not be seen. Only old mouse-face Alice had seen her creep in. The others had been too busy listening to the conversation and watching the

Queen for clues to when to laugh and when to applaud. Alice had rolled her eyes up in mock despair. Well, Alice had never been bold. If Nurse had told *her* to stay in and finish her embroidery, Alice would probably have obeyed.

A slight breeze stirred the pavilion over Queen Eleanor's head. Joanna wrinkled her nose and scratched it, still staring fiercely at the scene below. There was a larger crowd than usual. From Whitsuntide to the feast of St. John was the season of armistice between the barons, and the young unmarried knights had flocked to court, though Richard had not yet come. They were standing and sitting now along the stepped walks that led down to the center of the arbor. Below them, the ladies of the court sat on benches, their vivid gowns spilling over the dusty flagstones. The atmosphere was tense with the expectation of pleasure. Joanna sensed this without understanding it. Somewhere out of sight a voice was singing to the accompaniment of a viol. The sound came and went with the breeze. In the center of the arbor, beside the Queen, Marie was sitting in a high-backed chair. She was crowned with flowers and her little pet dog lay at her feet. She fanned herself gently with peacock feathers as she spoke.

"Sir Martin?"

A young knight stood forward and bowed. He looked self-consciously over his shoulder at his friends and then back at Marie, clearing his throat.

"My lady Countess, a friend of mine, a certain knight whom I will not name …"

"Of course." Marie inclined her head, smiling. The knight's friends laughed out loud.

"This knight swore to the lady he loved, as the hard condition of obtaining her love, that under no provocation would he boast of her merits in company. But one day, he overheard some detractors saying vile and untrue things about her. It was too much to endure and forgetting my vow in the heat of passion, I burst out in her defence. I mean," he amended hastily, "he eloquently defended his lady."

"Too late, Martin, too late!"

"Be quiet and let him finish," Marie said reprovingly.

"Well, this incident came to his lady's ears and now she has repudiated her champion. He admits he broke his pledge to her, but does he, in this instance, deserve to be driven from her presence? That is my question. Or rather, my friend's question."

"Well, ladies, how do you answer—his *friend*? Lady Isabel, what do you say?"

"I am in agreement with the lady. He has broken his vow, therefore he no longer deserves her love."

Joanna twisted her fingers together, thinking hard. Which mattered more, defending someone you loved or keeping a vow? A vow was sacred, she decided. No matter how hard, it should never be broken.

"Lady Rohaise?"

"I think he should be repudiated at first and then forgiven."

"Lady Adelicia?"

"I think the condition was too hard. Any lover who truly loves could not stand by silently to hear his mistress slandered. His fault sprang from too much love, not too little. He should be forgiven."

"I agree with the Lady Adelicia," said Countess Ermengarde.

"So do I," cried several other ladies.

"We seem to be almost unanimous here," Marie said. She smiled at the young knight. "The lady in question, who shall be anonymous of course, is at fault. We recommend that the lady reinstate you in her favor, Sir Martin."

Sir Martin grinned, sheepishly and returned to his place. His friends clapped and the ladies stared, smiling, at Lady Isabel and went back to their whispering.

"Next? Sir Joscelin? Very good."

"My lady, I am not ashamed to plead my own case. I was until recently favored by a certain lady whom I love. She is now, not of her own choosing, married, and since then she has avoided me and denied me the—er—solaces of love. Her husband is an honorable man and she claims her marriage vow must now take precedence over the vows we swore to each other. Is it right that through no fault of their own, two lovers should be separated thus?"

Joanna wondered who he was talking about. Alice would know. She looked down at Alice who was leaning forward with her forearms on her knees, her lips parted as she listened, fascinated.

Beyond her, Countess Ermengarde was saying, "The later contracting of a marital union does not properly exclude an early love, except in cases where the lady gives up love entirely and is determined by no means to love any more."

"And which of us is strong enough for that?" Marie said, smiling. "No, since we must love, and since love is not to be found in marriage, I think the lady should honor her previous vows to you, Sir Joscelin."

"Is it not possible to love one's wife?" asked a young knight, straightening up from the post against which he had been leaning. A shower of petals fell beside him.

"No, I think not," Marie answered decisively. "The essence of love is that a lover strive through his deeds to be worthy of his lady's favor. Why should a husband strive to earn the love of a lady who is already his by law?"

"Besides, love is a passion one does not choose, a madness that strikes where it will." Joanna could not see the speaker but from the voice she thought it was the Countess of Flanders. "What are the chances that this passion would be ignited by the spouse chosen by one's parents?"

"But what if my parents were to present three young ladies and ask me to choose one to marry?" the young knight persisted. "What if I loved one at first sight and strove, after our marriage, to earn her love? And what if she, loving me, tried to make herself worthy of that love?"

"What if roses were blue and cocks laid eggs?" called a male voice. Some of his friends laughed and Marie frowned slightly.

Joanna frowned, too, and hunched her shoulders. She looked like one of the little gargoyles on the new-style cathedrals. The stone step under her was beginning to feel hard and she shifted her weight a little.

"You must forgive Roger," someone said. "He is newly betrothed."

"Yes, I am aware of that." Marie fixed her eyes on him. "Well, time will disillusion him. I shall not." She waved away a page offering sherbet.

"Roger, a wife is required to submit to her husband and to be truly loved, a lady must be inaccessible."

"Not *completely* inaccessible!" said a voice and everyone laughed.

The page with the tray of sherbet was coming up the steps. He caught sight of Joanna in her hiding-place and winked at her. She looked longingly at the dishes of cool pale sherbet and her mouth watered but she dared not betray her presence. It was bad enough to be outside at all, but Nurse, she knew, thoroughly disapproved of these gatherings. It was partly this forbidden quality that gave them their allure for Joanna and partly her perception that here, for once, women dominated. Life so often seemed unfair in its treatment of girls and she was so often in rebellion against it: girls had to wear stiff, uncomfortable clothes; girls could not go out riding alone; girls when they married lost at one stroke their names, their families and their homes. But in love, it seemed, listening to the courtiers, women ruled supreme. She could not think, as Alice did, that it was the most important thing in life. She would have preferred something more heroic, like leading a crusade, but it was at least something where women counted, so she watched and listened and tried to understand.

"What does the Queen say? Let the Queen speak," someone called.

Joanna turned her eyes to where her mother sat to one side in a carved oak chair. She sat very straight, her back not touching the chair. Now she turned her head and her deep set grey eyes scanned the company. There was a rustling as people leaned forward to hear her.

"I hope Sir Roger will not be disappointed by his Constance," she said and her voice carried clearly to the outer edges of the arbor and beyond, "but I fear that his is an ideal which is seldom, if ever, realized in life. It would be admirable"—she paused and looked into the distance for a moment—"but I think, finally, impossible. No, even supposing it is there to start with, true love could not survive the trials of married life."

Joanna had been sitting up tensely, her blood strumming in her ears, tongue thrust out between her teeth. It was true that most married couples she knew bickered more or less constantly, yet there was a vow between them, an oath of love and loyalty. She was distressed by her mother's cynicism. Now she cried out suddenly, "But what of *Erec and Enide?*"

She had not meant to speak her thought out loud and was appalled by the sudden silence. The sound of the invisible viol stopped. Her sister Marie was frowning at her, and on the faces turned toward her she saw surprise, disapproval, and, here and there, amusement. The blood rushed into her cheeks. Her first impulse was to run and hide, but then she sat up stiffly and waited. Into the silence a cuckoo fluted his two notes.

"Joanna?" her mother called, not seeing her.

Joanna stood up reluctantly, holding her sticky hands flat against her dress and biting her lip to keep it from trembling.

"The child should be whipped," Marie said. "She has no business to be here."

"But, being here, she scored one through the ring, I think." A new voice, young and confident, spoke from behind her. "A touch at least, wouldn't you say so, Chrétien?"

Joanna knew the voice at once and whirled round, snagging the hem of her dress on a thorn.

"Richard!" she cried out. Her dress ripped as she started toward him, then she stopped, confused, aware that it was not her place to greet him first. She shrank back, clasping her arms protectively over her thin flat chest and stared at her brother.

Richard stood at the top of the steps, his thumbs hooked into his jeweled belt. The sunlight shone off his red-gold hair, making an aura around his head, and glittered on the gold thread of his tunic. He stood there for a moment, while below him there was a rustling on all sides as people rose to their feet and murmured "The Count!" Joanna thought he looked like a god. Smiling confidently, Richard stepped forward out of the sun. With barely a pause as he passed her, he reached out and pressed the tip of her nose.

"Stay put, little squirrel," he murmured for her ears only. "Don't run away."

He walked slowly down the steps. The women sank into curtseys and the men dropped to one knee, rising again as he passed, in one long continual wave. Joanna stood transfixed, wanting to escape now that nobody was watching her but waiting because Richard had told her to. When he reached the center of the arbor, he paused to pick two red roses.

"For the Queen of England and the Queen of the court of love!" he said, offering them.

"Richard, my son!" Queen Eleanor held out her arms to him.

He knelt briefly then rose and kissed her on both cheeks. Joanna noticed how he towered now over their tall mother. He had grown in the months since she had seen him and his beard was fuller. It had been little more than a reddish stubble at Christmas.

"Mother. Beautiful as ever, I see."

"And you more gallant than ever, my son."

Joanna did not ask herself why her mother glowed when this golden son appeared. It seemed inevitable to her that all who knew him should admire him. Wondering, she shot a sideways glance at Alice. Richard had not greeted her or asked for her. He never did. Alice stood with her head bowed, looking up from under her lids at Richard. Joanna could not read her expression. Beside her, her sister Marguerite scowled. Joanna had no trouble in reading *her* feelings. Marguerite was insisting on being called the Young Queen these days, now that it was definite that she was to be crowned with Henry later that summer. Richard had ignored her in saluting Eleanor and Marie as Queens. Besides, Marie was not really a Queen, of course, but only a Countess, and Marguerite thought she should take precedence over her now.

"Is no one going to answer my sister?" Richard called, turning back to the assembly. "Come on down here, Joanna."

Brushing a leaf from her dress, she stepped out. Everyone was staring at her and she cringed inwardly. Trying to hold herself with as much dignity as her brother, she walked down toward Richard. He took her shoulders and turned her to face the throng.

"What about *Erec and Enide*, the princess asks?"

Joanna felt her spirits lift at the word "princess". Everyone else called her child.

"Richard, leave her out of this. She's only a child."

"Surely her point is worth debating, Mother. Chrétien, it's no good hiding behind my aunt Emma. Step forward, man, and defend your work. On the one hand, my sister of France says that love in marriage is impossible. On the other hand, my sister of England points out that you have written a much-praised romance centering precisely on chivalrous love between husband and wife. Now, either you are writing arrant nonsense or you must declare Marie to be in the wrong. Which is it?"

Joanna could sense from his tone of voice and the way his hands gripped her shoulders that Richard was enjoying himself. He knew that Marie was Chrétien's patroness.

Chrétien stepped forward and bowed. His dark hair swung over his face and he brushed it back. His voice, when he spoke, was light and pure, a singer's voice.

"Neither one, by your leave, my lord. The noble Countess of Champagne is right, of course. How could it be otherwise? But in the case of Erec and Enide, the story hinges on Enide disobeying Erec. Now, a good wife owes obedience to her husband. So either Enide is a bad wife, which is not the case, or she must have some reason transcending her duty to her husband. In this case, she disobeys through love for him, for his own good. It is a *fantasy*, my lord. Not the reality, but an ideal view of marriage. You may find in a tale what can never be in life."

Tears pricked suddenly behind Joanna's eyes. "Well, I think it's beautiful," she said hotly. "If it's not the way it is, it's the way it *should* be."

Chrétien turned to her, surprised. He considered her a moment, then bowed.

"Thank you, my lady. What I took moments to express clumsily, you have said perfectly in one sentence."

At first Joanna thought he was mocking her. Then she saw that he was serious and warmth flowed through her.

"My lord," the Countess of Narbonne called, "why don't you cast the deciding vote? What are your views on love in marriage?"

Joanna saw Alice look up. Richard hesitated, then with a smile he said lightly, "Marriage? A necessary evil, if one wants heirs." He shrugged dismissively.

"And yet," said William Marshall, "many men might envy you, my lord. The Princess Alice is remarkably pretty."

"Alice? Yes, I suppose she is. Well, they have my leave to write ballads to her eyes."

Joanna blushed for Alice whose face so plainly showed the hurt and bewilderment she felt. Beside her, Marguerite nudged her and hissed something in her ear and Alice made an obvious effort to appear indifferent.

"Shall we go in, Mother?" Richard asked.

"Yes, my dear. I'll give orders for a feast tonight."

"It's already done. I spoke to Ralph when I arrived."

"Come in then and tell me all the news. Have you come from Bordeaux?" Still clasping Richard's hand, she turned back and spoke brusquely to her daughter. "Joanna, I should like to know two things. First, how are you acquainted with the work *Erec and Enide*? Second, why are you here and not with your nurse?"

Joanna looked up at her mother. The grey eyes looked back levelly. As usual, she felt tongue tied in her presence and especially so now, conscious of all the people around them listening to her.

Haltingly she replied. "I listened while Chrétien was reading it. I didn't hear all of it. But nearly all, I think."

"I see. You were eavesdropping. Like today." Someone behind her snickered and Joanna clenched her hands into fists.

"Does your nurse know you are here?"

"No, Mother," she replied in a small voice.

"You have no business to be here. You are only a child."

"On the contrary, Mother," Richard said, "it *is* her business to be here. Didn't King Louis expressly send Marie here as school-mistress for the girls? Isn't Joanna learning from Marie how to be a great lady? And where could she better learn than from you and Marie?"

"I don't think Louis had Joanna's welfare in mind when he sent Marie here," the Queen answered, partly mollified. "She's supposed to be in charge of Marguerite and Alice. Still, I see you wish the child to be spared a whipping this once."

"A general amnesty, to celebrate my return."

"Granted, of course. Joanna, run along. For the rest of the season you may join us without skulking. *If* you have completed your duties inside. Sit with Marguerite and Alice and behave yourself."

"Yes, Mother." Breathless, Joanna turned to go but Marie called to her.

"Joanna, was Scholastique with you?"

"No, I think she's in the schoolroom."

"You'd better tell her the same applies to her," Marie said grudgingly.

Joanna dodged behind the hedge. Slowly, led by Queen Eleanor and Richard, the company made its way up the steps from the rose arbor, the long trains of the women's dresses sweeping the flagstones. She could hear their talk and laughter, fading now as she ran between hedges toward the kitchen gardens. This was the long way round but out of her mother's sight, she picked up her skirts in both hands and ran.

She was so full of excitement and joy that she felt she could have run forever, down the slopes from the palace, through the maze of narrow hilly streets, jumping in one bound the Clain and Boivre rivers where they flowed together below the town and across the forest to ... No, there was nowhere in the world she would rather be. Richard had come home at last, there would be a feast that night, she was allowed to join the company. With any luck he would stay until St. John's, and certainly there would be tournaments and hawking, and in all the excitement she could easily avoid Nurse and stay up to hear the singing. Richard himself would probably sing and there would be crowds of people in the palace and marvelous sweetmeats at dinner. She leapt wildly over a bed of asparagus, not quite making it to the other side, and stumbled but recovered and ran on.

When Richard was invested as Duke of Aquitaine the summer before, Master Hubert, who had come to Limoges with them, had made an elaborate confection of pastry, a knight on horseback with a lady on either side, representing Poitou and Aquitaine, offering him shields with coats of arms on them. Joanna remembered it clearly, the cherry jewels gleaming on the ladies' gowns, the angelica plumes spilling from the knight's helmet, the whipped cream ermine trimming, the gold leaf on the shields. She skipped between beds of rosemary and camomile. As she passed, she pulled off handfuls of leaves and rubbed them between her fingers and sniffed them. She slowed down as she reached the palace kitchens and brushed the fragrant leaves from her hands.

The kitchen doors stood open to let the hot air out. As soon as Joanna entered, she knew that word of Richard's coming had reached them. Fires were lit in the two great hearths and there was noise and activity everywhere. From right across the room she could smell garlic. Two men, stripped to the waist, were preparing a flayed boar for the spit, brushing it with aromatic oils and inserting slivers of garlic and bunches of aromatic herbs into gashes in its sides. Another was stuffing a swan. Its long neck fell over the edge of the table, its head almost to the floor. The master cook was standing by the table, shouting orders. He kicked a dog out of the way, lifting it several feet across the floor. It ran yelping out the open door.

Backing up and watching the activity, Joanna cannoned into two scullions carrying a ewer of water. One of them let his end slip and water cascaded onto the floor. The cook wheeled on them, shouting.

"Keep out of the way, can't you, you clumsy brats?" He boxed the ears of the one nearer to him, the one who had not let the ewer slip. The boy, unable to defend himself, hunched his head down into his shoulders. His ears glowed red. He was about Joanna's age.

Hastily she said, "It was my fault really. I didn't see them."

Unappeased, the cook growled, "You don't have to see them. *They* have to see you. You, don't stand there gawping. Get that water where it's going and then come back and mop this or we'll all be slipping in it. Get on!"

He lashed out at them again and, jumping out of his way, they spilled more water on the floor.

Joanna edged her way more carefully around the kitchen and into a side kitchen where Master Hubert worked. She was a favorite of his and could usually count on him for a sweetmeat. Scholastique was afraid of him, but then she was a silly and hung back when he roared. Joanna had long since learned not to pay attention to that. Of course, Scholastique was at a disadvantage, being from Champagne and not speaking the langue d'oc.

Hubert was roaring now *and* tearing his hair. He was a short, rotund man, dark and hairy. Joanna waited until he noticed her and included her in his diatribe.

"And now you've come to bother me, too, as though I didn't have enough worries without silly little girls who aren't allowed in the kitchen coming and standing on one leg and smiling at me and thinking to wheedle some sweets from me. What do they expect? A miracle? I told Sir Ralph it can't be done. 'How many hours do you need?' he asks me. Hours! Days, it takes. God's teeth! I'll tell the young Count to his face. It can't be done. And these fools left a whole churn of cream where the sun got on it. Ruined, all of it. I'll have their skins for it. God's liver! I'm surrounded by fools." He took a cloth from around his neck and wiped his brow with it. "Here! You want some marzipan? Go, get out of here!"

Munching on the marzipan, Joanna skipped across the courtyard and into the palace, dodging servants who were taking up the rushes and sweeping the floors. It was dark in here after the bright sunlight outside and the open kitchens, but she was familiar with every inch of the way and did not wait for her eyes to adjust. Her long auburn hair had worked free of its snood and hung down her back, bouncing as she ran. Her thin leather shoes slapped on the cool stone floors. She hoped nobody had told them yet. She wanted to surprise them.

"Nounou! Scholastique!" she shouted, bursting in. "Richard's come and there's going to be a feast and I can join the grown-ups; Mother said so!"

CHAPTER ELEVEN

T o Joanna, the great Angevin treasure castle of Chinon was like an entire city. Its walls stretched along a high ridge above the river Vienne, a huge hilltop castle that was in fact three castles, divided from one another by moats. They were staying in the Fort St. George, the new castle built by her father. From its windows Joanna could see the Vienne winding south toward Poitiers and Limoges and the busy road that led west to the Île-de-France. Her mother had brought her with Richard and Geoffrey to King Henry's Christmas court at Chinon.

Her brother Henry, with Marguerite, was spending Christmas in Normandy, but he was making his existence felt here in Chinon. Joanna had heard her parents argue over him twice already and now they were at it again.

"His brothers have the freedom of their own provinces and he sees that. Richard was invested as Duke in Aquitaine a year ago and since then he has sat in on councils and traveled with me. And Geoffrey has Brittany now, since your lap-dog Conan died last year."

Joanna saw how Constance flushed and then went pale and bit her lip. The death of her father, Duke Conan, had been a bitter blow to her. Queen Eleanor did not notice the effect of her words.

"Exactly. Conan died. So Geoffrey is now Duke of Brittany. But *I'm* not dead. Does Henry expect me to step aside for him? Retire to a monastery, perhaps?" King Henry snarled. He paced the apartment again, limping slightly from an old wound where a horse had kicked him. It was bothering him again in this damp raw weather.

"You don't seem to try to understand his position. He's seventeen now and the principal heir, yet he's the only one with no place of his own. He wants England …"

"Never! I am King of England. It's enough that he will have it when I die."

"Well, then, Normandy …"

"Normandy? The heart of my domains? I can see Henry holding the Norman barons in check! He wouldn't last a sixmonth without disaster."

The Queen sighed. "Even Anjou … something."

"*Even* Anjou?" King Henry spun on his heel and stared angrily at her. "My birthplace, my patrimony. Do you forget that my ancestors were Counts of Anjou for generations? Do you expect me to yield up Anjou in my lifetime?"

"Henry, you are impossible. You have crowned our son King and yet you let him have no power. He feels his coronation was a farce and the crown only a plaything …"

"And that is how he sees it! Oh yes, he knows all about playing but anything that smacks of work brings on dreadful weariness! I tell you, Eleanor, he has shown no desire for responsibility, he has balked all my attempts to teach him the real business of kingship. Look how he spends his time, gadding about to Paris or Rouen or Arras or Poitiers. A vagrant, no less!"

"He has no land of his own. Where should he stay? He is only a pensioner on your bounty. Which, I gather, is none too generous."

"God's teeth! So now he's accusing me of meanness, is he?" Henry's voice started to rise and Joanna shrank inwardly. She fixed her eyes unseeingly on the needlework in her lap. "Let me tell you, that cub will ruin me with his extravagances. He has no more idea ... He spends money like water. And on what? Going from one jousting field to the next all over the continent, supporting a flock of hangers-on ..."

"Henry has a very generous spirit. I heard that he invited all the knights in Normandy with the name William to dine with him ..."

"You call that generous? I call it foolishly spendthrift. And this largess he distributes, it comes from *my* treasure chests."

"Of course, if you don't recognize a chivalrous gesture ..."

King Henry stopped in front of the Queen, breathing heavily. Joanna and Alice exchanged surreptitious glances. Constance glowered over her needlework.

"Now we come to the nub of it! Chivalry indeed! Chivalry is dead or almost so. The boy has been corrupted by visits to *your* court. Oh, don't think I don't know what goes on down there. He has his head stuffed full of Arthurian romance and unreal nonsense of knights-errant and women who fancy themselves to be goddesses. Real life is not tournaments and love songs, it's councils and law courts and the sooner he learns that, the better. They're all a waste of time, tournaments, troubadours, an idle distraction from duty ..."

"Unlike other men's distractions, they have at least the virtue of not being sins," Queen Eleanor observed icily.

The King glared at her and ignored the comment. "I banned tournaments in England and now I'm sorry I did not extend the ban to the Continent. That boy has been warped by the company you keep in Poitiers, idlers, adventurers, men like your precious uncle Ralph de Faye ..."

"I don't know why you can't leave him out of it."

"Because I suspect *you* don't leave him out."

"What exactly do you mean by that, Henry?"

Joanna sighed to herself. They had gone over the same ground again and again, needling each other, insinuating, arguing, and still her father would not cede any lands to the Young King. She sensed all the undercurrents of bitterness between them and wondered if it was always so between husband and wife. Instinctively she sided with her mother. Queen Eleanor remained dignified and outwardly calm in all these arguments while King Henry's color rose, he shouted and paced and gesticulated. Richard too supported his mother and it made the King even angrier to see how his children took her side against him.

He was shouting again now. Joanna wished she could leave, but was afraid of drawing attention to herself. They went on and on. They argued at dinner and during the masques, in public and in private. And not only with each other. Last night, at supper, her father had criticized Richard and Geoffrey for wearing their hair long. Geoffrey in his usual smooth-tongued way had tried to turn away his anger, but Richard, who had all the Angevin shortness of temper, had flared up and said it was his business how he wore his hair and that short hair was considered old fashioned now. Whereupon the King had burst into a rage, saying he supposed it was now old fashioned too for young men to be courteous to their elders and betters and not answer back.

"And that damned effeminate beard, too. Never mind that it looks like a scrubby strip of drowned cat fur, what's the sense in growing a beard anyway? It just looks as though you haven't taken the time to be shaved."

"I will not tolerate these insults, my lord," Richard shouted, his nostrils flared. "Besides, it's absurd to call a beard effeminate. By its very nature ..."

"Don't bandy words with me, you insolent cub," King Henry roared. "Are these the manners they teach you at Poitiers?"

Before either one could say any more, Queen Eleanor said, "Richard, you will leave the Hall. You should remember that men of gentle birth never shout at each other like serfs and especially not in the presence of ladies."

It escaped no one's notice that she had not reprimanded him for arguing with his father. Richard was silent, glaring, for a moment, then he spoke stiffly.

"I beg your pardon, my lady mother. I should not have allowed myself to be so easily provoked in your presence."

He bowed to her and left the Hall. King Henry shot an angry sideways glance at the Queen. He was aware that the rebuke had been aimed at least as much at him as at Richard, but could not say so without appearing a fool.

"Damned insolent cub!" he muttered. "In my day, we'd not have been suffered to speak so to our fathers."

"In *your* day, my lord," the Queen said, addressing him formally as she always did in public, "you were leading an army for your father against Stephen. Times were rougher then and boys had to grow up faster. Now, thank God, we have more time for the amenities of life."

"Such as growing long hair and choosing different clothes for every day of the week? Or listening to some cow-eyed poet sing that he is dying for love? Pah! Is that any occupation for a man?"

Joanna was in awe of her father. He seemed to her enormous, although he was not so very tall, in fact no taller than her mother. He was broad and stocky, with heavy shoulders and the beginnings of a paunch. Her chief impression of him was of his enormous energy. At dinner he could never bear to remain sitting too long but would stride up and down the Hall as he ate, pacing the center of the room between the long tables, bellowing his stories and jokes, a dig at a baron here, a more-or-less friendly attack on a knight there, a piece of ribaldry that had the tables in an uproar. He talked almost as incessantly as he paced and his voice would have carried over a battlefield. He would barely pause in his talking to tear off with his teeth a piece of meat from the hunk he carried. Even his eating had an energy and ferocity to it. He had a heavy jaw and big teeth—or so it seemed to Joanna— and with his head dipped over a meaty bone and his eyes darting around the room, he made her think of some great wild beast devouring its prey. From time to time he would stop in his pacing to put a foot up on a bench and trade banter with one of his men, then throwing his chewed bone to the dogs, he would grab another piece of meat and be off again, swinging his way down the room. His cupbearers had a terrible time of it. They had to keep far enough away not to be stepped on when he turned, but near enough to give him his cup when he held out his hand for it.

Joanna had little enough to do with her father. In Hall, he sat of course at the center of the High Table and she sat at the children's table at the other end. When he visited his children in their apartments, she stood stiffly, backed by her ladies-in-waiting, while he asked them a few questions about their schooling or their health. He never seemed to know what to say to put them at their ease and his visits were usually short. She was proud of him. He was, after all, the King, and in her mind the most powerful man in the whole world. Yet she was afraid he was not a good man. Since the death of Becket, she had felt herself irrevocably turning against her father.

ର ✿ ଚ

She was skipping down some dark back stairs in the castle one morning when she met her father coming up round a bend.

"Well, well! Joanna, isn't it?" He looked in a good mood for once.

One hand on the inner wall, she curtseyed awkwardly. The stairs were narrow at the center.

"What are you doing here?" he asked.

It crossed her mind to wonder what *he* was doing there, but she kept her head down and answered, "Exploring, if you please, my lord." She flattened herself against the wall and waited for him to pass.

"No, no. Talk with me a while. I so seldom get a chance to see my children, and never alone. I don't feel I know you at all. Let's explore together. How would you like to go up on the battlements? Would that please you?"

"Oh yes, please," she said eagerly, forgetting her fear of him for the moment. The battlements were specifically forbidden to her.

"You lead the way then. Your legs are younger than mine."

When they emerged onto the battlements, her eyes were dazzled by the light. She blinked and hesitated, shrinking back from the inner edge which gave onto sloping slate roofs. A cold wind blew on her face and stirred her hair. Overhead a huge grey cloud hung in the sky.

Her father picked her up and carried her to an embrasure. She stared amazed at how high they were. The countryside lay spread out below them, the little town of Chinon at the foot of the hill the castle stood on, the river Vienne winding away into the distance.

"That way, to the west," her father pointed, "lies Fontevrault. And that way, to the east, the Île-de-France. North, but some distance from here, lies Le Mans, where I was born."

She looked at him, leaning away in his arms, trying to believe he was once a baby. Above his ears, his reddish hair was turning grey. From close up, she saw that his forehead and cheeks were covered with freckles, so many that they almost seemed to merge into one. She studied the fuzz on his earlobes, the folds of flesh below his jaw, the lines at the corners of his pale blue eyes. He turned away from the view and she dropped her eyes.

"Well, little one?" He set her down. It was like the official visits again. She knew he did not know what to say to her and she stood silent.

"Let's sit a while." He sat down in the alcove of the embrasure and signed to her to do the same. "No, I hardly know my own children. It's one of the burdens of kingship. Especially the girls. They grow up and go off to be married so soon. Matilda now—I was fond of her, a sensible little thing. And Eleanor. She was so pretty." He studied Joanna. "You're not so bad either. Not as pretty as Eleanor but prettier than Matilda. And I suppose it'll soon be your turn to marry. Who shall we find for you, eh?"

Joanna knew it was a rhetorical question but his friendliness encouraged her.

"A king, please, Father."

He was startled and then laughed. "You want to marry a king?"

"Yes. I want to be a Queen." She did not add "like Mother" for fear of spoiling his mood.

He slapped his knee and roared with laughter. "Oh, that's good! Yes. I like a child who knows her own mind and sets her sights high."

Along the battlements, two guards came quickly into view. They saw the King and hesitated. He looked up and waved them away. They saluted and withdrew.

"So. A king. And what else, while you're at it?"

"I'd like him to speak French. I'm not good at learning languages, as Eleanor is."

"Very good. A French-speaking King. I suppose he should be rich too? Oh and, of course, I know you ladies," he reached over and pinched her cheek, "he should be young and handsome, too, eh?"

He laughed again and Joanna laughed, too, though she sensed he was making fun of her and her cheek stung where he had pinched it.

"Well, where shall we find such a paragon?"

She already had him in mind. King Louis of France's son and heir, Philip, whom they called the God-given, born the same year as herself, was her secret choice. She had never met him, but Philip himself figured very little in her fantasies, which centered on being Queen of France, as her mother had been.

Before she could say anything, her father spoke again. "Tell me, Joanna, does your mother say anything against me to you children?"

"No, Father," she said, instinctively blotting out the memories of her mother's criticisms.

"I have sometimes wondered." He looked out across the countryside. "Wondered if she were not turning them against me. Richard is hers, I know that. Geoffrey—well, he speaks fair but I don't trust him. But Henry—my heir." He seemed to be no longer speaking to her but to himself. "I've done so much for him but he is still ungrateful. At least there's John and he's fond of me."

In the distance a group of horsemen appeared on the horizon. Henry narrowed his eyes, watching them.

"Looks like the envoys from England I was expecting. More reports to read." He squared his shoulders and stretched. "I won't forget though. A king, French-speaking and rich, young and handsome." He grinned at her suddenly and she smiled back.

"Come. We must go down." He held out his hand and she put hers in it. His hand was large and warm and engulfed hers completely. She realized then that her hands were cold, and her feet, too.

They turned and went in.

CHAPTER TWELVE

In February, Joanna's brother John was betrothed. As usual, it was Alice who learned of it first and brought the news to the younger children in Joanna's bedchamber where they were playing.

"So now, Joanna," she announced, seating herself daintily on the chest that held Joanna's linen, "you are the only one in your family not married or promised."

"John?" Joanna exclaimed, sitting back on her heels and swinging her doll upside down by one foot. "He's betrothed?"

"Who to?" asked Scholastique.

"You should say 'to whom'," Alice observed maddeningly. "Her name begins with an 'A'."

"Agnes," Constance guessed. "King Louis' youngest daughter."

"No. In fact, her name is *Alice*, like mine."

"Alice? Alice of where?"

"Do you give up? Very well, I'll tell you. He is to marry the daughter of Count Humbert of Maurienne." Alice sat smiling with satisfaction at breaking the news to them. Joanna noticed for the first time, and with envy, that Alice's breasts were growing.

"Will she come here and live with us?" she asked. "How old is she?"

"I've never even *heard* of Maurienne," Scholastique said. "Is it a good marriage?"

"Yes, she's the *heiress*. Count Humbert has no sons and he has agreed to make John his heir when he marries Alice. Maurienne," she added, "is quite a large province. I'm surprised you haven't heard of it, Scholastique. It runs south from Lake Geneva, east of Italy to Provence, and almost to the gulf of Genoa."

"It sounds to me," Constance observed, "as though King Henry is trying to surround your father, with Normandy and Anjou in the west, Aquitaine in the south, and now Maurienne in the east."

"Never mind all that," Joanna said. "Tell us about Alice. How old is she and is she coming here?"

"She's only a baby. I don't know if she'll come here. She may stay with John and King Henry. *But*," she paused and looked around, making sure she had their attention, "we're all to go to Limoges this month for the official betrothal."

ભ ✤ ૭

Joanna remembered Limoges from her stay there for Richard's investiture. The city was divided into two by the river Vienne. She remembered how the procession had crossed the river from the older part of the city, known as the Chateau, to go to the cathedral of Saint-Étienne in the newer part, the Cité. It had been crowded then, the narrow streets lined with Limousins cheering their new Duke, but, she thought as she sat in her stationary litter looking out at the jostling throng, not as crowded as it was now. Somewhere ahead of them a procession of pilgrims come to pray at the tomb of St. Martial blocked the street. She could hear their chanting and the braying of their donkeys. All around her, people shouted and gesticulated. They had come in with a train of Italian noblemen following Count Humbert and there was pandemonium. A load of oranges being brought from

Spain to Limoges for the occasion had been torn off a packhorse in the press and trodden underfoot. She could smell the sweet sharp tang of the crushed fruit. Craning, she tried to look back and see Constance in the litter behind her but her view was blocked by horses. There was nothing she could do but sit and wait. Slowly, a foot at a time, her litter moved forward. The royal party edged past the massed horsemen and then the pilgrims, and climbed up to the fortified castle of the Counts of Limousin.

The castle itself was crowded to capacity. Alice told her that people were even sleeping up under the battlements. There were not enough poles to hang their gowns up separately and the ladies argued over that and over who should sleep nearest the fire. The February nights were cold. Joanna, curled up in the center of the bed before Alice and Constance, was asleep long before the arguments were settled and the candles snuffed.

The Hall was cleared after breakfast, the servants carrying out the trestle tables and benches. As more and more people piled in, Joanna resigned herself to not seeing anything but the broad back of the man in front. She stood flanked by two ladies-in-waiting listening to the talk around her. Two Normans were talking of the penance her father had done at Avranches for the martyrdom of Thomas. One of them had been there on the porch of the cathedral of St. Andrew's and had seen the scourging.

"He was wearing a hair shirt, too, under his clothes."

"Hmph! For show, I'm sure."

"Well, maybe. But the scourgings were more than just show. I saw them bloody his back. I tell you, there was hardly a dry eye among us. Even the cardinals wept."

"And the Young King?"

"No. No, he didn't weep."

Behind her, two other men were discussing the marriage contract they had been summoned to witness.

"Of course, this gives him control of all the mountain passes to Italy," one said.

"And to the Pope. It's a shrewd move. He'll be the equal of Barbarossa now. I think he sees himself as another Charlemagne."

"I heard a rumor that some anti-Barbarossa elements in Germany ..."

"Enough said. And now the whole southwest of France. That's a feather in his cap."

"Yes indeed. Who would have thought Toulouse would switch his allegiance to King Henry? He's King Louis' brother-in-law, too."

"Family ties give way to politics. Speaking of which, it looks as though certain family ties are strained to the breaking point. I hear the Young King is scarcely speaking to his father these days."

"Or his wife either, but that's an old familiar tale."

"He's a fool if he listens to that gossip. All the women are in love with William Marshal. It means nothing, he's a loyal man."

"William's loyal enough. It's his wife's loyalty he doubts. There's a story that she sent for William ..." he lowered his voice and Joanna could not hear any more.

A court official had pushed through the crowd and was speaking to the lady-in-waiting on Joanna's left. The lady nodded and bent down to Joanna.

"My lady, he says you are to go up on the dais with your family."

The man shouldered his way back toward the dais, shouting "Way for the King's daughter" and Joanna felt a sudden surge of pride as she saw how people made room for her to pass.

Flushed and excited, she sat down next to Constance. She stared out over the assembled crowd, the men of Maurienne on the left in their colorful clothes, the barons of Aquitaine in the body of the Hall and on the right, the men of the South, dark-haired and bronzed by the southern sun. Their fluent, lilting langue d'oc reached her as she stared down at them, wondering why so many were here. With a small shock, she recognized a familiar face in their front ranks. She creased her brow, trying to place him. Dark eyes, dark hair, a straight nose and rather thin lips. He looked about sixteen or seventeen, arrogant, and certainly of importance among the Southerners. Then he looked her way and she remembered him. The youth who had asked her for a token at Richard's first tournament three years ago. She could not remember his name but he was from Toulouse. He met her eyes and looked away with no trace of recognition. Either he had forgotten or he chose to forget. She felt slightly wounded.

Her father stood up and moved to the front of the dais. Queen Eleanor sat several places from the center, looking rigid and tight-lipped. The seat of honor next to the throne was taken by Count Humbert, a short plump little man, dark haired but already going bald. He sat with his hands arched together, smiling a little nervously now and then. Joanna's brother Henry sat next to him, leaning back in his seat as though dissociating himself from the proceedings. His handsome face showed his resentment all too clearly. Next to him was Marguerite, leaning slightly away from him and looking, Joanna thought, much prettier than before, though tense. Then came Richard and Alice and Geoffrey.

On the other side of the throne were two men whom Joanna did not recognize, but evidently, from their clothes and jewels, they were men of rank and importance, and the second of them wore a gold circlet on his head. Beyond them, her brother John sat in a chair far too large for him. His hands were on the chair's arms, aping his father's usual pose, and his plump little legs dangled well above the floor. Joanna observed with disgust how he smirked and preened, looking out at this vast assembly of nobles come to witness his betrothal. Queen Eleanor sat beside him. Joanna could not see the young Countess of Maurienne.

"We have summoned you here to announce to you all the alliance we have sealed with Maurienne. It has been several years since we have come into our province of Aquitaine and we are glad to see how many of our loyal barons are here today ..."

Joanna realized with surprise that the "we" did not refer to the Queen and himself. He was using the royal we which he did only rarely on formal occasions. She saw how the nobles of Aquitaine stirred and glanced at the Queen as King Henry spoke.

"... before you all, the betrothal of our youngest son John with Alice, the daughter and heiress of Count Humbert of Maurienne. In pledge of this, we have agreed to make a settlement of 5,000 marks in silver, which will now be paid over to Count Humbert, and he has promised to make John his heir in Maurienne."

Count Humbert had risen and stood beside King Henry. The King's Chancellor came up on the dais and with a bow gave the King a leather pouch which he handed to the Count. A noblewoman carried Countess Alice up onto the dais. Joanna saw that Alice was indeed a baby, perhaps one, perhaps two years old, it was hard to tell in her cap and ankle length gown. King Henry held out his hand to John who slid off the edge of his chair and came forward. The noblewoman set the child on its feet next to Count Humbert and the two fathers led the children face to face. In the body of the Hall, Joanna heard women sighing and murmuring. Their hands were joined and the King bent to say something to John. John's childish voice sounded clearly in the silence.

"Must I kiss her? She's drooling."

Some of the onlookers laughed and others clicked their tongues disapprovingly.

Reluctantly, John leaned forward and kissed the little girl. She turned, squirming, against her father and began to cry. The noblewoman came forward again and picked her up. Her cries could be heard as they left the Hall, diminishing with distance.

"My lord, before I swear to make John my heir," Count Humbert said in high accented French, "you must tell me what dower you mean to set aside for John."

There was a pause. Joanna could not see her father's face, only his back.

"He will have Ireland and the estates in England we spoke of …"

"Yes, but now. Nothing in France? His brothers all have portions in France. It is not right that John alone should have no land, no castles …"

King Henry answered firmly. "I will give him the castles of Chinon, Loudun, and Mirebeau and the land between them."

Young Henry drew his legs up and sat forward. "You cannot do that!" he exclaimed loudly.

The King half turned. "Cannot? Do you dare to speak to the King and your father like that?"

Henry leapt from his seat and strode forward. "You have no right!" he burst out. "Those castles are in Anjou and Anjou is my domain. I will not give those castles to John, now or at any time in the future."

"And I say you will!" King Henry thundered. "I am still King and you have not yet inherited Anjou. You will have all of

England and Normandy and you would begrudge your brother a paltry few castles ..."

"Paltry? The treasure castle of Chinon? You give with one hand and take away with the other. I am crowned King but I have no power. You give me Anjou and then take three strategic strongholds from my domains to give them to John, and I am supposed to assent gladly."

"Be silent, Henry!"

"I will not be silent! You wrong me constantly. I am not even permitted to select my own friends. You dismiss my household and banish them to their estates. I will never cede those castles to John."

"By God," the King began, but Richard had risen, too.

"My brother is right," he said, "and this affects me, too. These castles are on my borders and Mirebeau is in Poitou. I will not cede it either."

King Henry turned to the Queen. "And you, my lady? I suppose you support your sons in their insubordination?"

The Queen rose and stood very straight. "I support them in their refusal to allow their lands to be taken from them without their consent. I will not ratify this marriage settlement."

Geoffrey had come to stand beside his brothers. "Nor I," he said. "They should not be made to hand over their castles to John."

The King stood with his head lowered and thrust forward like a bull at bay. His hands were clenched into fists at his sides and he glared at the Queen and his three sons. John stood uncertainly, not smiling now, looking from his father to his brothers. Joanna held her breath waiting for the outburst that was sure to come.

"I will not tolerate this!" King Henry's voice rose into a scream that Joanna recognized. She cowered in her chair. "What I say stands and I say John gets those castles."

"Then I will leave," Henry shouted back. He turned to go but the King moved swiftly to intercept him. He seized him by the wrist and the two stood face to face, breathing heavily. The King leaned forward and spoke low, his voice hissing through clenched teeth.

"You will sit down and by God you will stay in that chair if I have to tie you to it."

They remained motionless, locked, glaring, for tense seconds. Henry looked out across the Hall where the King's men stood at attention all around the walls. Slowly his gaze dropped. The King released his grip and Henry returned to his seat. Joanna saw the red finger marks on his wrist as he sat, clasping the arms of his chair. Sullenly, the others took their seats again. The King turned back to Count Humbert.

"My word is still law in my family and I will be obeyed in this. John shall have Chinon, Loudun, and Mirebeau. You have my word on it." He added testily to John, who was still lingering nearby, "Sit down, sit down!"

Joanna was conscious of the seething silence around her. Count Humbert was speaking now but she did not listen. Under her lashes, she glanced sideways at her family, Geoffrey brooding darkly, Richard upright and angry, and Henry still rigid and flushed, his nostrils flared, his lips compressed. Beyond the throne, John sat sulking, his big day spoiled. Count Humbert was charging King Henry to take good care of his infant daughter. She was from now on to be raised in the English court and considered as one of King Henry's family. Joanna remembered Alice's words, that she alone of her family was not yet betrothed. She dreaded it, dreaded being sent away to a strange court and a strange family, and yet she felt hurt and belittled to be the only one not promised. Of course her brothers' marriages were more important. She was only a girl and the youngest of the girls at that, but she could not repress a feeling of unfairness that she was of so little importance in the scheme of things. If she were Queen of France, she would not be neglected so.

The two men on the other side of the throne rose now. King Henry was saying something about settling the feud between them. Joanna listened dispiritedly as he introduced the one with the gold circlet as the King of Aragon-Barcelona but her interest was aroused when she heard that the other man was Count Raymond of Toulouse. She looked down into the Hall and saw in the front ranks the Count's heir. She remembered his name now, Raymond of course, like his father, Raymond de Saint-Gilles. He was very like his father in appearance, too.

Her thoughts wandered and she shifted restlessly in her chair. It was all taking too long. There was a stir of interest in the assembly. She yawned and focused again on the dais. The King of Aragon-Barcelona had sat down and now Count Raymond stood facing her father, his back to the Hall. Someone had brought in the relics from the chapel. She recognized the jeweled reliquary that stood between them and understood with surprise that the Count was about to swear fealty to her father. Was he not King Louis' man? An oath was serious. She was shocked that Toulouse should change his allegiance. And she remembered Alice saying that he was married to King Louis's sister. She looked instinctively at young Raymond, wondering what he thought of this desertion of his mother's family. He was watching intently but without expression.

"Do you wish without reserve to be my man?" King Henry asked,

"I wish it," the Count answered. His voice was deep and resonant, with the rich southern lilt.

He knelt before the King and held out his joined hands. King Henry clasped them in his own, above the sacred relics. The Hall was hushed as everyone strained to listen.

"I promise by my faith that from this time forward I will be faithful to King Henry and will maintain toward him my homage entirely against every man, in good faith and without any deception."

The King leaned down and raised the Count to his feet and kissed him. Together they faced the crowd in the Hall. Joanna shifted to the other side of her chair and began to pick her nose. She saw Nurse frowning at her from the side of the room and put her hands in her lap.

� ❀ ഌ

There was a banquet that night. Joanna was wearing her best jewels, a necklace and bracelet of heavy gold set with sapphires. Nurse had brushed her hair until it gleamed. Holding her train in her left hand, as the ladies did, she went into the Hall. The fresh rushes on the floor were sprayed with perfume and the walls were hung with tapestries, between which the wall cressets flared. The trestles were already set up and covered with white cloths. Behind the central seat of honor at the High Table, an embroidered baldaquin had been erected. Servants moved down the long tables setting silver spoons and bread trenchers colored pink with sandalwood. Half way down each table stood a jewel-encrusted boat-shaped salt cellar.

Joanna saw Richard and Raymond de Saint-Gilles in the middle of a group of young men. They seemed to be teasing Raymond about his costume, a yellow silk tunic with ornamental borders, over which he wore a dark blue cloak fixed on one shoulder with a silver fibula. Joanna walked toward them, head high, confident in her jewels and long-trained gown. As she came near them, she heard Raymond say, "Oh God, are children coming to the feast? I thought they'd all be in bed by now."

She walked on by, cheeks burning, straight over to a group of musicians tuning their instruments in one corner. Their bows did not assuage her feelings. She kept her back turned on the room, angrily wondering how she could in her turn snub Raymond, until she heard the room fill with chattering guests.

The ewerers started to circulate with their bowls of warm water with floating flower petals, going first to King Henry and then to the most important guests. Constance came up and took Joanna by the arm.

"Let's sit down there," she said. "I want to be as far away from them as I can."

A trumpet fanfare announced the first course and the sons of the Limousin nobles started to serve the High Table, with double portions for all the honored guests. Farther down the room, the men pulled out their knives and looked around for the cupbearers. Joanna let Constance drink first, as she was older, and then took the half-full cup.

"They've been arguing for hours," Constance said. "King Henry has banished some more of Henry's followers to their own estates, did you know? He has replaced them with his own men. Henry is furious."

Joanna said nothing. The servers had reached them now and were offering platters of salmon belly, porpoise and peas, roast lamprey and other fish, since it was Lent. Joanna had no appetite. She watched as Constance heaped their trencher with half a dozen items, then took a fritter for herself.

"Is that all you're eating? Don't wait for the subtleties. They won't get down this far."

At the High Table, the panter was cutting the upper crust from the bread to offer to the King. Of all the people there, only Count Raymond seemed to be enjoying himself. He sat easily in his chair, selecting delicacies from the dishes offered him and savoring the wines. On either side of him, Joanna's parents were grim and silent.

On the far side of the room, Henry and Richard were in the midst of a noisy group of young men. Joanna saw them arguing and gesticulating. King Henry was watching them too. She saw Raymond de Saint-Gilles' dark head and yellow tunic at the same table and frowned angrily. Alice saw where she was looking and leaned across the table.

"You missed your chance there, Joanna. He's getting married this year. Still, your father has Toulouse's allegiance now."

Joanna did not answer. She had never mentioned to Alice or anyone her dream of marrying Philip of France. She wondered what Philip looked like. Not as handsome as Raymond, no doubt, but still, a king ...

"What's so funny about wearing yellow?" she asked suddenly.

The young man next to Alice looked across with a smile and Alice giggled self-consciously. "Joanna, don't you *know*? It means success. Success with a *lady*."

"You mean, because he's to marry this year?"

They laughed again. "Oh Joanna, you're such a child."

She felt left out and stared sulkily down at the table, pleating the cloth between her fingers. She hoped they would soon go back to Poitiers.

CHAPTER THIRTEEN

Joanna left with the other women three days later. The King abruptly decided to leave for Chinon the next day and had insisted that Henry accompany him. Henry was virtually a prisoner. The King would not let him out of his sight, even making him share his bedchamber. They heard that he had escaped at night from Chinon and was supposed to be heading for France. King Henry had sent relays of riders after him. Queen Eleanor decided to pack up and ride immediately for Poitiers.

Someone must have posted fresh horses for Henry. When they were back in Poitiers, the news came that he had safely crossed the French border. Shortly after this, Richard and Geoffrey left. Joanna did not know if her mother had sent them away or if they had chosen to go. She knew that they were going to Paris to join Henry at King Louis' court and she envied them their freedom of movement. For her, there was no choice. She had to stay here in Poitiers and await the consequences, and she was afraid.

Her father would be furious with King Louis for helping his sons against him. Her feelings led her to side with Richard and yet she knew it was wrong for sons to rebel against their father. She thought of Philip of France, completely out of reach for her as long as her father and King Louis were enemies. If it came to war, she hoped it would leave Poitiers untouched, though even Poitiers was no longer the haven of peace it had once been.

More and more often, Joanna found that there was impassioned talk of war at court instead of music and recitals. Young men no longer brought their grievances to the court of love. The older courtiers were leaving, slipping away one by one to their own estates. She wondered why men always seemed so focused on battle and power struggles instead of all the other rich and fascinating aspects of life.

Joanna gave up sweetmeats for Lent and made herself eat fish, which she disliked. She went every day to chapel with Nurse and knelt on the stone floor, beside her cushioned prie-Dieu, to pray for a reconciliation. She knew there was nothing she could do, but somehow she felt that her suffering, little as it was, might help to avert catastrophe.

Easter came and the reduced court celebrated with all the usual splendor. Queen Eleanor had ordered that nothing should be omitted, and for a week there was feasting at night and tilting at the quintain and other games during the day.

A week after Easter, on the Monday of Hocktide, news came from Paris and everyone assembled to hear it. Even Nurse came in and sat on a bench by the wall, her pudgy hands clasped in her lap. Joanna sat beside her, biting her nails. Outside the long windows, clouds scudded in the sky and the wind shook the new buds on the trees.

"My lady mother," Marie said, "my husband bids me return to France. He is in Paris, at court. It seems my father the King has summoned all his foremost bishops and barons. He wants me to return at once."

"Yes. I expected this." Queen Eleanor rose and paced the floor. Joanna had never seen her so restless. Her eyes glittered and there were shadows under them. "You know why he wants you back? He thinks it's no longer safe here. It's all beginning now, the uprising. Henry, young Henry, has defied his father openly and Louis is supporting him. Henry, it seems, sent bishops to ask

Louis to send young Henry back to Normandy. Louis asked them, 'Who makes these demands of me?' and the bishops answered, 'The King of the English.' 'That cannot be,' Louis said, 'for the King of the English is here with me.' It will mean war."

Joanna cringed. War between her father and her brothers? Whose side would she be on? Her father was King and had to be in the right, but her sympathies were with her brothers and she saw her mother was also with them. Not that it mattered what she thought, she knew. But how would it affect her and their life here in Poitiers? She listened intently.

"What will King Henry do?" someone asked.

"Wait for Louis to move. What can he do? He will not invade France. I suppose he is defending his borders, but I hear that he is out hunting and hawking every day."

"My lady, my husband says that at the Easter court, young Henry rewarded those who came out in support of him with endowments of land. His seal is in King Henry's keeping but my father has had a new seal made for him and he has granted Kent and the castle of Dover to Count Philip of Flanders ..."

"Yes, yes, I have the same here in my letters. And Lincoln to Philip's brother, the Count of Boulogne. And the County of Mortain. Mostly, it's with England that he is generous and is keeping his continental domains for himself. I know young Henry doesn't care for England. Not surprisingly. But this is unwise, most unwise. It will make all the English rally to Henry."

"It won't be enough. Henry is finished. Scotland against him in the North, King Louis and the Franks against him in the East, and Brittany has risen, too. I think he has only Normandy on the continent now. The South will support you. Have you heard the sirventes Bertran de Bom has written, calling on everyone to rise and fight for their rightful ruler, Queen Eleanor, against her English husband?"

"How could I not have heard it? Everyone is singing it." The Queen turned sharply and folded her arms. "Don't underestimate Henry. He has experience and he moves fast."

Joanna tried to follow. Scotland against her father in the North and France on his borders here? He was surrounded. What would become of him? She watched her mother.

"He will have to move fast to hold both the Scots and the Franks. Besides, he's an old man now. The old lion, they are calling him."

"Not so old," Queen Eleanor said, raising an eyebrow. "He turns forty this year, I believe, and he is still strong. Don't forget that I know both him and Louis well. Louis will hold his ground if all goes well, but he doesn't have Henry's energy in adversity. And young Henry was just eighteen a month ago. For all his prowess in tournaments, he has no real experience in war. No, it is far from a foregone conclusion. The old lion is not toothless yet, I am afraid."

"When will it start?" Joanna cried out.

"Oh, not until the summer. The Franks fight by the almanac, you know. They don't like the discomforts of rain and cold. And that's another advantage that Henry has. I never knew a man who cared less for such things."

CR ❀ ꝏ

Marie left that week, taking with her Scholastique and Chrétien the poet and her chaplain André and all her ladies and household from Champagne. The Countess of Flanders left, too. Joanna embraced Scholastique, her throat tight with misery. Scholastique's plain face was pale and tears stood in her eyes.

"Joanna, I shall miss you. Don't forget me."

"I won't. Will you go to Paris?"

"Yes, to my grandfather's court for a while. And then home to Troyes. But this seems like home to me now."

"'Tere de France, mult dulz estes pais,'" Joanna quoted. "Remember?"

"Yes, of course, but you've got it wrong. 'Tere de France, mult estes dulz pais.' Land of France, you are a very pleasant land." She began to sniff and hugged Joanna again. "'A grant dulor ermes hoi desevrez.'"

"To our great sorrow this day we shall be parted," Joanna repeated. "That's Oliver speaking to Roland when he was dying, isn't it?"

"Yes. Oh Joanna," she burst into great sobs. "Shall we ever see each other again?"

"Cheer up!" Joanna urged her, though her throat ached. "*Munjoie*, Scholastique!"

"*Munjoie!*" Scholastique echoed Charlemagne's battle cry, smiling wanly through her tears. She let herself be led to her litter.

Joanna waited until they were out of the bailey, then she ran up the stairs, up to the top of the Maubergeonne Tower, and leaned from a window. The tears ran down her face unheeded as she watched the procession of tiny silent horses creeping east across the plains below Poitiers. She watched until they were mere dots disappearing into the woods on the horizon. First Eleanor, now Scholastique.

Perhaps it was better not to make friends, not to love at all, since separations seemed inevitable.

It was not for safety but for schooling that Queen Eleanor sent her to Fontevrault, or so she said. There were plenty of other clerks in the palace who could have taught her after Marie left with her chaplain André, but Joanna did not protest. Perhaps in an Abbey she would be safer if war came to Poitou. Nurse, for one, was happy.

"Anjou again, after all these years! These are terrible times but I can't but be glad to think I shall see my village and my own folk again," and she sighed heavily, belying her gladness.

Joanna hugged her tightly. "You won't leave me, will you, Nounou? Everyone else is going. I couldn't bear it if you went, too."

"No, no, of course not, child. I'll leave you for a while at Fontevrault to visit my own people but I'll come back and stay with you as long as they allow me to. Don't you fret, lambkin. The Lord is watching over you."

"And whose side is He on, Nounou? Will He make my father or my brothers win?"

"Let us hope they think of Him and come to their senses before there is any question of winning or losing. But I've said it before and I'll say it again, it's a shocking thing for sons to rebel against their father. Whatever he may have done, he's still their father."

They left in late April, under a heavily armed guard. The weather had turned fine and spring flowers were blooming everywhere. It was in the same season that she had traveled this road before, she and Eleanor sharing a litter when they first came to Poitiers from Fontevrault. She looked around her as her litter bumped along, thinking that perhaps some sight half-remembered would bring back memories of that journey. She could not remember it, could not remember Fontevrault either, except a dim recollection of two great round kitchens. Five years had passed since she and Eleanor had ridden out from Fontevrault. The old melancholy crept over her, no longer painful now but almost welcome in its familiarity. Eleanor had been Queen in Castile for almost three years now and all Joanna could remember of her was a gentle smile.

The Abbess herself came out to lead them to the royal apartments at Fontevrault. The apartments were near the west entrance to the Abbey. Beside it were the guests' kitchens and the guesthouse, and beyond that, the school, and then the Abbess' house and her private garden. The buildings clustered around the Abbey church. In the northeast corner was the infirmary and next to it, east of the church, the cemetery. Next to that again, the vegetable garden and the henhouse. The various farm buildings attached to the Abbey sprawled along the south side. Closer to the Abbey church itself were the nuns' quarters. The kitchens that Joanna remembered stood a little distance from the refectory to lessen the risk of fire. The sacristy and library were at the east end of the great Abbey church and the almshouses near the west door.

Joanna's days were marked by the sound of the Abbey bells. She rose at daybreak when they rang for Prime, and even at night, though she slept heavily as children do, she knew in her dreams that Matins and Lauds rang and the Ladies were awake and praying for her family and for peace in their time.

She had been there a month before she saw the Abbess again, except at a distance. She was somewhat in awe of the Abbess, not because Mother Audeburge came from one of the greatest families in the land but because like Queen Eleanor, she had an air of natural authority. The young nuns in the cloister would fall silent and bend over their breviaries when she passed through.

She never said anything to them; it seemed her mere presence sufficed to create order and silence around her. Joanna remembered her mother saying, "Mother Audeburge is a fine judge of people, jewels, and wine." She had added, laughing, "What more could you ask of an Abbess?"

Joanna was drawn by the smell of lilacs into the little garden behind the Abbess' chambers. The heavy clusters of blossoms drooped over the wall but not low enough for a young girl to reach and smell them. She looked around for a large stone or stool to stand on. Intent on one thing at a time, she had not seen the Abbess when she came in. Mother Audeburge was sitting in the shade against the wall, motionless and staring before her. Joanna thought she was in prayer or contemplation and started to creep away. Without changing her position, or even looking at Joanna, the Abbess called to her to come back.

"No, no, child, don't run away. Come back here. Come and sit beside me a while. I haven't had a chance to talk with you yet."

Joanna sat down beside her on the stone bench and they looked at each other with the candid stare of the very young and the very old.

"Let me see now, you can't be Eleanor, you're too young. You must be …?"

"I'm Joanna, Mother."

"Joanna. Yes, yes, of course." She looked in front of her again and half-closed her eyes. They sat there in silence for a while and Joanna studied her intently. Her black habit, where the sun was beginning to catch the folds of its skirts, had a sheen that she recognized as silk. Were nuns not supposed to wear simple cloth, to avoid the sin of vanity? But perhaps it was allowed for an Abbess. The Abbess' hands were not modestly folded in her sleeves but lay in her lap. They were old hands, almost transparent, with dilated blue veins running across the backs of them and swollen knuckles. She wore splendid rings on one hand, a great ruby set in gold on one finger and no fewer than five emeralds in a row—Joanna counted them—on another. Her other hand was bare but for her spousal ring, a plain gold band that sealed her as the bride of Christ. Joanna thought it a curious contrast. Her face was soft and crumpled, as Joanna called it in her mind, with pouches beneath the eyes, and her chin and cheeks puffed out slightly above her wimple. When she looked at Joanna, though, her eyes were clear and steady.

"Your sister is prettier than you."

This was true so Joanna did not answer at first. Then to even the score a bit, she said, "I am cleverer."

"Cleverer, are you? Then you'd better go into the Church."

"No, I don't want to."

"Perhaps you're not all that clever then. It's either that or marriage. You know what that means for a girl like you? You'll be sent off from your family when you're twelve or even younger, to marry some rich and powerful man. Not a king, I think, as you're the youngest and not the prettiest. A count, perhaps, or a duke, if you're lucky. He'll be old enough to be your father or maybe even your grandfather. He won't care a fig for you and he may not even speak your language. He'll come to your bed when you don't want him and leave you bruised and your face scratched by his beard. If you do want him, likelier than not he'll be in someone else's bed. You'll have to put up with him when he's drunk and hold your tongue when you know he's wrong or foolish. And don't think you'll find love elsewhere. You'll never be alone or unobserved. He'll have other women, you may be sure, but it's as much as your life is worth to play that game yourself. Perhaps in Aquitaine. They take those things more lightly there. But it's your brother who's going to be Duke of Aquitaine so you won't be going there. No, it's a hard life and few pleasures. You'll have to entertain your husband's guests even if you despise them and manage his castle, and when he's away at war, which he will be half the time, you'll have to do all his work as well as your own. Even to standing a siege. The world is full of dangers. Every year or two you'll risk your life in childbed. You'll lose some of your children to sickness and the others, inevitably, when they grow up and leave you.

"There's nothing permanent, you see, but death. Only one love that will never fail you. If you were wise, you would choose it at the outset. 'For I am persuaded that neither death nor life, nor angels, nor principalities, nor powers, nor things present, nor things to come, nor height nor depth, nor any other creature, shall be able to separate us from the love of God, which is in Christ Jesus our Lord.'"

"'But lay up for yourselves treasures in heaven, where neither moth nor rust corrupts, and where thieves do not break through nor steal,'" Joanna quoted somewhat pertly. The sermon the previous Sunday had taken this text or she would never have known it.

The Abbess looked at her steadily. "You say it but you don't understand it. Perhaps you will when you are older." She looked into the sky. Her voice took on a dreamy monotonous note. "Here we know peace and safety. We are respected, even admired. If you love learning, we have books and libraries and the time to use them. We have music, not the frippery minstrels' songs that you young people like these days, but real music. And art—you can spend your days working on fine manuscripts if that is your bent. Beauty, calm, and an ordered existence."

Beneath Joanna's hand, the stone of the bench felt rough and warm. She picked at a bump on the surface and watched an ant run onto her finger. The scent of lilacs was very strong now. She kept her head bent, soothed, entranced even, by the Abbess' droning voice. The Abbey was a quiet peaceful place compared to a castle but she could hear everyday noises in the background, the kind one never notices except in still moments such as this. There were shouts and the clanking of pots from the kitchens, the murmur of young voices in unison from the scriptorium where Sister Ermengarde was teaching the catechism, a rooster crowing nearby, and farther away the metallic ring of a hammer on metal, no doubt the blacksmith at work.

The Abbess smiled suddenly and held up her hand. The ruby on it flashed fire-red in the sunlight. "I know what they say about us Benedictines. But I praise and thank God daily for all His gifts. God gave us rubies and gold and silk, and God gave us the ability to paint and carve and sing and make wine. The essential is to love the Giver more than the gifts. Out there in the world you may lose sight of that. My left hand reminds me." She turned the single band slowly on her finger.

Behind them, the Abbey bell began to ring with startling suddenness. Two or three birds flew shrieking from the lilac tree.

"Vespers already?" The Abbess rose, briskly for her age, and smoothed the skirt of her habit. "Have I been wasting my time here or have I sown a seed that will in God's good time grow into a beautiful flower?"

Joanna stood and stared at her, not knowing what to say.

"God be with you, Joanna. Be a good girl and say your prayers every day." She folded her hands into her sleeves and walked slowly away.

The bells were ringing and the birds flying up into the air and the lilacs scenting everything. The Abbess went around the corner, slowly, her skirts swaying. Joanna brushed an ant from her hand and looked up at the birds. The sun dazzled her. When she looked back, the Abbess was gone. Joanna stood there alone in the sunlight.

Joanna folded her lips obstinately. Eleanor would have agreed with the Abbess, she knew, and Eleanor was cleverer than she.

CHAPTER FOURTEEN

J oanna came home to Poitiers for the feast of St. John, the 24th of June. Five days later, the rebellion flared into open war in Normandy, the heart of King Henry's domains. When the messenger arrived, he was brought directly to the dais. The courtiers rose to their feet and pressed forward to hear the news. Interrupted in mid-sentence and quite forgotten, the poet who had been reciting to them stood to one side. Joanna climbed on a bench to see over the heads of the crowd. The messenger knelt before the Queen. Little runnels of sweat streaked his dusty face and his tunic stuck to his back in sweat-stained patches.

"My lady Queen," he said, "Count Philip of Flanders has invaded Normandy."

Joanna saw the Countess of Flanders clutch her neighbor's arm. The Queen did not move. She sat upright and still, but Joanna saw how her jeweled fingers, clasped in her lap, were white around the knuckles from pressure.

"He laid siege to Aumale on the 29th of June and has taken it."

An "Ah!" went up from the listeners.

"King Louis and the Young King, your son, are attacking Verneuil. Your sons and the Counts of Poitou and of Brittany, are with the Count of Boulogne, laying siege to Drincourt. The whole country is up in arms. The barons of Brittany are marching on Dol."

"Henry?" the Queen asked crisply. "Where is King Henry?"

"My lady, we do not know for sure. He is seeking mercenaries. Perhaps he has gone to Chinon."

"To his treasure? Yes, that is likely. So he needs mercenaries. Will his English vassals not come to his aid?"

"My lady, the English are hard-pressed on their own borders and begging him for help. The King of Scots has formed an alliance with the Earls of Chester, Derby, and Norfolk, and I hear that many castles have fallen into their hands."

The Queen rose and paced the dais, fanning herself as she walked. Joanna watched her nervously. She could see the tension in her mother's posture, and if she was worried, it must be serious indeed. The air in the Hall was hot and still, despite the open windows.

"They will have to move fast. Forty days, that's all they have and then the balance tips in Henry's favor."

"My lady?" the Countess of Flanders asked.

"Forty days," she repeated impatiently. "I say nothing against your husband Philip. He is loyal enough to our cause, he and his brother of Boulogne. But Louis—once the forty days of military service his vassals owe him expire, do you think he will dip into his treasure to support my sons? Not he! He will withdraw to Paris. But Henry will empty his entire treasure, if need be. There is too much at stake for him." Her fan swished sharply through the air. She turned back to the messenger, who was still on one knee. "Go now and get some wine. My Chamberlain will see that you are paid."

"I thank you, my lady." He bowed his head and rose, backing awkwardly down from the dais.

Forty days, Joanna thought, was paltry service. If *she* were a man and had sworn an oath of allegiance, she would not give up so soon.

Every other day of that July, fresh news arrived. The Breton barons had seized the fortress of Dol, on their frontier, and were holding it. King Henry had put his jeweled coronation sword in gage to hire mercenaries. The Count of Flanders was moving on Rouen itself. King Henry had recruited an army of mercenaries in Brabant, twenty thousand according to one report, ten thousand according to another, but all agreed they were moving south by forced marches into Normandy.

Joanna was not there when news of the collapse came. She had been at the stables and, hearing the bells ring for Vespers, ran back to the palace. In the Great Hall, knots of people stood about talking anxiously. There were no signs of supper. From upstairs she could hear women weeping,

"What is it? What's happened?" she asked Alice, when she found her sitting in a window with Constance.

"The Count of Boulogne ..."

"King Henry's Brabantine army came on them at Drincourt ..."

"He's dead. His army smashed ..."

"Who's dead? I don't understand," she cried. "Is Richard all right? He was at Drincourt."

"Yes, yes," Constance said. "Geoffrey and Richard are safe. They are fled to France, as far as we know. But the Count of Boulogne was killed and because of that, his brother the Count of Flanders has withdrawn. The Countess is leaving here tomorrow."

"And my father? Where is he now? And King Louis and my brother Henry?" Joanna looked from one to the other.

"King Henry marched on Verneuil after his victory at Drincourt," Constance said.

Joanna looked at Alice who stared out of the window.

"My father has withdrawn," Alice said bitterly. "King Henry said to the French heralds, 'Go tell your King that I am at hand, as you see!' and my father retreated. Well, now it is the turn of Brittany. King Henry is heading west, they say."

"Oh my God!" Constance exclaimed and buried her face in her hands.

"One cannot help admiring him, though," Alice said. "One day he is surrounded by enemies on all his borders, the next he swoops down on them one by one and defeats or drives them all away."

"But ... it's not the end?" Joanna asked. "They will come back? King Louis will come back? My brothers, I know, won't give up."

"My father won't be back until the spring. Meanwhile King Henry will have re-established himself everywhere and fortified his borders. *He* doesn't fight by the almanac."

"But ... Brittany? The King of Scots? The rebellion in England?" Joanna stammered.

"He'll tackle them one by one. Your mother was right. They underestimated him, and he's not an old man yet."

CR ✿ ℇ

It was August, hot drowsy weather. The Countess of Flanders had gone back to Arras with all her retinue and the diminished court waited. From the high windows of the Maubergeonne tower, Joanna watched the peasants bring in the harvest. In the palace, quarrels broke out and tempers flared. The week of the feast of the Assumption, they heard that King Henry's mercenaries had recaptured Dol from the Bretons. The King himself, racing from Normandy to Brittany with incredible speed, took a host of captives.

Constance was in despair. "What shall we do? What shall we do?" she wailed.

"Do?" Queen Eleanor raised an eyebrow. "Well, you obviously can't go back to Brittany, unless you want to join the captives."

"But should I go to Geoffrey in Paris?"

"I see no reason why you should think of running if I do not," the Queen said tartly.

Joanna admired her mother's courage. Constance was often on the verge of hysteria these days, Alice was bitter over what she saw as her father's cowardice, and Nurse was horrified by the whole rebellion. The Queen seemed to be keeping everyone in the palace calm by the strength of her own indomitable will.

In September King Henry met his sons, accompanying King Louis, in the traditional meeting-place under the elm at Gisors in the Vexin. Although King Louis recommended that the sons make peace with their father, there was no settlement. Young Henry and his brothers rejected their father's terms and rode back to Paris with King Louis. It was Michaelmas, the 29th of September, when they heard of it in Poitiers.

"Oh why would they not accept?" Constance grieved. "Now it will go hard on all the captives."

"They were generous terms too, in the circumstances," Alice said, and Joanna's Nurse agreed.

The Queen thought otherwise. "Bribes," she snorted. "Henry simply will not see that what young Henry wants and needs is power. A kingdom of his own. The right to make decisions. All these offers of allowances, of honors, of freeing his captive household, are beside the point. Besides, I think they're waiting for results in England. The rebellion is gaining headway there."

"Is that what you're waiting for, too?" asked Joanna's aunt Emma.

"Yes, I suppose I am. Henry may have to go back there soon."

But King Henry turned south instead. Now the news became grim reality to Joanna. As her father moved methodically across Touraine, storming castles, razing their walls to the ground, and burning their ruins, refugees began to arrive in Poitiers. As the King moved down into northern Poitou, the refugees moved on, seeking asylum in the Île-de-France.

"Now you must go, my lady, now before it is too late," they urged the Queen as they took their leave of her. Joanna looked at her anxiously. They should leave before her father arrived, shouldn't they?

"And throw myself on Louis' mercy?" She smiled a little grimly. "I hate to do it. I will wait a while longer and see what happens."

The week before Joanna's birthday, the castle of Faye-la-Vineuse was stormed and taken. The Queen's uncle and confidant, Ralph de Faye, had already fled to Paris. The Queen was silent when she heard the news. She sat and drummed her fingers on the arms of her chair. Joanna saw the dark shadows under her deep-set grey eyes as she stared unseeingly before her.

By breakfast the next day the Queen had left. The first Joanna knew of it was when she came into the Great Hall, still rubbing the sleep from her eyes, and saw Marguerite in the seat of honor on the dais. She stopped abruptly, scowling, and a page bumped into her. Alice was on the dais with Marguerite but Constance was sitting alone at one of the half-empty long tables. Joanna sat beside her.

"Where's Mother?" she hissed, dreading the answer.

"Gone," Constance said briefly, through a mouthful of bread. She swallowed it and added, "Left before sunrise, with a few knights. She went disguised as a man."

"Has she gone to Paris?" Joanna asked in a small voice.

"Yes."

Joanna crumbled her bread and stared down at the table. Her appetite had left her and her stomach hurt.

"Why am I left behind?" she asked.

"Because you'd slow her down. Think how easily she would be caught traveling with children and litters and baggage-wagons."

"She didn't say goodbye."

"I'm not surprised. Your mother doesn't seem to have feelings herself, so she never thinks of others' feelings."

Joanna looked up at Constance. "You don't like her, do you?"

"No, I never have. She's a cold, hard woman."

Joanna thought of her mother. Into her mind came an image of her riding away, in something like man's attire, turning back and laughing. She looked around the Hall, at the empty tables. Here and there, groups of knights, squires and pages, poets and musicians ate greedily, their heads bent over the table. On the dais, Marguerite and Alice and her aunt Emma sat in silence. They all appeared fragmented, sparkling, drowned. She wiped her eyes with the back of her hand.

The days passed slowly and, for Joanna, miserably. Her mother had gone, fled to Paris to join Richard and Geoffrey and Henry there, without a thought for her. It was because she was a girl, she knew it. Parents did not care about their daughters. They loved their sons, so she was left here and her mother did not care what happened to her. She cried herself to sleep at nights.

On All Hallows' Day, travelers from the court of Paris stopped on their way to Compostela. Rain covered the sound of their arrival and Joanna was surprised to see them in the Hall at supper. Patiently, they repeated for the newcomers what news they had. The Queen was not in Paris and was not expected. The young Plantagenets had settled in Paris for the winter. King Henry was in northern Poitou. No, they had heard no news of Queen Eleanor on their way here. A band of knights? There were so many on the roads these days. Who could tell?

Joanna was not alarmed at this, as everyone else seemed to be. She remembered the ambush, the day they had arrived in Poitiers. Her mother was invincible; she was in hiding somewhere and would reappear eventually, laughing and chiding them for their lack of faith.

Joanna's aunt Emma sent out reconnoiterers north and east from Poitiers. In the palace, they waited for nine tense days. By St. Martin's Day, they were all returned and all brought the same news: The Queen and her knights had vanished without a trace.

It was a mild wet winter in Poitou. In the castle, life went on as before. The grooms swept out the stables and the smiths banged away in their forges; the servants emptied chamber pots and brought in fresh rushes for the floors, the laundresses pounded tablecloths in their wooden troughs, and in the kitchen the cooks turned the spits and prepared soups and stews in great iron cauldrons. To Joanna it all seemed a parody. The center of the dance was gone and this was only pointless capering.

She began almost to long for her father's arrival, so that things could be more definite again. Then she would know what had become of her mother and what was to happen to herself and the others. But now that he was so near, he seemed in no hurry to come to Poitiers.

Lent came, and Easter. Daffodils sprang up along the foot of the palace walls. Joanna picked great handfuls of them and set them in the window of her chamber. Their trumpets made a brave splash of yellow against the stone walls. Staring over them, she wondered for the thousandth time from what window her mother was looking out. Was she free to stroll among the spring flowers or was she a prisoner somewhere? The daffodils withered and still there was no news of the Queen.

On Whitsunday, the 14th of May, Joanna had gone to Mass in the morning with the rest of the household. After it, she escaped on her own, as she was more and more in the habit of doing, and wandered on the slopes below the castle walls. It was a perfect day, clear and sunny, but not hot. Sounds carried perfectly. Joanna did not consciously hear the sounds of human activity from the town below or the castle above, but she heard the woodpeckers laughing across the fields and the frogs croaking by the streams. She came across a puddle left by the spring rains and stopped to watch the tadpoles in it. Absorbed, she squatted beside it, seeing that some already had tiny legs while others had barely developed tails. Sometimes they floated on their backs, their tiny mouths gulping air and their bloated iridescent bellies turned up. Sometimes they lay motionless, their translucent heads and far-apart eyes just resting on the water's surface. She poked them with a grass blade and they flicked off at once, tails wiggling, little dark commas diving to the safer depths of the puddle.

There was a sound like distant thunder. Joanna looked up at the sky. It was a clear light blue with no clouds in sight. The faint rumble continued, more like drums than thunder now. It was Sunday, and Whitsunday at that, so no one was working today. She stood up, smoothing her skirt. From up above, she heard shouting on the battlements. She looked out over the town of Poitiers, but the slate roofs of its houses and shops and churches blocked her view. Suddenly she picked up her skirt in both hands and ran. She scrambled up the slope and through the gatehouse into the bailey, across the bailey and into the Hall, up the stairs, panting now, and into the Tower solar. Leaning from the window, she saw what she had expected.

Dark lines of horsemen moved across the plains far below. The thundering of hoofs reverberated off the hills and walls of the city. They came on in a mass, sweeping across the vineyards, scattering the animals out at pasture, churning up the new green ears of wheat in the fields. She watched until the leaders crossed the river, then she went down.

The household assembled in the Hall. There was little talking. Joanna edged behind Alice and Constance at the far end, where they stood with Marguerite and Emma of Anjou. They waited nervously. Through the open doors came the shouts of the seneschal in the bailey and farther off, the shrill squeal of pigs as the townspeople hurried their livestock off the streets. Presently they heard the clatter of iron-shod hoofs on cobbles. The sound swelled until it drowned out all others. In the Hall they shifted uneasily and stared at one another. Long moments went by. Then the bailey outside was suddenly filled with noise: neighing and stamping, shouts and commands, blare of trumpets and clatter of arms and jingle of harnesses. There was silence in the Hall. When they heard the first swift steps in the porch, those who were sitting rose to their feet and instinctively they all moved back against the walls. King Henry strode into the Hall.

He paused just inside the doorway and surveyed the room, his left hand on his sword hilt, his head jutting forward. Then he walked slowly down the cleared centre. He seemed larger than before, in a chainmail hauberk with a simple green surcoat over it. His head was bare. His hair was pushed back from his brow where he had dragged off his mail hood, which lay folded on his neck. Joanna saw the broad streaks of grey hair winging back from his temples. His chief barons followed him. The tramp of their mail clad feet sounded harsh and heavy as they came down the Hall. They looked contemptuously around them at the men against the walls with their waved hair, colorful clothes, and long-toed soft shoes.

The King stopped two thirds of the way down the Hall. His sister Emma stepped forward to greet him but he turned from her, ignoring her. He slapped the gauntlet he carried against the palm of the other hand, staring slowly round at them. Finally he spoke.

"No one is to leave the castle. We will tell you what our decisions are concerning each one of you when we have made them. You are all dismissed."

That was all. He turned back immediately to speak to the baron behind him. Glancing at one another, the Poitevins filed from the Hall. Joanna and Alice fled upstairs to the solar.

The King made some of those decisions swiftly. By suppertime the court hangers-on were gone, banished from Poitou. The knights and squires of her mother's court, the troubadours and minstrels, were sent on their way. The palace became a military fortress. Some days, men in chains were led in and then days later marched away to prisons in Normandy and Anjou.

In June, orders came for them to pack. Alice tried to find out where they were to go but all she could discover was that they were heading north for Normandy.

"You see? I told you so. We'll go to Rouen, to the court there, or to Caen," she said. Alice was cheerful at the prospect of court life again, hunting and hawking, music and dancing and civilized conversation. Joanna thought of the dreary castle of Bures in Normandy. Wherever they went, it would not be the same as Poitiers, she knew that.

The day before their departure, they dined with the King at last and it was then they learnt that they were bound for England.

"England?" Joanna said involuntarily, dismayed.

"Yes, England. Is that so surprising?" Her father stared at her. "Where did you think you were going?"

Joanna stared down at the tablecloth, her lower lip thrust out. Alice answered for her, hesitantly.

"We had thought, to Normandy, my lord."

"Well, it's England. That should knock some of the nonsense out of you." He leaned across the table and glared at Marguerite, his brows beetling. "Let's hope we're there before your husband."

"My lord?"

"Your precious husband, so I hear, is planning an invasion of England. Or rather, the Count of Flanders is, since I doubt that Henry could successfully invade anything stronger than a whorehouse." He laughed loudly but Joanna saw no real mirth in his face. Marguerite flushed and bit her lip.

Joanna did not speak for the rest of the meal. All she could think of was England, that distant, cold, and barbarous land.

ଓ ⚜ ଚ

They left on the feast of St. John. Joanna was shocked that they should travel on a feast day, but her father was in a hurry for them to leave. She remembered the summer season of previous years at Poitiers, that magical golden season that began on St. John's Day, the tournaments, the feasting, the palace filled to overflowing with courtly knights and their silk clad ladies.

As their procession wound slowly out of the gatehouse, Joanna craned from her horse for a last look. By now, she was comfortable on horseback. The clandestine riding lessons with Richard had long since been replaced by official sessions with a groom. Today though, she was riding astride. This was no time for ladylike sidesaddle riding. It would be a long ride.

The morning sun struck the high windows of the tower. The sweet scent of roses came to her overpoweringly from her mother's bower. Her throat ached with the effort of keeping back her tears. They clopped slowly down the narrow cobbled streets of Poitiers, across the bridge and finally out onto the plains. The escort went ahead, two hundred men in arms, then the royal party, her aunt Emma, Marguerite, Alice, Constance, Joanna herself, and all the other ladies who had remained in Poitiers. There were no litters for them on this journey; they all rode on horseback. Behind them came their households, seneschals, chamberlains, and chaplains first, then the almoners, wardrobe mistresses, butlers, panters, ushers, tiring-women, marshals, doctors, pages, and clerks. They were followed by the cooks and bakers, the brewers, tailors, and candle makers, and riding behind them with the baggage-wagons and sumpter horses came the laundresses, grooms, and servants. More armed men brought up the rear. The King and the bulk of his men remained in Poitiers. They would catch up with them later.

It took them almost two weeks to reach Barfleur on the Norman coast. Barfleur was crowded, noisy, and stinking. King Henry's army was encamped all around it. Their tents spread across the downs and the evening air was filled with their shouts and singing. The town smelled of the sea, of rotten fish and seaweed and salt-soaked rocks. The inn where Joanna slept smelled of fish, too, and of urine and wood-smoke and unwashed bodies. She and Alice and Constance were lodged there. Marguerite was taken somewhere else, they did not know where. They slept together in one bed. There were no sheets, only dirty blankets, and the room smelled of cats.

They were roused before daybreak and breakfasted on bread and ale. The sun was just coming up as they reached the docks.

Barfleur faces east, from the peninsula of Coutances, and the sun seemed to come up out of the water, sending blood-red streaks of light across its surface. The boats rocked, their masts outlined against the orange light.

Joanna heard a sailor murmur, "Red at night, shepherd's delight; red in the morning, shepherd's warning."

They stood in lines everywhere, soldiers, children, officials, sailors, babies with their nurses, knights and horses, captives from Normandy. Joanna saw earls and countesses and barons in chains, some surly, some dignified, some ranting and weeping. She watched Constance scanning their ranks, presumably for familiar Breton faces. The sea crashed endlessly on the rocky coast and sucked at the piers below them. Sometimes she felt its spray drift across her face. The wind blew strongly off the land and the smacks tugged at their ropes.

The crowd pushed aside to make room for the King's party to come through. He was arguing with his chief mariners.

"I tell you, we cannot wait for the weather, man. My son Henry and the Count of Flanders are in Flemish ports waiting to invade England. We have the wind. We sail today."

"Sire, remember the White Ship. The Channel was not as big that day as it is now, but she went down right out there …"

They went on by. Joanna wrapped her mantle more tightly around her arms against the wind. Her hair felt damp. She looked out at the grey-green choppy sea with its lines of white-crested waves. Henry, the present King's grandfather, had lost his only legitimate son, William, when the White Ship went down, and half the young nobles of England with him.

Behind the King came his officials. Joanna saw her younger brother John with them and a child she thought must be Alice of Maurienne. They were followed by a smaller group, of officers with a slim straight figure in blue in their midst, not chained, but obviously under guard. Joanna's eyes narrowed suddenly. The woman wore a hood and she could not see her face, but she looked like …

"Mother!" Joanna shouted.

The woman looked her way. It was indeed Queen Eleanor, pale and grim, but upright as ever. Joanna gasped. All this time she had believed in her mother's invincibility. She had wanted to be like her, a Queen, powerful, independent, and admired. What was there to emulate now? Her mother was one of King Henry's captives. Her guards would not permit her to stop. She smiled a little wanly as she went by. Joanna watched her straight blue back until the crowd surged round them again, blocking her view.

The scene was pandemonium but gradually the ships were loaded. The horses screamed and the babies wailed and the sailors cursed. The mercenaries filled most of the ships. Joanna and the other royal captives were all embarked on one ship with their households and their guards. Next to them was the royal flagship. The lions of England flapped stiffly on the aftercastle and King Henry's personal standard streamed out from the masthead. The King himself paced the forecastle. Overhead the clouds massed and scudded, dark at their centers, the edges torn and worried by the chivying wind.

King Henry raised both arms to the sky. "Lord, if in my heart I nourish plans which will bring peace to my people, if the King of Heaven has decreed in his infinite mercy that my arrival shall mark the return of peace, then may He grant that I come safely to harbor. But if He does not mean to vindicate my wrongs, if He is opposed to my purpose and has decided to punish my kingdom, then may I never be allowed to reach its shores and may the sea overwhelm my boats with all that is in them."

His men looked hesitantly at each other, then one of them said, "Amen." The others echoed it and they all crossed themselves. From ship to ship the gesture was repeated with murmured prayers. *"Domine miserere nobis ..."*

Someone at Joanna's elbow laughed quietly. "Was that a prayer or a challenge?" a cool voice asked.

"Mother!" Joanna cried and stopped. Her mother's face was pale and there were lines running between her brows and from her nose to her mouth. She had aged in the nine months since Joanna had seen her.

"Joanna! You look older."

Joanna bit back the first answer that sprang to her mind. She remembered how Richard always greeted their mother. "You look as beautiful as ever,, Mother," she said, looking anxiously at her.

The Queen did not smile. She looked back at the port of Barfleur. Her eyes seemed sunken and hollow.

"Where were you all this time?" Joanna asked.

"At Chinon. A prisoner in all but name."

One by one, the square sails were hoisted on each ship, the anchors raised, the hawsers coiled. Outside the harbor, the swell hit them. The boats pitched and rolled. The gulls wheeled, shrieking overhead. Joanna stood on the aftercastle with her mother, gripping the rail. The shoreline tilted one way, then the other. They drew slowly away. Barfleur became a huddle of roofs, then a group of small, square dots, then a pale patch on the long green coast of Normandy.

The floor of the aftercastle came up hard under one foot, then fell away. She learned to ride it, bending at the knees. The spray hit her face and the wind blew her hair around. She held it with one hand. On the decks below them, Alice and Constance and Marguerite sat huddled, their faces all pale green. Here and there, groaning figures hunched, retching, over leather buckets. Joanna's ears rang with the constant buffeting of the wind. In spite of her sadness, she felt exhilarated. They stood there together, riding out the storm. The Queen held her hood close at the throat with one hand and with the other gripped the rail.

"It was a day like this when I first sailed to England," the Queen said. "Worse, in fact. It was December and bitterly cold. December the 7th we sailed from Barfleur. Twenty years ago this year. The ships were all separated at sea. Henry and I were heading for Southampton but we landed in some harbor below the New Forest. At least we landed." The wind snatched the words from her and hurled them away. "We were crowned the Sunday before Christmas, I remember. I wore white and gold." She stared at the almost invisible coastline of France. "We had to live in Bermondsey because Westminster had been wrecked by Stephen's followers. Henry was born there in February."

Joanna had never heard her mother say so much about the past. She had always lived for the present.

"Are you afraid, Mother?" she asked.

Her mother looked at her then. She stood balancing effortlessly on the heaving deck of the aftercastle, her face still and composed though the wind screamed around her and the long horizon behind her angled steeply one way, then the other.

At last she said, "God has seen fit to make us women physically weak. I see no reason why we should make ourselves morally weak too."

Joanna felt like cheering.

In the evening, sitting on stools in the forecastle, they saw the coast of England come into view, not the white cliffs that Joanna had expected, but a green coastline that could have been Normandy. It seemed like the entrance to a vast river. The land on the left was the Isle of Wight, on the right England itself. The evening tide brought them into Southampton.

Part Two
Winchester, England 1174

CHAPTER FIFTEEN

Joanna was awakened by the bells. She lay and stretched her toes. No one else stirred. Nearby, Nurse snored lightly. The nights in summer here in England were short and Nurse complained every morning when the first light came that she had not had long enough to sleep. The bells were still ringing. It could not be for Prime. Perhaps it was some local English festival, some saint's day they celebrated in Winchester. What was it now, the 16th of July? She counted the days mentally. Yes, they had been in Winchester a week.

She remembered the confusion of their arrival. It was late and they were tired, but it was still light, the strange drawn out twilight of northern countries in summer. There were crowds of serfs milling around, unloading the ships and shouting to one another in their incomprehensible tongue. With any civilized language, you could recognize words here and there because of the closeness to French and Latin, but this language was quite alien, barbaric.

They were to ride on at once. The King was giving orders. A horse was brought for Joanna, no cushioned litters here. A soldier threw her up into the saddle. She clung to the pommel, dazed, weary, her lips caked with salt, her blood still rocking to the surge of the sea. Looking around, she saw groups forming. At a distance, Queen Eleanor sat her horse, demurely sidesaddle, her back straight, her head high. She was surrounded by guards. Unconsciously, Joanna sat up straighter. Her mother turned and saw her, lifted a hand in farewell. Then she rode away.

Joanna and Alice rode the twelve miles from Southampton to Winchester together. Alice was pale and silent from the sickness of the crossing. The countryside seemed veiled, the light hazy, the colors muted except for the deep soft green everywhere. In Aquitaine in the summer the grass turned brown and the sharp clear light pouring down from a blue sky etched the rocks and pine forests and vivid flowers. Even the sounds of their progress were muffled. The horses' hoof beats were absorbed by the thick lush undergrowth on either side of the good straight Roman road, bracken and brambles, hawthorn and bindweed and old man's beard. A low mist hung in patches over the fields and wreathed itself through the oak trees. The distances were blurred, softened by the moisture that hung in the air.

Tuesday, July the 8th, a week and two days ago. They had reached Winchester at night. Daylight was fading, withdrawing gradually, draining the color from the landscape until it all appeared as grey as the long walls of the city. The towers of the cathedral and the castle rose above the walls. They went in by King's Gate and clattered through a city shuttered for the night. Joanna and Alice shared a bed. The sheets felt clammy and they curled together for warmth. Joanna slept fitfully, dreaming of shipwrecks.

In Winchester, Joanna found that her ladies-in-waiting from Poitiers were gone. She was to be assigned a new household. They lined up for her to meet them on the Friday after her arrival, long-nosed Norman officials, stern-faced ladies, and younger maids. They bowed as she went down the line, trying to remember all their names, Robert and Hugh and Reginald, Agnes and Maud and Isabel. The maids, she supposed, were Saxon. The first one, rising from a curtsey, caught her eye. She looked hardly older than Joanna herself, a slender, fair-haired girl with a lively intelligent look. Joanna smiled at her and she smiled back without shyness or hesitation.

Joanna turned to the steward at her elbow. "Does she speak French?" she asked.

The maid herself answered. "Yes, my lady. I am from Normandy. Adèle de Laigle, at your service."

"*De* Laigle?"

"My father is the Baron de Laigle."

Joanna frowned. "And you are a maid?"

"No, my lady." She smiled that quick friendly smile. "I am to be one of your ladies-in-waiting here."

Joanna liked her instantly. She was the youngest of all her ladies, only a year older than Joanna herself, and there was an openness and friendliness about her. When they discovered their mutual love for *The Song of Roland*, their friendship was sealed. Adèle had shared her chamber since that day.

The bells rang on, the high tones cascading rapidly down the scale over and over while the deep notes chimed in more slowly. The ladies were stirring now and Joanna's tiring-women came in. Nurse still lay hunched under her covers, uttering little grunts of complaint.

"Hurry, hurry, I'm freezing," Joanna urged her women, as she stood naked in the center of the room. "My God, if it's like this in summer, what will winter be like?"

"Take not the name of the Lord in vain," Nurse intoned from her blankets.

"I thought you were asleep, Nounou."

"Even if I were, do you think the Lord Himself is not listening? Whatever is all that racket?"

"I hear say that it's a great victory in the North" said one of the tiring-women. "De Glanville has taken the King of the Scots."

"Yes, I'll wear a mantle until I warm up." Joanna lifted her chin while her woman fastened the mantle at the neck with a brooch. "But what of the northern earls? Are they defeated, too?"

"That I don't know, my lady. Shall I brush your hair?"

"No, Adèle will do it, won't you, Adèle? She's gentler than you."

She sat on a stool and held up a mirror to look at herself while Adèle, behind her, brushed her hair with long sweeping strokes.

Staring at the polished metal, Joanna saw a heart-shaped face with a little pointed chin, wide-set green-blue eyes, a hint of freckles across her cheekbones and the bridge of her nose.

"How long is my hair now, Adèle?"

"Down to here." Adèle touched her back just above the waist.

Nurse lifted her face from the basin of cold water and frowned disapprovingly. Water dripped from her eyebrows and the end of her nose. She took a linen napkin from one of the women.

"Vanity, vanity ..."

"Yes, I know, Nounou. I'm just *looking*. I want to be tidy to go to chapel, don't I?"

"I'd tell you if you weren't. You don't need a mirror for that." She struggled into her surcoat. "I swear this thing is shrinking. It seems to get tighter every day."

Adèle giggled. "There, is that enough?"

"Yes, thank you, Adèle."

They went out, leaving Nurse arranging her wimple, and Adèle accompanied Joanna to the entrance of the royal gallery in the chapel.

"See you at breakfast," she said, and danced away.

Joanna went in. Her aunt Emma was there, at prayer, and her brother John, who gave her a sly, smug smile. She ignored him and knelt. Down below, the household was filing in. Looking through her fingers, she saw Adèle slip in. The smell of incense came to her. The priest, who had been kneeling before the altar, rose and turned to face them.

"We give thanks this morning to Almighty God in that He has granted victory over our enemies to our Lord Henry, by the grace of God, King of England and of his other possessions overseas."

Emma raised her head and stared at the priest, then she looked at Joanna and lifted an eyebrow. Joanna stared back, her eyes wide. *"By the grace of God"*? Since when had her father allowed himself that title? Not even King Louis called himself King by the grace of God. It was an Emperor's prerogative. "Pride is hateful before God and man." Her father had added another mortal sin to his list.

At breakfast in the Hall, they talked of that and of the news of victory. Emma sat on the dais. Joanna and Adèle joined Alice, halfway down the Hall. John came and sat opposite them. They looked at each other and sighed. He helped himself to bread and chewed for a while before speaking.

"I suppose *you* were sorry to hear of this victory," he said at last. "I'm surprised Father didn't shut you up with the other traitors."

"I am *not* a traitor," Joanna said hotly, rising to the bait.

"Everybody in Poitiers was a traitor. I heard Father say so. You and Mother and my brothers. They were just fighting to keep me from getting what Father promised me. But he will make them give me my share."

"What a self-centered little creature you are!" Alice said. "I suppose you think the King of Scots and *my* father are fighting against you, too? You're just a child. You don't understand what it's all about."

"I do! I bet I understand more of it than you. You're only a girl. I know that Henry was supposed to land at Dover and he didn't and there weren't two fronts and that's why Ranulf de Glanville won, and I know it's not just King William but all his barons, it's all over in the North, the whole thing is finished in a single day, so there!" He spread butter on his bread.

"That's disgusting. You'll get fat if you eat butter on your bread," Alice observed.

"Don't care. I like it." Defiantly, he added another thick scoop of pale greasy butter. "It isn't fair! Henry and Richard and Geoffrey get everything, just because they're older, and they don't want me to have even a little piece of France and all I get is Ireland and who wants Ireland?"

"I should think Ireland is just the place for you. They probably even put butter on their bread there," Adèle said and she and Joanna laughed. "Can't you see it? 'A little butter for the Lord of Ireland's bread!' 'Yes, Sir, and how about a little hog fat for the royal breakfast?'"

"Some bat's blood to drink, my lord?" Joanna supplied.

"A little subtlety of spun sugar and squashed snails, perhaps? Oh, I forgot, they wouldn't have spun sugar in Ireland. Just the squashed snails." They laughed again.

John flushed angrily. "I may be the youngest but at least I'm not a girl. Anything would be better than that. And I hope your husbands all shut you up in towers."

"Speaking of husbands," Alice said, "where's your baby bride? I've only seen her once since we got here."

"She's sick again. She's always sick. I hate her."

"No doubt it's mutual," Adèle said smoothly. "Well, this has been delightful, John, as always, but we must take our leave of you."

Joanna and Adèle left the Hall arm in arm, giggling.

ᚲᚱ ✣ ᚱᚲ

The King was at Westminster. On the 1st of August, the forces that had been assembled in the Channel ports to invade England turned east and besieged Rouen, under the direction of King Louis. King Henry left at once for Normandy and entered Rouen. King Louis, the Count of Flanders, and the Young King folded their tents, burned their siege engines and withdrew. King Henry's victory was complete. By September he had rounded up his sons and brought them together at Montlouis.

John was jubilant. "You see? I get my share after all, just as Father promised. And Henry and Richard get less than they were offered the first time. That will teach them to rebel."

"Constance must be glad to hear that Father has released the hostages," Joanna said, ignoring John. "I wonder how she's doing in Devizes."

"Richard and Geoffrey have sworn homage to Father again," John said. "Henry didn't have to, because of his royal title. So that's the end of your rebellion."

"Don't start that again. It isn't *my* rebellion."

"Father will be back in England soon. Then he'll deal with you."

In November the King came to Winchester. Joanna and Alice prepared themselves nervously to meet him in the Hall before supper.

"How do I look, Joanna?" Alice asked anxiously. "Will he be angry with us, do you think?" She pinched her cheeks to bring color into them.

"You look beautiful, Alice," Joanna said, admiring her. Alice's hair hung gleaming down her back. She wore a simple circlet on her head and a gown of dusky rose silk that flowed smoothly over her supple body. "How about me?"

Alice scrutinized her. "You look good. Wait, your ear is poking through your hair." She rearranged Joanna's hair for her and they went down together.

The King was in a good mood. He stood with one hand on John's shoulder, a cup of wine in the other. His sister Emma was with him, smiling but looking wary.

"Come here, come here! Don't be afraid," the King called to them. They curtseyed before him. "Joanna my dear." He kissed her and pinched her cheek. "You've grown. And Alice." He kissed Alice and held her from him, his hands compressing her shoulders. Joanna saw his face become serious as he stared at Alice. "You've become quite a beauty, Alice. Yes, indeed. It will be a lucky man ..." He checked himself, then he took his hands from her shoulders and laughed shortly. "God's body, I was quite forgetting, it's Richard who's to be the lucky man." He stared at her, his eyes narrowed. "Yes, indeed. My own son. How old are you now, Alice?"

"Fourteen, my lord."

"Fourteen, eh? I promised your father you should not wed till you were fifteen. So there's time enough before we have to think of that. As for the rest of you, I'll find husbands for you all soon enough. You too, Emma. I have in mind for you a Welsh prince ..."

"Welsh, Henry?"

"Yes, Welsh. I need the alliance and he's a good man ..."

"You can't do it, Henry." Emma was distraught. "I'm your *sister*, for God's sake. I'm the daughter of Geoffrey of Anjou. I won't be shut away with some primitive tribe in the hills of Wales ..."

"You will do as I say," the King thundered. "And if you ask me, he's just what you need. He's a strong leader, a fighting man, and he won't stand any of your nonsense. Don't think I don't know what sort of thing went on in Poitiers, pretend courts of love—pah!"—he spat into the rushes—"and goddamn pansy boys reading poetry and men with nothing better to do than swearing fealty to idle, wayward women, of all the addlepated

165

notions! The game is over and you can come down from your pedestals now. You're not too old to bear children, Emma, and that's a woman's job in life."

"Oh Jesus!" Emma exclaimed. They stared at each other, breathing heavily. Then the King turned away, his mantle swinging.

"What are we waiting for? Let's eat."

The trumpeters lined up and raised their instruments. The King turned back to them and spoke over the blare of the fanfare.

"We'll talk of it later. No need to spoil the evening with arguing. You are all to sit with me on the dais tonight." He looked at them. "And you, Alice, you shall sit beside me."

Color rushed into Alice's cheeks and she looked at the ground. "Thank you, my lord," she murmured. "You do me too much honor."

Joanna reflected that in Poitiers there would have been a gracious response to this, but the King said nothing. He washed his hands in the ewer held before him and walked away, drying his hands as he went. He tossed the napkin to one side where it was deftly caught by a page.

They sat at the table on the dais, looking down at the long trestles in the Hall. The procession of servers began. Joanna sat next to John. He drank first, being a boy, and she was repelled to see grease float from his lips onto the surface of their wine. She turned the cup round and sipped cautiously from the other side.

Joanna looked around the Hall. New frescoes had been painted on its walls for Henry and Marguerite's coronation in 1172, but it was not as elegant as the Hall at Poitiers, with its graceful arcades and long windows looking onto the pleasances. She sighed, thinking of it. Her mother, whom she had thought invincible, shut up in Salisbury Tower, Marie back at her husband's court in Troyes, Marguerite and Constance in Devizes, the Countess of Flanders back in Arras where, they'd heard, the Count had had a man hanged for daring to practice the principles of Chaplain André's Code of Love. Now her aunt Emma was to be married off to a Welsh prince. Only she and Alice were left. She looked at Alice. Alice was sitting in the Queen's place, she thought suddenly. The King offered her his cup and smiled as she drank from it.

CR ✿ ℘

When the King left for France, Alice complained that it was dull after all the excitement of his visit. By the end of the month, the castle of Winchester was even more somber. Alice of Maurienne, John's sickly fiancée, died suddenly one night after a few days of whooping and wheezing. Joanna put on a black mantle and went to her burial mass. The little coffin lay before the altar and Joanna, from the gallery, stared down at it. Alice lay like a waxen doll, her hands crossed piously on her breast, her hair arranged over her shoulders. She was two and a half years old.

At the feast following the burial, the courtiers came one by one to John to offer their condolences. John sat in a great chair, trying to look serious. When it was Joanna's turn, she said awkwardly, "I'm sorry, John."

He leaned toward her. "Are you? I'm not," he muttered. "I never liked her. She always cried whenever she saw me."

"I'm not surprised," Adèle whispered behind Joanna. She said it softly but John heard and shot her a venomous look.

CR ✿ ℘

In December John was summoned to Argentan in Normandy for the Christmas court. All of Joanna's brothers would be there. There was no mention of the girls going.

"I expect I shall get lots of gifts," John boasted. He eyed Joanna and saw that she was disappointed and envious. "They have sent fourscore deer from overseas for the feast. Imagine that! It will be a huge feast. All kinds of sweetmeats, I expect, and subtleties and marzipan."

When Joanna did not answer, he went on, "The whole family will be there. All the *men*, that is. Of course we don't want *girls* there."

This time Joanna answered angrily, "I don't want to go anyway. We'll have a better time here on our own without you, won't we, Adèle?"

"Girls are stupid," John said scornfully, sensing that he had hit a nerve. "Who wants girls around? I expect Father hates them, too."

"That's all *you* know," Adèle said and she giggled.

Alice usually giggled at remarks like that, but she was bitterly disappointed, too, that they were not going, so she was silent and stared pensively out at the frost-limed roofs of Winchester.

CHAPTER SIXTEEN

When spring came, it seemed all the more of a miracle by contrast with the long bleak winter. The first snowdrops poking through the grass in the castle bailey were like a shaft of light penetrating a long-sealed dungeon, promising eventual release. First it was the snowdrops and pale sunshine behind high flying clouds, and then one day there were daffodils and the birds were singing and the sun shining. Joanna and Adèle skipped round the bailey like wild creatures, joined hands and spun in circles until they were dizzy and fell on the grass, laughing breathlessly, cheeks flushed.

Alice had re-established herself as a source of information here. Joanna never knew where she heard all the news, but it was Alice who knew first that the King was coming for Easter and Henry with him. In the castle, great preparations were made, the closed-off rooms were aired, silver was polished, wall hangings were taken down and shaken by the maids in the bailey. Alice started to preen herself, brushing her hair a hundred strokes every day, complaining to her women about the fit of her gowns that were now too tight in the bosom.

Marguerite arrived from Devizes. The two sisters greeted each other ecstatically, but in a few days they were arguing as they had always done. The months of isolation had not changed Marguerite. She made herself unpopular at once with the steward by criticizing the lack of formality in the Hall. She took the seat of honor on the dais and kept an eagle eye on the pages and ushers for infractions of the proper ceremonies. She reproved Joanna and Adèle for giggling and behaving like a pair of hoydens and took exception to the tight fit of Alice's gowns, to the length of her hair, to her constant use of the mirror, in fact to almost everything about Alice's appearance. She was jealous, Joanna and Adèle agreed.

The week before Easter, the King rode into Winchester with Henry at his side and a swarm of earls and knights in his train. Marguerite and Alice and Joanna went out onto the porch steps to greet them. The King swung down from his horse with all his old energy, tossed the reins to his marshal and took the steps two at a time. Henry followed more leisurely. He stood almost a head taller than his father, a handsome fair-haired young man. He smiled pleasantly but there was a look of petulance about his eyes.

Henry and Marguerite exchanged a cool kiss. The King took Henry's elbow and spoke to them in a jocular tone.

"Come now, that won't do, my boy. All these months apart and a feeble kiss like that? Or are you saving yourself for tonight? I want a grandson, you know ..." He leered at them. "Where's your hot young blood? Why, at your age ... or even at my age ..."

He gave one of his great bursts of laughter and his eyes slid over Alice, standing beside Marguerite. "I'm not too old yet to show more enthusiasm for a pretty girl than you do, by God's body!"

He seized Alice in his arms and bent his head to her. The group on the porch stood immobile as the seconds drew themselves out and the King still held Alice, turning his head as though he would bore his mouth into hers, bending her slender body backwards until it seemed it would snap. Joanna watched, fascinated as his square hands slid down Alice's back to her hips and pulled her against him. Henry stared at his father, his expression unfathomable, and Marguerite seemed to hold her breath, her nostrils flared, her lips thinned. The King straightened up at last. A thread of saliva hung from his lips. Color flooded Alice's throat and face. She stared hypnotized at the King, like a rabbit at a snake.

"Well?" the King said shortly. "Are you all struck dumb or what? Let's go inside."

He turned to Joanna and kissed her on the cheek. "How are you, little one? Let me look at you. They say you have my eyes." He bent his knees and crouched at Joanna's height. "Yours have more green in them. Pretty eyes. Like a cat's, wide apart and green and unblinking. Yes, you'll be a pretty girl. Not a beauty like Alice, but certainly no disgrace to the family."

രു ✿ ฌ

After the abstinence of Lent and the all-night vigil in the cathedral on Easter Eve, the week that followed was a riot of games and feasting and gifts. The courtiers presented the King with gifts and the King in return gave feasts for them. Down on the Itchen river, below the city, there was tilting at the quintain in boats, with the watching crowd laughing and cheering when anyone fell in the water. The nobles hunted in the New Forest and at night they danced and acted in improvised masques. Alice was in her element. She loved to hawk and sing and she was a graceful dancer. Joanna noticed how the King's eyes followed her as she danced.

Hocktide Tuesday was his last night in Winchester. The King had drunk heavily at supper. Joanna went upstairs at the end of the meal while the servants were clearing and folding the trestles. As she went past Alice's apartments, she heard Marguerite's voice raised in anger.

"Stay away from the King."

"Why should I? There's no harm in it."

Joanna stopped in the doorway and watched them. Alice was brushing her hair and Marguerite sat on the bed.

"Of course there's harm, you silly child. You know as well as I do what kind of man the King is."

Alice flipped her hair back and stared impudently at her sister.

"Whatever are you suggesting, my dear sister? I sit beside him at table and he stares at me when I dance. Yes, I know he does.

It's flattering, but surely not harmful? Your imagination is running away with you. A man may stare at a pretty girl, may he not?"

"Not in the way he stares at you, if you are the daughter of a king and betrothed to his own son, besides."

"Do you think he's not aware of that? There's nothing in it. He's amusing himself."

"No doubt he would like to amuse himself in your bed."

Alice put her brush down. There was a moment's silence.

"Are you crazy, Marguerite?"

"No, I'm not crazy. *I* know and *you* know that you would never do such a thing. But others may not know. There is gossip already. You are disgracing our family's honor. Do you want to know what they are saying about you?"

Two spots of color burned in Alice's cheeks. "No, I don't want to know. And if you talk of disgracing the family, what about you throwing yourself at William Marshal? Oh don't act the innocent with me! It was the talk of Poitiers! Everyone knows what was between you two …"

Marguerite jumped to her feet. "There was nothing between us," she shouted. "William is far too honorable. How dare you suggest such a thing?"

"Nothing? Then I suppose he didn't ask you, as I'm sure it wasn't from lack of willingness on your part. Do you close your eyes when you're in bed with Henry and try to imagine he's William?"

Marguerite stepped forward and slapped Alice's face. "How dare you?" she said through her teeth. "You're no better than a slut. Thank God our mother never lived to see what you've become. You killed her then, and if she had lived, this would kill her, too …"

"For God's sake, don't throw my mother's death up at me again. Can I be held responsible for that?"

"If she hadn't had you, she wouldn't have died. You are not *fit* for her to have wasted her life on you."

Marguerite turned and ran from the room. Joanna flattened herself in the doorway but Marguerite never even noticed her. Alice sat heavily on a stool.

"Joanna, is that you? My God, did you hear her? She's hysterical! She's never forgiven me because our mother died when

I was born, and now she resents me because I'm prettier than she is. Can I help either thing?" She spread her hands helplessly.

They went down together. The servants had removed the trestles and driven out the dogs. Groups of courtiers were dancing to the music of vielles. Joanna and Alice made their way to the far end of the Hall, avoiding the whirling skirts and outflung arms of the dancers. The King, leaning on one arm of his chair, was talking to Henry of the tour of England they were to start on the next day.

"We'll visit Thomas' tomb first, then from Canterbury to the assizes of Kent. I want you to inspect the Welsh marches with me this time, too ..."

He broke off as the two girls came up. "But we can talk of this tomorrow. We don't want to bore your sisters. Alice, come and sit by me." He snapped his fingers for a stool, which was brought at once. "I shall miss watching you dance. Still, life is not all pleasure. Even Henry here has learned that at last, I think." He smiled affectionately at Henry. Joanna, watching them, thought that Henry's answering smile was somewhat reluctant. "This tour will be all business, no tournaments and feasting, I'm afraid, just synods and assizes and councils, but I want Henry to see it all working and I want the people to see and know him. My heir. Well, that's enough of that. Have some wine, my dear."

He offered his cup to Alice, leaning toward her. Joanna saw him put his hand on Alice's knee as she sipped the wine. Casually, his hand moved up her thigh, crushing the thin silk of her gown.

Alice returned the cup and looked levelly at him. "And Richard, my lord? You have not spoken to me of him."

The King took his hand from Alice's thigh and sat back in his chair. He drank some wine, looking at her speculatively over the rim of the cup, belched, and wiped his mouth on the back of his hand. "Have I not? Perhaps because until now you have not asked me about him. Why this sudden interest in him now, I wonder? Richard is in Aquitaine, where he should be. He has his work cut out for him, restoring order there. He won't be back in England this year. Does that disappoint you?" He leaned toward her again, leering. "Are you in a hurry to be wed? You will have to wait a little longer for that pleasure."

Alice colored and would not meet his eyes. The King drank again, then got up abruptly and moved down the room. They saw him stop and put his arm around the Earl of Clare's beautiful sister.

In the morning he and Henry and all their train left Winchester. Alice was fretful and short-tempered but Joanna and Adèle were not sorry to see them leave. They settled to a quiet routine of lessons and sewing and riding, and when they could, escaping to the various hideouts they had created and reading to each other and talking and dreaming of their futures.

"I wish I had not been born a girl," Joanna said, as they sat side by side on the floor leaning against the wall in a little unused chamber high under the battlements. "They don't let you do *anything* if you're a girl."

"I'd rather be one. Boys have to go off and fight. You wouldn't want to do that, would you? You might be wounded or even killed. If you had a leg wound that turned septic, they'd chop your leg off. Can you imagine how awful that would be? No, I'd much rather let the men fight the battles and wait safely in a castle for them to come back. Besides, if you're a girl, you can wear pretty gowns."

"Gowns!" Joanna snorted. "That's not much of a reason to be a girl. There isn't anything *important* a woman can do. I used to think being a Queen would be wonderful, but look at Mother—shut up in Salisbury Tower and there's nothing she can do about it."

Adèle pulled her knees to her chest and wrapped her arms around them. "There is one important thing a woman can do, Joanna. Men can't have babies. And women do have some sort of power over men, if they make themselves loved. That's the best thing. A lover will do *anything* for …"

"But don't you see," Joanna interrupted, "it always depends on some man! My mother says sons are a woman's weapons, *you* say lovers will get you what you want, but can't a woman ever have a life of her own? I don't *want* to depend on men all my life. I don't trust them! They don't love you for ever and then what? When you're old and no longer beautiful, they shut you up in a tower somewhere."

Adèle was silent for a while. "That's the way life is," she said at last. "There's no point in fighting it. The only place a woman can be independent of men is in a convent and who wants that?"

"There are so many things I'd like to do," Joanna said reflectively. "I'd like to travel and see the world, especially the Holy Land. I'd go there on a pilgrimage. If I were a man, I'd go on Crusade if they had one. I wouldn't mind fighting ..."

"You wouldn't really want to, would you?"

"Yes, if it were for something I believed in. That's what I'd like to have, something definite, something real, with a purpose, not just being a—sort of ornament at some King's High Table."

She leaned her elbows on her knees, moodily. "The worst thing is that one day I will have to leave and go and marry. You, too, I suppose. Just as soon as I get fond of someone, we are separated. Eleanor, my sister, went to Spain five years ago and I have never seen her since ..."

"I know. My sister, too, was married and I cried for days ..."

"I didn't know you had a sister. You never told me. And I had a friend in Poitiers, Scholastique, she was my niece in fact, and she's gone. And my mother ..." Joanna took Adèle's hands. "Promise me you won't leave me, too."

"I can't promise. If my father sends for me ... And you will soon be married, Joanna."

"Then swear fealty to me, as men do. Then I'll know, wherever you are, even if we're apart, that you will always be my liege."

Adèle knelt on the dusty floor of the little unused chamber high under the battlements and placed her hands in Joanna's. In her high, clear voice she repeated the oath familiar to them both and solemnly Joanna raised her and kissed her.

ᙢ ✹ ᙣ

At first, news reached them of King Henry's movements. He and Henry had visited the Martyr's tomb together. From there they had gone to London, then west to Gloucester. The last they heard was that the King had arranged the betrothal of John to Isabelle of Gloucester. It was a good marriage—Gloucester, the King's cousin, was England's premier Earl—and John, predictably, boasted of it.

After that, they heard no more. Plague was spreading through the country. The great fair of Winchester was not held and travelers were stopped at the gates. The city virtually sealed itself off, but toward the end of the summer Joanna and Adèle heard the bells tolling daily. On most days there were seven or eight funerals at every church in Winchester. They never left the castle any more. There was no more hunting and hawking. The almoners and the steward's men, who had contact with the townspeople, tied cloths around their noses to keep from breathing their air, and the castle was sprayed daily with perfumes to keep the pestilence away. In the chapel they prayed each morning that God would deliver them and every day the death toll in the city rose. Joanna and Adèle listened to the knells and counted the strokes that told the victim's age. When it was a child, they bent their heads in silence and crossed themselves.

As more and more people died, the livestock were left untended and the harvest was not reaped. The grain rotted in the fields and famine set in. The crowds around the castle gates begging for alms grew larger and noisier, but in the castle too they had little enough for themselves and none to spare and the soldiers drove the beggars away.

At Michaelmas the King and Henry returned to Winchester. At the beginning of October Alice turned fifteen but no one mentioned her marriage to Richard. The gossip in the castle was open now. Joanna heard it but ignored it. She remembered Marguerite's words. "I know and you know that you would never do such a thing." Alice and the King were more and more often seen together. He would stare at her until she looked up and met his eyes, then he would smile and she would blush and look down again. She could not be faulted for modesty, and yet Joanna sensed that it was a form of flirtation more provocative than open smiles and touches and she was angry with Alice, for her mother's sake, for Richard's sake, for all their sakes.

She said as much to Alice one day on one of the rare occasions when they were alone together. Alice did not defend herself as Joanna had expected she would. There was a tangle in the silk she was sewing with and she pulled at it savagely, snapping the thread. Disgusted, she put it down beside her in the window embrasure and stared out. In the countryside beyond the city, the trees were turning red and gold. Lines of swallows perched on the walls, whistling and fluttering about. Soon they would be gone. The sun shone but there was a coolness in the air.

"For Richard's sake, you should not ..." Joanna resumed but Alice interrupted her. Bouncing to her feet, she swept away from the window. Her sewing fell unheeded to the floor.

"For Richard's sake!" she cried, angrily mimicking Joanna. "Why should I care about Richard? What has he ever done for me? He has always slighted me, always. I don't think he has ever once paid me a compliment, but Henry says I am beautiful. He is kind to me and takes an interest in what I do and talks to me ..."

"Henry?" Joanna said. "Do you call my father Henry?"

Alice hesitated, playing nervously with the end of her belt. "He asked me to call him Henry. When we are alone together." She looked up quickly and defiantly.

Joanna sat very still in the window and watched her. Alice paced up and down, head bent, picking at her belt.

At last she burst out, "There's no one I can talk to, Joanna. No one but you. We were friends in Poitiers, remember? Joanna, I don't know ... Oh my God. I know it's wrong. But he's the King. He frightens me. I can't refuse him."

Joanna did not pretend not to understand. "You must. Alice, you *must* refuse. He won't insist. He knows how wrong it would be. Why, he's practically your father!"

"He is *not* my father. Richard and I are not married. And he does insist. He's so overpowering, Joanna, you can't imagine ..."

"Alice, you must tell him clearly, tell him it's not possible, he must not dream of such a thing."

"It's too late, Joanna." She paced again. "Do you understand what I'm saying? It's already too late. It has happened."

She came over suddenly and sat opposite Joanna. "I'm his mistress. There, I've said it now."

Joanna stared at her, aghast. Alice looked as she always did, her color a little heightened perhaps, her expression distressed. Should there not be some outward sign of this change in her? Alice and her father ... Her mind skipped sideways from the image.

"Tell him it must never happen again. To sin once can be forgiven but to repeat the sin ..."

"Once? Once?" Alice laughed hysterically. "Twice the first night alone and that was a month ago. He has come to my room almost every night since ..."

Joanna covered her ears. "I don't want to hear it. You must tell him it must stop."

"I'm frightened of him. He's so big and powerful and he's the King."

"Just tell him."

"You don't understand, Joanna. I don't want it to stop. Don't hate me. Please don't hate me." She breathed rapidly and the tip of her tongue showed between her lips.

Joanna stared at her. "I thought you said he frightened you."

"He does. He does. You can't imagine how exciting that is ..." Alice's eyes glittered strangely.

Joanna felt sick. "Oh my God ..." she said.

She flung her sewing down and got up and ran from the room. She ran blindly through the castle until she found Nurse. She threw herself into Nurse's arms, crushing the linen she was folding.

"Why, whatever is the matter, lamb? You're trembling all over. There, there, Nounou will take care of you."

"Nounou, I don't ever want to grow up," Joanna said passionately. "Not ever ever."

CHAPTER SEVENTEEN

As a child, Joanna had seen things in black and white. If you sinned, you were wicked and you went to hell, and lust was surely the worst of the deadly sins. Now it seemed less simple. True, there were many people around who were easily recognizable as Satan's tools, the lame, the cross-eyed, the hunch-backed and deformed. There were those who, possessed by demons, would fall to the floor writhing and foaming at the mouth, who could only be exorcized by whipping and asperging with holy water. But Alice? Painfully, Joanna struggled to accept the new situation.

It was mid-November and bitterly cold. Joanna, coming into the solar, interrupted a conversation among Marguerite's ladies who sat there sewing.

"If he gets his divorce, does he mean to marry ..."

The speaker was shushed into silence as they saw Joanna in the doorway.

"I swear if it gets any colder, I shall wear *two* fur cloaks," one of them observed.

Women's gossip, Joanna thought, but a divorce was a rare occurrence and she was curious. "If who gets a divorce?" She asked, sitting down.

No one spoke. Heads suddenly bowed over their sewing, they seemed not to have heard.

"Am I not supposed to know? I'm not a child any more."

Marguerite looked straight at her. "It's your father, Joanna," she said flatly. "He wants to divorce Queen Eleanor."

Joanna felt as though her heart had stopped.

"Divorce?" She whispered. Her breathing fluttered and she pressed her hands flat against her stomach. "Father wants a divorce?"

They were all looking at her now. She thought of her mother and sat up very straight and firmed her trembling lips.

"You may as well know it," Marguerite said. "Everyone will know soon enough. The Cardinal is here to arrange it."

"On what grounds? My mother has given him no grounds."

Marguerite shrugged. "Consanguinity, no doubt. Does a king need grounds? The Pope will grant it, if it's advantageous."

"Would we go with her to Poitiers?" she asked.

"To Poitiers? You don't think the King would risk losing the whole south-west of France, do you?"

"But it's hers," she cried indignantly. "He can't take that from her."

"That's true. If he divorces her, she is still Duchess of Aquitaine in her own right. Worse yet, she might remarry and the south would be held by someone else."

"Then what ..."

"Fontevrault. He wants her to go to Fontevrault." Marguerite watched Joanna narrowly. "Oh not just as a nun, of course. She would be Abbess. If she cedes her lands to the King."

"A nun? Mother? She would never do it."

"What's the difference between that and being shut up in Salisbury? If she doesn't agree, King Henry will keep her there until she dies. She's not young, you know, your mother. What is she now, fifty-three? And the King only just into his forties. No, it's Salisbury Tower for the rest of her life or the abbacy of Fontevrault, with all the respect and comfort and power that that entails. I think I can guess which she'll choose. She's been in Salisbury almost two years now and must be desperate to get out."

"*Despair* is foreign to my mother's nature," Joanna said, with all the dignity she could muster, though her heart was thudding and tears pricked behind her eyes. She rose, stiff-lipped, and left the room. Once out of sight, she ran until she reached her own chamber and flung herself on the bed and wept abandonedly.

It was the worst of winters. The cold grew daily more intense. By Christmas, snow lay thick on the ground. At night it froze and in the day it snowed again. The snow grew deeper and deeper. The soldiers dug paths across the bailey and out from the castle gates. Icicles hung from the shutters and frost patterned the chapel windows. And still it grew colder. The Itchen river froze and young men tied animal shinbones to their feet and slid on its surface. The water they brought Joanna in the mornings to wash in was filmed with ice and the hot bricks to warm her bed were cool by the time they reached her chamber. Joanna's forehead ached from the cold. Her breath steamed whenever she spoke. The ladies sewed briefly, got up and stamped about to warm their feet, went back to their sewing. There was no sign of a thaw by Candlemas.

The King did not restrict his traveling. He went as usual on his circuits of the courts of justice, descending on Winchester from time to time. Whenever he was there, he ate little and drank heavily and was impatient, even with Alice. The Queen had refused to enter a convent. She refused to agree to a divorce.

"She'd rather do anything than see him marry Alice," Marguerite said. "And I can't say I blame her, even though Alice is my sister."

"Marry Alice? He couldn't. He wouldn't," Joanna exclaimed.

"I don't know if he could, but he certainly would. You know what I think he wants? A new family of Plantagenet sons. He's never trusted Henry—well, one can see why. Henry's so irresponsible, no sense of duty. Not like someone like William ..." She checked herself. "But Henry and I are already crowned. Nothing can stop Henry from succeeding him." She added as an afterthought, "God willing."

CR ❀ ℥

Suddenly it seemed, in one day, winter was over. Joanna had heard that Easter court was to be held in Winchester and all her brothers and her mother would be there. When she looked out of the windows, the day seemed beautiful. There had never been a day like it. She no longer saw the dirty patches of snow, only the flowers; nor the clouds, but the fleeting glimpses of blue beyond them.

Scorning a litter, Queen Eleanor rode from Salisbury to Winchester. Joanna heard the crowds cheering in the city streets. She was beside herself with impatience, giving little jumps and hugging herself and Adèle alternately as they waited on the porch that led to the Hall. There was a clatter at the gatehouse and the Queen came in suddenly. She sat upright, reining in her horse and waving to the assembled crowd. She was smiling widely.

Close up, the Queen had aged but it was not significant. She was thinner, Joanna saw, and there were new lines on her face, but her eyes glowed and her chin was firm. She greeted her daughter as though it were Joanna, not she, who had been away.

"There you are, Joanna! After all this time! Let me look at you. How tall you are!" She observed her critically, at arm's length. "Yes, that color suits you. I believe you look like me. Doesn't she, Henry?"

"She has my eyes."

"No. No, I don't think so. Yours are so little. Hers are large and much greener. Yes, I think she has something. I always thought Eleanor the pretty one, but when Joanna is older ... She has good bones. My bones, you see. But you should use lemon juice on those freckles. Come and kiss me, child."

Joanna stepped forward to embrace her mother. She was startled to find that she stood as high as the Queen's shoulder now. Holding her mother, she felt her tense, quivering with nervous energy. Her gaze was already going over Joanna's head, searching the Hall.

"When does Richard come?"

The King shrugged. "He will be here before Easter. And Geoffrey, too."

"It will be like old times. All the family together again. Except Matilda and Eleanor, of course. To think that Matilda is a mother now. That's what you always used to call her, Henry, do you remember? 'Little mother.' I never knew whether it was because she was named for your mother or because she looked like a little mother even when she was a child. How I wish I could see my grandson. Otto. Such a barbaric name. Do you think he will be very German? And Eleanor—how strange it is—her children will all be Spanish. Europe will be filled with our grandchildren, Henry. What do you mean to do for Joanna? Surely it's time to think of that?"

Joanna had never heard her mother prattle on so nervously, almost feverishly. As though she had had no one to speak to for months.

"I'm thinking of it. I'm not ready to make an announcement yet."

Joanna looked quickly at her father, but his face gave nothing away. The subject was not mentioned again. There was too much else happening. Every day brought fresh excitement. Richard's arrival, full of his successes in Aquitaine; Geoffrey and his Breton followers; Constance from Devizes, unlike the Queen, spoiling her reprieve with recriminations. Joanna had never seen Winchester Castle so fine. The Bishop of Winchester celebrated mass in the cathedral built by the Conqueror a hundred years before. The great nave, the longest in England, was crammed with Norman nobles, Englishmen now in all but language, Gloucester and Norfolk, Chester and Kent; the Bohuns and Bigods, the De Veres, De Vescys and De Mandevilles; Fitz-Alans, Fitz-Stephens and Fitz-Walters; and the King's bastard sons, Geoffrey, Bishop of Lincoln, and William Longsword.

They feasted afterward. The Queen looked splendid in scarlet robes and grey fur and enough jewels to ransom a king. The High Table was filled with princes of the church and state. A baldaquin had been erected over the King's chair. He was in a good mood again today as he looked along the table at his sons.

Joanna was not at the High Table, but, as befitted her rank, she sat near the head of one of the long tables that ran down the Hall. She looked at her family, seated in a row behind the High

Table. Henry, next to the Bishop of Winchester, as usual looked sulky. He was conspicuously not speaking to Marguerite beside him. Joanna knew why. All the court knew why. She looked at William Marshal, a little way down the same table talking and eating at once, the center of attention of all those around him. She looked back at the High Table, at Marguerite nibbling demurely at her food, her fingers raised. Could it be true? Once she would have dismissed the rumors as absurd, but since the business of Alice ... Perhaps even Marguerite, prim as she seemed, was capable of sin. Marguerite looked up and Joanna caught the momentary flicker of expression on her face as she looked at William and then quickly away. *Yes,* Joanna thought, *it could be true.*

Richard and Alice sat beyond them. Richard was leaning forward across the table, shouting down to his father something about his exploits in Aquitaine. The King had asked whether his harshness there had been justified and Richard was defending his actions. Joanna had been startled when she had seen him. In the two years that had passed—or was it three?—Richard had become a man. He was as tall as Henry, with long arms and legs, and broader than Henry. He would be heavy in the shoulders and chest, like the King. His beard was full now, a curly red-gold beard merging into his golden mane of hair. Command and success had given him an air of authority. He looked satisfied, even exultant. Clearly, no one had dared tell him about Alice.

Geoffrey and Constance were talking to each other. They had at last an interest in common. Constance lapped up all he could tell her of Brittany. There was an awkwardness, a self-consciousness, in their movements and glances today. Tomorrow they would be bedded for the first time. They had been married five years, but Constance had been only twelve years old when Geoffrey fled to Paris with his brothers and their marriage had not been consummated.

The Queen was talking of Otto again, their first grandchild.

"But no Plantagenet grandsons," King Henry complained. His voice carried into the Hall and people glanced up.

"I wish you would not use that ridiculous nickname," the Queen said tartly. "It is not dignified for a king to call himself by the name of a common weed."

"It was good enough for my father and it's good enough for me," the King said obstinately. "Five sons and still no Plantagenet grandson."

"Five is rhetorical. You can hardly count poor little William, God rest his soul."

All those listening, except King Henry, crossed themselves. The King took another drink of wine.

"Well, Henry then. He and Marguerite have been married since 1160 and still no heir."

"They were five and three in 1160," the Queen pointed out acidly.

"They're not children now, are they? Why, when you were Marguerite's age, even that pasty-faced Louis had managed to give you two daughters. No sons. It took me to give you sons."

"Your memory is at fault. Louis and I were married eight years before Marie was born and even then it was a miracle for which I prayed to Our Lady."

"I suppose it *was* a miracle for Louis. No doubt he thought prayer alone would do it. Eh, eh?" He thumped his hand on the table and his great laugh cracked out. Everyone at the dais end of the tables was listening now and there was an answering shout of laughter. "I suppose it took that monk the first seven years to figure out what he was supposed to do. Eh?" He laughed again and the company duly laughed back. "Well, it didn't take us eight years or a miracle to produce a son, did it?"

Near Joanna, a man said quietly to his neighbor, "Unless it were a miracle to produce a son three months after the marriage."

She glared at him.

"And Geoffrey? What about it, Geoffrey?" The King shouted down the table at him. "Your turn is soon to come. Let's see if you can make a grandson for me before your brother does."

"Richard is older than Geoffrey," the Queen observed coolly. "And Alice is of an age to marry now. Why are they not married yet?"

She knows, Joanna thought suddenly. There was an awkward silence at the High Table. The King shifted in his chair and Alice sat very still, staring at her plate. It was Richard who answered.

"Time enough for that on my next visit, Mother. Aquitaine is no place for me to take a bride to yet. There are still several castles in the south to be reduced …"

"One thing at a time, Eleanor." The King had recovered his composure. "I have in mind another marriage for our family this year."

Heads lifted all round that end of the Hall. Joanna froze. "Yes, I have chosen a husband for our youngest daughter. An excellent match." He rubbed his hands together in satisfaction. "Couldn't be better. We have been in touch since Christmas …"

Joanna dug her nails into her palms. *Not here, not now,* she begged him silently. *Not with everyone watching. Not without warning like this. Philip, Philip—was it to be Philip?* Her whole frame shuddered with the effort of maintaining her composure. Adèle was far away, below the salt, and beside her John was watching her curiously. She could not bear it.

The Queen bent toward the King and spoke to him in a low voice. He looked at Joanna and nodded and spoke to her in a low voice.

"Well, it's not settled yet, so I'll not announce it. Many a slip twixt cup and lip, eh, as the Latin has it. But it was Pope Alexander himself who proposed the match, so I think it will soon be definite."

Joanna could not eat any more. John, summing up the situation, pulled their trencher to him and ate her share as well as his. Her pulse thundered in her ears and she felt sick to her stomach from the tension. The rest of the meal passed in a daze. She heard nothing, focused on nothing. The scraping of benches as people rose startled her into awareness. Her father came down from the dais toward her.

"Come, Joanna, come with me. Let's go somewhere quiet where we can talk."

He held his hand out to her and she took it. His hand was warm, the palm calloused from riding. It enveloped hers completely. He led her from the Hall into his council chamber. The room was furnished only with a table and a number of stools. There was a pile of papers on the table and a big pewter inkwell holding them down. There was a half-finished fresco on one wall:

a great eagle with spread wings being attacked by four eaglets. Joanna and her father sat on stools facing each other.

"I shouldn't have sprung it on you like that," her father said. "I meant to talk to you first. Still, you must have expected it?"

She stared at him. Every detail of the scene etched itself on her mind's eye: a notch scored in the edge of the table, the angle of the stack of papers, a hair growing out of her father's nostril. In the distance, the noises from the Hall: the musicians tuning their instruments, talk and laughter, the clash of dishes as the servants cleared away.

"I think you'll be pleased, Joanna." He was smiling at her, had taken her hand again. Strange that he could be so kind to her and yet lock her mother up in Salisbury and fornicate nightly with Alice. How *could* one person be both good and bad?

"Nothing to say? You don't ask me who he is?" he teased her.

"Who, Father?" She said at last, holding tightly to his hand. Now was the moment. *Philip, Philip of France,* she willed him.

"William of Sicily." He watched for her reaction. "Well? What do you say?"

It was hard to breathe. Joanna stared unseeing at her father. Conflicting emotions jostled in her mind. She was not to be Queen of France, then. The waiting period was over and real life rushed toward her. She felt fear, excitement, disappointment, and over all, blotting these out, a kind of blankness, an emptiness.

"Sicily ..." she said numbly, trying to think. "It's an island in the Mediterranean?"

"Haven't your tutors taught you any geography? Of course it is. But a large island. And the kingdom includes the South of Italy."

"He's a king, then?"

"Didn't I promise you a king? Yes, indeed. You will be Queen Joanna of Sicily. *And* he's rich. Richer than I am, in fact. And young. And I hear he's very handsome. There! Did I do well for you?"

The numbness had passed and her blood was racing now. A kind of excitement seized her ... Queen Joanna. Not Queen of France, but still, she would be a Queen after all.

"Does he speak Italian?"

"Good Norman French. I promised you, didn't I? He's a Norman. The De Hauteville family from Normandy, which means he's technically my vassal."

"How old is he, Father?"

"He must be about twenty-one."

"I thought you said he was young?"

The King laughed. "That *is* young. To me. I should warn you, it's not completely settled. He wants to know first 'if you are pleasing.' His envoys are on their way here, and I suppose they mean to look you over and report to him. But we don't have to worry about that. I swear you're getting prettier every day. Right now, with the color in your cheeks and your eyes shining, you're as pretty as any of them. No, there's no doubt but that he'll have you. Well, are you pleased?"

"Yes, Father." Not Philip, but still a rich, French-speaking King. She must be pleased, she supposed. She smiled stiffly at him. "Yes. Thank you."

CHAPTER EIGHTEEN

Joanna stood as still as she could, her arms held out from her sides, while they fussed around her. The cloth of her gown felt stiff and scratched her through her linen shift. It was heavy with gold thread. Her women fluttered around like so many sparrows, diving in for a quick peck and then darting away again. Nurse, relegated to a corner, sat on a stool and watched, dabbing now and then at her eyes with her apron. Opposite Joanna, planted stolidly on the only chair in the room, the Bishop of Winchester also watched.

"Too much jewelry, do you think?"

"No, no. Not enough, if anything. You don't want them to think King Henry cannot afford the best for his daughter."

"And gold thread in her hair?"

"Yes. That's good. Your shoulders back a bit, my lady."

"If they speak to you in Latin, answer in Latin."

"Keep your eyes down, but don't bow your head. You should look modest but royal."

"And don't smile. It looks foolish and immodest."

"But have a pleasant expression. You must not appear sulky or too serious."

"Curtsey when you are presented, but not a deep curtsey. Your rank is higher than theirs."

Joanna was not listening. She heard their advice only as the twittering of birds. She stared unseeing at the door. Down in the Hall, King William's envoys were waiting for her. The gown she was wearing had been made especially for this occasion. For weeks now they had filled her head every day with the history of Sicily, the geography of Sicily, the politics of Sicily, all so that she could appear well informed today.

It was Whitsun. The Easter court had ended in turbulence. King Henry had raised the question of his divorce. The Queen had adamantly refused ever to consider one and had contemptuously rejected the monastic life. Her sons had all upheld her and an angry shouting match had broken out. The Queen had been peremptorily sent back to Salisbury. They were all gone now, the King, Henry and Marguerite, Richard, Geoffrey and Constance. Joanna, Alice, and John remained.

"Have done," the Bishop said gruffly. "The girl looks well and we have kept them waiting long enough."

He stood up slowly. Joanna's women fell back, their heads cocked on one side as they studied her. She lowered her aching arms to her sides.

"Pinch your cheeks a little. You look pale. And bite your lips."

In the Hall, talk ceased as Joanna and the Bishop came in. Every one stood. There was a fire blazing in the hearth. It was May, but cold and damp in Winchester. Three men who had been warming themselves at the fire turned. The others fell back, leaving these three in a row facing her. Joanna swallowed nervously. She stood as instructed, head up, eyes lowered.

Archbishop Rothrud of Rouen came bustling forward. He had joined the envoys in London and accompanied them here.

"My lords, this is the lady Joanna. My lord Bishop, may I present the Bishop-Elect of Troia, the Bishop-Elect of Capaccio, and the Royal Justiciar of Sicily, Florian of Camerota?"

The Bishop of Winchester moved down the line, embracing each in turn. Joanna still stood like a statue. Anger was rising in her, a Plantagenet pride that would not tolerate being treated like a costumed puppet and made to wait for inspection. The men had finished their greetings and turned toward her. Before anyone could speak, Joanna stepped forward.

She said clearly, "In the name of my father the King, I welcome you all to Winchester, my lords."

She curtseyed, not briefly enough to be insulting, but not a deep one either, and noticed as she did so that there were no rings on the hands of the Bishops-Elect. That was good. She would not have to kiss them. She straightened up and looked at them all. Out of the corner of her eye, she saw Rouen and Winchester exchange dismayed looks, but the three men opposite her did not hesitate. They knelt before her. Triumphant, she held out her hand for them to kiss.

As they rose, she moved toward the fire.

"How is your lord King William? Well, I trust. And his lady mother, Queen Margaret? I was most interested to hear of the portrait of Our Lady painted by St. Luke. She has endowed an abbey to house it, has she not?"

"Your Highness is very well-informed," the Bishop of Capaccio murmured.

She snapped her fingers as she seen her mother do and when she felt the chair against the backs of her legs, sat without looking behind her.

"Pray be seated, my lords."

"Your Highness, it is not the custom in Sicily to sit in the presence of royalty."

"No?" She smiled at them. "But you are in England now. And you have had a long hard journey from London. You have my permission to sit."

Stools were brought for them.

"Tell me about King William's new foundation, his abbey outside Panorme, a Benedictine abbey, I believe. How is it progressing? Does it have any monks yet?"

The Bishop of Troia answered her. "Your Highness, the first monks for the Abbey of Monreale arrived this spring. One hundred monks from La Cava. Yes, it is a Benedictine abbey, run on the Cluniac model. It is built in the royal deer park just outside ..."

She had chosen a good topic. Around them, at a respectful distance, the court listened amazed as she elicited descriptions of Monreale, enquired after her countrymen Archbishop Walter of Panorme and Bishop Richard of Syracuse, praised what she had heard of the beauties of Sicily and the virtue of its King. When she felt the moment was right, she ended the interview and rose to her feet.

"I thank you all, my lords, for your instructive talk. I have learned much and look forward to hearing more of your country at supper tonight. Until then, my lords, I take my leave and trust that you will find your lodgings here as comfortable as your ranks and honors demand."

"Your Highness is most gracious," they murmured, kneeling again.

Joanna left the Hall. She went up to the solar. Her women followed, several paces behind. They were silent at first but as they went up, she heard the buzz of talk begin and grow. She threw herself on the window seat in the solar and laughed delightedly.

"There! That should show them! That stuffy old Bishop of Winchester—I don't think he would have let me speak at all if he had had his way."

"Joanna! You were marvellous!" Adèle rushed to her and embraced her. They rocked together, laughing. "I swear I was frightened of you myself! You played the Queen to perfection. Truly you did!"

"Well, I thought it a most unseemly display," Nurse sniffed. "Pushing yourself forward among all those men like that and you still a young girl! Do you want them to tell their lord that the King of England's daughter is a forward hussy with no modesty or manners?"

"I think they liked it," the Countess of Pembroke said thoughtfully. "I confess I held my breath at first. If they had been Normans now ... But it seems in Sicily they have a different view of royalty."

"Yes, did you hear them? 'Not sit in the presence of royalty,' indeed! Whatever do they do at dinner?" Another lady said and they all began to laugh.

"And the way they said 'Your Highness' this and 'Your Highness' that! Did you ever hear anything like it? Positively Byzantine."

"I only hope they approved," Nurse said dourly. "If they were only play-acting—and I wouldn't put it past their Byzantine deviousness—and give you a bad name, you'll be in trouble, my girl."

It seemed that they approved. King Henry, on his return to Winchester, was delighted to hear their reports of her beauty and queenly bearing. He hugged Joanna when he told her of the impression she had made.

"I didn't know you had it in you. You were always such a quiet little thing. But blood will tell and you *are* my daughter."

"And Mother's," Joanna amended silently, smiling back at him.

"I'm proud of you, Joanna. Is there anything special you'd like to ask of me? Some palfrey that you fancy? A falcon? A brooch or circlet that you've set your heart on?"

"There *is* something. Father ..." She twisted her belt nervously. "Will I be able to take my own people with me? Adèle ... I want Adèle to go with me. She wants to go, too. We've talked of it. Please, Father."

"Adèle? De Laigle's daughter? We'd have to ask her father, but I don't see why not. You should have your own women with you. Mind you, I can't promise how long King William will let them stay. That's in his hands. And in yours and theirs, too. Don't let them make themselves unpopular, you know, stand aloof from the rest of the court and don't criticize or meddle in politics. It wouldn't be the first time a Queen's foreign followers caused trouble at court and got themselves thrown out. Though in Sicily I should think they'd hardly notice, they've such a mixture there already. Norman, Lombard, Greek, Jew, and Arab ..."

"Not at court, surely?"

"Yes indeed. I gather the palace is staffed by Moslems, and the King even has a band of black slaves."

Joanna was horrified. "But you said the *Pope* approved this match ..."

The King pinched her cheek. "Ah, you're still young, Joanna. The Pope's a prince and a prince without an army, what's more. He needs the support of powerful kings. If William has Arabs in his service, that's his business. He's a good Christian in spite of it."

ભ ✤ ૭

It was a busy, confusing time. Sometimes she was impatient to leave Winchester and start on the great adventure and the days seemed to crawl. At other times, she was afraid. She thought of leaving all the familiar places, leaving her parents and her brothers for an alien court and the stranger who was to be her husband. At those times, the days went all too quickly.

Joanna had to submit to endless fittings of thin silk gowns in the drafty rooms of Winchester Castle. It was summer, but the thick stone walls of the castle kept it cool even when the sun was shining outside, and the English sun, Joanna had learned, was unreliable.

Inexorably, the days passed. Lammastide came, the 1st of August. Joanna's wardrobe was ready. Her gowns and linens and mantles were packed in chests that filled an entire chamber. Her jewelry was all locked in leather boxes under the care of her treasurer. The ladies and household officials who were to accompany her were ready and all the coffers packed, gifts for King William, casks of Bordeaux wine, English wool and Flemish cloth, money and plate, linens, armor, dismantled beds, rugs, furs, candles, hay for the horses, and even a portable altar for the journey.

To Joanna it all seemed unreal, a dream that she walked through like a ghost. She still followed the same routines, but she had a sense of no longer belonging. She had already begun to withdraw from Winchester and the Norman court there. Yet she could not imagine the court in Sicily. One thought sustained her: she was going to Poitiers. Her mental count of the days was timed to her arrival in Poitiers; beyond that she could not think.

In mid-August a special court was held in Winchester. Her mother came out of Salisbury again to attend it. The time had come at last and Joanna, stiff and miserable, went through the ceremony like a puppet. King Henry was traveling and it was the Bishop of Winchester who formally surrendered her into the care of the Bishop of Capaccio and Florian of Camerota. Gifts were exchanged. In the King's name, the Bishop presented the Sicilian envoys with gold and silver, fine clothes, cups, and horses.

She said goodbye to John, who smiled nastily and said, "I'm glad we shan't have to see *your* ugly face around here any more." In a quick flash of understanding, she saw his unhappiness. She gave him a hug and said, "I shall miss you too, John." She left him standing there, suddenly serious, biting his knuckles and staring after her, wide-eyed.

Alice cried openly. "Don't hate me, Joanna," she whispered in her ear. "I wish I were going with you to Poitiers. It was all so simple then. Now everything is such a mess." Joanna embraced her, too, for the first time in many months. She remembered the early days in Poitiers when Alice had been kind to her. Here in Winchester she had hated Alice for taking her mother's place with her father and had avoided her, but suddenly she felt guilty about it. Alice was unhappy and what right had she, Joanna, to judge her?

"I'm sorry, Alice," she murmured and they clung together.

On the 25th of August the procession set out on the first leg of the long journey to Sicily. Now they were actually on their way, Joanna felt less nervous. She rode beside her mother, who was to come with her as far as Southampton. It was an imposing procession. The soldiers of the escort guard went first, then Joanna's official escorts, the Archbishop of Canterbury and the Archbishop of Rouen, resplendent in scarlet; the Bishop of Evreux; Joanna's uncle Hameline, the King's bastard brother; the Sicilian envoys and their followers. Behind Joanna and her mother came her ladies and her household, then all the servants, the pack horses and the baggage wagons, and more soldiers. The procession was strung out for a mile through the countryside of southern England.

In the fields on either side, Saxon serfs stood in silence and watched them pass.

"They are such a sour-faced people," Joanna said. "Don't they ever cheer or smile?"

"They have little enough reason to love us," her mother observed.

They rode on in silence for a while.

"I envy you," the Queen said at last. "I shall be back in Salisbury tomorrow and you will be on your way to the warm south. How I miss Aquitaine! The sunshine, the wine, the flowers. When you are in Poitiers, go and see if the rose bower has been cared for and send me word, if you can. I hope you will be happy with your William. He's still young, that's good. But he's been King since he was twelve, that's not so good. He will be used to having his own way. Try to win his mother over. She was Regent once and probably still influences him."

Joanna nodded. They were silent again for a while.

"He will have women there," the Queen said suddenly. "You must expect that. He's twenty-two and you—how old are you now?"

"Eleven this year, Mother."

"Yes, that's right. I remember. So you're too young to be a wife to him yet awhile. But even afterward, there will be many other women. For us, it is a different story. Love, for women, is rare and risky, but all the more sweet for that. Like licking honey from thorns." She sighed. "Kings have so many opportunities. They have to be saints to resist them. Louis, I think, was faithful to me and what a bore *that* was. I remember what a contrast Henry was, his energy, his virility ... like a breath of fresh air in that fusty court in Paris. He talked of his campaigns and strode up and down all the time. He was only nineteen then. I was very attracted to him. And he to me. I know he was. It wasn't just Aquitaine that drew him. But he's like all men. We could have ruled an empire together, but he couldn't stand having me as his equal. So now that I am past bearing sons for him, he shuts me up in Salisbury. He's afraid of me. Is it true he's sleeping with Alice?"

Her mother looked at her. Joanna could not tell what she was thinking. The grey eyes were hooded, one eyebrow slightly raised, her mouth a straight line. Joanna looked back at her uncertainly.

"No, you need say nothing. It's clear enough in your face. You must learn to guard your feelings, Joanna. We women cannot

196

afford to be transparent. Our power lies more in deviousness than directness, though I wish it were not so."

"But if one is Queen ..." Joanna said. "I always wanted to be a Queen. Like you. But so many people have told me it is more important to be good than powerful."

"Only those without power would say such a thing. Goodness is usually dullness and is an invitation to others to step on you, besides."

She was silent for a while, looking ahead. A cloud of midges swam above her and dust swirled around the horses' hoofs. There was an overpowering smell of honeysuckle from the hedgerows on either side. As far as the eye could see, the endless soft English green stretched out, fields running out to humped uneven hedges, hedges merging into straggling coppices and beyond them, darker green in the distance, the sprawling shapeless oak forests. There were no sharp edges to stop the eye, no straight lines, no definition. Joanna looked sideways at her mother's profile, the straight nose and flared nostrils, the high cheekbones, the sweep of her dark brow against the pale golden skin. She did not belong here, any more than a lily would belong among the tumbling tangled wildflowers at the road's edge.

"I will never forgive him," the Queen said suddenly. "The others ... they were unimportant. But Alice ... his own son's bride. Does Richard know of it?"

"I don't know, Mother, but I don't think so."

"No, I think not. That settles it. There will be no divorce. Not under any terms. I will not free him to marry that conniving little bitch. He thought I would tire of it but I have found a certain strength in solitude. There is time to think. Now I suppose he thinks he will wait me out, but I'll not die to please him."

They had reached the crown of a hill and below them lay the coast. In the harbour of Southampton, a row of masts rocked side by side. Flags flew from some of them, but they were too distant to recognize the colours. Among them were the seven ships waiting to take Joanna's party across the Channel to France.

CR ✾ ℘

The screaming of the gulls, the salt smell, the heaving of the deck under her feet and the creaking of ropes brought back to her vividly the day two years ago when she had sailed to England. Now she was reversing that journey, across the Channel to Barfleur. She had slept in Southampton and come aboard in the morning. She had embraced her mother, caught her whispered "God be with you, Joanna!" and now she stood at the rail, looking down at her where she stood on the dock between the Archbishop of Canterbury and Hameline Plantagenet, the King's brother.

The ship moved smoothly away from the dock. Queen Eleanor raised a hand, then let it drop and turned and walked briskly away. Her cloak fluttered out behind her. Joanna still stood watching, but the Queen did not turn back again.

It was a much calmer crossing than that other time and she had better accommodation when she got there. Her brother Henry had come to meet her and he rode with her across Normandy as she retraced her journey through Bayeux and Caen where the Archbishop of Rouen left them, Falaise and Argentan with its faint memories of a Christmas spent there many years before, Alençon and Le Mans and Chinon where her father had promised her a king. Each day brought them closer to Poitiers and Joanna became more impatient and excited.

They were well into September before they finally emerged onto the plain below Poitiers. The late sun struck across its walls and steeples so that it appeared to Joanna like a golden city in a fairy tale. Eagerly, she pointed out the landmarks to Adèle at her side.

"Look, that's the cathedral of St. Pierre and there's Notre Dame la Grande. It looks finished now. They were still building it when I was here. And there—there, Adèle!—that's the Maubergeonne Tower, the highest part of the palace. The palace is in the center of the town."

As they approached the gates, a group of horsemen rode out to meet them. Richard was at their head. Together Joanna and Richard rode through the gates of Poitiers. The streets were lined with cheering townspeople and women and children leaned from the upper stories, waving and calling to them as they passed.

"Did you choose it on purpose, Joanna? To arrive today, I mean, on my birthday?"

"I had quite forgotten. So it is. Oh Richard, I have no gift for you." She looked behind her. "Well, I have plenty with me. I'm sure King William won't notice one item less from the store of things we're bringing him."

"I am nineteen today. It's taken me two years to restore order here, but I've done great things, Joanna, you will see. And I think even Mother would approve of my court here. There aren't as many ladies as there used to be, and none like Mother or Marie, of course, but we have fine poets and minstrels from all over Aquitaine and Provence. How is Mother?"

"She's very well."

"An amazing woman." Joanna noticed that as usual he did not ask after Alice. "I shall never forgive him. Mother, of all people, to be kept confined in Salisbury. He couldn't have chosen anything crueler. He must know how she thrives on society and conversation and elegant company. I swear I will free her one day, when it is in my power to do so."

"She knows that. She gave me letters for you. They're in my baggage. I'll give them to you when we reach the palace. Oh Richard, you can't think how glad I am to be here! I've looked forward to this for four months. It's all so beautiful. And warm. I hated England."

"Yes, a cold uncivilized place. I don't envy Henry at all. I wouldn't trade my Aquitaine for England at any price. I was born there but I don't care if I never set foot there again. Unless it were to rescue Mother." He looked sideways at her. "You look good, Joanna. And you ride well. Do you remember when I taught you to ride, in the bailey here in Poitiers? You were such a funny little thing, hanging on so determinedly! How long will you stay here?"

"Till my birthday," she answered promptly. "I want to celebrate it here."

"October? You see, I remember, little squirrel! And I shall have a gift for you even though you forgot all about mine!" He reached out and pinched her cheek. "And how is Mouseface?"

"Mouseface?" Joanna asked, startled. "Oh you mean Alice. I had forgotten that nickname. She's well."

"That's too bad. Yes, I know all about Alice. She's Father's mistress." Contempt crackled in his voice. "Alice was always an idiot but this goes beyond everything. I'm damned if I'll ever marry her now. I'd rather lose my right arm than take Father's cast-off whore as my wife."

"My God, Richard, think of the problems that will cause, if you reject King Louis' daughter and after all these years …"

"Blame Father for it. I despise him, Joanna. How could he be married to a woman like Mother and dally with all those sluts year after year, and then Alice … He has no more control than a dog when it meets a bitch in heat." He pulled savagely at his horse's head and it reared up, neighing.

"But let's not talk of that. We have a month together here and I mean to make it one you will never forget."

It was a perfect month. Joanna took Adèle all over the palace and showed her all her favorite childhood haunts. The rose bower was at its peak and now Joanna, instead of hiding on its steps, sat at its center while pages knelt before her with sherbet and minstrels beguiled the languorous afternoons with their songs. They went to the kitchens to see Master Hubert who called Joanna "my lady" and stumbled through French compliments until Joanna interrupted him in the langue d'oc. Then he grinned and together they reminisced over her raids on the kitchen and he ended by giving her and Adèle a piece of marzipan as he had done in the old days. The enchanted month ended with a great birthday feast at which a roast peacock, fully feathered, with its tail spread, was served, and a swan with silvered body and gilt beak, swimming on a green pastry pond. Master Hubert had made, especially for her, a subtlety representing a crown of marzipan covered in gold leaf, with cherries for rubies, and whipped cream for ermine round its base.

At the end of October Richard set out with her on the journey south. She had felt few pangs on leaving Winchester but then she had had Poitiers to look forward to. Now, she suffered. She had dreamed of Poitiers in the years at Winchester, dreamed of going back there one day. She had gone back, for one month that had passed all too quickly, and now she was leaving it forever. Leaving her childhood, her mother and brothers, her

200

home, France, everything that was familiar and everything she loved. For miles she wept, sitting slouched on her horse, and did not care who saw her. Adèle rode beside her. She did not speak but her presence was comforting. At last Joanna wiped away her tears and sat up. Adèle was with her and so was Nounou. Perhaps it would be tolerable.

She had never been further south than Limoges. From here on it was all new. The countryside grew wild and somber. They went through gorges where the road ran alongside streams between high walls of shale, through quiet dense forests where the only sound was the rustling of the leaves of many different trees.

Hills stood out in sharp relief and villages clung to their slopes, their red walls and roofs bursting from the green like unfurled poppies. From Périgueux to Cahors they rode past volcanic peaks and through misty green valleys and oak forests turning russet. Once they passed a huge field of sunflowers as tall as a man, their dying yellow heads all turned south.

There were few towns in this area but the road was busy and it was covered with horse and mule droppings. Every day they rode past wandering friars and students, peddlers carrying their wares, chapmen and tinkers and quacks, beggars and cripples, seasonal workmen and serfs out of bond, discharged soldiers, and long caravans of merchants going to trade fairs with their trains of pack animals and muleteers. They met swift papal envoys galloping north and sometimes knights and their ladies on horseback. Lepers in black costumes with white patches and tall scarlet hats, carrying their wooden clappers, stood off to the side as they passed, keeping as far away as they could. Beyond Cahors they crossed the main pilgrim road running between Conques and Moissac and came on a band of pilgrims returning from Compostela, staffs in their hands, cockleshell badges on their cloaks, and purses on their belts. They marched behind a bagpiper, singing canticles and ringing their little bells.

On the border of the County of Toulouse, they were joined by a group of riders headed by the Count's son, Raymond de Saint-Gilles. Joanna's heart sank when she saw him. Riding beside Richard had been a delight to her and now she was afraid that he and Raymond would ride together and ignore her. She remembered how he had twice snubbed her. Whether her status as Queen-to-be altered things, whether he felt obliged to show hospitality on his own ground, or simply because they were both older now, Raymond was as courteous as she could have wished. He had come to escort them safely across his father's lands to the port of Saint-Gilles. Her father had told her that King William was a handsome man. Looking at Raymond de Saint-Gilles, Joanna wondered if William could possibly be as handsome as this.

Beyond Millau they passed olive groves and vineyards, low thorny plants and scrub. The mild air smelled of thyme and rosemary and boxwood, and the sun shone on white walls and the dusty road winding south ahead of them.

They came into Nîmes across a vine-planted plain. It was their last stop. From there they rode to Saint-Gilles. Joanna had come all the way across France from the grey-green choppy waters of the Channel to the blue Mediterranean which now lay before them. Twenty-five ships were waiting in the harbor for her. She was greeted in King William's name by the Bishop of Syracuse, Richard Palmer, and the Archbishop of Capua. It was the second week of November and the moment she dreaded had come at last. A cold wintry wind was blowing off the sea. Raymond stood back tactfully as she embraced Richard, tears in her eyes.

"Chin up, little squirrel," he encouraged her in langue d'oc. "Remember, Queens don't cry. Good luck, Joanna."

She stood for a moment, taking a last blurred look, then resolutely turned and stepped onto the gangplank and off the soil of France.

Sicily 1176

CHAPTER NINETEEN

The journey was worse, far worse, than Joanna had expected. When she heard of the disaster that had struck the Bishop of Norwich's party, she had some qualms. Two of the ships escorting him back from Sicily had sunk in a gale and all the rich gifts that King William was sending King Henry were now at the bottom of the Mediterranean. Because of this, the master mariner had decided they would not risk the open sea, but would sail along the coast.

Her sickness began the day they sailed. At first it was no more than queasiness as she sat with Adèle, watching the waves tilt endlessly one way, then the other. She stopped watching the sea and tried to look at the ship, the sailors, the deck, anything else. The ship was too small to fill her field of vision. It rose and fell, slapping hard into the waves. She closed her eyes. If anything, that was worse. There was nothing to concentrate on but the lurching of her stomach and the smell of the meat they were bringing out for dinner.

The first time she vomited, she was relieved, thinking that that would end it. Somewhere around the thirtieth time, she lost count. Her stomach ached with the pain of dragging up yellowish bile from its depths. The cold wind chilled her and her hair stuck to her scalp. The carpenters had built a small cabin for her on the deck and she lay there on a pallet, covered with fur rugs, a bowl beside her head.

Outside her cabin, they erected a table at mealtimes. She heard the clatter of pots and goblets and knives, but was too ill to eat anything but bread. The smell of the sailors' sardines and onions made her retch painfully again. She heard them shouting to one another as they worked, meaningless commands, part of the endless noise of the voyage, the slapping of the waves, the howling of the wind, the rattle of the lanterns on the mast.

By Christmas they had reached Naples. Joanna was thin and pale. There were dark rings under her eyes and her hair looked stringy and lifeless. They stopped in Naples over Christmas. Joanna recovered slowly at first and then, as her appetite returned, the color came back to her cheeks and she began to fill out. She ate hungrily, making up for lost time. By the end of a week, she felt herself again, though still thinner than when she had set out from France.

In the New Year, the ships sailed without them. Joanna had insisted on going the rest of the way overland, as far as possible. Joanna and Adèle rode side by side. Joanna's spirits were high. It was enough for her not to feel nauseated, to breathe deeply the fresh thyme-scented air, to look forward to the next meal. She looked out at the Mediterranean, relieved to be riding a gentle palfrey instead of tossing sickeningly on the unquiet sea. The weather was mild with frequent showers. The landscape was quite different from England and northern France. There were no dense forests of oak, but gently undulating open country, little hills crowned with castles and crowding villages, outlying farms and vineyards, isolated monasteries by streams, wide plains of scrub and beech groves. Near the end of January, they rode into Reggio, between rows of marble villas and palaces, and Joanna looked out across the straits to Sicily, where Etna showed up, snow-crowned, on the horizon.

There was no way of avoiding the sea crossing to Messina, but although they advised her that the road from Messina to Panorme was rough and tedious and that most people made the voyage by sea, Joanna was adamant. She would sail to Messina, since she had to, but from there on she would ride.

They had been traveling now for over five months. Joanna was apprehensive again, with the end of the journey so near. The landscape with its pines and prickly pears was alien, and so was the architecture. She remembered the cool grey skies of Winchester, the plainness of its Norman arches, and felt a thousand miles from home.

It was night time when they reached Panorme at last. The locals called it Palermo, but the Norman rulers knew it as Panorme. Her palfrey had been richly caparisoned and Joanna herself wore her best jewels. Her hair fell loose over her shoulders under a gold circlet and her scarlet mantle hung over her palfrey's tail. Adèle had fallen back with her ladies and Joanna rode between Richard Palmer, the tall spare Englishman who had become Bishop of Syracuse, and the Archbishop of Capua, a heavyset dark-haired Lombard. She was tense and nervous and her fingers felt stiff on the reins.

As they came down toward the city, Joanna thought at first it was on fire. Lights blazed everywhere in the streets and were reflected in the dark waters beyond the city. The lights spilled out of the gates and she saw they were thousands of flickering torches. The walls were lined with them. The whole city was ablaze. As they came nearer, she saw the men carrying the torches. They spread out before the gates of the city, forming a great semi-circle. At its center, a single figure stood out in front of them, sitting his horse and waiting.

Joanna held her breath. Light flashed off his rings as he raised a hand to signal his men to wait. His horse stepped forward. Joanna saw what she thought were long earrings, swinging by the King's head. As he came closer, she saw that he was wearing a high Byzantine tiara with jeweled pendants hanging from it on either side. Dazed, she took in the rest of his costume, the long robe of scarlet silk with its wide border embroidered in gold, the pearl-edged dalmatic crossed on his breast and tied around his waist, its fringed ends hanging to his heels. It could have been the Emperor of Byzantium himself. She was aware that on either side they were looking at her. She dug her heels into her palfrey's sides and urged it forward until she was a few feet from the King. His face had been in shadow and she was dazzled by all the flaring torches behind him, but as she stopped by him, his horse turned sideways and she saw his face. King William was not a handsome man; he was the most beautiful being she had ever seen.

His eyes were large and fringed by long thick lashes, his brows perfectly arched. She had expected him to be dark but his hair was as fair as any Norman's. It hung in a fine silky sweep to his beardless jaw. His skin was as smooth and pale as a woman's. Joanna had never seen a man like him. Her father and her brothers had freckled faces and necks burnt red from riding out in the sun, but William's neck, above the scarlet silk, was as white as her own. The perfect lips curved into a smile that did not reach his eyes.

"Welcome to Panorme, Joanna."

She jumped, hearing the apparition speak. Somehow, it would have been more fitting if he had sung like an angel or remained as silent as a statue. His voice, however, was quite normal, a light attractive voice. He leaned toward her and kissed her. Close up, he smelled of perfume and rosewater. She was suddenly conscious of the dust on her skirts and the simplicity of her jewels and was glad that she was riding sidesaddle instead of astride, as she had done on previous days.

It was a bewildering ride. The city was thronged with people and lights and the noise was deafening. The tops of the buildings were lost in the velvety black sky but what little she could see looked distinctly Arab. Joanna rode in a daze. She was shivering as though from cold, despite the mild air, and could think of nothing to say.

"I am taking you to the palace I have had prepared for you and your household," King William said. "We call it the Aziz. That's Arabic for 'magnificent.' My father built it. My mother is waiting to greet you there."

Torchbearers lined the streets and behind them crowds that she could not see for the light roared and cheered. The King languidly raised a gloved hand, on which rings glittered.

"I mostly stay at Favara at this time of year," he went on. "My grandfather built it as a sanctuary for birds and beasts and it has a large lake which I keep well stocked with fish, which makes it a good place to spend Lent. In the summer I go to the Parco or to Mimnermo. It is shady there in the hills, and in the summer it's very hot at sea level."

"My father moves around a lot, too," she said. "All over England and Anjou and Normandy, for the assizes and so on."

He looked at her, his great liquid eyes dark in the torchlight. "These are not other cities I was speaking of but my palaces in and around Panorme. As for the assizes, I leave that to my ministers. I go to the Parco for the hunting—we have deer and goats and wild boar there. Mimnermo is my summer pavilion."

Joanna was silent, dazed. Four royal palaces in one city?

"At the moment, of course, I am living in the royal palace itself, until our marriage is celebrated," he added. He gave her a slow appraising glance and she blushed in the darkness. Inside this strangely androgynous-looking Byzantine figure, with his tiara and silks, his perfume and his smooth soft skin, there was undeniably a man. She had seen that expression on her father's face when he looked at Alice.

They were above the city now. The air was fresh and cool and faintly lemon-scented. She could hear the splashing of water on either side. In front of them rose the somewhat forbidding palace, with square towers at each end and a row of recessed arches. A great Arabic inscription raised in white stucco ran round the entrance arch.

"The Aziz." William said simply. "We are here."

He saw her looking at the inscription. "I had that put there. It says, 'This is the earthly paradise that opens to the view; this King is the Musta'iz; this palace is the Aziz.' Musta'iz means The Glorious One in the Arab tongue."

The strangeness was back again. She was in a dream, she thought, and pinched her wrist, but it hurt. The Hall of the palace, which was upstairs instead of on the ground floor as was normal in England and France, had a high honeycombed ceiling and niches around it roofed with tumbling Saracen stalactites. The walls were covered with a frieze of marble and multicolored mosaic. On the end wall were three medallions against a background of decorative arabesques, in which archers shot at birds and peacocks pecked dates from palm trees. From a fountain in the wall, water trickled down into an ornamental marble channel.

Joanna withdrew her gaze from all this splendor and concentrated on the woman coming to meet her. At least Queen Margaret looked normal. Short and slight, brown-eyed, in her late forties, she would not have been out of place in Poitiers or Rouen. She was nothing like her son, except in her large dark eyes and long lashes. There were pinched lines between her brows and at the corners of her mouth and the faintest of moustaches on her upper lip.

Joanna curtseyed tiredly. Her head was beginning to ache and she was bewildered by all the new impressions. She had a terrible feeling that she might cry. Queen Margaret took her arms and raised her, then brushed her cheek against both of hers in turn without kissing her. She was no taller than Joanna.

"So. You have come at last," she said. She still spoke with the soft sibilants and extra half-syllables of her Spanish origins. "You look tired. And thinner than I expected." She studied Joanna, still holding her arms. "Well, we have a fortnight to put some flesh on you and some color back in your cheeks."

Joanna said nothing. She stood there, disoriented, exhausted, apprehensive.

"I will leave you in my mother's hands," William said. "She will know what is to be done. If there is anything you need, you have only to ask. I hope you will be happy here, Joanna."

He smiled at her and she felt her whole body relax suddenly. She had not realized how tense she was until she saw the kindness in his eyes. She had the impression that he understood her feelings and sympathized. He took her hands and bent and kissed her, a gentle kiss on the lips. "I wish you a good night."

She pulled herself together enough to drop a little curtsey. "Goodnight, my lord."

The Queen herself led Joanna to her chamber. Joanna stopped on the threshold with a gasp. It was a large room by the standards of the castles she was used to. Candles burned steadily all around and lit up the sumptuous mosaics that encrusted the upper walls and the vaulted ceiling. Centaurs, leopards, peacocks, lions, and stags chased each other through palms and orange trees in perfect Byzantine symmetry. The room glowed with blues and greens and gold. The hangings of the large bed were pure silk, embroidered in gold, and the covers gorgeously woven with scenes of hunting and hawking. The floor was marble, patterned in geometric designs. There was a small table inlaid with ebony and ivory and two chairs, one covered with tooled leather, the other with green and blue velvet fixed with gilt nails. There were carved chests and a prie-Dieu with a velvet cushion, and more cushions on benches and window-seats. Joanna had never in her life imagined such luxury. Even the candlesticks were works of art, one the image of a child in silver sitting on a gold chair holding a candlestick, another an enameled sheep standing on a silver-gilt base, with a candlestick on its back. Joanna could only stare, speechless.

"This is a little grander than what you have been used to, I dare say," Queen Margaret asked slyly, watching her reaction.

Joanna let out her breath. "It's the most beautiful chamber I've ever seen," she said honestly.

For a few seconds, her view of the world was transformed and the center of civilization wrenched from its accustomed place. Her father's realm, England and Normandy and Brittany, Anjou and Maine and Aquitaine, was the greatest kingdom she knew, indeed the only one. She had thought of Poitiers as the center of everything and imagined no palace could be more elegant than the palace there. Now she saw how it must appear to someone from the kingdom of Sicily, a pleasant and graceful place but plain and lacking in comforts, and as for England, it was a bleak and barbarous realm on the very edge of the civilized world. It was only a flash and then she relegated Sicily again in her mind to an exotic and luxurious island on the periphery of Christendom.

Adèle was awed. When Joanna and her women were left alone, she whispered, "Do you think we are dead and gone to paradise?" She touched the walls as though they might dissolve at any moment. "Joanna, this is real gold! And *two* chairs! How will we ever sleep with all these animals crawling all over the ceiling?"

"I could sleep anywhere tonight," Nurse said firmly. "I'm that tired. And Joanna, you must get to bed at once or you'll look fit for nothing in the morning."

"You'll have to remember to call me 'Your Majesty'," Joanna said, giggling. "I have a feeling they'd die of shock if they heard you call me Joanna."

"You're not Queen yet," Nurse answered, unperturbed. "And don't you lecture me on how to treat you in public, as though I didn't know my place. But Queen or no, in private you'll always be my lambkin that I nursed as a baby. It hardly seems any time ago and here you are about to be married. Oh dear!" She sighed heavily. "And a good thing I've come with you, by the looks of all this. Remember Dives and Lazarus and don't let your head be turned by worldly vanities. It's harder for a rich man to pass through the eye of a needle and I'm thinking the Devil will strew your path with temptations here."

Adèle was exploring the chamber and with exclamations of delight, had found a cedar-paneled closet for the wardrobe with a bar for hanging folded linens, and in yet another closet, a garderobe. "Look, Joanna, no more wandering down long draughty corridors to garderobes in the corner turret!"

Nurse was unimpressed. "I think that's plain disgusting," she sniffed. "Whatever heathen would put a garderobe right next to the chamber? Think of the stink! We'll be driven out of here in less than a week!"

"It doesn't smell, Nounou. And listen—there's running water down below. I can hear it."

"Not yet it doesn't, but it will. Garderobes always smell bad and that's a fact. Now say your prayers and get to bed!"

CHAPTER TWENTY

Joanna knelt on the marble steps before the gilded rails of the choir. Despite a velvet cushion, her knees were growing stiff. Carefully, she shifted her weight. Her heavy mantle rustled and the fragrance from the flowers garlanded around her neck momentarily overcame the smell of incense.

Before her, Archbishop Walter of Panorme intoned in Latin, "If any man can show just cause why they may not lawfully be joined together, let him now speak or else hereafter for ever hold his peace."

There was silence in the Palatine chapel. Somewhere at the back someone coughed and feet shifted on the marble floor. Joanna stared steadily ahead, at the rows of candles on the altar, the crucifix above it and behind that, the mosaic of the Virgin Mary looking down from the apse.

The Archbishop peered from under his craggy brows, then resumed his chanting. Joanna's hands felt cold, though they were pressed together in front of her. On either side of the altar were columns topped by leafy gilded capitals and, rising from them, arches covered with colorful geometric designs and medallions of saints and leaves and stars and flowers and angels. Not an inch of the chapel—floor, walls, ceiling, was unadorned. She was becoming used to the profusion of color and pattern now, after eleven days. She had arrived on the feast of the Purification and now it was St. Valentine's Eve and her wedding day. It was only the second time she had seen William since her arrival.

From her window at the Aziz, she could see the royal palace, rising white as a dove from the water's edge. Her first view of the city from her window, that first morning, had been almost as startling as her chamber. Adèle had called her over and she had wrapped a cloak around her, hastily plucked from the clothes pole, and run to look. It was a sunny morning, cool and crisp and clear. The city lay spread out below them, red-tiled roofs, minarets, and gilded cupolas, palm trees and citrus groves, flowers spilling red and purple and orange over dazzling white walls, and beyond it all, the Mediterranean sparkling in the morning sun.

"Can you *imagine*," Adèle said, "that it is probably *snowing* in Winchester? Do you remember this time last year? The ice on the ewers? And those itching chilblains?"

"And the smelly fur rugs on the bed," Joanna added. "And nothing to look at outside but grey walls and leafless trees. I think you were right, Adèle, it *is* paradise."

Paradise, but also a prison. Used as she was to coming and going freely, to exploring, to frequenting the kitchen or forge or mews at will, she found the constraints on her movements here intolerable. She had seen only the state rooms and her own chamber in the Aziz and had not been alone once with Adèle or Nurse. Always, the ladies-in-waiting that Queen Margaret had sent her on the first day were in attendance. Queen Margaret herself had visited her every day and always seemed to find something to criticize, smiling that narrow smile of hers.

"You must not mind if I tell you this, Joanna. I stand, after all, in place of your mother now. It is not seemly for a Queen to run ... I think the King my son would not like to see you twine your feet around the chair legs. You are not just a youngest daughter any more, you must remember your position, you are

Queen of Sicily now and that is a great honor ..."

And then there was Constance, the King's aunt and heiress to the throne of Sicily. Constance attended Mass twice a day without fail and spent most of the rest of the day in seclusion in her apartments, meditating perhaps or sewing. However, she felt obliged to come out of her seclusion regularly to visit Joanna, not to advise her on etiquette, as Queen Margaret did, but to cross-examine her on the state of her soul. "I didn't see you in chapel for Vespers today, did I, Joanna? I have brought you a copy of the Lives of the Saints, which I am sure you will find inspiring. I thought we might pray together this morning. I have brought my holiest relic, one of Saint Apollonia's teeth." Joanna found it both embarrassing and irritating.

Adèle, too, was obliged to be more formal. On the first morning, breakfast had been served to Joanna in her chamber and she had told Adèle to sit and eat with her. Queen Margaret came in when they were almost at the end of their meal and at once apprised Joanna of her mistake. Ladies-in-waiting, it seemed, did not sit at the same board with royalty. They stood respectfully to one side and watched.

"You must do better than that, Joanna. We don't want the King my son to be disappointed in you, do we? Of course, I know in Northern courts ... But he will expect you to behave properly once you are his wife. You must remember your position, my dear, and try to do him credit at all times."

Joanna had to fight the rebelliousness she felt. It was only for a few days, after all, and then she would move into the royal palace with William. She hoped, and thought, that William was not as critical as his mother made him sound.

Joanna was very aware of him beside her now. Out of the corner of her eye, she could see his mantle. It was of white silk, so encrusted with pearls and gold thread that it stuck out in stiff folds around his kneeling figure. He was speaking now, his clear musical voice echoing in the chapel.

"Ego Guillermus prehendo te Johanna ..."

They said he spoke many languages, not only French and Latin, but also Greek and Italian and Arabic. She wondered if he knew langue d'oc. She turned her head a little and looked up at his pale slender hands with their heavy rings, up above them to his face. He was bareheaded, his smooth, fair hair shining in the light of massed candles. She studied his pure profile. There was a boyish look, childish almost, to the curve of his cheek seen from the side, the long lashes, the small straight nose, the curved lips and slender neck. He could have been a carved cherubim …

The Archbishop was speaking to her and she brought her attention back to the present moment and promised to honor and obey for the rest of her life the stranger at her side. The Archbishop blessed the ring and gave it to William. She held out her right hand and he slid it onto her middle finger. It was too loose and she crossed her thumb under her palm to hold it on. The Archbishop took his stole and wrapped it round their joined right hands, raising them so that all those standing behind them in the chapel could see. It was done. They were man and wife, *in nomine Patri et filii et spiritu sancto.*

The choir burst into song so suddenly and so near her that she jumped. *Laudate Dominum*, they sang. Praise Him in the sound of the trumpet, from one side of the choir. Praise Him on the lute and harp, from the other. Their high voices soared to the ornate ceiling. She looked at their plump smooth faces as, hand in hand, she and William followed the Archbishop to the altar. That was another thing she was not used to yet. She had never seen a eunuch, as far as she knew, in France and England, but the Aziz was staffed by them, as though the King did not trust men to serve in the women's palace.

Christus vincit, Christus regnat, Christus imperat …

It was not over yet. The Archbishops of Capua and Salerno led her to the two thrones facing the altar. They took from her the mantle and the garland of flowers. The choir chanted and the Archbishop came slowly toward her. She knelt before him, her hair flowing down over her shoulders, and he anointed her with oil on her hands, her breast, and her head. She stood again while the assistants dressed her in her coronation robes.

The Archbishop held the crown of the Queens of Sicily over her head and there was a hush in the chapel. He lowered it slowly and settled it on her head. It felt heavy and, despite the velvet with which they had padded it inside to make it smaller for her, sat low on her forehead. The pendants hung to her shoulders. Beside her, William was also wearing his crown and ceremonial vestments, a white robe that reached his feet, a scarlet tunic, pearl-encrusted white gloves, a rich dalmatic patterned in gold and purple, and over all, a white cloak lined with miniver and fastened by a sexfoil gold brooch. In his right hand he held a gold rod surmounted by a finial of leaves and in his left an orb with a white cross. Carefully, they ascended the steps to the thrones and sat side by side.

A great shout rang out from the four corners of the chapel. *Vivat, vivat Regina! Vivat Rex, vivat Regina!* With a soughing like waves on a beach, everyone knelt.

Joanna sat beside William and looked out over all the bent heads. She felt hot, her pulses raced, and she dared not move for fear the crown should slip. *Domine, in virtute tua,* the choir sang triumphantly. "The King shall rejoice in your strength, O Lord … You have given him his heart's desire and have not denied him the request of his lips."

King William rose and Joanna came to stand beside him. The congregation stood again, the regalia was placed on velvet cushions and they set out to walk through the city in procession. At first Joanna was concerned with not going so fast that the noblewomen bearing her train would wrench it from her shoulders, nor so slowly that the silk canopy borne over their heads would go ahead of her. Then she remembered that she was Queen now, the noblewomen and the canopy bearers had to adjust to her pace, not she to theirs. She relaxed a little and involuntarily smiled.

On either side of the street, the crowds, held back by lines of soldiers standing with their legs spread and pikes extended, cheered and waved. She wished her mother could see her now. At the thought of her mother, her head went up and she stood as tall as she could.

Ahead, at the foot of the street, she saw a glint of blue water. A pale spring sun shone on the sea and on the whitewashed walls of the royal palace, and a slight breeze stirred the palm trees. A rich and beautiful country and she was its Queen. The thought kept coming back to her. Queen Joanna! She breathed deeply, inhaling the odors of lemon and sea air and olive oil. Despite the cool air, her skin felt flushed and warm from excitement. She had achieved her ambition and could imagine nothing beyond it but a life of ease and pleasure.

They were before the palace now and its steps were lined by black guards in scarlet uniforms. The sun glinted on their weapons as they stood stiffly to attention. William stopped and she looked up at him, questioning. Beneath the ornate tiara, his face was blank and beautiful. He took her hand and they turned to face the crowd before going in to the feast. The crowd was jumping up and down and its wild cheering had settled into a steady chant.

"*Vivat Regina!*" they shouted. "*Vivat Regina! Vivat Regina!*"

CHAPTER TWENTY-ONE

J oanna leaned her head against her chair and with the back of her hand, lifted the hair off her neck. The July heat was stifling. The sun blazed down on the marble paving in front of her and the fountains sparkled. Two eunuchs had sprung to fan her. The slight breeze was welcome at first but soon felt as warm as the still air. She stared out over the shrubs in the courtyard. They looked faded and tired, despite daily watering. There was a strange thorny bush in front of her and near that a plant with pale fleshy swords rising to sharp points and then a short fat palm which seemed to have compacted itself under the fierce sunshine. Vivid dabs of red and pink stood out here and there from these stiff, prickly plants. Behind them, on the other side of the courtyard, the fretted arches seemed to jump and waver in the heat. She looked up at the tiled roof and the pale walls and the endless glaring blue sky.

"Your Majesty would perhaps be cooler inside the palace?"

She moved her eyes without turning her head. Around her, in the shade of the cloister, her ladies sat on benches and steps, embroidery frames in their hands, bright skirts trailing on the swept stone floor. The clerk who had been reading to them had fallen silent, his hands flat on the open book. The speaker was looking up at her. He sat on a low stool, a man of fifty or so, deeply tanned, his carefully trimmed dark beard shot through with grey.

"Not yet, Nicholas, not yet. I've been inside ever since dinner and I want to be outside now."

"Your Majesty perhaps did not rest for long enough?"

"Too long. I'm not used to it yet. In France and England, we never went to bed in the middle of the day." She thought briefly of her father with all his energy and impatience consenting to lie in bed from dinner until after Nones like these Sicilian lords. "Besides, I couldn't sleep because of the bells. When will they stop?"

"They are to ring all day, on His Majesty's orders." He looked at her, his dark eyes narrow under heavy grey brows. "It *is* a great diplomatic victory for him, Your Majesty."

She sighed. "I suppose so."

He said, as though explaining her lack of enthusiasm, "Of course, Your Majesty has never known a time where there were not two Popes."

"There was only one true Pope," she said sharply. "The Emperor Frederick supported an anti-Pope. Even he has admitted as much now, by abjuring him and acknowledging Pope Alexander."

"You are of course quite right, Your Majesty. I stand corrected."

"So the Pope actually received Emperor Frederick in St. Mark's. I should like to have seen that meeting. After all these years. Eighteen years of schism, is it not?" She wanted to show him that, although young, she was not ignorant. "I never thought about it much before. I never thought much about Germany at all."

"Quite so, Your Majesty. I never think about it either, if I can help it."

Joanna looked at him quickly. She had never heard him express a personal opinion before. William had sent her Nicholas of Athens to be the Chamberlain of her household. He was always perfectly deferential but she sensed concealed amusement, or even mockery. It made her uncomfortable. At first, she thought it was because of her age, then, disagreeably, she saw that it extended to all her retinue. He did not care for Germany. She wondered what he thought of France and England.

"I wish we could go hawking," she said suddenly.

"In this heat? It would be unbearable," Adèle said, raising an eyebrow.

"I don't think so."

"But very harmful to the complexion." That was one of the Sicilian ladies Queen Margaret had wished on her.

"We can't even go this evening, because of the banquet." In the summer, Joanna had learned, they hunted and hawked only in the early morning or early evening. In the middle of the day, all activity ceased and everyone rested, a custom that made her impatient. "Well, at least I can walk around this cloister. That's better than sitting still all day."

She jumped to her feet and her embroidery fell to the floor. One of her women retrieved it. Nicholas was on his feet as soon as she was. For an old man, he was remarkably agile, she thought. He was lean and graceful. For some reason, she often found herself comparing him in her mind with her father, perhaps because they were close in age or because they were so different. Her father was stocky, would no doubt be fat if he were not constantly on the move. His shoulders were hunched and his legs bowed from years in the saddle. She looked at Nicholas, standing straight and slim before her, at his lean dark face and the blend of deference and superiority in his expression.

"Come and walk beside me, Nicholas, and teach me more about Sicily. There is so much I still have to learn."

"Your Majesty, if I may say so, is a most apt pupil."

"You don't *have* to compliment me, you know."

"It is impossible to keep myself from doing so, Your Majesty," he answered smoothly.

They turned the corner and started down the next side of the cloister. Joanna walked slowly, her dress trailing on the smooth stone. The air was hot and still. In the sun-filled courtyard the fountain water fell straight as a silver arrow and the plants cringed in the fierce heat.

"Tell me truthfully now, Nicholas, don't you secretly think we Northerners are all barbarians?"

"Your Majesty ..." he murmured deprecatingly.

"And *now* you are thinking that only a barbarian would ask such a question!"

He laughed. At least, she supposed it passed as a laugh for him, though it was a far cry from King Henry's thigh-smacking, gut-wrenching bellow. He walked beside her and just half a pace back, matching his stride to hers, his hands clasped behind his back. As usual, he was richly dressed and jeweled, though he wore his finery lightly.

"You have me at a disadvantage," he said at last. "I have been trained since childhood to conceal my feelings, to speak diplomatically, to deal in half-truths and omissions rather than the whole plain truth. What you ... Northerners usually call Byzantine deviousness." He smiled at her. "Yes, of course we know how you despise that. As for what I truthfully think—even with a fellow Roman, I would not venture so far. Nuances, hints, unfinished phrases. It is seldom necessary to spell it out. But *truthfully* then, I have great admiration for the energy and directness of the West. The King your father is a man of enormous talent as a lawmaker and a soldier, and King Louis is a devout and honorable monarch."

"I begin to understand. One listens for what is *not* said as well as what is."

Nicholas looked up at the carved and vaulted roof above them. Presently he said, "I have often found that Northern women are much quicker in learning the language of subtlety than Northern men. I met your brother Richard once."

Joanna laughed out loud. "Now there's a not very subtle link of ideas! Yes, Richard is the least devious of men. Certainly, the least devious of my brothers."

"And because of it, he will be a great leader. Men may not agree with him but they will know where they stand. He will never hesitate or prevaricate."

"So you have been to France?"

"Yes, indeed. To the Île-de-France several times and to your father's domains."

"And to Byzantium, I believe?"

"I was a page at the court of the Emperor Manuel," he said.

She was becoming accustomed by now to his inflections and heard the awe in this simple sentence.

"Is Byzantium as beautiful as they say? More beautiful even than Panorme?"

He looked sideways at her and again she felt like a naïve provincial. After a moment, he answered. "There is no comparison. Palermo is a rich and beautiful city but Byzantium is the queen of cities. As far above all others as the august Emperor Porphyrogenitus is above all other Christian kings. Is that," he asked slyly, "honest enough for you? Now you see why we Romans despise the Germans. Holy Roman Emperor indeed! Constantine moved the Roman Empire to Constantinople in 324 and it is still there!"

"So that is why you always refer to yourself as Roman rather than Greek?"

"*Civitus Romanus sum*. The Roman Empire was secure in Constantinople while Europe was being overrun by Huns and Goths and Vandals."

"But that is all in the past. What of the Christian kings of Europe now?" she asked curiously.

"The Emperor is God's vice-regent on earth."

"And the Pope?"

"Pope Nicholas I was excommunicated by the Patriarch Photius in 867. There has been a schism between our two churches since 1054. Compared with that, the 18-year schism between your two Popes is nothing. We recognize one God, one faith and one empire. Under the Emperor, the Patriarch is the leader of the one true Christian church."

Joanna blinked a bit. "Then why, if you feel like that, are you here and not in Constantinople?"

He grimaced. "Your Majesty is still young enough to think men can be consistent."

"Or Norman enough?" she teased.

He acknowledged this with a tilt of his head. "I suppose it is because here I have position and wealth and respect, to a degree I could never have hoped for in Constantinople. I am a bastard, you see. Here, that doesn't signify. My father acknowledged me and made me a page at the Imperial court, but I could never inherit, never rise to anything. It is a hierarchical society, fixed, traditional. This is a young society and much more vigorous, flexible, tolerant. Here, you can make your way with talent and energy, regardless of your origins or religion. The King himself is only four generations removed from a Norman vavassor. Besides—I can admit this, having lived here for so long, though my fellow Romans would not—the power is passing to the West. I felt it when I first went to Paris in 1149. Paris, of course, is not a city to equal Constantinople. A small dirty town with small dark houses, full of drunks and beggars and slaughterhouses and pillories. And the stench of it! The filth underfoot in the muddy streets and the open sewage trenches, that was what I noticed first. But once I got used to the evil smells, I began to notice other things, the friendliness of the people in the taverns, the liveliness of the students. They came from all over Europe. I was a student myself then. Paris was the place to go. We would sit up all night over a jug of wine, arguing, debating, discussing everything under the sun quite openly. In Constantinople one weighed one's words. There were spies everywhere. And enthusiasm was somehow suspect, uncouth. We Romans were too dignified for that. I have never seen a city half as beautiful as Constantinople, but it is locked into the past, frozen. The future lies with the West. It's hard to tell where. They're all small struggling countries now, but if they could unite ... The Spanish kingdoms, say, or the Frankish ... Your father King Henry seems on his way to creating an empire, young Henry in Normandy and Anjou and Maine, Geoffrey in Brittany, Richard in Aquitaine, and now he has proclaimed John Lord of Ireland."

They were still pacing slowly around the cloister.

"My mother ..." Joanna said suddenly. "She must have been Queen in Paris when you were there."

"Yes," he said, "she was. That was partly why I went there. I wanted to see her again."

"Again?" Joanna stopped and stared at him. "What do you mean?"

"You see, you have drawn me into plain speaking after all. Perhaps it is because in some way you remind me of her. To speak plainly then, I idolized your mother. Oh, don't misunderstand me." He raised a hand apologetically. "I should perhaps have said I worshipped her. She never spoke to me. I suppose she never even noticed me though she did once smile at me. I was a fifteen-year-old page at the Imperial court when the King and Queen of the Franks came to Constantinople with the crusaders. They did not stay in the Imperial palace itself, the Boukoleon, but one of the other palaces, called the Blaquernae, by the Golden Horn. But they came often to the Boukoleon for feasts and other ceremonies. She was—no, she was not the most beautiful of women. There were many women in Constantinople more beautiful. Somehow they were all alike. They walked with tiny steps, their eyes lowered, their backs curved, their stomachs thrust forward. They tittered behind fans when anyone spoke to them and never looked you in the eye. I was captivated from the first moment Queen Eleanor walked into the triclinium they were to dine in that night. She had such a light, swinging step and was so straight and upright, looking around her and smiling openly. I think it was her sheer vitality that I admired. She enjoyed everything so frankly. The girls I knew thought she was lacking in dignity, hoydenish. I thought she was everything a Queen and a woman should be. There was a feast for King Louis' patron saint, Dionysius the Areopagite, and the Emperor had sent a chorus of Greek priests to sing for them, I remember. King Louis was reclining awkwardly—in Constantinople they still dine in the Roman fashion, on couches—but Queen Eleanor looked quite at ease, resting on one elbow and leaning forward to talk animatedly to the Emperor. She was talking about the famous golden tree behind the throne, the one with the little golden birds that sang so cunningly. I was kneeling before her couch, to offer some delicacy, I forget what. We all had to kneel at the same time and rise at the same time. It was quite a ritual. I was looking sideways for the signal and just could not resist one quick glance up at the Queen, though of course we were supposed to keep our eyes down. And that was when she smiled at me. I have never forgotten it. And now I have the great honor of serving her daughter."

"Thank you for telling me that," Joanna said. "I can imagine it. When I think of my mother, I think of her smiling, too. On horseback, erect and smiling." Impulsively, she put her hand out to Nicholas. He went on one knee and kissed the back of her hand.

The bells stopped suddenly. She had become so used to them she no longer noticed them until they stopped. In the unaccustomed quiet, the gushing waters of the fountains sounded loud. Then from one of the city churches, Vespers rang.

"I must go and dress for the banquet," Joanna said. "I enjoyed our talk."

Cɾ ❧ ʀO

As she mounted the stairs to her chamber, she met Queen Margaret, her head veiled, missal in hand, followed by her ladies. Queen Margaret looked her up and down.

"You are not going to chapel for Vespers, Joanna?"

"I went this morning, my lady."

"Now, Joanna," Queen Margaret advanced upon her with a thin smile, "I thought we had agreed that you would call me 'mother.' Your family is here now, you know."

"Yes, my lady mother," Joanna murmured, fighting the rebelliousness she felt. Her mind was filled with the visions of her own mother that Nicholas had conjured up and it did not come easily to call this slight, hard-mouthed woman mother.

"You must wear your best tonight to honor the peace the King my son has made with the Holy Roman Emperor."

Joanna ground her teeth, but submissively answered, "Yes, my lady mother."

The Queen went on, her ladies dipping into curtseys one by one as they passed Joanna.

"Oh, I shall *scream* if she says 'The King my son' one more time!" Joanna exploded, clutching Adèle's arm. "Why can't she call him William for once?"

"Everything in Sicily is more formal," Adèle said soothingly,

"She's no more a Sicilian than I am! She was a princess from Navarre, and what's Navarre? A nothing kingdom, a tiny little place poked away in the Pyrénées that I'd never even *heard* of until a year ago! And she thinks she can tell *me* what I should wear, as though I …"

"Ssh!" Adèle hissed warningly. Joanna glanced back and saw among her own women the Sicilians the Queen had given her. She lowered her voice but went on angrily.

"There, you see! She sets spies on me. She doesn't trust me. I am never alone, with just you and my own women."

She had entered her chamber and sat down with a thump on her tiring-chair.

"I have a headache," she said shortly to her women, "wait in the ante-chamber. Adèle will brush my hair for me a while."

They withdrew, but she noticed they left the door between the chambers open.

"Adèle, you are always so sensible. Say something to calm me down. She always makes me bristle."

"Well … I think you are partly right and partly wrong. In a way, they are spies. But I think Queen Margaret was sincere when she said you would need them to advise you with local customs and so on. It's quite normal for you to be assigned some local women. Everything she does is mixed like that, and I dare say she herself could not separate out her various motives. She wants you to do credit to her son and she also wants you to make mistakes. She wants to help you and advise you but at the same time she resents you. The thing is, *you* don't have to worry about her either way. *You're* the Queen now."

"So what should I do? Tell her to stop pestering me? Tell her I shall scream if she says 'The King my son'?"

"Of course not. Try to please her. Thank her for her advice. Praise the King—she dotes on him, of course, that's obvious. And if you still can't please her, then that's her fault, not yours. She is not a happy woman, I think. It shows in her eyes and the lines around her mouth."

"You make it sound so straight-forward." Joanna picked up a glass and studied her face in it. The wide green eyes stared back at her. There was the faintest sprinkling of freckles across the bridge of her nose. "She thinks I am not beautiful enough for her son, I'm sure."

"I dare say she does," Adèle answered, brushing briskly. "But she would think the same of any woman in the world. And she may even be right. He is quite extraordinary. Unreal, almost. I thought he used cosmetics—his lips are so red and his complexion so smooth. You've been closer to him than I have. Does he?"

"No, I think he's real enough. But I can't begin to tell what kind of person he is. He never shows any expression. Not that I have seen much of him. Just at banquets and ceremonies. He is very polite and impersonal. First, he asks after my health and then if I am comfortable at the Aziz. Then he gives me news of my family, if he has any. That's all the talk we've ever had. I wonder if he *has* any feelings?"

She was dressed when Queen Margaret came in and her women were fixing her hair. Adèle gave her a quick nudge in the ribs and respectfully drew back.

"I should value your advice, my lady mother," Joanna said, "on what jewels to wear this evening. You know so much about the court here and what is fitting and also what would be most pleasing to the King your son." She saw Adèle turn away to hide her smile.

The Queen's face lightened. "I should be glad to help, my dear. Let me see—the coronet the King my son gave you on your wedding day. That would be perfect, since you are wearing white. But you need some color. Not rubies, I think. They would bring out the red in your hair." Joanna bit her lip and stared at the beautiful ruby necklace Queen Margaret was wearing. "Nor sapphires. Your eyes are not blue, are they? Of course. Emeralds. What do you have? This?" She pursed her lips. "Too heavy for you. When you are older, it will do. You need something dainty— *this* is perfect! What a lovely piece! Old-fashioned, of course, simple—but it will do." She had picked up a delicate necklace of amethysts and pink tourmalines set in gold. "This will do very well for a young girl."

"It belonged to my grandmother," Joanna said.

"The Empress Matilda?" Queen Margaret handed it carefully to Joanna's chief tiring-woman. "It's of German make, perhaps? Pretty enough, though the workmanship is somewhat crude."

She supervised the choosing of rings for Joanna and the arrangement of her dalmatic, then they went downstairs together. By now Joanna was becoming used to the rows of slaves and eunuchs lining the halls and prostrating themselves as they passed, to the water running in marble channels down the center of the rooms, to the glittering tesserae covering the walls. She still felt strange arrayed as a Byzantine Empress.

Outside the palace, they were mounted on palfreys with jeweled bridles and rode side by side through the city to the towering royal palace with its arched stories rising from among the palm trees.

Inside the palace, servants backed away from her, opening doors as she led the way, and her arrival in the Hall was signaled by a fanfare from the trumpeters. King William came to meet her, kissing her on both cheeks. She saw Queen Margaret watching with pursed lips as William led her to the throne next to his own.

The envoys returned from Venice, Count Roger of Andria and Archbishop Romuald of Salerno, were the honored guests at the banquet. They sat garlanded with flowers at the High Table and recounted again, in detail, how the Emperor Frederick had waited at the church of St. Nicholas on the Lido, how he had been escorted by a delegation of cardinals to St. Mark's, how he had prostrated himself before Pope Alexander and received the kiss of peace. He had signed a fifteen year peace with Sicily and a six year truce with the Lombard league.

Joanna knew it was important for Sicily but she had heard it before and found it boring. She occupied herself with seeing how many names and faces she could remember now. With the archbishops, she did not do very well. There were no fewer than six present and she could remember only Walter of Panorme. The nobles were not much easier. She remembered the King's cousin, Count Tancred of Lecce, a villainously ugly, short, dark man. She lost track of the rest, Count Roger, Count Richard, Count Robert. It was all very confusing and too many of them had names beginning with an R. She did better with the high palace officials.

Caid Richard, the King's Great Chamberlain, was unmistakable, and Matthew the Chancellor, Florian the Justiciar and Margaritus the Emir. She remembered Margaritus because he was handsome and because of his unfamiliar title. She had asked William about it.

"It's an Arabic term," William explained. "Margaritus is in charge of the fleet. The full title is Emir-al-Emirs, but the Normans here usually call him Amir-al."

Joanna was brought back to the present by the mention of news from France.

"I hear that your sister the Young Queen Marguerite was brought to bed of a son in Paris last month," William said, selecting a stuffed date from a gold-plated tray.

"A son? Henry and Marguerite have a son at last?" Joanna exclaimed, clasping her hands. "Oh, that is good news! My father will be pleased. What have they named him?"

"Unfortunately, the child lived only three days," William went on imperturbably. He turned to talk to the Archbishop on his left.

Joanna sat without eating, her thoughts a thousand miles away. Her mother would have had the news long since, in Salisbury. Henry and Marguerite would at least be brought together by this, she hoped. And Alice, in Winchester, would be grieved for her sister.

"You are comfortable at the Aziz, I hope?"

Joanna jumped. "Oh yes, indeed, thank you, my lord."

She looked at the beautiful expressionless face beneath the ornate tiara. She remembered her father's rages, Alice and her nervousness, Henry sulking and petulant, Marguerite with her fussy self-important ways, Richard, marvelous Richard, confident and swaggering, and her mother, smiling, vivacious, proud ... Real people, all of them, unlike this puppet. A feeling of irritation swept over her, a desire to shatter that imperturbable facade and see what lay behind it.

"I don't think your mother approves of me," she said, on impulse.

There was no emotion on his face but at least he was paying attention to her.

"No, no, Joanna, you are quite mistaken. She has the greatest respect for you. She told me so herself."

"She did?"

"Yes. In fact," he leaned slightly toward her and there was a trace of a smile on his perfect lips, "between you and me, she is a little afraid of you."

It was Joanna's turn to be surprised. "Afraid of me? How can she be?"

"Easily. You are, after all, the daughter of the most powerful King in Europe. And you have lived at so many great courts: Poitiers, Winchester, Rouen, Chinon. My mother, you know, came from Navarre and she feels that you, perhaps, look down on her."

"My lord," Joanna was astounded at the idea. "I never thought ... I don't know what to say. I was in awe of her ... she is so correct and I ... my family is much less formal ..."

"But you have a certain way with you, you know. I have been quite in awe of you myself, at times." Now he was definitely smiling. "My mother is a small woman and you stand so straight and tall and look down your nose. It is a very beautiful nose, of course, even with the freckles."

Joanna blushed deeply. What would Alice answer? She looked down at her plate and twisted her fingers in her lap. "My lord ... I want to please her, of course. But I shan't be with her much longer."

She thought he looked wary. "What do you mean?"

"Why ... I mean that I shall be living here, now that we are married ... shall I not?"

His smile had gone. "No. You will be staying at the Aziz. I see no need for you to move into the royal palace until we are man and wife in more than name."

Joanna stared at the table. How many years would that be?

"You are disappointed?" He was smiling again. "I want you to think of me as a friend, Joanna. Our marriage has been followed by peace with the Holy Roman Empire, the greatest threat to our kingdom. What can I give you in return? Ask something of me."

She raised her eyes to his. "I should like to go ... which was the palace you said was your favorite in the summer? I should like to hawk there, if I may."

"Of course. We'll go tomorrow. The Parco, you mean."

"Tomorrow? Don't you have to ... well, talk to the envoys, sign papers, things like that?"

He dismissed the idea with a wave of his hand. "My ministers take care of these things for me. I take care of celebrating. Yes, we'll go tomorrow. I didn't know you liked to hawk. And is that all you want?"

She hesitated. "I wish we could have a minstrel from the South of France. To sing in the langue d'oc. Not that this isn't beautiful ..."

He nodded politely, but his attention was swinging back to the Archbishop and she was not even sure he had heard.

☙ ❀ ❧

Back in the Aziz, after the banquet, she sat on the bed in her shift, swung her feet up and leaned back against the pillows. Adèle came to take her jewels off her.

"I thought it would never end. I'm exhausted from it all. What a strain! I feel stiff all over. What I really want is a bath. A long soak in warm water. Did you notice Margaritus of Brindisi? He's handsome, isn't he? Though not as handsome as King William, of course. Oh Adèle, we're not going to the royal palace, he says. We're to stay here."

Her women moved about the room, talking quietly to each other as they put away her jewels and folded her clothes. Nurse had been wrong about the garderobes. The servants poured buckets of water down them every day and sprinkled perfume all around. She closed her eyes and wriggled into a more comfortable position. There was no creak from the leather straps on the bed. The deep soft mattress enveloped her body. *It must be filled with down,* she thought lazily. Her father had said William was rich, but she had not imagined such luxury and elegance. She had thought in terms of more silver, bigger jewels, gold plates at dinner, not things like down mattresses, perfumed garderobes, and piped-in water. The hardest thing to get used to was the unvoiced assumption that all this was normal and civilized and that she herself was the somewhat primitive product of an intolerant northern land. And the defensive nervous fear that she shared with no one, that perhaps they were right.

There was a knock at the door and she heard one of the women cross the room. Something heavy was being carried in. She opened her eyes. Two of the palace eunuchs were bringing in a great wooden tub. They were followed by a row of servants with steaming pitchers.

"What's this?" she said, sitting up.

They all bowed deeply. "The bath you ordered, my lady."

"I didn't order a bath—did I?" She hesitated. "Yes, I did say I wanted one—I didn't think ..."

The servants poured the water into the tub and withdrew. Joanna watched, her eyes narrowed thoughtfully, as one of the Sicilian women Queen Margaret had sent her poured perfume into the water. A simple wish and it had been realized immediately. It was like a fairy tale and like one, she knew, it could have its complications. She had a sudden vision of her father, roaring in his fury for someone to rid him of Thomas Becket. Her mother had been contemptuous and she was right. All those years a King and he had not learnt to guard his tongue. She remembered one time when he had actually rolled on the floor in a rage, stuffing the rushes into his mouth, full of dirt and dog shit and everything ...

She stood up and let them pin up her hair. The water felt good, warm and relaxing. They drew the curtains round her and the perfumed steam rose gently. She leaned back against the warm, smooth wood. The edge came up to her neck.

With her eyes closed, she called out, "Put a folded napkin under my neck."

It was brought at once. Hands lifted her head, the napkin was slipped under it. She lay relaxed, her arms floating on the water. So far, it was good to be a Queen, but she promised herself she would remember Thomas and never grow careless or proud. Thomas had been a proud man but he had worn a hair shirt and had maggots in his sleeves. Her thoughts went round and round dreamily. What about this bath? Was that not luxury and comfort that Thomas would have scorned? One had to be on one's guard at all times. She started to pray silently. *Miserere mei, Deus*, Lord, have mercy upon me. Then she thought it was unseemly to pray in her shift and in a bath tub. She was really very tired. Her thoughts were hardly making any sense at all.

She leaned forward and drew back the curtain. "I want to get out now."

They wrapped her in linen towels and she sat on a chair while they brushed out her hair. Then they brought her a clean dry shift and put it on her.

"I'm really very tired, I'm going to lie down and rest for a while," she said.

Her women helped her onto the bed and covered her with a fur rug. She was still awake, but just barely, when they brought the boy in. He was dark-eyed and slender, fourteen years old or so. She opened her eyes and stared.

"What's this?" she asked, for the second time within the hour.

One of the women curtseyed. "His Majesty the King sent him to you. He is a minstrel, from Provence. He sings in the langue d'oc. His Majesty thought you would like that."

"Langue d'oc?" She sat up. "Oh *yes*. I should like that very much." Her throat constricted. She waved a hand to indicate he should sing and lay back again, closing her eyes. She thought of the songs she had heard in Poitiers in the long arcaded Hall. She remembered the rose garden and Master Hubert and Richard riding into his first tournament and her mother presiding over what they came to call the Courts of Love.

> *Lancan vei la folha*
> *Jos dels albres chazer*
> *Cui que pes ni dolha*
> *A me deu bo saber*

Tears gathered in her closed eyes. She had heard that sung to her mother in Poitiers. Now it was her turn. The minstrel was singing for her as once they had sung for her mother. She was Queen and would wear beautiful gowns and sit at the High Table and all the young knights would pay court to her and do her bidding…. Imperceptibly, she slipped into dreaming sleep.

CHAPTER TWENTY-TWO

It had happened suddenly and Joanna did not know how or why or even when. Certainly by the end of the first week at the Parco, she was obsessed by William. Perhaps it was Adèle who led the way, that first night when she and Joanna were in bed together, reminiscing over how he had looked, what he had said, the exact angle of his right profile that was most becoming, the lift of an eyebrow when he said such and such. Perhaps it was the change in William himself. Before this, she had only seen him in state robes. Or it might have been the kindness he showed her. True, she was his Queen and it was her due, yet it was heady stuff for her to be singled out for attention by this man who was doubly the cynosure of all who saw him, for his looks and his rank.

Joanna had ridden up to the Parco in the comparative cool of the evening after the banquet for the Venice peace. Servants from the royal palace had gone ahead to join the small staff already at the Parco. Queen Margaret had stayed behind at the Aziz and so had Nurse. William had warned Joanna to take only a small party as the Parco was a small, simple place. "Only a pavilion, really," he said. So Joanna had chosen her favorite Poitevin ladies and, of course, Adèle, and had left the Sicilians. She felt liberated and happy even on the way up there. They wore large hats to keep the late sun off their heads and rode at a leisurely pace.

Everything delighted her, though away from the well-tended and watered city, the land was barren, dry, sandy soil and low-growing shrubs, dusty olive trees and reddish rocks and lizards that scuttled for shelter at their approach. Presently they were up among pine trees and her nostrils were filled with the smell of sun-warmed pine sap. The needles rustled under the horses' hoofs and the thin shrill rasping of the crickets sounded loudly in the still air. Panorme lay far below them, a huddle of red-tiled roofs and golden domes on the edge of the bright blue sea. At this height, one could see patterns in the water, swirls of deeper blue, rocks showing through the clear shallow water, and, further out, patches of green and indigo.

She had imagined something like her father's hunting-lodges in Normandy, but what was small and simple to a Sicilian was sumptuous to a Norman. The Parco, like the other palaces here, was built around a central open courtyard. The arches of the cloistered walkway were carved and the inevitable fountains burbled into their marble basins. It was surrounded by shade-giving trees and set among lemon groves and pleasure gardens where peacocks strutted. The air was always faintly lemon-scented and filled with the sound of running water.

They were up early in the morning. William was not at breakfast, but from the crowds of young noblemen present, she knew he had come. She saw Count Roger of Andria laughing loudly among a group of Normans, and she recognized the ugly little Tancred of Lecce, who bowed to her solemnly when he caught her gaze on him.

It was barely an hour past dawn when the laughing eager throng, forty or so men and women, arrived at the mews, set at a little distance from the Parco itself. Here, everyone fell quiet, not wishing to disturb the falcons. Joanna was riding a beautiful little palfrey. The falconer came out from the mews and bowed low to them. Some of the men started talking to him about the new birds in his mews and the likelihood of good sport that day.

When William rode up with a small group, Joanna would not have recognized him at first if it had not been for the reaction of the courtiers around her. He looked tall and slim and ordinary in a blue silk tunic with yellow embroidery, low boots and leather gauntlets and a soft feathered hat pulled down to his ears.

He greeted the company gaily and swung off his horse and came over to Joanna.

"Come and let me show you," he said. "I am proud of the mews here. This is Mauger, my chief falconer. How's that new young brancher doing, Mauger?"

"She's fine, Sire, but a little restless. She's still in a sock."

He held his hand up to Joanna and helped her to dismount. They passed a bird that was being weathered, tied by a leather strap to a stone block by the door, and entered the mews. It was dark and cool inside. There was one window, high up. Joanna felt sand scrunch under her feet and heard rustling and fussing around her. A hand took her elbow.

"Your eyes will soon adjust," William said, very quietly. "Stand still until you can see."

She waited and gradually, in the semi-darkness, made out the perches of various sizes and heights around the room. Some were high and far out from the wall, others near the floor.

"These are some eyases taken from their nests a week ago." Mauger was beside them, pointing to the low perches. The nestlings' eyes were seeled and they were attached by leather jesses to their perches. Sensing a new human presence, they moved uneasily and tried to scratch at their heads. The little bells on their feet tinkled.

An assistant came forward from the back of the room to soothe them, stroking them and crooning over and over the bar of a song. They walked on, being careful to make no sudden movements. At the back of the room, another assistant was walking a hooded falcon, talking gently to her. As they watched, he fed her a chicken leg, stroking her as she ate.

"This is my precious. Look at her! Isn't she a beauty? I call her Vitesse." William pointed to a magnificent gerfalcon on a high perch. They went over to it and he sang a few low notes. The falcon turned its hooded head from side to side and stepped delicately on its perch, making the bell on her jesses ring.

"We have a lot of short-winged hawks here," William explained, "because it's mostly wooded country, but I thought today we might go down by the lake and raise some waterfowl, herons, cranes, ducks perhaps. What are you used to? A merling? We have several here. You should have your own bird, so she can get used to you. Or he. Perhaps you would prefer a tiercel, as they're less aggressive, or do I insult you? I never fly any but females myself. Mauger, I'll take Vitesse today."

"Yes, Sire."

"This one is beautiful," Joanna said, pointing to a young peregrine standing quietly on its perch.

"Does this one fly free, Mauger?" William asked.

"Yes, Sire. She's a good bird, learned quickly."

"She was still on a creance when I was last here," William explained. To Mauger, he said, "Give her to the Queen and see how they suit."

Joanna felt a sudden thrill at being so casually referred to as the Queen. She held out her left wrist as Mauger transferred the peregrine from its perch. She felt its claw grip the heavy leather and instinctively began to talk to it.

"There now, my pretty, it's all right, we'll be all right, you'll see."

The bird cocked its head, listening to her.

"These are her call notes, my lady," Mauger said and he whistled softly.

She listened. "Like this?" she asked and tried to repeat it. She ran it through a few times, to be sure of it. "She likes me, I think. Look, William, how docile she is!"

She was suddenly abashed at having called him William, a thing she had never done before, but he paid no notice.

"She's yours, then. What will you call her?"

"I think—that I will call her Bellebelle," Joanna said, handing her back to Mauger.

William was very still. He stared at her and even in the semi-darkness she could see how the lines of his face had hardened.

"Bellebelle?" he said harshly. "Why that name?"

Near him, a bird tossed its head and bit at its jesses.

"Because she's beautiful," Joanna stammered. She had said something dreadfully wrong, she knew, but was not sure what. Mauger had turned his back and William was still staring at her.

"My lord, I am sorry if I have said something to distress you. I did not mean it. Perhaps the name reminds you … I will call her something else." She searched her mind and remembered Richard's palfrey at Poitiers.

"Gracieuse! May I call her Gracieuse, instead?"

"My dear child, call her whatever you will," he said lightly and turned to go.

A moment ago, she had been the Queen and now she was his dear child. They left the mews together. Outside, the sunlight was dazzling. She screwed up her eyes against it.

A few at a time, the courtiers entered the mews to retrieve their birds. Then they all trotted off, falcons perched on their leather-clad wrists, to the spot where the huntsmen waited for them with the hounds. The dogs were pulling at their leashes, tongues out, eager for the chase.

They rode sedately through the park and then into the shady trees through wide alleys. William drew alongside her.

"You sit your horse well," he said after a moment. There was no sign of the brief awkwardness in the mews.

"Thank you, my lord," she said, unreasonably pleased. "My brother Richard first taught me to ride."

She was riding astride, away from the public eye. The bells on Gracieuse's jesses tinkled and the horses' hoofs thudded softly on the turf. They emerged suddenly from the trees. The ground sloped down to a vast still lake surrounded by bushes. In the centre of the lake was an island with an elegant little pavilion on it.

"It's beautiful!" She exclaimed. "I didn't know this was here."

He looked pleased by her praise. "I had it made," he said. "It's an artificial lake. We go out on it in boats sometimes."

"Oh, I would like that!" She cried. "Could we do that while I am here?"

He raised an eyebrow and smiled. "Of course. We'll go tomorrow, if you would like. We can have a cold dinner served on the island. It's best in the morning, as there are too many insects in the air in the evening."

He rode away from her as they came down toward the lake. The nobles spread out into a semi-circle, positioning themselves, talking to their birds.

"Now, Gracieuse," Joanna murmured, stroking the bird on her wrist, "now, girl, pretty girl." She crooned its call notes to it and looked around her. Some of the other birds were already aloft. She slipped the hood from Gracieuse's head and untied her jesses. Gracieuse soared up at once and Joanna shaded her eyes, watching a little nervously. But Gracieuse had been well trained. She circled overhead, waiting on the hounds, seeming at times almost motionless, then tilting smoothly. The huntsmen unleashed the greyhounds and they raced toward the bushes, barking loudly. There was a crashing as they plunged into the undergrowth and then the sound of wings flapping. Birds rose into the air all round, mostly ducks.

"Now, Gracieuse, now," Joanna shouted in excitement, half standing in the stirrups.

Gracieuse circled again, then stooped so swiftly that Joanna could not see where she had gone. She looked around. It looked like chaos, but the hounds and birds were trained to work together. The falcons dived to strike the ducks in the air, the hounds retrieved the fallen prey and killed them if they were not already dead, and the huntsmen took them from the dogs. Joanna scanned the air but could not tell if Gracieuse was aloft again. At that distance, the hawks all looked alike to her. A huntsman ran up and dropped a white crane at her horse's feet.

"Mine?" she asked, amazed.

"Yes, my lady. That's your peregrine, isn't it?" He pointed to a bird circling high above them.

"I think so. Wait a moment." She put her head back and whistled Gracieuse's call notes. The bird dropped straight to her upheld wrist, folded its wings, cocked its head and stared her in the eye.

"Oh Gracieuse," she said softly, "you gem, you beauty! Huntsman," she leaned slightly from the saddle, "give me the crane's heart."

"Yes, my lady." He took his knife from his belt and slit the crane open. Blood flowed sluggishly over its white feathers. Gracieuse watched intelligently. Joanna extended her right hand and the huntsman placed the heart on it.

"There, Gracieuse, there, my lovely," Joanna murmured, stroking the bird as it fed.

"A crane at the first stoop? That's excellent." William had drawn rein beside her and sat watching. His approval put the seal on her triumph. She looked across at him, laughing. He had taken off his hat and run his hand through his hair. His blue tunic was open at the neck and she could see a sheen of sweat on his collarbones and on the tendon that stood out as he turned his head to her. She had a disturbing sensation, longing for something and not knowing what she longed for, or as she put it to Adèle later, like feeling homesick when you are already at home.

"Shall we move on round the lake?" he said. "I think we've raised all the birds in this area."

They made some half dozen drives in all before retiring to the shade of the trees for an early dinner. The servants were waiting for them in a clearing where they had spread clean white cloths on the ground and set out plates and cups. Joanna reluctantly yielded Gracieuse to her falconer and drew off her heavy gauntlet. One of the grooms led her horse away. The group gathered, chattering loudly, around the cloth as first William, then Joanna, washed their hands in the proffered basin. When William sat, everyone followed suit. Joanna sat beside him on a cushion. She was ravenous. The servants brought them food, cold roast meats and capon and partridges, little mounded heaps of lemon rice with almonds, figs stuffed with cinnamoned eggs, olive bread, humble pie, cheese and fruit, and fresh-baked bread. Joanna accepted everything. There was wine, cooled in the lake, and mulled pear cider, which she preferred.

William had publicly praised her for that first crane and everyone, even Count Roger, who never seemed to notice her, had congratulated her. As she would have guessed, Count Roger was a superb horseman and had brought down more birds than anyone. They sat around the cloth, tearing at capon legs and tossing the bones back to the greyhounds, eagerly discussing the morning's hunt.

After the meal, they lay back lazily in the shade while musicians played for them. The greyhounds dozed, crickets chirped, the servants quietly cleared away, the huntsmen drank their ale. The day's catch of cranes, herons, ducks, and snipe, lay in neat piles. Beyond the trees, the lake surface sparkled in the sun.

The next day they went to the island. The wide boat was tricked out in gold and silver and the sails were silk, though they were furled for lack of wind. She remembered the dreadful Mediterranean voyage from Saint-Gilles—the heaving deck, the smells of rope and sardines and salt, the cold spray—and she could hardly believe she was on a boat. There was no wind. The servants rowed smoothly as she and William lay back on velvet cushions. The ripple of the water mingled with the music of vielles. They dropped anchor out on the lake and fished from the boat, sitting under silk canopies. Joanna had never fished before and, good-naturedly, William helped her, when she got a bite, reel in a pike. They dined in the pavilion on the little island and afterward Joanna and Adèle took off their shoes and waded in the lake, holding their skirts up and laughing to feel the soft mud squeezed between their toes.

It was a relief not to be on display. Here away from the city and the people, waited on by disciplined slaves and discreet servants, they could relax. On the island, William sat bare-headed, legs stretched out before him, sipping wine and talking in a desultory fashion with some of the younger nobles. Life could not be improved on, Joanna thought. Hawking one day, boating another, and no mother-in-law to criticize or advise her. She was profoundly happy.

CHAPTER TWENTY-THREE

Joanna and Adèle sat side by side on the floor of Joanna's chamber, with their backs to the window and their long hair hanging out over the sill.

"The sun will bleach it," Adèle explained. "It will make your hair more golden." Tactfully, she did not add, "and less red."

"A good thing Nurse can't see us," Joanna said. "She'd say we were addling our brains."

"Yes." Adèle giggled. They sat in silence for a while. "Did you notice how *he* never came down to breakfast?"

William had left the Parco to return to Panorme after only a week. He had told Joanna of his decision at dinner, the day of an unsuccessful boar hunt, and misunderstanding her visible disappointment, had urged her to stay on as long as she liked. He left the next morning.

Joanna stayed on for another three days. They seemed interminable. In the mornings, she and Adèle rode out in the park, with an escort at a respectful distance. In the heat of the day, they rested and lovingly fingered the treasures they had stored, two dice that *his* hands had touched, a white feather from the crane that Gracieuse had killed on the first day, some pressed flowers from a later open-air dinner and, best of all, a missal that he had actually kissed. On the fourth day they left, needing to replenish their fantasies with a view of the reality. They did not in fact see William. He had left the day before for his summer pavilion at Al-Menani.

Joanna sat now with her eyes closed. The sun, beating down on the crown of her head, was making her feel drowsy and far-away. She said nothing.

"Do you *think*—perhaps he had a woman there?" Adèle murmured.

"Not one of the ladies, I'm sure."

They would have known. All week they had watched every smile, every turn of his head. He was unfailingly polite to all the ladies, but favored none. When they danced after supper, he led out a different lady each time.

Adèle must have reached the same point in her thoughts. "He *did* retire early from the dancing most evenings. And his apartments were on the other side of the palace from yours."

Joanna moved her head. "Perhaps you're right." She sat up suddenly and turned to Adèle. "And he calls her Bellebelle, I'll wager. That's what I was going to name Gracieuse and he looked at me very oddly and asked why that name. I could tell he wasn't pleased so I changed it to Gracieuse."

She sat back again and laid her head against Adèle's. Dreamily, they began to fantasize in broken sentences, William leaving the dancing early, William finding Bellebelle waiting for him in his chamber ... Tacitly, they evaded the central issue in their thoughts, risking a bold image sometimes and then retreating to the comparative safety of the tone of his voice or the sweep of his long eyelashes on his cheeks as he lay, eyes closed, next to Bellebelle. It was strangely titillating to Joanna and not at all disturbing. She had no sense of William as her husband and it did not seem odd that she and Adèle should daydream together over his attributes. He was still a godlike figure, despite the comparative informality of this past week, and old, older than any of her brothers, having just turned twenty-three a month before. He was beautiful and he had been kind to her and in return she idolized him. They both idolized him. They treasured every smile, every compliment, and told them over like a rosary when they were alone together.

"And perhaps that's why he lives in the royal palace and you at the Aziz," Adèle persisted.

"You mean he keeps a mistress at the royal palace?" Joanna was both shocked and excited at the idea.

"He wouldn't dare."

"I don't see why not. Look at your father and Alice. That was public knowledge."

"Yes, but different. Alice, after all, is noble. Father wouldn't have kept a common mistress in a royal palace."

"Perhaps Bellebelle is a lady, after all. A nickname for one of the ladies. Countess Adelaide ..." They collapsed into giggles. Countess Adelaide was fifty and fat.

"Get your heads in from that window this minute! Whatever are you thinking of? The sun is too strong. It will make you sick, you know it will."

Nurse stood surveying them, hands on ample hips. Her face was flushed and there were dark circles of sweat under her arms.

"Nounou, we're only making our hair fairer ..."

Nurse tossed her head like a horse. "If God wanted your hair fairer, He would have made it so. This place will be the ruin of your character, I knew it from the first."

"Nounou, this place is paradise. Have you ever seen such comfort? Down mattresses, piped-in water, velvet chairs ..."

"Paradise, indeed! Those are tools of the Devil and it's hot enough here to be the Devil's own place." Nurse sat on a wooden chest, spurning the velvet chairs, and fanned herself. "It stands to reason," she said, "if you enjoy life here on earth too much, it takes your thoughts off the life to come and that *can't* be good. I'm not saying I wish you any sorrows, God forbid, but it's my belief we're living too soft a life here. It's all pleasure, pleasure, pleasure ..."

"Not all," Joanna said, standing up and stretching. "What about that dreadful toothache I had a fortnight ago? *That* wasn't 'pleasure'."

"And a fine fuss you made about it too! That's what I mean—a big girl like you putting off having a tooth pulled for weeks just because you were afraid of a little pain! Anyone would have thought it was an arm or a leg you were losing."

"It wasn't a little pain, it hurt a lot."

"I don't know what your father would have said. He has his faults, God knows, but fear of discomfort is not one of them. We all have to lose a tooth from time to time. It's just one of life's little tribulations, to be borne with fortitude."

"William hasn't lost any of his teeth yet and he's older than I am."

Nurse cocked her head on one side. "Yes, you're right. But that's unusual. Look at the Lady Constance now, she's the same age as the King and she must have as many teeth out as in. And I'll wager *she* didn't make such a song and dance about it as you did! There's a lady you could do worse than imitate. All this soft living hasn't turned her head, though I don't know how."

Joanna sighed. She had heard this many times before. Although they lived in the same palace, Joanna's and Constance's paths seldom crossed. When they met, mostly at dinner, Constance talked little. As Nurse had pointed out, she had lost several teeth and was very conscious of it. When she talked, she habitually covered her mouth with her hand and she never smiled if she could help it. She was a tall gawky woman, stooping to conceal her height, which made her appear round-shouldered. She had fair hair that frizzed a little round her temples and hung limply at the sides, and fair eyebrows and lashes that were almost invisible. Her long nose, pale watery eyes, and narrow jaw made her look perpetually sad. Since Joanna's return from the Parco, she had stopped visiting her to enquire into the state of her soul, convinced, as Adèle put it, that she was a lost cause. With the influx of young men to the palace, Constance ate dinner less and less often in Hall, preferring to eat in her own apartments. She was ill at ease in the company of men, especially young noblemen whose main interests were hawking and dalliance.

"She'd make a perfect nun," Adèle said. "Too bad for her she's the heiress, but you'll see, as soon as your first child is born, she'll enter a convent. I'm sure of it."

Joanna looked now at Nurse where she sat foursquare on the wooden chest.

"And all the bathing you do isn't good for the skin," Nurse said, "let alone the soul. Too much pampering the body. The blessed martyr Thomas had maggots in his sleeves and didn't complain of them."

"However, he *was* ashamed to show them to the Queen," Joanna pointed out, "and here, *I* am the Queen. It would hardly do for me to have maggots, now would it, Nounou? Constance, I might add, would do well to bathe a little more often."

It was true that a definite odor of unwashed feet hung about Constance. In Normandy or England, it would not have been noticeable, with all the castle smells of dogs and garderobes and putrefying matter in the floor rushes, but here where all the noblewomen smelled of perfume, Constance was the exception.

"And what are you going to do today?" Nurse asked, changing her line of attack. "A hawking party? A dress fitting? Listening to some foolish love tale about Lancelot and that faithless Queen Genevieve, instead of the lives of the saints?"

"Guinevere," Joanna said automatically. Sometimes she wondered why she wanted Nurse to stay. Indeed, in an argument a few days before, she had suggested to Nurse that she would be happier if she returned to France.

"Happier?" Nurse had said indignantly, puffing up like a pigeon. "Happy has nothing to do with it. Yes, I know that's all you think of, but I thank the Lord I know my duty and it's my plain duty to stay here and act as the voice of your conscience since you don't seem to heed your own."

Joanna pouted. "To please you, Nounou, I will go and work at my embroidery and they shall read me the life of Thomas the martyr. There! Is that a suitable occupation for a Christian Queen?"

Nurse nodded dourly. "You're a good girl at heart," she said at last. "In spite of everything. In the end, that goodness will prevail. I know it will. I pray for you every day."

"Nounou!" Joanna held out her arms.

Nurse pushed on her knees and levered herself up from the chest. She had grown very stout. She came over to Joanna and kissed her forehead. They were the same height now and she had to reach up to do it. Joanna flung her arms round her and squeezed her, feeling the solidity of her, the strength, the safeness.

"Don't ever leave," she said. "Even if I get cross and tell you to. I need you here with me."

"There, there, lambkin," Nurse murmured, patting her back.

ℭ ❀ ℬ

The reader droned on and Joanna and Adèle had moved to the window seat of the Hall. Here they could murmur to each other unheard by the ladies-in-waiting scattered round the large room. It was a week since they had last seen William. They were eking out the days of separation with memories of that occasion, what he had said, how he had looked. They praised not only his undeniable attractions, but attributed to him manly qualities he did not possess, a deep voice, broad shoulders, skill as a horseman. The truth was, he was no better than average on a horse, his build was slender, and his voice rather light, though pleasant enough.

By mutual consent, they did not mention his beard. Even their admiration could not disguise the fact that it was, so far, a pitiful failure. He had been growing it for three months now and it was no more than fair fuzz on his cheeks and chin.

Joanna stretched and yawned. The reader broke off and looked at her uncertainly.

"Oh, that's enough, that's enough!" she said impatiently. "Let's go and walk outside for a while, Adèle."

She slid off the window seat and all round the room her ladies rose, folding their needlework. The reader stood with his head bowed.

"Count Tancred of Lecce, Your Majesty!" the guard at the door intoned.

"Oh no!" Adèle groaned beside her. "Your faithful lapdog is here again!"

Adèle was convinced that Count Tancred was in love with her, but Joanna guessed that it was her position rather than her person that attracted him.

He came into the room aggressively, as though he were breasting a swirling stream. "Bantam cocks are always the fiercest," Adèle had said of him more than once. The ladies bowed their heads coldly. He was not a favorite of theirs.

"Good morning to you, my fair cousin," he said and bowed slightly to Joanna. Involuntarily, she ground her teeth. She was always irritated by his insistence on their relationship and by his attempts to ape the courtly style of the younger noblemen. He dressed too young for his age, too, she thought, looking at his bright colors and pointed toes and curled beard.

"Good morning, Count Tancred," she said shortly.

"Come, come, not Count, please. That is too formal. I shall be offended, you know." He wagged a finger at her and smiled archly.

She looked at him without smiling. "I was just on my way out when you arrived," she said, "cousin Tancred."

"Ah, I see." He glanced around him, took a book from under his arm. "I brought you this, my lady. It is not worthy of you, of course, but if you would deign to accept it, I should be most honored."

Tancred's stance was as cocky as ever, his head was up and his jaw jutted at her, but the eyes in the ugly face were a dog's eyes, pleading, uncertain.

Silently, she took the book. It was bound in leather ornately tooled in gold. She opened it and looked at the title page. Unlike most women, Joanna could read and could not help being proud of it. It was written in Latin, with elongated capitals in blue and gold. "For the most excellent, virtuous and fair Queen Joanna of Sicily, this book was made to the order of Count Tancred of Lecce, her humble and devoted cousin and servant." She turned the page and stared. It was a collection of poems in the langue d'oc, beautifully written, one to a page, with delicate illustrations of birds and beasts and flowers. The words jumped up at her.

Can par la flor, justal vert fuelh
E vei le tems clar e sere …

She looked at him. The man really did try. A book was a precious and rare gift. As far as she knew, her father had never owned even one. It was not, after all, his fault that he was so ugly. She saw suddenly that he knew he was not liked and felt sorry for him. She closed the book.

"Thank you, cousin Tancred. It is a beautiful and thoughtful gift and I am very glad to accept it. I was going to walk in the gardens. Perhaps you would care to join me?"

"There is nothing I should like more. What could be more delightful? To walk in a garden of beautiful flowers with a lady more beautiful than any of them, more perfumed than the jasmine, more delicate than the rose, more modest than the violet …"

She bit her lip, already regretting the invitation, and turned from him. Behind his back, Adèle rolled her eyes up drolly.

Out in the gardens, they walked in silence. The gravel of the long alleys crunched under their feet. Behind them, Joanna's ladies trailed along in groups, talking idly, stopping to smell the flowers.

"I am fortunate to find you alone," he said at last. "The Aziz has become a magnet for our young nobles since you came here. And who can blame them?" He leered at her and his eyes flicked briefly up and down her figure.

"Not only young nobles come here," she answered coldly. "Archbishop Walter was here yesterday, and Chancellor Matthew has come."

It was true that the Aziz was becoming a livelier place. They came in twos and threes at first, then in groups, young nobles who appeared at the dinner table and after dinner crowded round her, wanting to be seen, wanting her to remember their names and faces, just a word in her ear, if they could: about cousin Hugo who had been in exile for two years and if she could see her way to reminding the King of him, or sister Agatha who would so much appreciate a place at court, surely one more lady-in-waiting would not be too many and they would be eternally grateful, not that they were not already her loyal servants, of course …

"Be careful what you promise," Tancred said, as though he could read her thoughts.

"I was born and bred in courts, Count Tancred," she said angrily. A whiff of rosemary made her think of Poitiers.

"I beg your pardon. I presume too far but you are young ..."

"There are many things I do not know, but flattery, bribes, favor-seeking—I have known it all my life and recognize it when I see it." She looked at him levelly, trying to put significance into her gaze.

"Of course, dear cousin." His ugly face split into a smile. "We who are born royal become used to that at an early age."

She continued to look at him, suppressing the words that jumped to her lips. Born royal, indeed! Born a bastard. Tancred had short legs, though his torso and arms were of normal length. His simian appearance was enhanced by brows that almost met and by the thick dark hair on his hands. It was hard to believe that he and William were cousins.

They rounded a corner and suddenly were face to face with Queen Margaret. Joanna saw the nascent smile on her lips vanish abruptly as she looked at Tancred.

"My lady Queen!" Tancred said. "An unexpected pleasure!"

Queen Margaret's gaze passed over him as though he were not there.

"Joanna, my dear, should you be out walking without a sunshade held over you? This sun is ruinous to the complexion, you know."

"I think perhaps it is time I left you," Tancred murmured smoothly. "Thank you for deigning to accept my gift." He kissed her hand and as she looked at him, gave a tiny shrug and conspiratorial smile, as though to say: old ladies have their whims, humor them but do not take it seriously. His steps crunched on the gravel as he walked away from them.

"What gift?" Queen Margaret asked sharply.

"Count Tancred brought me a book of poems in the langue d'oc, my lady mother."

Queen Margaret stared after Tancred's departing back. "He is not to be trusted, Joanna. Do not allow him to become too friendly. He speaks fair but would tell any lie if it served his purpose."

Joanna thought that Queen Margaret was probably right but as usual her obstinacy was aroused by the Queen's advice, so she answered, "King William seems to trust him. He has given him command of the fleet."

"My son has a magnanimous spirit. Too much so, perhaps." Her mouth hardened. "If it were my decision, I should never have allowed him to return."

"Return?"

The Queen hesitated, looked about her. "Shall we sit over there and talk awhile?"

Joanna gestured to her women to wait for her. She sat beside the Queen on one of the marble benches, looking out over the love-knots of thyme and basil. The sun was high in the sky and the air was hot and filled with the scents of herbs and lemon.

"Count Tancred is lucky to be here at all," Queen Margaret said, with that same tightness about her mouth again. "He is a traitor. My husband exiled him. He should have put him to death."

Joanna looked into the hard black eyes. "*Tancred* exiled? What did he do?"

"There was a revolt right after my husband, King William, came to the throne. The Norman barons resented my husband's choice of a new Emir of Emirs, a man called Maio, the son of a merchant from Bari. The Normans despised him although he was an able man and well-educated. The Pope supported the rebels, but my husband defeated them and Pope Adrian was forced to sign the Treaty of Benevento."

"Yes, I've heard of that," Joanna said. "They tried to teach me about the history of Sicily before I left Winchester."

"It was a good treaty. I have to say that for Matthew."

"Matthew? The Chancellor?"

"He drew it up. He was one of Maio's protégés, a young notary from Salerno. Tancred was among the rebels and he was imprisoned. After that, Maio handled the affairs of the kingdom. My husband," she hesitated and pinched her lips into a little moue of distaste, "preferred more frivolous occupations."

Joanna thought of William. *Like father, like son,* she thought.

"The next conspiracy was against Maio himself. They wanted to give some status to their rebellion, so they chose Bonnellus to kill Maio. Bonnellus came from one of the oldest Norman families in the South and he was Maio's intended son-in-law. Maio trusted him."

Joanna looked at Queen Margaret, startled. The Queen's voice had thickened and she stared ahead of her, rigidly. Joanna smelled the sour sweat of strong and unpleasant emotion. She wondered what Maio had been to the Queen.

"Animals! The people are such animals. He was killed on St. Martin's Eve, near the Porte St. Agatha, where the street narrows, you know. Hacked to pieces. And then the mob came out and threw his body about and kicked and spat on it. William—my husband, that is—acted fast for once. He got Maio's wife and family out of their house and into the palace before the mob reached them."

No, it was not Maio's death, Joanna thought, that moved her so. There was anger in her voice, certainly, but she had not blinked or hesitated in speaking of it.

"It was too dangerous to avenge Maio's death. Not right away. The people supported Bonnellus. And while we waited for the right moment, Bonnellus made his move.

"The palace, you know, was built as a Norman fortress and the palace guard was loyal. Bonnellus decided there was only one way in—through the dungeons below it. Tancred had been there for five years. They released and armed all the prisoners and Tancred—*Tancred* led them into the palace. He knew his way about, of course. They seized my husband. He was in the Pisan Tower. And they—took us."

Queen Margaret's head had sunk onto her chest. Joanna barely heard her last sentence. She sensed that they were close to the source of her emotion now, but the Queen lifted her head and went on firmly.

"The palace was completely ransacked. All the gold and silver, everything, was taken. There was nothing left. There was a great silver planisphere that Edrisi had made for King Roger. That vanished, too. How they took it, I can't imagine, as it was immensely heavy."

She was speaking fast, as though the torrent of words could hold some worse memory at bay. "They burnt all the records in a giant bonfire in the palace courtyard. And they put all the palace eunuchs to the sword. The Normans had always hated the Moslems. They massacred them everywhere, even men like the poet Yahya Ibn al-Tafashi. They used to live everywhere in Panorme; now, as you know, they are crowded into one narrow Moslem quarter of the city. And Roger ..."

Her voice broke suddenly and she swayed back and forth in anguish. Joanna watched her. When the Queen spoke again, her voice was little more than a husky whisper.

"They had decided to make Roger King, you see, in William's place. Roger—he was nine years old. My eldest, little Robert, had died. Four sons and only one left to me now. My husband never cared for me, you see." Joanna thought that the Queen had forgotten her now. She leaned forward, gazing into the distance, and tears ran unheeded down her cheeks. "I was pushed aside, neglected, ignored, from the beginning. He was not a good man. A great terrifying bear of a man with a bushy black beard. I was afraid of him, though I tried to be a good wife to him. When he turned from me, I gave all my love to my sons."

She choked again and was silent for a moment. "As long as I live, I shall mourn him. One never gets over it entirely. Poor little Roger. I blame his father. It was the worst day of my life. We were held prisoners in the palace and they had paraded Roger through the town as King. It wasn't his fault, poor little boy. He had no choice in the matter. He was such an earnest, loving child, fair hair, big eyes, and a few freckles, and so well-meaning. His father shook him as though he were a rat and pushed him away, in front of the tower windows and that was when the arrow struck him. In the eye. Oh my God! I sat on the floor beside him—after they took the arrow out—and held his hand. He was in such pain and afraid. He stared up at me with his one eye. 'Mother, will I die?' he asked. I loved him so much. I wanted to comfort him but I knew I had to prepare his soul. 'My dearest son,' I said, 'tonight you will be in paradise with the blessed angels. And I pray that I will soon be there with you.' Sweet Jesus! The pain of it will never leave me until I do join him there."

Joanna found there were tears in her own eyes and her throat was tight. Instinctively, she reached out and put a hand over Queen Margaret's. The Queen clutched it convulsively.

"He went to a window and spoke to the crowd. He asked them to go home, to allow the rebels to leave, said he had pardoned them. He did all that while his son, his own son, lay dying on the floor behind him."

There was a silence.

"Where was William in all this?" Joanna asked.

"William?" the Queen said vaguely. "Little William? He was there all the time. He was with Roger and me when they arrested us and he was beside me when Roger died. He was much attached to his brother."

Joanna thought of William's expressionless face, of the smile that never reached his eyes, and tried to imagine him as a six-year old boy watching his beloved older brother die.

Queen Margaret seemed exhausted. She sat with drooping shoulders, her eyes on the ground.

"What happened then?" Joanna prompted her.

The Queen stirred listlessly. "William re-established himself. His terms were generous. No executions, no imprisonments. The leaders were exiled, including Tancred."

"Is Bonnellus still alive in exile?"

"Bonnellus? He wasn't exiled. He was pardoned and received back at court," the Queen said tiredly.

"*Pardoned?* After all he'd done?"

"He would have attracted more rebels; the thing would never have ended. He swaggered about Panorme for a few weeks and then he disappeared. They put him in the Ring."

"Not the palace dungeons?"

"No, William never made that mistake again. Those dungeons have never been used since. Now they use the Ring. Bonnellus was blinded and hamstrung and left to die in his cell. And that should have been Tancred's fate."

Joanna sat still, turning the story over in her mind.

"I thought this such a peaceful place," she said at last, "with Moslems and Jews and Greeks and Lombards and Normans all getting along together so amazingly well. At home, we were always hearing of rebellions and ambushes and sieges, and that was all one race. Often all one family," she added.

"Sicily peaceful? On the surface it is. The Norman barons resent the Italians and the Greeks for getting all the plum administrative positions. The Latin churchmen, who are more powerful now than they used to be, are intolerant of the Jews and the Moslems and the Greeks, the Greeks despise the Normans and Italians, and the Jews distrust everyone. But William is loved by the people. He is truly the kingpin. In his presence the nobles are courteous to each other, but without him, it would all fall apart and they would be at each other's throats. William is a good man. I tried to raise my sons to be kind, considerate men because I hated that lack in their father."

She turned to Joanna and squeezed the hand that still held hers. "I think you will be lucky in this marriage. He will love his children and cherish you."

"Mother," Joanna said, moved. She wanted to reassure her, to promise her happiness in the future to compensate for her past suffering, but the Queen went on, nodding her head.

"He will be a good husband. A good kind husband."

CHAPTER TWENTY-FOUR

Half her lifetime ago, Joanna had asked her father for a king as a husband, a young French-speaking King. Her father had added, teasingly, that he should be rich, and handsome, too. They had found their paragon, but until now Joanna had not really thought of William as her husband. He was the King, he was a man who had shown her kindness for which she was grateful, he was the golden idol she and Adèle adored. But although she knew it was to come, she had not directly perceived of him as the man who was to share her bed and father her children. That was a distant event, something that would not happen until she was a woman. Imperceptibly, to herself at least, she had become a woman. Not yet in the fullest sense, but she was as tall as any, taller than Nurse and Queen Margaret, and her breasts had grown. She would be fourteen in October.

She began to feel self-conscious in William's company. Adèle was no help. She seemed to delight in telling Joanna how William had stared—so!—at her, Joanna, while she was dancing, how he had asked her age or initiated enquiries among her women as to her physical development. Adèle's mind tended to run on such things these days. She was in love with a young squire, a year older than herself, of a noble Southern Norman family. The squire was considerably more accessible to her than William had ever been and quickly responsive to her stares and giggles. Adèle's whispered confidences to Joanna were no longer of an arched eyebrow or a tilted head. Instead, she told her of palms touching, of knees pressed together under the table.

A few months before Christmas, her monthly flow of blood began. At first she was excited but then she found that it gave her a terrible stomach ache each time and, moreover, precluded most of her normal activities. She learned to fold the bulky linen clouts and wind them between her legs and fasten them on her stomach with a pin, like a baby's diapers, but it was hard to walk without waddling and the cloth rubbed the tender skin on the inside of her thighs, especially after multiple washings and scrubbings. She could not ride or dance or hunt. The first day or two, she would spend lying on her bed with a hot brick wrapped in cloths held to her stomach while her women brewed her camomile tea with poppies and honey and oil of juniper, which was supposed to relieve the ache.

She should not have been surprised but it still came as something of a shock when William suggested October as the month they should begin to live as man and wife. They had been talking of other things, of her family, of Richard's astounding capture of the hitherto impregnable castle of Taillebourg earlier that year, of King Louis' visit to Canterbury in August where her father, King Henry, had met him.

"Strange to think of the two rival kings kneeling together at Thomas' tomb," William said, "the king who supported him and the king who—opposed him."

Joanna noticed the slight hesitation and guessed what he had almost said. She said nothing.

"I wonder what they thought. Did they remember him as they knew him or pray to him as a saint? It must be strange to know somebody well and then he is made a saint! I wonder if anyone I know will become a saint one day? Anyway, it seems that Thomas answered King Louis' prayers. His son is recovering and they have rescheduled his coronation for All Saints' Day. Also, he is to be married, I hear. Philip, that is. Speaking of marriage, I think it is time you moved into the royal palace."

"The royal palace?" Joanna repeated stupidly. "But I'm quite happy at the Aziz."

"I dare say you are. But it is usual, you know, for a man and wife to live under the same roof." He smiled at her teasingly, but she was too nervous to smile back. "Anyway, I will see that it is arranged. For October, perhaps, your birth month. I will have to ask my astrologer for a favorable day."

That was all. He was as casual about it as if he had been suggesting a hunt.

When the day chosen by the court astrologer came, she rode through Panorme to the royal palace in a long procession. The populace knew what her move entailed and they thronged to see her go by, with much cheering and laughing and a few raucous encouraging shouts from tavern goers who had come out to watch. She looked ahead with what she hoped was a pleasant dignified expression but out of the corner of her eye, she could see men commenting slyly to each other and knew she was blushing.

The banquet was even worse. The knowing glances of the men, the smiles of the women, the way they looked from her to William and back, all embarrassed her deeply. She had chosen to wear a pink gown that night and now she regretted it, knowing that her cheeks must match her dress. Her women had fixed her hair up from the sides to the crown of her head with late pink roses tucked into her gold circlet and let the rest hang loose down her back, interwoven with a long trailing spray of roses. It had looked pretty and youthful in her chamber but now she felt like some kind of pagan sacrifice.

In fact, the whole evening had pagan overtones, or so it seemed to her. Everyone was drinking more than usual and there was a great deal of noise, which made it hard to hear the musicians singing of young love as the spring from which all valor flowed, of faint-hearted lovers too shy to speak and maidens taking pity on them. Everywhere she looked, Joanna saw couples with their heads close together or surreptitiously touching. She wondered if it was always like that and she had not particularly noticed before this evening. There was Tancred, halfway down one of the long tables. He had his arm round the girl beside him, there was no doubt about it, and was tickling her. He looked up and saw her watching him, raised his cup in a salute and grinned at her. She looked away hastily and saw Tancred's wife Sybil opening her mouth to accept a tidbit from the fingers of the young knight next to her.

She could not bring herself to look at William, even when he spoke to her. The songs were getting bawdier, their theme being love's ultimate solace, and shrieks of laughter resounded through the Hall. Against it all, William's voice went on, smoothly, calmly, talking of his day's activities, a hunt he had gone on. She listened not so much to the words as the tone of voice and found it reassuring, even soothing.

The courtiers started dancing. William had indicated that he would not dance but they might. Joanna watched them, still listening to the calm even voice beside her. She thought she had drunk too much. Everything seemed at once too bright and blurred. She was very hot.

"One last cup of wine before we go to bed," William said.

She looked up, alarmed. "No more for me, thank you, my lord. I've already had too much."

"What is too much, on one's wedding night?" He smiled at her. He was already holding the cup out to the page to fill. "Now, for me, that's another matter. But I've been abstemious, though I doubt you noticed. Drink this to our union."

He kissed the cup, looking at her over the rim of it, turned it round and held it out to her. She bent her head and drank, vague irreverent thoughts of the Mass running confusedly through her mind. William set the cup down and stood up. The music broke off and the courtiers, interrupted in mid-dance, stood around the Hall in little groups, turning to face the royal dais. A faint cheer sounded from one corner and someone laughed. Joanna rose to her feet, trying not to catch anyone's eye. Caid Richard came hurrying forward, a smile on his plump dark face. A page pulled their chairs away from behind them and a fanfare sounded as they left the Hall, their attendants following.

In her chamber, Joanna stood silent and nervous as her women undressed her. Her chamber here was darker and less ornate than the one at the Aziz and there was no garderobe, only dressing-rooms opening off it. Wrapped in a white mantle, she sat on a velvet chair while they unpinned the wilting roses from her hair, fussing and clucking around her like a bunch of excited hens. They had drawn back the hangings on the bed. They gathered around in a tight giggling circle as they removed her mantle and pulled back the sheets for her to climb in. The linen felt smooth and cool to her hot skin. She pulled the sheets up to her chin and sat back against the big pillows. One of her women brushed her hair again so that it fanned out across the pillows.

There was a noise of men's voices outside and then a loud thump on the door. Joanna had been hot a moment before, now suddenly her hands, clutching the sheets, felt icy.

"He's here, he's here!" the women exclaimed, bustling about the room, putting her brushes and clothes out of sight. One of them opened the door. Joanna took one quick glance and then looked away again. William was wrapped in a long mantle of blue silk and wore a gold circlet on his head. Did he wear it to bed, she wondered, and was suddenly afraid, with the wine and her nervousness, that she was going to giggle. She tightened her clutch on the sheets so hard that her knuckles turned white and stared at the mound her legs made under the bedclothes.

William's attendants were disrobing him, gathering in a tight circle around him and holding up the wide mantle to shield him from the eyes of the ladies clustered by the door. She felt the bed dip and rustle as he slid in beside her. The Archbishop advanced to the foot of the bed and raised his right hand. Solemnly, he invoked God's blessing on their marital bed, on the covenant between them and on the issue of their union, which he prayed it would be God's will to bestow. Joanna could not concentrate on the exact words. A candle sputtered and crackled, subsiding into its melted tallow.

The prayer ended and there was a general sense of relaxation in the room. Joanna could hear people murmuring to each other and a few giggles. Her women were filing out and the attendants were moving round dousing the candles.

"Leave that one," William said, as someone came to the side of the bed.

"Very good, my lord." It was Caid Richard. She recognized his high voice. "Is there anything else you require, my lord?"

"Not from any of you." A burst of laughter from the nobles at the door greeted this and William added, "I think I can manage this on my own."

There was a muttered comment at the door that Joanna only half-heard. It brought another shout of laughter. They were leaving now. She heard their voices receding through the ante-chamber.

"Then I will wish you both a very agreeable night. Good night, my lord. Good night, my lady."

The rings of the scarlet silk hangings rattled along the rails as Caid Richard closed the bed curtains. The light by the bed made it seem as if they were in a tent glowing red. Did he always sleep with a light in his chamber? She would have preferred the dark at this stage. She heard the latch click shut. There was a metallic clash outside, the guards on the door presenting arms, she supposed, as they took up their post for the night.

She closed her eyes and lay very still. She knew what would come now. All the young brides, when they exchanged confidences with the other ladies, told more or less the same tale. He would roll toward her and there would be some fumbling and fondling under the sheets, rough or gentle, brief or prolonged, depending on his temperament, and then ... So she was startled when he pulled the sheet from her fingers and flung it back. Her first instinct was to try to hide her nakedness with her hands and then, when that seemed useless or at least uncompliant, she covered her burning face with her hands. Then at last she felt him move toward her. He lay close beside her and put his arm round her.

"Joanna ..."

He began to stroke her and murmur to her as one might soothe a flustered hawk. He stroked her hair, smoothing it back from her brow, and put his head close to hers on the pillow, murmuring into her ear. "It's all right, Joanna, relax, I'm not going

to hurt you, there's nothing to be afraid of, it's all right, my dear."
Gently, he pulled her hands away from her face. His fingers were
on her wrists. "Why, your heart must be pounding like a trapped
bird's."

"I'm frightened," she said involuntarily. It was the first thing
she had said since her women had undressed her.

"Yes. I know." He laughed suddenly and added, "I'm not
Isabelle's husband, you know."

She was surprised into looking at him. Isabelle, fourteen like
Joanna herself and recently wed, had enthralled the younger ladies
with stories of her middle-aged groom's bizarre demands.

"Oh yes, I hear things. In fact, I hear pretty much everything,
I suppose. Still, even a king has no right to interfere with what
goes on between a man and his wife. There *is* one particular
demand I should like to make of you," he said. She was stiff again
at once, apprehensive. "I should like you to try not to look so
unhappy. Am I such an ogre? It's not so terrible, is it? This is new
for me, too, you know, don't think it isn't. My first and probably
only wedding night. And the bed blessed by the Archbishop, no
less. *That* was somewhat discouraging, though I suppose it's
perverse of me to feel that."

His hand was sliding over her again. She was beginning to feel
heavy and relaxed, with the wine and sleepiness, and his gentle
stroking was really rather pleasant. Even when his hand closed on
her breast, she did not move, though she became more wakeful.
Very slowly, he bent his head and kissed her, on her eyelids and
then on the lips. His body covered hers. She moved her head
sharply and he began to murmur again, between light little kisses,
in a new deep thickened tone. Her body trembled but she
acquiesced, whimpering slightly at the tearing sensation of his first
thrust. He gave a long sigh and then for a long while there was no
other sound but his ragged breathing and the rhythmic creaking
of the bed. She lay with her legs up as he had pushed them, her
eyes closed, feeling nothing, no panic, no pleasure, a little soreness
perhaps, and a little disappointment. Was this what all the fuss
was about? It hardly seemed worth it. Now at least she knew and
would not be afraid the next time. She had heard from the others
that it improved with time, that one came to desire it.

Something was wrong with William. He was gasping and his body jerked convulsively. Alarmed, she opened her eyes. The light still glowed redly through the curtains. She turned her head until she could see his face. He lay with his weight on his right shoulder, his face a few inches above hers, his perfect features drawn into a mask of agony, unrecognizable. His eyes were screwed shut, his mouth was open, grimacing. As she watched, frightened, he seemed to sob and the mask dissolved, his features blurred and softened and flowed together and his mouth hung slack, then his head dropped to her shoulder and his weight relaxed onto her. She could feel the rapid thudding of his heart.

"Are you all right?" she asked anxiously.

His only answer was a muffled grunt that sounded more like a snort of laughter than anything. Presently he rolled from her and lay beside her, his right arm still under her neck. She turned her head to look at him and saw his profile, returned now to its normal purity of line. His eyes were closed and his long lashes lay on his cheeks. There was a slight film of sweat on his brow. As though aware of her gaze, his eyes fluttered open and he turned his head to her. He smiled lazily.

"Yes, I'm all right." He laughed a little. "Very much so, thank you. And you? It wasn't so terrible after all, was it?"

She shook her head silently. He pulled his arm from under her neck, kissed her on the forehead and then moved over to the side of the bed, opened the curtains and blew out the candle. In the darkness, she felt him move back beside her. His head rolled onto her shoulder and one arm lay round her waist. In spite of the wine and her drowsiness, he was asleep before she was.

CHAPTER TWENTY-FIVE

The Hall was crowded. All the courtiers who could squeeze in were there. Joanna walked slowly up the central aisle, with two of her ladies holding her train, to join William on the dais. Queen Margaret was in the front row, smiling at her, and next to her, Constance, her head poking forward awkwardly like a chicken's. Archbishop Walter was there and Chancellor Matthew and Bishop Richard and further back she could see Count Tancred. Her gaze passed on rapidly, not focusing on anyone.

"My lords, I take you all to witness that I, William, King of Sicily, do hereby on this nineteenth day of October in the year of Our Lord 1179, bestow and settle on my Queen, Joanna, here present, who is now my wife in the eyes of God and of man by the consummation of that marriage that was contracted between us some two and a half years ago ..."

Off to the side, she saw a row of clerks scribbling furiously, taking down his words. A noble, his eyes on her, leaned toward his neighbor and murmured something and the other looked at her too and smiled. She looked away hastily, up at William, trying to concentrate on his words.

"... which is her traditional right as a Queen of Norman blood ..."

He looked magnificent again, as he had when she had first seen him, swathed in pearl-embroidered white silk from head to toe, his gloved hands with the great rings on them crossed before him, the pendants on his tiara hanging like long earrings to his collar. The only part of him she could see was his face, the smooth cherubic curve of his cheek, the delicate line of lip and nostril, all empty and expressionless, as usual. Suddenly, inappropriately, she remembered the mask in the night, the dribbling snarling mouth and screwed-up eyes, the sobs and jerks and gasps. There was something that moved him then, something that could break up the blandness of that perfect face. She felt a sudden surge of power and with it, unmistakably, desire. Her crotch tingled, her thighs felt weak, and she was hot all over. She kept her eyes fixed on the floor, hoping the rush of hot blood to her throat and face would be mistaken for maidenly modesty. Which, she thought, it might well be, considering what he was saying now.

"... and in recompense for that gift of her virginity with which she has honored me ..."

It was humiliating to have to sit here on this dais, in front of everyone while he talked of virginity and consummation, publicly announcing to all these avid curious listeners what they had done last night.

There was a gasp from the back of the room that rippled through the whole crowd. All the heads were turning away from her at last and people were pushing for a better view. Relieved, she lifted her head and felt her blushes fade. Her eyes widened in astonishment. Six men were carrying in a golden throne. Behind them came others and she could see more men just outside the door. The people at the front of the crowd, before the dais, pressed back to make room as her marriage settlement gifts were laid out, a gilded table more than twelve feet long, the golden throne, a dinner service of twenty-four gold and silver plates and cups, bags of gold tari coins, she did not know how much. In addition, the bed and its furnishings were hers, though for obvious reasons not brought into the Hall, and she was to have the revenues of the County of Mont St. Angelus ...

The scribes wrote busily. William took her hands and kissed them. There was a murmur of mingled approval and dissatisfaction from the crowd. He kissed her on both cheeks and suddenly the crowd was cheering, clapping, stamping.

Joanna was accepted. That night William came to her chamber again and it was unexpectedly worse than the first time. She was very sore and had not drunk enough wine to numb her, as on the previous night. Whatever she had felt that morning of excitement or desire was completely lacking. William had wasted no time on reassurance or teasing and she had found the act decidedly painful. The third night was better. They had danced and drunk for several hours after supper and Joanna had been titillated by the open admiration of a young Count from Southern Italy. Instead of falling asleep after his climax, William had lain awake talking to her and after a while, had made love to her again, more slowly and gently. She had come to think she might soon grow used to it.

On the fourth night, after dismissing her ladies, she lay waiting for him but he did not come. She had left one light burning, as he liked, and eventually she fell asleep. The candle burned itself out in the night. It was of course Sunday, she excused him to herself, and she tried not to feel slighted.

There was no pattern to it; sometimes he came to her, other nights he did not. After a while, she thought no more of it. The fairy tale had come true, beyond all her rosiest expectations, and she was living happily ever after. She longed to prove herself worthy of this god-like creature who seemed to have no faults. Sometimes in chapel she had to catch herself back from blasphemy, finding that her prayers of adoration were addressed to William rather than to God. She understood now St. Paul's saying that the head of every man is Christ and the head of the woman is the man. He was indeed her head, her lord, and she worshipped him. And secretly, when she watched him surrounded by admiring courtiers, she hugged to herself the strange power she had over him, that could reduce all that majesty and beauty and calmness to quivering, gasping flesh.

In spite of living daily with him in the royal palace, she did not feel she knew him any better than when she had first come to Sicily. He was pious, he was kind, as Queen Margaret had promised, but he never spoke of himself. His talk to her in bed was strangely impersonal. He never spoke of his childhood or asked her about hers, though he listened politely enough when she talked of it. Nor did he ever ask her thoughts or feelings about anything, or share his, except in the most superficial and perfunctory way. If she asked him about affairs of state, he would shrug his shoulders and say, "I leave all that to Matthew."

He shied away from personal feelings even when they were expressed impersonally in song or verse. Once, in the Hall, they were listening to a ballad, a particularly moving ballad about a youth going off to war and taking leave of his beloved and then he hears that she is married to another and he dies far from home, twice pierced to the heart and welcoming death as the lesser pain. Many people had wept and she had looked at William beside her on the dais, his face as unmoved as ever, the slightest of smiles curving his lips like a stone angel. William had applauded languidly and called for something more cheerful.

Joanna did not see this as a lack in him. It would have seemed almost sacrilegious to expect ordinary passions in him like any other man. She still had Nurse or Adèle to confide in and, increasingly, Queen Margaret. Since the day when William's mother had wept and told her of little Roger's death, Joanna had had warmer feelings toward her and more and more she went to her for advice. It had been her ambition to be a Queen like her mother, influential, admired, and wise. Now she had modified that ambition: she wanted only to be the best possible Queen for William.

She thought she was fulfilling all her functions. William seemed satisfied and she knew she was popular at court and with the people. She took her place at ceremonies, she attended Mass regularly, she greeted guests and was charming to envoys, she was always compliant when William came to her bed at night and never questioned him when he did not. Until she had children, no more could be expected of her. The rest was pleasure.

Each month she waited eagerly and somewhat nervously to see if she had conceived and each month her hopes and fears were washed away in a flow of blood. A son would have completed her happiness, but these were early days yet. Sons and daughters, all as handsome as William himself, would complete the fairy tale. Otherwise, it was as near perfection as could be.

Joanna sat on the brink of a fountain, trailing her fingers in the water. Her ladies, talking among themselves, sat at a discreet distance. It was autumn, the best time, when the fruit was ripe and the sun no longer burned and her natal day came round again. She ran a finger over the smooth marble she was sitting on. It left a trail of water that glittered in the sun. Down by her feet, there were weeds between the paving-stones. The gardeners had missed them; that was unusual. She looked out over the courtyard, the neat clipped box hedges lining the stone walkways, the lemon trees with their branches drooping laden with fruit, the palm trees and flowers and, around the sides, the rose trees in wooden boxes that had been brought out now that the heat of summer was past. The roses made her think of her mother, who had been held in Salisbury Tower for over six years now. She could not imagine her mother as powerless. Even in Salisbury, she must be organizing and civilizing those around her.

Lost in her thoughts she did not hear Tancred approach and started when he spoke to her.

"My dear cousin. All alone out here? You have missed the news."

"News?" she asked, straightening herself languidly. Tancred's smile reminded her of something, someone. She could not quite pin it down.

"King Louis of France is dead. He died last month. You know, of course, that he has been half paralyzed since his return from Canterbury last year."

"Yes, of course." She crossed herself automatically. "So Philip is King."

Once she had wanted to marry Philip. If she had, she would now be Queen of the Franks. Shut away in the dark, old-fashioned Cité palace with an ugly king who could barely sit a horse. She thought of the long sunny days in Sicily, of her

William, William the Good as the people called him, and smiled slightly.

"I wonder if Philip will press for his sister Alice's marriage, now that he's King?" Tancred said.

She remembered suddenly what Tancred's smile reminded her of: her brother John, picking the wings off flies, and smiling as he watched them stagger crazily in circles. She felt momentarily chilled, although the sun was still strong.

"Alice ... My God, I had almost forgotten her. It seems so long ago, so far away. That draughty castle in Winchester ... She was born this month, too. Just like me. She must be twenty now. I can't believe it. I've been here four years already."

"And it's more than ten years since she was betrothed to your brother Richard. King Henry must be running out of excuses by now."

Joanna looked him in the eye. Tancred, she was sure, knew that scurrilous story, but not for a moment would she discuss it with him.

"Richard will marry her when the time comes," she said. "He has been occupied in Aquitaine. That is his first concern."

"Oh yes, he is quite the conquering hero in Aquitaine. It's a pity in a way that he is not the heir. The Young King, I hear, does nothing but drag his knights from one tournament to another while Richard is fighting real battles. He must be envious of Richard."

Joanna stood up abruptly, shaking drops of water from her fingers. She did not want to hear any more veiled criticisms of her family. Her contented mood was spoiled. Tancred was like John in that he took pleasure in destruction for its own sake, whether of flies or of other people's happiness.

Tancred walked beside her. Joanna observed him covertly. His knee length tunic made his legs look even shorter and his arms hung like an ape's to his thighs. The straggling black hairs over the top of his nose where his brows almost joined gave him a frowning look. His thick lower lip drooped open like an idiot's. He looked across at her and their glances met. His eyes were shrewd. It was as though another being inhabited this misshapen body and looked out through those eyes.

"It's strange," she said abruptly, "how unlike you and William are, since you are cousins. He is so ..." She had spoken without thinking and now she caught back what she was going to say. "... so fair and you are dark," she finished lamely.

"Fair. Yes, William is fair," he said. "Fair of hair and fair of face. And tall and slender and young and popular. And he is King. Deservedly. A man with every virtue and advantage." Somehow, he made it sound like a criticism.

"You, at least, have every reason to be grateful to him, I suppose, since he brought you back from exile."

In a flash she saw that he hated William. It was there in his eyes.

"My cousin has been most generous to me. I am everlastingly grateful to him."

Had she imagined it? There was nothing there but obsequiousness.

"He is a good Christian," she said.

There it was again. All he said was, "Yes. Yes, indeed," but she sensed dark currents swirling unseen beneath the smooth surface.

"One might almost say the very model of a Christian King." A sly sideways glance at her. "Almost."

She was floundering out of her depth in cold water. Tancred was going to tell her something unpleasant, she felt it in every tense muscle. She knew she should prevent him, could in fact prevent him by turning back, by calling to the others, but perversely she wanted to know. Her mind circled it like a tongue round a rotting tooth.

Tancred was staring up at the sky, through the branches that arched above the alley. He scratched absent-mindedly in his dark beard. "You should ask the King if you could visit the Shiraz some time. The silk workshop, you know. I hear it is a most interesting place." His voice was casual.

Joanna was infuriated by this sudden change of subject. She had braced herself for something—Bellebelle kept by William in some house in Panorme, perhaps—and now it seemed she was not to hear it after all.

271

"That is not what you were going to tell me, is it, Tancred?" she asked bluntly.

He looked at her then. "Oh yes, it is," he said. Tancred smiled, a little crooked smile that curled up one side of his thick mouth. "The Shiraz, you see, is his most Christian Majesty's harem," he said pleasantly.

"Harem?"

She did not know what it was. He explained it to her. Not one Bellebelle, but a hundred Bellebelles. Beautiful young women, Moslems for the most part, but some Frankish girls who, he understood, usually converted to the Moslem faith after a while. All of them for the King's use, as he put it. And the other courtiers, of course, but it was understood that the King always had first choice, first rights to a newcomer, sole access to his current favorite. When he traveled, he always selected a few to take with him.

"His boast is that has never spent a night alone since he was sixteen," Tancred said.

It was hot even here in the shade, but Joanna's hands felt cold. The gravel crunched under her feet as she turned to face him. There was a smell of boxwood in the air from the little hedges that lined the alley and other fragrances from unseen flowers. Somewhere a peacock shrieked.

"Bellebelle?" Joanna asked hoarsely. Her mouth was very dry.

Tancred considered. "Yes, there is a Frankish girl with that nickname who was his favorite for a while last summer. I believe she was on that visit to the Parco when you were there." He leered at her. "She's long since been superseded, though I suppose he still lies with her from time to time. Currently, I hear, it's a Greek beauty named Eudocia."

His soft voice slid around her. She found she was trembling and clenched her jaw.

"But he's a Christian ..." she protested.

Someone had called him a baptized Sultan; she could not remember who. Was that what he had meant?

"Not too Christian not to see the advantages of other systems," he said, leering again. "Who can blame him? It was there waiting for him. It's a pity, of course, that he prefers it to the business of governing his kingdom. Still, he's a young man and his blood is hot …"

Something was making Joanna's breathing difficult, a great lump expanding in her chest. She sucked air into her lungs. Her fingers were curling into claws. Tancred had smashed her idol. She saw William's face, that beautiful guileless bland face and the agonized nighttime mask. She had thought that power over him was all hers but now it seemed she shared it with hundreds of others. Images floated across her mind, Alice years ago in a meadow in Poitiers saying "They do it lots of times. I think they like it". Alice and her father … But even her father, with all his mistresses, would never have condoned anything as monstrously unchristian as this.

"All this practice, of course, must make him an excellent husband." Tancred leant toward her, openly leering now.

She drew back her right arm and hit him in the face as hard as she could. He rocked back a little but did not move. The mark of her fingers sprang out red on his cheek. The red spread, obscuring her vision. She could not breathe and her whole body vibrated with tension. Turning, she walked swiftly back along the alley. It seemed dark under the trees as though the sun had gone, and everywhere was streaked with red. Her ladies drew apart, fluttered, spoke to her as she passed. She ignored them all, walking faster and faster. She crossed the terrace and burst into the palace. Guards sprang to attention. She swung past them and took the stairs at a run, holding her skirts high. Like an animal, her instinct was to run for her lair. There were no guards at her chamber. She flung the door open so violently that it crashed back against the wall. There were maids in the room, smoothing the sheets on the bed, checking for fleas. She stood there, chest heaving, for a moment while they scurried back, bowing, clutching their aprons and staring at her.

A great bubbling scream was rising in her throat and the red mist covered everything now. She picked up the first thing that came to hand, a great gilt candlestick, and hurled it at the wall, splintering the mosaics. Vaguely, she heard the women exclaim, saw out of the corner of her eye their startled movements. Energy was pulsing through her arms and she felt strong enough to tear anything or anyone apart. She picked up a chair and swung it against the bedpost with a resounding thwack and flung it from her. She tore the silk hangings down from the bed and ripped them apart, scattering the pieces everywhere, rampaging through the room, kicking the walls, overturning the tables, hurling the prie-Dieu at the shutters.

The scream in her throat reached her lips. It came out as a low roar through her clenched teeth.

"God's teeth, I'll tear him to pieces, the bastard, the whore-mongering bastard, to treat me, the daughter of the King of England, God damn his soul to hell, I'll not stand for it, Christ's liver, I hate him, I hate them both, the God damn fucking bastard and he calls himself a Christian, I spit on him, may his teeth rot and his prick wither, I hope he never repents, I want him to burn in torment for eternity …"

Her voice had risen gradually to a shrill scream. On the periphery of her vision, people moved around her, but they were blotted out by the swirls of red across her eyeballs. There were voices, snatches of dialogue heard but not understood.

"… her father, the old King, he was just the same …"

"… used to roll on the floor and bite the rushes, so I've heard …"

"… possessed by a devil …"

"… family of Anjou is descended from the devil's daughter, they say …"

She felt possessed. The strength of her rage twisted her body like a violent pain so that she bent almost to the floor. Her hands stuck out stiffly in front of her, clawing into the air. The tendons of her neck stood out and spittle hung on her chin. Obscenities she did not know she knew spilled from her.

It was beginning to ebb. She could see again. She searched for a stronger blasphemy to fan the ashes into flame again.

"Christ's balls!" she screamed. "I'll kill that son of a whoring bitch."

Queen Margaret was standing just inside the doorway, watching her. How long she had been there, Joanna did not know. She stood very still, her hands folded in front of her, her dark eyes staring without expression. As Joanna looked up at her, she made a gesture with her hand to the women. They filed silently out, looking back over their shoulders.

Fury blazed up again in Joanna. "The King my son, the King my son!" she chanted. "Do you know what the King your son is? I'll tell you. Your precious Christian son spends his nights rutting like a goat. He doesn't care about the kingdom, he doesn't care about you or me, he doesn't even care about God's commandments or his own soul. He's a lazy, lascivious, selfish, lying, whoring, foul …"

She was having difficulty breathing again. A bubble of air seemed to be stuck in her throat. It came out as a high-pitched laugh. "I won't endure it! I'll go back to my father, I'll denounce him to the Pope, I'll make all Europe see him for what he is. I care not a fart for his soul, but I won't be made a fool of before his own court, they all knew, everyone knew but me, all sniggering behind their hands, laughing at me, pitying me …"

She was shaken by sudden laughter again. It confused her. She did not feel like laughing. She gasped for air. The room was turning dark. She was either laughing or sobbing, it was hard to tell which. William, that perfect, priceless, Christian King … The rich, handsome, young monarch her father had promised her. She had loved him. More than that, she had worshipped him. The golden idol with feet of clay. At one stroke Tancred had destroyed him for her. She staggered to the bed and fell face down on it, weeping. The sobs tore themselves from her, great dry heaving sobs. Her body shuddered and her throat ached. She felt exhausted and infinitely sad.

"My dear, my dear child." Queen Margaret had come to sit beside her. She stroked her back rhythmically, soothingly. "Joanna my dear—I'm so sorry."

Gulping still, Joanna sat up and pushed her hair back from her face. The room was in chaos. Bits of torn silk hung from the overturned chairs, an ivory table lay with its legs smashed, mosaics were chipped, and there was a great dent in the bedpost. Tancred's book with half the pages torn from it lay face down on the floor and other objects, brushes, ornaments, cushions, were strewn everywhere.

Abashed, she looked at Queen Margaret, half afraid to face her condemnation. The Queen looked back at her. There was nothing but pity on her face. She reached out and stroked Joanna's cheek.

"My poor child," she said. "My daughter."

Tears spilled easily at last. Leaning on Queen Margaret's shoulder, Joanna wept like a child while the Queen stroked her hair. The torrent of tears washed away the last remnants of anger. She felt tired but purged.

"You knew?" she asked.

Queen Margaret handed her a lace handkerchief to wipe her eyes. "Yes, I knew. He is not a bad man really. This is not the moment to tell you so perhaps, but there are worse faults."

"Forgive me. Please forgive me. I didn't know what I was saying. What you must think …"

Queen Margaret silenced her with a raised hand. "There is nothing to forgive. I know exactly how you felt. This—harem of William's, he inherited the custom from his father."

They were silent for a moment.

"But William does care for you. In that at least, you are luckier than I was."

Joanna pushed the hair back from her face. "Tell me what I should do, mother."

"Do? Nothing. There is nothing you can do. Ignore it. Don't fight with William over it. You will only cause bitterness and strife, and you will not change his ways. Be dignified, be virtuous and pray. Who knows, after all? Even holy St. Augustine was a sinner in his youth. It is not for us to judge. And we all have our sins. William is guilty of lust and sloth and they are grave sins indeed, but so is anger."

"I could not help it, it just came over me like a wave."

"So does lust. Let him who is without sin throw the first stone. We are all sinners. Holy Mary, Mother of God, pray for us miserable sinners, now and at the hour of our death." She crossed herself.

Joanna did not follow suit. "I will not go to supper tonight. I can't. Someone must make my excuses. Say I am indisposed, no matter what. I am not ready to face him yet."

CHAPTER TWENTY-SIX

In the morning when Joanna awoke, she stretched luxuriously in her bed before she suddenly remembered. The Shiraz, the harem, all those women who shared her husband with her. A cold determined fury possessed her. Queen Margaret had told her to do nothing, to ignore it, never to bring it up with William.

No, no, no, she could not do that. She was a Plantagenet, she was the daughter of a long line of kings, and she could not tamely accept this. What would her mother have done? And she was a Christian. It was intolerable. It was her duty to obey her husband, but did a good wife stand by and watch her husband endanger his immortal soul? She thought of Erec and Enide and how Enide had disobeyed her husband for his own good.

Abruptly, she swung her legs out of bed and rose. She took a light breakfast while rehearsing in her head what she would say to William. When she was ready, she went in search of Caid Richard.

"I wish to speak to the King, Richard. Where can I find him?"

"I regret, Your Majesty, but the King left early this morning.

He has gone to the Aziz to visit his aunt, the lady Constance."

Caid Richard was studying her face as he spoke. She thought that everyone knew of her rage of the previous day and she knew why William had left. He was unwilling to face her and would avoid any talk of his harem and her reaction. Frustrated, she felt anger boil in her again. She took a few turns about the room and came to a sudden decision.

"Richard, I want you to escort me to the Shiraz. This morning. Now."

"Majesty ..." Caid Richard, usually so smooth, stammered and looked dismayed. "I think this is not wise ..."

"Am I not free to order a silk gown if I want one?"

"Of course, but I can order the seamstresses to come to the palace for a fitting, if that is your desire ..."

"No, I want to see the place."

"But, Majesty ..."

She ignored him. "And tell those two to accompany us." She indicated two beardless plump young men. Caid Richard looked from her to them and she saw understanding on his face.

"The King will not ..."

She interrupted him. "I take all the blame on myself. Fear not, Richard, I will exonerate you."

"I still think ..."

Exasperated, she looked him in the eye. "Richard, I wish it. That is all."

At the gate, they stopped to pick up a small armed guard. The Shiraz was within walking distance apparently. Caid Richard was still clearly uncomfortable and she knew that William would be angry with him for not stopping her. But she was angry, too, and she would make it clear to William that Richard could not stop her.

From outside, the Shiraz was an entirely unremarkable building. Inside, she found a large workshop where several young women were busy at long tables. They all stopped in their work and gaped at her. A eunuch bustled forward, looking amazed and fearful.

Joanna spoke before he could.

"Your name is?"

"Yahya Ibn, Majesty." He bowed obsequiously. "But if Your Majesty is interested in some silk, I will have samples sent ..."

"No, Yahya, thank you. I am here to see the Shiraz, not to order a gown."

Yahya and Caid Richard exchanged glances that clearly said, "What can we do?"

"Very well, Majesty. At this end, we have the worms. They feed on these leaves ..."

Joanna looked briefly at the worms on a pile of leaves under a gauze layer and passed on to the next section where there were cocoons attached to a frame. The girls—they were no more than girls for the most part—watched her in silence. She noticed the one thing they had in common, their beauty; whether fair Northerners or darker skinned, dark-haired Arabs, they were all beautiful.

She passed rapidly by vats of steam where the cocoons were treated and sinks where the silk threads were washed. Several girls had been occupied in spinning the thread but they had all risen to their feet at her entrance. Past the looms, there were great sheets of silk and dying vats.

"Your Majesty, can I show you some finished silks and ..." Yahya Ibn Fityan was clearly nervous.

"I wish to see the girls' living quarters, if you please."

The eunuch wrung his hands. "Majesty, it is not appropriate ..."

Joanna confronted him. "That is for me to decide."

Yahya had given himself away with a swift glance at a curtained recess at the back of the workshop. Joanna strode over to it, with Yahya fluttering beside her, and flung back the curtain. She opened the door behind it and stepped from the crowded dim workshop with its high narrow windows into a different world.

Exquisitely carved Arabic arches surrounded a large central space with a burbling water channel running down the middle. Flowers tumbled over the sides of huge stone urns set on the patterned marble floor. She saw couches with silk cushions on them and footstools and a small stage that she guessed was for dancers. Overhead in the side cloisters, the ceiling glowed with blues and yellows against the white marble and on the walls, riotous mosaics depicted the act of love in many forms. She hastily averted her eyes from the more lurid scenes.

The atrium was surrounded by many small rooms, and from these girls now started to emerge. They all stopped in amazement on seeing her and clutched their gauzy shifts more closely to their lithe bodies.

Yahya was touching her elbow. "Majesty, you have seen it, now go, please go."

Joanna raised her chin. "Certainly not. I will speak to the girls."

She chose one who looked older and more confident than the others. "Don't be afraid, I just want to ask you a few questions."

The young woman looked uncertainly at Yahya. "This is the Queen," Yahya said. "Do as she asks."

The Queen! A gasp went up from the assembled girls and a whisper, hastily stifled, started to spread.

"Are you well treated here? Are you happy?" She realized swiftly that the answers were all going to be yes and yes. How would they dare say anything else?

"Where are you from? How do you come to be here?" She turned to a group of younger girls.

"From the village of Caltagirone, if you please, my lady."

"And how do you come to be here and not in your native village?" She turned to another girl. They were all clustering around her now.

"The man came …"

"The man? What man?"

"I don't know, my lady. An official, well-dressed. We were very poor and there were too many children in the family. The man offered Papa money to take me to court in Palermo."

The girls around her all nodded in agreement. Joanna seethed. Their fathers had sold them, essentially into slavery.

"And are you well treated here?"

"Oh yes, my lady. We never had food like this at home."

"Are you allowed to go out?"

A quick look at Yahya. "Sometimes. In groups. If Yahya is with us and some guards."

Joanna spotted a very young girl hand in hand with another on the outside of the group. She beckoned to them.

"And you two?"

"If you please, my lady, this is my little sister. The man agreed to take both of us. There were already five girls in our family and my father thought he would never be able to find husbands for all of us."

The younger one spoke up. "It's nice here, but I miss my Mamma and my friends."

"Can you go back to your villages?"

Again those quick looks at each other. The other girl cast her eyes down. "They would not take us back. We are ... dishonored now, you see. No husband would want us."

Joanna was about to ask what happened to them when they got older, but she saw all eyes swivel past her to look at someone behind her. She turned. William stood in the doorway. There was a look of barely suppressed fury on his face.

"You will come with me. Now." He spoke through his teeth, no honorifics, no "my lady".

He was angry, but so, she thought, was she. She deliberately turned her back on him and spoke again to the two sisters. "If you had a choice, where would you go now?"

The younger one slid a hand into Joanna's own. "If you please, lady, I would like to come with you."

Joanna smiled down at her. "Perhaps you will. I'll see."

William had reached her side and took her elbow, none too gently. She allowed him to lead her out. Not a word was spoken on their fast walk back to the palace. As soon as they reached a private room, he whirled on her.

"What were you thinking? This was outrageous. You will never never do such a thing again."

"Outrageous? As outrageous as your behavior in maintaining a harem? In buying girls from their families to be used as your sex slaves?"

"This is none of your business. Stay out of it. You know nothing about the matter and I will not have you interfering or daring to criticize me."

"Not my business? On the contrary, it is entirely my business. You are my husband. Everything you do concerns me. Apart from the vows you swore on our wedding day, I cannot let something as monstrous as this go on without trying to stop it."

"And you are my wife. You swore to obey me. I will not have you interfere in my life. You will obey me in this as in everything else."

"Even if I know that my husband is endangering his immortal soul?" She saw him flinch slightly. "Have you read *Erec et Enide*? The wife disobeys her husband because saving him comes above obeying him. Was she right? Should I say nothing and let your soul be damned? That is what you are saying. I warn you, William, I will not do it. I will not stand by and tolerate such a monstrous, unchristian thing as this harem of yours."

"This would be nothing in Constantinople or ..."

She interrupted him, blazing. "Indeed. You are a Christian king, William. The souls of your subjects are in your hands. And you use them to serve your carnal appetites. Is this Christian? Good enough for some luxury-loving Oriental potentate, but not for you."

She sensed his hesitation. "And another thing, William. You know what the people call you? They call you William the Good. The *Good*. Because you don't interfere in their lives, you don't overtax them, and Matthew sees to it that law and order are maintained. And what part of all that are you responsible for? None of it. Be a King, William. It is high time for you to stop playing in your harem and rule your kingdom. Become William the Good."

Pacing up and down the chamber, she went on, her voice raised.

"You are a Norman king, William. You and I are only a few generations removed from Norman conquerors. What would they think of this luxury? Is it befitting a man? They would despise it. And I do, too."

Another turn and she was back to face him. He was staring at her now, fascinated.

"And you know what it means to be a Norman, William? It means we have Viking blood in our veins. We are Vikings, you and I, William. Viking men treated their women as equals. Viking women were strong and proud. Yes, they were often brutal. There was rape and pillage and plunder of captive peoples. But this sort of thing? Never!"

William let out his breath. "You are magnificent, Joanna! I swear it. You look every inch a Viking Queen!"

There was silence as they faced each other. She saw the open admiration on his face. She had won the battle. It was her triumph but she saw him now as weak. He was weak and self-indulgent and she no longer felt any love or respect for him.

"And another thing, William. Those two young sisters—I want to bring them here to the palace. I will find work for them."

Despite, or because of, their violent argument that day, when William came to her chamber that night, their love making was more passionate than she had ever known it. Her feeling of having done the right thing in a difficult situation gave her energy and her passion rose to meet his. Perversely, the thought of him embracing all those beautiful young girls and the memory of the erotic mosaics excited her and she responded to him with ardor.

"My Viking Queen!" he exclaimed as they clung together sweatily, limbs intertwined. "My magnificent Viking Queen!"

CHAPTER TWENTY-SEVEN

Montroyal was the peace offering. Joanna knew it as soon as William suggested it to her. It was the morning of All Hallows and the two of them went ahead of all the court to the altar rails. As they knelt side by side, Joanna stole a sideways glance at him. William's face was lifted, his eyes closed, his expression rapt. She looked at his pure profile, the long lashes lying on his cheeks, the short, straight nose, the clear cut curving lips, the fuzzy dark blond beard outlining his chin, the slender neck. *Every* night since he was sixteen? Had he meant that literally? Surely not holy days? What about Easter, Advent, Lent?

Archbishop Walter, standing before them at the altar, dipped awkwardly and rose again. He turned and was coming toward them. William's eyelashes fluttered slightly. He crossed himself and opened his mouth. What did he tell his confessor, she wondered? She herself had confessed her burst of anger and had done penance for it.

"Hoc est enim corpus meus ..." The Archbishop was placing the host on William's tongue. Could he be absolved if he were not

penitent? Did he promise week by week to reform and then confess all over again the next time? Or did he simply never mention it? *How* could he accept the body and blood of Christ with such a sin on his conscience?

The Archbishop was moving over to her. Guiltily, she lowered her eyes and ordered her thoughts. It was the All Hallows Mass and here she was, thinking carnal thoughts, judging others. She crossed herself hastily. The familiar awe came over her as she took the body of the Lord into her mouth. Holding it on her tongue, she looked up at Christ Pantocrator surrounded by angels and the evangelists in their squinches. Beside her, William was already being given the cup of wine. She swallowed the bread. It was dry and stuck to the roof of her mouth. The Archbishop held the cup before her. She leaned her head forward and put her lips round the thin warm gold. The cup was tilted and wine ran into her mouth. She was always apprehensive that she would spill it but she never had. She screwed her eyes tight shut and swallowed the blood that was shed for them, and for many, and for the remission of sins.

To come to the Lord's table having sinned was one thing—they were all sinners, more or less—but having sinned and intending to repeat the sin, that very night perhaps, that was quite another thing. How could he reconcile it with his conscience? Or did he think, being King, he was above certain restrictions? Pride was another sin. She opened her eyes. William crossed himself and stood up and she followed suit. He took three steps backwards, genuflected, and crossed himself again. How much was expected ritual and how much sincere devotion? Joanna's skirts dragged on the five steps down into the nave, then they walked in silence to the royal dais at the opposite end of the chapel. The first line of nobles went forward to the sanctuary rails. Joanna put her head in her hands and tried to pray. She still could not understand it but knew it was between William and his Maker.

In the Hall after Mass, William came toward her, bent, and kissed her on both cheeks. She sat very still, trying not to move away from him. His face was as bland as ever. He sat down beside her and said, without any preamble, "I was thinking you might like to visit Montroyal." He smiled at her, that peculiarly sweet, guileless smile of his. "I should very much like to show it to you." She knew then that he had been told of her outburst and knew too that they would never talk of it. It was frustrating to her Angevin nature. She would have liked to bring it out into the open, hear his explanations, but she could never ask him about it.

"Yes," she said, "I would love to see Montroyal. Thank you."

Perhaps, more specifically, it was the mosaics, not the visit itself, that constituted the peace offering. They rode up there several days after All Hallows, with Chancellor Matthew and Bishop Richard in attendance and of course the usual train of ladies-in-waiting and courtiers. Tancred, she was glad to see, was not among them.

Chancellor Matthew rode beside her. Joanna never felt quite at ease with Matthew although he always treated her with deference. He was a clever man, an ambitious man, and, she guessed, a self-interested man. The Norman nobles despised him because they thought he gave himself airs. On the face of it, it seemed an irrelevant criticism. He was the King's right-hand man and entitled to at least as much show as they. Yet she knew what they meant. If he wore bright colors or costly fabrics, it was not, as for the Normans, simply because they gave him pleasure or because that was what he was used to. With him, everything was deliberate. There were subterranean layers of motives and meanings behind all his actions. His finery was a statement; more than a statement: an assertion, a challenge.

"Monreale," he said enthusiastically, giving it its Italian name, "is a masterstroke. The whole point of Monreale—no, I should not say that. I do the King an injustice. He is undoubtedly sincere in wishing to build a cathedral to the glory of God. Everyone knows how pious he is." He glanced sideways at her. He, too, she thought, had heard of her outburst. Was there anyone who had not? "And I think he also wants to emulate his grandfather, King Roger of glorious memory, who built Cefalu and the Palatine chapel. But, of course, as his premier statesman, I cannot help observing that Monreale will be an enormous help in curbing the power of the Church hierarchy."

"I don't understand," Joanna said.

"It's a new archbishopric, you see, my lady. Its incumbent will be equal in rank to Archbishop Walter himself. But Sicily's strength lies in tolerance, in keeping a balance between its various peoples and using the best in each of them, Norman soldiers, Jewish financiers, Greek scholars, Arab administrators, standing at the crossroads of Europe ..."

He smiled self-deprecatingly. "Forgive me, my lady. I am a true patriot and get carried away by my enthusiasm at times."

The enthusiasm was real enough, Joanna reflected, but she could not see him as a man to let himself be carried away.

"Balance of power is vital here. It takes a strong central authority to hold together all these different laws and languages, religions and customs."

Joanna glanced at William riding ahead of them, fair, slender, upright, with his air of aloofness, indifference. He was not, she noticed, a very good horseman. Too stiff. He treated the horse as though it were a chair, not a living moving creature. She sighed sadly. Only a fortnight ago, she had thought him the acme of humanity, beyond criticism. She looked back at Matthew, dark, stocky, intense, his head hunched into his shoulders, and wondered with a sudden shock if he thought of himself as the strong central authority he had spoken of.

Joanna had heard Monreale described but she was unprepared for the sheer size of it. The cathedral was magnificent, not especially beautiful to her eyes, but certainly impressive. A square Norman tower rose above the long nave. The walls stretched away, indented with ornate blind arches in reddish lava. To her right, as she stood at the West end of the cathedral, she could see the red-tiled roof of the cloister. The Abbey buildings were surrounded by other temporary huts and workshops. Slabs of stone and lengths of lumber lay in heaps and there was dust and rubble everywhere. The cathedral looked finished from the outside but stonecutters were still chiselling stone blocks into decorative corbels and bosses while their assistants held metal templates in place for them. Smiths were heating irons in their fires for cutting stained glass and she could see the row of kilns that were used for firing the painted window sections. She had picked her way round a pile of mortar and past various tools, axes, mallets, and saws, to the West portal and was looking in through the great yawning gap into the dark interior when William came up, his step light and bouncy. Smiths, masons, and carpenters watched him as he went by, but none stopped work.

"Well, what do you think? Isn't it grand?"

She had never seen him so enthusiastic. "It is certainly most impressive."

"Here, you see, there will be bronze doors. I haven't commissioned them yet. I want to get someone really good. There's a man from Trani, Barisano, who is working on the doors for the north portal. I'll show you afterward. And of course the windows are not in yet. You have to use your imagination. But the main thing will be the mosaics."

He took her arm and led her inside. It was cool and dark. Sounds of hammering echoed off the high stone walls and there was a thud and diminishing whine of vibration as someone dropped a heavy beam. Sand or grit crunched under her feet and the whole place smelled of mortar and freshly-sawn wood. Her eyes quickly grew accustomed to the gloom. There was in fact quite a lot of light from the high windows not yet glazed. She felt disappointed by what she saw. The long walls stretched out flat and unadorned above the marble inlays on their lower sections. There was nothing to break the uniformity of that monotonous expanse.

William was waving his hand up at the central apse under which they stood. "Here will be Christ Pantocrator, a gigantic figure. Can you see the outline? His right hand alone will be more than six feet high. And below him, saints—that isn't decided yet. And up there, above where the thrones will be, on each side of the eastern arch, a portrait of me offering this cathedral to the Mother of God."

Suddenly Joanna saw it. The great outline of Christ, so huge that she had not been able to focus on it properly, sprang out on the apse above her. Once she saw it, she saw the other sketches. The walls were covered with them. She went closer to look.

"Why, this is Christ walking on the waters. And the disciples watching him from the boat. And the washing of the feet and the agony in the garden and the betrayal."

William beamed. "Yes! The whole Bible. Or very nearly. Everything from Adam and Eve—over there, do you see?—to the Acts of the Apostles. Most of the artists are Greek, of course. Byzantium is the only place with enough organized mosaic workshops to undertake such an enormous task. But there are some Italians. I want to encourage local talent. Those three pictures you were looking at, on the lowest row there, washing the feet and the agony, those are the work of an Italian. We haven't got them all sketched in yet, as you can see."

Joanna studied him as he talked. She had never seen him like this, radiating energy and excitement. Watching him, she found that suddenly, shockingly, in the middle of his new cathedral, she was imagining that energy and excitement put to profane uses. Her stomach muscles tightened and the skin on her nape prickled. Images of William in bed swam before her. She thought of him with all those unknown women and she remembered the touch of his hands on her own body. Her legs felt weak and sweat trickled between her shoulder blades. She blinked and stared at the walls, but the lewd visions, mostly William in his harem, but sometimes her father and Alice, superimposed themselves on the swirling iconography. Think of something else, she admonished herself, horrified. Think of ascetics, of Fontevrault, of Thomas the martyr ...

"... I haven't decided. Perhaps the Evangelists. But there is room for more than four figures. So, if you would allow me, my dear, I would like to let you choose the first figure. Your favorite saint. Your patron saint. Whichever you choose."

He paused, looking at her.

"I'm sorry?" she said. What was he talking about? He was amazingly handsome. And gentle. And even if he had all those other women, she was still his Queen and not, she thought, unpleasing to him. For the first time, she wanted him. The blood beat in her throat. She wanted to lie down on the dusty floor and couple with him. She dug her fingernails into her sweating palms. Here, of all places to be thinking such thoughts. At least it was not consecrated. She thought of Thomas again, of the maggots in his sleeves and Our Lady coming to mend his hair shirt for him.

"The figures to go below the Christ Pantocrator, around the apse. I should like to put your favorite saint there, if you agree."

"Thomas," she said. "Thomas the martyr."

"Thomas?" He looked at her curiously. "But your father ... I am a great admirer of Thomas myself. Would your father be offended? That his son-in-law would choose to honor his old enemy ... Still, you are his daughter and you choose him."

"They are not enemies now," Joanna said. She had her emotions fully under control again. "They are reconciled. Father has done penance and Thomas is sanctified. Why, there are hundreds, probably thousands, of pilgrims going to Canterbury now and Father doesn't resent that." Or does he? Thomas, after all, had won. It was momentarily very clear to her. Thomas had been driven into exile, reduced to poverty, and finally murdered. Her father was King. He had his life, he had power, wealth, followers and freedom. But it was Thomas who had won and because of it, men and women would come to pray at his tomb for centuries ahead.

"You're right. Yes, it is a good choice. A man of our times for a new cathedral. A man of uncompromising virtue, who died for his faith—I have it!" He clapped his fist into the other palm. "Martyrs! We will have Thomas here," he strode excitedly across the floor, "and opposite him, here, Saint Peter of Alexandria who also returned from exile to face martyrdom. And Stephen and—and—who else? Lawrence. And of course, Thomas was an archbishop, so we must have Nicholas of Bari, who was one of the chief patrons of our kingdom. And Martin, since it's a Benedictine abbey. And—well, we can decide on the other two later, but it's a perfect plan. A tribute to the most recent saint and martyr. I like it. I have always admired those who give up everything for their faith."

There was no doubting his sincerity. Some part of her, Joanna thought, had meant the choice of Thomas to be a reproach to him. The irony of it seemed lost on him. Now he was taking her arm again, leading her back to the entrance.

"I want you to come and see Barisano. He's just finished a door panel with Saint Paul on it and I swear it looks just like Archbishop Walter!"

CHAPTER TWENTY-EIGHT

"We must never forget, my dear Joanna," Constance said, "that in our position, it is up to us to set an example."

Joanna stifled a yawn. William had kept her awake later than usual the night before and Constance's conversation was not the most stimulating at the best of times. Joanna did not think Constance enjoyed these visits any more than she did, but a sense of duty brought Constance once a week to the royal palace. As usual, she was exhorting her to deny her usual pleasures and pray more.

"Where we lead, others will follow. I know you attended Mass daily during Lent, but I notice you gave that up after Easter and only go once a week now. Is it enough, do you think, to observe the minimum, like any vassal, and spend the rest of your time in frivolous pursuits?"

Joanna turned her head away, catching the unpleasant smell of Constance's breath. "I am grateful to you, of course, for your advice, but you see, my position is an awkward one. If my lord wishes to organize a hunting-party and I refuse to join it, would it not seem as if I were reproaching him? For you, it is different. As St. Paul says, 'The unmarried woman cares for the things of the Lord, but she that is married cares how she may please her husband.' Perhaps," she added wickedly, "you should go and talk to William about frivolous pursuits."

"But a wife by her example ..." Constance was beginning when Adèle burst into the room, her hair unpinned, tears running down her face, a crumpled letter in her hand. Ignoring everyone, she ran straight to Joanna. "Joanna, the most terrible thing has happened—oh my God, I can't bear it!—it's a disaster—you must prevent it—I won't go!—I'd rather kill myself, I *will* kill myself ..." The words came hysterically, interrupted by choking sobs. Joanna got up, alarmed, and took her by the elbows.

"Adèle, what is it? What has happened?"

Adèle began to weep. Mutely, she held out the letter to Joanna who took it from her. Joanna felt herself grow cold as she read the first words. Numbly, she read the whole letter through and then stood staring at it. Adèle's father had chosen a husband for her. She was to return to Normandy immediately. The marriage would take place before Michaelmas.

The thought of losing Adèle was intolerable. "Who is he?" she said at last.

Adèle drew the back of her hand across her eyes. "A neighboring baron. I've never met him," she gulped. "He's a widower and *old*—oh, in his thirties, at least. He has *children* my age. He has a seat not far from my father's castle and lots of land, so he's rich. But I won't go!" she cried passionately. "I'll—I'll refuse! I'll marry Alan. I'll run away. Anything! You must tell him you need me here, Joanna, you won't let me go."

Joanna stood very still. Even in that first moment she had the cold conviction that she could not prevent it. Constance, whose mouth had dropped open revealing her rotten teeth during this interchange, now closed it and frowned at Adèle.

"Adèle," she said earnestly, "it seems to me that, whatever your personal feelings may be, you have a clear duty to obey your father and ..."

"Oh, what would you know about it?" Adèle shrilled, rounding on her. "An old maid like you! I dare say you would jump at the chance of any marriage …"

"On the contrary," Constance said frostily, forgetting for once to hide her mouth with her hand as she spoke, "I am mindful that St. Paul told us it is better to remain unmarried and that is what I should prefer. But if ever I am required to marry, for family or state reasons, I hope I shall acquiesce with a good grace and fulfill my duty without complaining."

"That's easy for you to say! You've never been in love!"

"I should hope not, indeed! A young woman cannot be too careful of her morals, if she is not to be thought loose, and to encourage some frivolous young man with talk of love and other unholy nonsense …"

"Oh, it's hopeless!" Adèle turned back to Joanna. "Joanna, you must help me! I won't go, I swear it! I'll tell my father I am with child and then the baron won't want me."

"Are you?" Constance asked, her features drawn into an expression of distaste. "Then *nobody* will want you."

"Of course I'm not, you stupid cow! But Alan would want me anyway."

"Alan—if you mean Alan FitzJohn—strikes me as a basically sensible young man. He may want you but I doubt if he would marry you if it meant being disinherited."

"He would, he would! Oh, it's so unfair!" She burst into tears again and Joanna led her away, trying to calm her.

ℭ ✾ ℭ

Adèle left in the month that Pope Alexander died and was succeeded by Pope Lucius, "a very old man, with a modicum of learning", as Matthew rather nastily described him. For Joanna, the weeks between Adèle's receiving her father's letter and her departure were like a dream, or rather, a nightmare, from which she was unable to awake and had to go through it to the end, unable to run, unable to scream. She watched in frozen misery as Adèle alternately wept and raged her way to sullen despairing resignation.

Eleanor was very much in her thoughts. She could no longer remember her sister's face but she remembered clearly her anguish when Eleanor had gone to Castile. And then leaving her mother in England and Richard in France.... So many farewells. Involuntarily she felt herself growing a protective shell against the pain. When Adèle left, she did not weep.

Outwardly, life went on as before. She felt not so much sorrow as the absence of happiness. With the summer, the court moved up out of Panorme into the cooler hills, to the Parco or to Mimnermo, al-Menani as the eunuchs called it. Joanna moved with them, at the very centre of them and yet always apart. When she rode out hawking, the young nobles crowded round her, eager to hold her gloves or to help her dismount, and at night they vied to dance with her and recited poems in her honor. Yet she was aware that for all their compliments and attentions, hers was never the hand they reached for beneath the table nor were her kisses sought behind a tree in the park. Whether he was physically present or not, William was an invisible shield between her and any admirers.

William ... Her anger and resentment against him had faded and they had reached an amicable state of truce. He was polite in public and kind in private, but he parried all her attempts to engage him in more revealing conversation with easy imperturbability. Soon she gave up trying.

There was no one she could talk to. She could have confided in Adèle, but Adèle was gone and no one had taken her place. Isabelle perhaps could have been her friend but Isabelle had died in childbed that summer, a bad death. She had screamed for three days and nights before dying with the baby still locked in her too-slender body.

When Joanna was young, she had run to Nurse with all her pains and problems, but she was too old for that now. Nurse often seemed to her an alien being, an anachronism, in the glitter and luxury of the Sicilian court, a heavyset, red faced figure plodding sturdily from one dull chore to another, grumbling and criticizing. And then Joanna would castigate herself for thinking so about the woman who had loved and raised her with such devotion. In an excess of guilt that Christmas, Joanna had given Nurse an extra generous present, a jeweled cross on a gold chain. Nurse would not have welcomed jewels as adornment, even if they had been fitting for her station, but Joanna rightly guessed that jewels for the glory of God would be acceptable. The front was studded with gems and gold filigree. The back was a flat piece of silver with the image of Christ crucified engraved on it.

Joanna herself felt homesick at Christmas because her family had been in Caen, even Matilda. And Adèle. It had been the biggest Christmas court for years. To judge from Adèle's letter, Christmas here in Panorme had been a much more peaceful affair. It was typical of Adèle that she had not hesitated to dictate to her scribe all the gossip, but then it was probably common knowledge anyway.

Joanna put Adèle's letter down and sat dreaming for a moment. Then she crossed to the window of her chamber and looked out, over the palm trees bending before a stiff wind, over the gilded domes and minarets and stark white walls of Panorme to the Mediterranean where brightly painted fishing boats bobbed on the foam-crested waves. She looked to the horizon where the sea met the pale sky. Over there, to the northwest, lay France, sweet France. She remembered when she and Adèle had first come here, how they had exclaimed over the glittering mosaics on the walls, the marble floors inlaid with gold and silver, the endless sunshine, the vivid flowers. Paradise, Adèle had called it then. It had not changed. But for a moment it seemed less real to her than the vision in her mind's eye of the green fields of Normandy among their little hedgerows, the grey stone castles dominating the hills and the sprawling dirty crowded towns.

"What news from home?"

Joanna turned back from the window. Nurse stood in the room with a pile of freshly ironed linen in her arms.

"Why do you do that work?" she asked irritably. "Leave it to the servants."

"And what should I do, sit and twiddle my thumbs? There is no disgrace in honest work and I'd rather make myself useful." She crossed the room and lifted the lid of a chest and started to arrange the linens.

"Do you miss it? Anjou, I mean?"

"Miss it? Of course I do," Nurse said briskly. She closed the chest and set her hands on her hips. "You look sad, chick. Is the news bad?"

"No. No worse than usual. There was a great scandal, Adèle says, at the Christmas court. The old rumor about Marguerite and William Marshal. William did not come in Henry's train for once; he arrived later and in front of the whole court, publicly, appealed to Father to let him defend his honor and Marguerite's in single combat."

"Oh dear, oh dear. Men think to solve everything by fighting. Well, I suppose it's the right of any vassal who is accused to settle it in combat, but one would have to be very sure the accusation was true before challenging William Marshal."

"Exactly! No one accepted the challenge. So Henry pointed out it was hardly a fair trial, since William is an acknowledged champion and then William offered to fight with the forefinger of his right hand cut off, for three days without respite. If he won, his reward would be to clear his name; if he lost, they could take and hang him. He is a brave man, that William Marshal."

"And what happened?"

"Still no one would accept his challenge. Henry was furious, of course, and William Marshal said he scorned to defend his innocence in mere words since the man's way was denied him and he left the court to go to—let me see—the shrine of the three Magi in Cologne. Of course, Father is against these trials by combat or ordeal, anyway. He has a new system of trial by twelve of your peers."

"What a way to start the Christmas court! I hope things were more peaceful after Marshal left."

"No, it ended in such chaos that Father broke up the court before the year was out. Henry and Marguerite were not speaking to each other. And Henry and Richard quarrelled, apparently over Richard's new castle at Clairvaux. And then Father summoned Richard and Geoffrey to do homage to Henry and Richard refused. So Richard and Henry would not sit down at the same table together and all their vassals were at daggers drawn. The end of it was that Father cut short the court and went to Le Mans. Henry swears he will take the cross."

"Hah! It might be the best thing he could do, if he meant it, but I daresay it's just a threat to bring the King your father round and win some concession from him."

"Am I being selfish keeping you here, Nounou?"

"I promised to stay with you as long as you need me, didn't I? So of course I will."

"But don't you wish you were there instead of here?"

"Wish—want—that's you all over. What difference does it make what one wishes? One can do God's work here as well as there, and there's always something I can turn my hand to. Now where's that gown, the one you were wearing yesterday? I've just time to mend that ripped seam before dinner. And what are you going to do with yourself today? Surely not stand there and stare out of the window?"

"I might as well be Mother, shut up in Salisbury Tower."

"Tsk, tsk! Shame on you! How you can complain, when your life is nothing but pleasures and advantages, and a lord as courteous as my lord the King! And pious, too. No, you're a lucky girl. I thought him stiff at first—well, in all that fancy get-up he wears, like some heathen Greek King instead of a proper Christian—and he certainly doesn't have your father's rough-and-ready ways, no offense meant, but he can be a kind man in his distant way, well, you can tell to look at him, a face like an angel, *that* couldn't hide a wicked heart, could it? Anyway, he condescended to speak to me and I thought he hardly knew who I was, I was standing back in the corridor to let him pass, but no, he stops and says to me, 'Mistress Jeanne,' he says, 'I want *you* to come to the consecration of my new cathedral and no skulking at the back. I shall see that my officers give you a good place where you can see it all. I know how much you do for my lady,' he says, 'and I thank you for it. And besides, you're a better Christian than most around here.' Well, as to that, I wouldn't like to say, though there are some I could mention that I haven't seen in chapel since Twelfth Night, and as for those big black heathens, they still give me the creeps. But for a King to thank me, just as if I were a lady! Oh, he's a lovely man! And what *you* need," she added shrewdly, "is a child. *That* would stop you maundering on about France and wishing for this and wanting that."

Joanna did not answer. She was keeping to herself her suspicion that she was at last with child. She had missed only one month's flow and was waiting to be certain before saying anything, but she felt a tingling in her breasts and queasiness in the mornings and felt sure of it herself.

The King was as good as his word. Joanna, from her throne below the main eastern arch, could see Nurse standing to attention in a newly starched coif, with Joanna's silver crucifix round her neck and her prayer book in her hands. In the front row stood Constance, her mouth firmly closed over her bad teeth and her eyes closed in prayer, and next to her was Queen Margaret, small, bird-like, her hair magnificently dressed for the occasion and her great dark eyes fixed on her son William. Joanna thought she looked thin and pale and much aged. Archbishop Walter had come, Joanna noticed. He had refused to participate in the ceremony and was seated, on account of his age and rank, across the nave from them, where he stared in front of him, glowering, his chins sunk in folds on his neck, his hands clasped over his silk-clad paunch. Joanna saw Tancred's ugly, beetle-browed face in the front row, too. His wife Sibylla was beside him and they were flanked by Chancellor Matthew, looking as satisfied as if the cathedral were entirely his own creation, and Sibylla's brother, Count Richard of Acerra. The nobles had come en masse to the consecration. She could see Count Roger of Andria standing foursquare, his thumbs in his belt, an honest and intelligent face, but arrogant, like all the Normans. Their colors, green and crimson and blue and gold, enlivened the cathedral's gloomy interior. At the far end, the doors stood open and shafts of sunlight struck the cipolin columns. They were wooden doors, temporary ones, as Bonnannus of Pisa had not yet finished his bronze ones. In the north porch, the doors of Barisanus were hung now; she had seen them earlier this year.

The abbot, now the archbishop of Montroyal, was coming to the end of his sermon. She looked up, above the heads of the crowd, to the mosaics on the walls. Less than a quarter of them were completed, but St. Thomas was up there, where they had planned, the second figure to the right of the central window, next to St. Sylvester. She stared at him. He gazed, not straight ahead of him, but off to the right somewhere, his expression serene. She tried to remember what the real Thomas had looked like. A tall skinny long-shanks of a fellow, her mother had called him. Probably the artist had never seen him, anyway. With the two portraits of William, above her head, they had really tried. On the left, William was shown receiving his crown from Christ and on the right, offering his new cathedral to the Mother of God. She could not see them now but remembered them clearly. The artist had striven to show William's individual features, his great eyes and perfectly arched brows, his rounded face and short straight nose, his fair sparse beard, but the parts did not add up to the whole.

"In nomine Patri et Filii et Spiritu Sanctu ..."

Joanna slipped from her seat to her knees as the whole rustling congregation knelt. It was over. She had time only for one quick prayer—"Holy Mary, Mother of God, grant that this child is a son"—before William offered her his hand to lead her from his new cathedral out into the bright April sunlight.

At the banquet that night, Joanna was seated by Queen Margaret. Joanna saw how frail she had become. The bones showed in her hands like a bird's claws, and the skin of her face was drawn taut and almost translucent like old parchment. When she turned her head, the skull showed beneath the skin, in the lines of jaw and cheekbone and the deep sockets of her eyes. She took the old Queen's hand.

"You look tired, my lady mother. Are you unwell?"

"I am in pain much of the time and sometimes long to die. These Arab doctors are very clever. They have a draught of poppies that can take away the pain and make one dream, but I take it only when it is more than I can stand. God would not send this pain without a reason so I should accept it willingly, but sometimes I am weak. Perhaps He wishes to purify me by suffering before I stand in His sight."

"Mother, my lady mother," she said, "you must not talk of dying."

"Nonsense! Not talk of dying? What else is life for, if not to prepare for that? No, no, I look forward to it, to being reunited with the sons I lost and with my own dear mother and so many others. You are young and have not come to terms with death, but God willing you have time. I thought at the consecration, 'mine will be the first burial here.' William means it to be the royal burial-place, you know, he told me so. He is going to move his father's body there from the Palatine chapel, and his brothers' bodies so we shall all be together. The one thing I want to see before I die is that you and William have an heir. I am afraid I will not live to see it."

And then, as Joanna made a protesting move of her hand, "No, no, child, I am content, if it were not for that. It is not when one dies, but how, that matters and I want to die well. As I say, I am content to go but I pray for a grandson first. Four sons and only one left to me now and that one childless …"

Joanna leaned close to her. "I have told no one this as yet, but I am with child. Let me tell William first and then we will make it official. A grandson, perhaps in time for your birthday."

Queen Margaret turned to her, beaming. "Is it really true, my child? I have prayed for this. Now I have something to live for and will hold off this illness that has been consuming me. Once I have held the child in my arms, I can go happily. I expect mine will be the first burial in this beautiful new cathedral that was consecrated today."

It was not to be. All that summer, as Joanna grew bigger and bigger, the hot weather distressed her. She spent most of her time at the Parco where slaves fanned her day and night. William came sometimes to visit her. He was buoyant over this pregnancy and solicitous for her wellbeing.

By the spring she felt she could hardly walk. The child twisted and kicked inside her and pressed against her lungs, making her breathing shallow. She was relieved when at last her pains began. She had been confined to her chamber for a month since and longed for it to be over. The midwife rubbed her belly with oil and helped her into a sitting position. All the pins were taken from her hair and all the doors and cupboards in the room kept open.

It felt as though a vise had seized her and kept squeezing past the point of tolerance. The midwife murmured comfortingly to her and advised her to pray to St. Margaret. Between the pains there were moments of rest, then it would seize her again, for longer and longer. She tried not to think of poor Isabelle who had died after three days of this pain, probably worse than Joanna's own. The midwife had assured her that the baby was well positioned.

At last, she felt the child slipping from her as though all her internal organs had dropped out and then there was relief. There was a faint cry.

"A boy! It's a boy, Majesty!"

Joanna felt the tears spring to her eyes. An heir for William! She held the tightly wrapped little bundle in her arms. He seemed so tiny.

"Is he healthy?" she asked.

"A fine boy, Majesty," they answered.

William came that evening and strode around the chamber laughing and drinking wine. "Bohemund! I shall name him Bohemund. You have done well, Joanna."

The next day Bohemund was feverish. Joanna saw them fussing over him on the other side of the room. They let some blood but the fever worsened. A priest was sent for and the baby was hastily baptized. A deepening sense of urgency and despair gripped Joanna and she swung her legs out of the bed and stood up. Blood gushed from her and she felt faint. Her ladies rushed to her and put her back to bed and swaddled her again. The wet nurse came but the baby would not take the breast. He wailed and coughed and wheezed. Joanna listened to him as they bound her breasts to stop the milk. They fed him honeyed water dripped from the end of a rag, then they took him away.

Joanna slept but her sleep was tormented by dreams. She took little red-faced Bohemund to a cool stream and dipped him into the water. Then she held him under the water to stop his wailing. When she lifted him out, he was quiet and very pale and cold and still ... She awoke sweating and shaking. There were several people at the foot of her bed and she knew at once from their faces what they had come to tell her. She screamed once and then started to sob convulsively and could not stop.

"My lady, my lady, you must calm yourself ..."

"It is God's will, it must be accepted." That was the priest.

"You are young, you will have other sons yet ..." She didn't want other sons, she wanted this one, they didn't understand.

They went on and on, but she would not be consoled. It was Queen Margaret finally who came and said nothing, but held her and wept with her and then she was able to stop crying. Her throat was sore and her head ached and she felt empty.

So the first funeral in William's fine new cathedral was their baby son. Joanna, newly risen from her bed, sat and watched as the tiny coffin was carried in. He did indeed look pale and still now, as he had in her dream. And so tiny ...

"I wish it could have been me," Queen Margaret said to her. "I am ready to go. I had so much hoped to hold a grandson before that happens."

Not when, but how. Joanna remembered her words as she walked behind Queen Margaret's bier into Montroyal less than a year later. She had died well. Joanna wondered if she herself could be so stoical in her acceptance of pain. For weeks before her death Queen Margaret had refused all medication and at the last, she had asked to be moved into the chapel. She had received extreme unction there, still conscious, before slipping into the coma in which she lay for a day and a night, breathing so lightly that the end, when it came, was barely perceptible to the watchers around her.

William knelt beside Joanna in the cathedral, his face set and his eyes dry as he watched them lower his mother's body into the tomb. The hollow grating of the stone lid being set in place echoed around the cathedral. *William will be buried here too one day,* Joanna thought, *and then I myself one day. And our children after us, if we have them.* She found herself praying, not for the repose of Queen Margaret's soul, but for a son, a son and heir for William. She thought that Queen Margaret would not have minded. And as always, she prayed for little Bohemund though she knew that in his innocence he would have gone straight to heaven and was waiting for her there.

Joanna had been spared the familiarity with death that most people had. She had never known her little brother William who had died nine years before she was born. She had been saddened but not shocked by the deaths of Queen Margaret and Isabella. Queen Margaret was old, and childbirth, like war, was always dangerous. But even after the gap of six years since she had left

France, she was shocked by the news that reached them that July.

Her brother Henry was dead. When the messengers brought the news, he had been buried for a month already, his body with the Dukes of Normandy in Notre Dame of Rouen and his eyes, brain, and entrails in the monastery of Grammont, beside the gravesite that their father King Henry had chosen for himself. She remembered Henry vividly, his loose-limbed way of walking, the lock of golden hair that fell across his brow and the wide mouth that could smile so charmingly when he wanted to please, but that she remembered downturned in a petulant moue, and his clear, light, blue-grey eyes flashing in barely contained rage. Poor Henry, he had always been angry: angry with their father for not giving him more power, angry with Richard for his arrogant success in Aquitaine, angry with Marguerite for preferring William Marshal to him.

Henry was a young man in his prime, twenty-eight years old, strong, active; he had died not in a war or a tournament, but of a simple fever. It could happen to anyone, she knew that with her head, of course; now she felt it, too. If to him, then to anyone, herself for instance, young and healthy as she was. Mortality laid its cold touch on her.

Henry died in rebellion against his father. When the fever took him, in the little town of Martel, they sent messengers to fetch the King, but King Henry, afraid of treachery, sent his ring and stayed away himself. Faithful William Marshal had been with him at the end and was even now on the way to the Holy Land with Henry's cross, since Henry could not himself redeem his pledge to God.

"King Henry has called on Duke Richard to yield Poitou and Aquitaine to his younger brother John," the messenger said. He knelt before the table where they were eating. They had heard Mass said that day for the repose of Henry's soul.

William nodded silently, his mouth full of meat, but Joanna sat forward sharply. "How can Father ever think Richard will agree to that?"

William swallowed. "Reasonable enough. Richard is now heir of England and also Duke of Normandy and Count of Maine and Anjou."

"Heir ..." she said, struck. She had not realized it before. "Yes, he is heir to the throne. But Aquitaine will always be his first love. He will never let it go."

"My lady is right," the messenger said. "He has refused. And Queen Eleanor supports him. As Countess of Poitou and Duchess of Aquitaine, she will not give her consent to transfer her lands from Duke Richard to Lord John."

"What news else of my mother?" Joanna asked. "She must have taken the news of Henry's death very hard."

"Queen Eleanor knew of his death before the messengers came. Or so they say. She learned of it in a dream. She saw him wearing two crowns, of which one shone with an unearthly brightness."

William crossed himself. "Poor lady! Yet one should not feel too sorry for her. She has done great wrongs in her time."

"The wrongs were done to her," Joanna said indignantly. "Shut in Salisbury for nine whole years ..."

"Come now, Joanna, everyone knows she stirred her sons up against their father. A terrible waste, it always seems to me. Between them, with all their energy, they could have built a great Empire. But she threw it all away for personal vengeance. That's a woman for you."

"I don't know," Joanna said obstinately. "She may have done that. I was only a child, I don't know all that passed. But the wrong was not all on her side."

"Oh, I'm not arguing that your father is perfect. But he is King and her husband. There was no excuse for her."

CHAPTER TWENTY-NINE

For months Joanna was depressed, grieved as she was by the loss of her baby son, sobered by her brother's death, and unsettled by the news of the birth of a child to her old friend Adèle. It was thinking of her mother that finally helped her to overcome this with a somewhat brittle determination to enjoy to the full her role as Queen of a rich and peaceful kingdom. She and William might yet have children. They were all in God's hands.

It was easy enough to enjoy oneself in Panorme if one were young and a Queen and had a husband who encouraged the pursuit of every pleasure. Joanna pushed her sadness for Bohemund into a hidden corner of her mind and looked upon her need for a friend like Adèle as something childish she had outgrown. With William at her side, she danced, she hawked, she rode. Of all these things she loved best to ride. She thought of her mare, Cigale, as more of a friend than most of her attendants.

Cigale was the color of burnt cinnamon, with a long ash-blond mane and tail. She stepped lightly and elegantly, picking up her feet, and never stumbled or shied from a jump. In the hills outside the city, Joanna would give Cigale her head and they would gallop across the dry springy turf, with no sound but the thud of hoofs and the wind and the crying of skylarks wheeling high above them. Joanna never carried a whip, Cigale knew instantly what was wanted of her by the slightest nudge of a knee or turn of the head. Joanna was a better rider than any of her women and they would fall back while the younger noblemen accompanied her.

William seldom came on these rides. He loved to hunt, but did not enjoy riding for its own sake and was, moreover, an indifferent horseman. But he put no obstacles in her way and was even amused and pleased by the extravagant praise showered on her by his nobles. He never criticized anything she did, even when that Christmas she and her ladies dressed as Moslem women, with colored veils, gilt slippers, henna on their fingers, and kohl around their eyes. They meant it as harmless amusement, but Nurse was scandalized and said so.

"Dressing like heathens, like wantons, would be bad enough at any time, but on the day of Our Lord's birth! How could you do such a thing?"

Joanna shrugged. "It was just for amusement. William didn't see any harm in it. And we didn't go to church in that costume."

"I should think not indeed! I know you think I'm old-fashioned but I hope I will never bring myself to approve of such goings-on."

Joanna did think Nurse old-fashioned and more and more she avoided her, but she felt guilty about it. In Lent she threw herself into fasting and prayer with twice her usual zeal. She also felt guilty that, unlike her mother, she knew little of the affairs of Sicily or the world. But when she tried to talk to William of such things, he answered indifferently and turned the subject.

When Easter was over, there was a great feast and after the feast, dancing. Joanna was surprised to see Constance dance. She was always punctilious in attending feasts but usually excused herself as soon as the meal ended. Even more surprisingly, she danced gracefully, in a dignified gliding style of her own. When the dancing stopped for an ode to be recited in praise of William the Glorious One and his new cathedral, Constance came to sit beside Joanna, smiling a closed-lip smile and fanning herself with a new ivory fan. She looked better than Joanna had ever seen her look, her cheeks flushed from dancing and her fair hair swept up under a thin, silk veil. There were other changes too: she was wearing more jewelry than usual and a new gown, lavishly embroidered in gold thread.

"You are looking very fine tonight," Joanna murmured to her. The ode was long and platitudinous and after the first few stanzas she felt no need or desire to listen to any more of it. "That gown is beautiful."

"Yes. Do you like it? I'm glad. You have such good taste and I have never studied such things. William's own embroiderer did it for me himself. Yahya Ibn Fityan. He runs the Shiraz, you know. Wasn't it kind of William? He sent him to me himself."

Joanna felt the familiar knot of pain in her stomach at the mention of the Shiraz, dulled now by years of acceptance, but still there. She was also surprised that William should send his own embroiderer to Constance who, by her own admission, was not interested in such things, when he had never offered his services to Joanna. There was, of course, the awkwardness of the Shiraz; perhaps he had thought it more discreet to avoid reminding her of its existence.

"He has done an excellent job. But is all this in honor of Montroyal? I don't think I've ever seen you dance before, not even at our wedding feast."

Constance was actually blushing. Joanna stared at her, amazed.

"It seems I have to take my place in the world, after all. If I could choose, of course, I would rather dedicate my life to the Lord, but things are not always what one would choose and not for a moment would I consider shirking my duty, whatever my own feelings. William has spoken to me, you see." She looked down and fiddled with the fan in her lap. "He wishes me to marry."

"Marry? I thought that ..." Joanna's voice trailed off. She had indeed thought it was too late for that now. A few heads turned their way. She had exclaimed more loudly than she had intended.

"Yes. I thought so, too. I had put the idea out of my head. With some relief. Now it seems I must learn again to hold court, to dress like a peacock, to dance and talk of idle worldly things. You have no child, you see, Joanna. I'm so sorry, I should not speak of it. But you are young and have many years ahead to produce an heir for him."

The ode had finally ended and the poet was bowing. A group of acrobats came forward and positioned themselves in the centre of the Hall.

"But I do not have much time," Constance went on. "I am thirty already, so William has decided I should marry and have children, God willing, in case you do not give him any."

Joanna took it in. It was reasonable, she could see that, but she felt a sense of failure. William had not mentioned it to her and that seemed a tacit reproof.

"Do you know who? Has William someone definite in mind?" she asked. "Someone here at court?"

Constance gave her a shocked look. "He wants a powerful ally," she said. "There's no advantage to my marrying someone here at court. No, it will be a king or a king's son."

Joanna thought swiftly. England—her brothers were all married or betrothed. France—King Philip was married. Could he possibly be aiming as high as the Holy Roman Empire or Byzantium? With Byzantium at his back, he could face the Western kingdoms as at least their equal and all this land had once been Byzantine. It was natural and yet surely not now? The time could hardly be worse.

"Byzantium?" she said, thinking aloud. "It isn't possible."

Constance crossed herself swiftly. "Great heavens, would you have me marry that monster Andronicus? Besides, he's married, to that poor little French princess who was betrothed to Alexius."

"No, it's confidential," Constance went on, "but I think I can tell you. William has in mind for me the Emperor's son. I mean, of course, Emperor Frederick's son."

"Ah." Joanna inhaled sharply. "Henry. Henry of Hohenstaufen. He will be Emperor after his father. You will be Holy Roman Empress, Constance." She looked at her, impressed. So William had chosen to throw in his lot with the Western

Empire. It would set the Eastern Empire against him. "You will have to live in Germany, Constance. Will you like that?"

"No. But if I must, I must."

Joanna accepted the news with equanimity. Her grandmother Matilda had been Holy Roman Empress before she married Geoffrey Plantagenet. It seemed natural to her that William should choose to ally himself with one of the two great Empires, but the rumor, spreading through the court, caused instant consternation. She had never seen Matthew so shaken out of his usual composure.

"It's a disaster," he fumed. "The King is courting disaster. The people will never accept it. What is he thinking of? Does he not see that he is handing Sicily to the Germans on a plate? It will mean the end of the kingdom of Sicily. I beg your pardon, Your Majesty. What I mean is, in the event Your Majesty remains childless, which pray God will not be the case, and in the event that the lady Constance succeeds the King, then Sicily will belong to her husband. It will become part of the Holy Roman Empire, another province, nothing more."

Joanna's old friend Nicholas was equally aghast. "They are a tolerant people, the Sicilians. A Norman King now, or a Frank or a Spaniard ... But the Germans are their traditional enemies. I have to agree with the Chancellor in this. Much as I dislike the man, he *does* understand the feelings of the Sicilians. They would be losing their independence to an Empire they have always considered barbarian."

The Imperial envoys arrived that winter with the formal proposal from Emperor Frederick for the hand of Constance on behalf of his son Henry. There were no cheers for them in the streets of Panorme and the atmosphere at court was tense. Matthew, visibly, could hardly bring himself to be civil to them. Archbishop Walter was the only one who openly supported the King in this matter and Joanna suspected he only did it to spite Matthew.

Joanna herself went through her part in receiving them without feeling anything one way or the other. When she spoke to William of the opposition to Constance's betrothal, he was unconcerned.

"I know they do not like it," William reassured her, "but they will come around. Besides, it's far from certain that Constance will ever come to the throne. You and I will have many sons yet, God willing, so don't worry about it. If I don't worry, why should you?"

Why indeed? Except that he had put his finger on a nerve. Bohemund was ever-present in her thoughts. Adèle had a child, a daughter named Berthe; Joanna's sister Eleanor and King Alfonso had a daughter, Berenguela; Geoffrey and Constance also had a daughter, Eleanor; and her sister Matilda, of course, had any number of children, Henry, Otto, William, Matilda, and the rest. It seemed to Joanna that she alone was cursed with childlessness.

By the following spring, Joanna and the whole court knew what lay behind the German marriage. It was war, war with Byzantium. The time was right at last for William to give vent to his long-nursed grudge against the Greeks and he wanted a sure truce with the Roman Empire before he attacked them. The languorous days in Panorme were over, hawking was abandoned for practice at the quintain, and poetry readings were replaced by eager discussions of strategy.

In the autumn, Constance's betrothal to Henry of Hohenstaufen was formally announced at Augsburg and there were no longer any public objections in Panorme.

Soon after, William left for Messina, where the fleet was being assembled. Tancred had also gone. He was to have command of the fleet and his brother-in-law, Count Richard of Acerra, was joint leader of the army with Baldwin, a hairy boastful man of low birth who had risen to high rank by distinguishing himself in arms over many years. In William's absence, Chancellor Matthew continued to run things as efficiently as before.

"Admit, Matthew," Joanna said, "that the King made a wise move in betrothing the Lady Constance to Henry of Hohenstaufen."

Matthew pursed his lips and stared down the almost empty Hall. "If it were necessary to make war on Byzantium, then yes, it would be wise to have an alliance with the Germans first to cover our backs."

"Necessary ...? But Andronicus is a monster. No Christian King could stand by and allow such things to happen."

"I am not a soldier, my lady. I am a lawyer. I believe in parley before fighting."

"I don't believe anyone could parley with Andronicus."

"True." He nodded his head. "The time was right. And the King has long nursed a grudge against the Greeks, ever since the failure of his marriage to poor princess Maria, God rest her soul."

Joanna dropped her knife onto her plate with a clang. "His marriage? Maria? Do you mean that William was married before? I never heard of it."

Matthew shrugged. "It came to nothing, but I am surprised you never heard the story. Yes, he was to marry Emperor Manuel's daughter Maria. The Emperor first proposed it in 1167 when Maria would have brought the whole Empire as her dowry, but by the time it was settled, in 1171, Maria's brother Alexius had been born, so it was not such a brilliant match. Good enough, though. She was still the Emperor's daughter."

A better match than the youngest daughter of the King of England, Joanna thought. She watched Matthew spear a piece of meat with his knife and convey it to his mouth.

"The King went to meet her with his brother Henry," he said, chewing. "Archbishop Walter and I went with them. To Taranto." He swallowed neatly. "She never came. No explanations, no apologies. We waited and waited but she never came. The King was furious at the insult and to make it worse, his brother Henry came down with a fever and died. The King took it very hard. Henry was the last of his three brothers and they had been very close. He has always held Byzantium responsible for his brother's death."

Joanna felt a sudden rush of pity for the young William, hurt so many times, a witness to his brother Roger's painful death and then his younger brother Henry. No wonder he had withdrawn into himself and suppressed his feelings.

In June, William sailed back from Messina to Panorme. Joanna went down to the harbor to meet his ship. She had not seen him since the previous autumn and was surprised by the degree of pleasure she felt on seeing him again. She watched with pride as he came swiftly across the gangplank, lifting a hand in acknowledgment of the cheers from the small crowd of townspeople who had gathered. A hot wind blew his tunic back against his legs and lifted the fair hair beneath his embroidered hat. She wanted to run and embrace him but she stood and waited. He came across to her and took her hands and kissed her lightly on the forehead.

"Well, they're off," he said, without preamble. "Eighty thousand men, the largest fleet we've ever mustered. And a division of mounted archers. How have you been? You look well."

She opened her mouth to speak but without waiting for her answer, he turned to Matthew.

"They sailed a week ago. The ports can all be opened again now to outgoing traffic. By this time, they will be near Durazzo and it's too late for anyone to get a warning to the Greeks."

Matthew glanced about him. "My lord King," he began.

"No, no, it's no secret any longer. It doesn't matter who knows it now. Durazzo. And after that, the Via Equatia, all the way across to Constantinople!"

He turned back, smiling, to Joanna and took her arm. "How have you been? You look well."

"Where is Durazzo, my lord?" she asked, trying to share his excitement.

"Durazzo? It's the Byzantine Empire's main port on the Adriatic. The Via Equatia starts there. The Imperial road, you know. That *my* army will be marching along before long!"

William was right. Durazzo surrendered without a struggle. By the beginning of August, the army had marched across Greece and was encamped before the walls of Thessalonica. On August 24, the Sicilian troops entered Thessalonica. William was not in Panorme to hear the news; he had gone to escort Constance with all her retinue, and five hundred packhorses and mules laden with her dowry, to Salerno. By the time William returned to Panorme, the vanguard of the army was less than two hundred miles from Constantinople itself and the fleet was in the Marmara waiting to join up with them. The forces Andronicus had sent to block the Sicilian army's advance had retreated to the hills and watched helplessly.

It was September. William danced with Joanna while the courtiers stood around the Great Hall and clapped their hands to the measure. Outside the windows, the leaves on the poplars were beginning to turn red and gold and every day the swallows gathered in ever larger numbers.

At the doorway a knot of men conferred with a travel-stained messenger. William and Joanna went hand in hand to the dais and sat down, flushed and smiling. The messenger was brought forward. His face was somber. He knelt, keeping his eyes on the King, and twisted his cap nervously in his hands. The music stopped and gradually, around the Hall, the talk ceased and the courtiers stood in a silent ring. William was no longer smiling. He stared at the messenger.

"What news, man?" he said at last.

The messenger licked his lips. "My lord King," he hesitated.

"Go on. Speak your message."

"My lord, Andronicus has been murdered."

There was an exclamation from the assembly. The messenger looked around him and went on quickly. "The Emperor's cousin Isaac Angelus has been proclaimed Emperor."

William sat very still. "And?" he said.

The messenger swallowed. "Emperor Isaac put his ablest general, Branas, in command of all the armies. Sire, he took our men by surprise and routed them."

All eyes were on William as he sat tightlipped and still. To the men below the dais, his face revealed no emotion, but Joanna, seated beside him, knew the effort it cost him. She remembered her father's rages and watched him, aching for him.

"What of the army now?" he asked.

"Sire, Baldwin agreed to discuss peace, but the Greeks attacked him without warning. The army ... the army was cut to pieces, Sire. There are many prisoners. Baldwin himself is taken prisoner, and Count Richard of Acerra. Some were drowned trying to cross the Stymon, which was in full spate after the rains; the rest fled."

"Fled?" William's voice was tight. "Where to? Where is the fleet?"

"The fleet was still lying off Constantinople, the last we heard."

"So if the men manage to reach the coast, there will be no ships to take them off?"

There was a very long silence. At last, William said, "God's will be done." He rose and withdrew into his own apartments.

Day by day the magnitude of the disaster was revealed. The men who managed to get back to Thessalonica found no ships to take them back to Sicily and the Thessalonians took their revenge for the atrocities the Sicilians had inflicted on them when their city was taken. Of William's enormous army, the greatest he or any Sicilian king had ever mustered, only a small number of stragglers found their way back.

The only redeeming aspect was that the fleet, which had waited for seventeen days in the Marmara, had returned intact. Tancred, who had command of it, was received with acclamations when he returned to Panorme. Joanna heard them shouting for him in the streets outside the palace.

Neither in public nor in private would William discuss his army's defeat. It seemed as though he had put it behind him, and all that winter he flung himself determinedly into a round of pleasures. More than ever, Joanna prayed for a son. A son would give William back the confidence in himself that she knew he had lost, but the months went by and there was no sign of one.

In the spring William sent the fleet against Cyprus, where Isaac Comnenus, another member of the Imperial family, had seized the throne and declared himself Emperor of Cyprus. This time the fleet was under Margaritus of Brindisi. In Jerusalem the situation was so bad that the Patriarch Heraclius himself had gone to England to appeal to King Henry to come to their help.

"King Henry should go," William said decisively. He spat some grape seeds out on the ground.

It was a Sunday and they were sitting in the garden. The sound of church bells came from the city and, closer at hand, the twittering of birds busy building their nests. Joanna put her head back to feel the spring sun on her face. The air smelled fresh and clean.

"It is his Christian duty, of course," Count Roger assented. He stood, leaning against a marble urn on a pedestal. "I don't see how he can hesitate. As premier Christian King of Europe ..."

"I doubt that King Philip would like to hear you say that. He is King Henry's overlord." That was Matthew, standing to one side, self-contained and neat, but gaudily dressed as usual.

Count Roger shrugged. "In theory, of course. But in practical military terms, King Henry is the one with experience, men, and money. King Philip is only a boy. Of course the Patriarch went to England."

"I thought that was primarily because of King Henry's family ties to Jerusalem." Joanna had closed her eyes. She opened them now and brought her head down to look at Sibylla, who had just spoken. Sibylla, Tancred's wife, rarely spoke. She was a small, mousy woman, devoted to her sons and generally unobtrusive. She blushed now to find that everyone was looking at her and added determinedly, "The boy King Baldwin *was* King Henry's cousin, after all. That must count for something."

"True, true," Matthew said, nodding his head. "Their mutual grandfather Fulk of Anjou ..."

"What does it matter who their grandfather was?" Count Roger interrupted. "It's obvious to anyone that Guy de Lusignan is incapable of holding off the infidels and who better to go to his help than King Henry?"

Joanna had been only half-listening to their talk, but now she sat forward. "Is it the same Guy de Lusignan?" she asked. "I mean, is he from Poitou? That Lusignan family?"

"Yes. And now he is King of Jerusalem."

"He tried to kidnap my mother once and hold her to ransom. I was a child. I remember it well."

There was a moment's polite silence before the discussion came back to the present situation in Jerusalem.

William said quietly to her, "You're not very interested in this, are you?"

"Not very. To tell you the truth, I have trouble remembering who rules the three Frankish kingdoms there. Levantine politics are hard to follow."

"You're more interested in the West. What news from Adèle? I saw you had a letter from her."

"Marguerite is to marry King Bela of Hungary." Joanna laughed. "I can't imagine Marguerite in such a semi-civilized country."

"On the contrary," William assured her, "King Bela's court is considered one of the most brilliant in Christendom."

"But he only converted to the Church in the last decade. And Marguerite is so punctilious. She will not even have the consolation of seeing her son King, if she has one, as King Bela already has a family by his first wife."

"What of your own family?"

"Geoffrey is still living in the Cité palace with King Philip." She did not add that Geoffrey's wife Constance was pregnant again; it was a subject she was sensitive about. "Richard has Aquitaine under control ..."

The others were listening to her. "Now there's a leader, by God," Count Roger said. "If King Henry will not go himself, perhaps he will send his son. Richard is the one to go."

ଦ୍ଧ ✿ ୫୦

In September she was at Mimnermo. It was hot still, though autumn would be beginning in northern France, a hot windless dry day. Her hair crackled when she touched it and the distant lake shimmered in the haze. A messenger brought another letter from Adèle.

"Read it to me," Joanna said lazily, "I am too tired."

She shifted a little in the chair they had set for her in the shade. Behind her, two black slaves, who had momentarily stopped fanning her, began waving their wide peacock feather fans again. In front of her, the fountains splashed endlessly in their marble basins, the only moving thing in the still, sunbaked gardens.

"To Joanna, Queen of Sicily, Adèle, Baroness of Bec, sends greetings. It is with the greatest sorrow, my dearest Joanna, that I write to tell you of the death of your brother."

Joanna sat up with a gasp. Richard was dead! She could imagine how arrogantly he led his men, riding out before them, scorning to stay in safety, confident in his own strength and expertise. And now she was to hear of his death in some siege or skirmish. Her throat was constricted and her breathing fluttered.

"Geoffrey Count of Brittany died last week in Paris, on August 19, in a tournament. I write this from Paris where I have just seen him laid to rest in Notre Dame. I was not at the tournament but those who were there say that he was thrown to the ground where he was trampled on by the horses and died shortly afterward of his injuries. His widow Constance, who is with child, was not able to attend his requiem mass, being in Brittany, but the whole French court was present and he is obviously much mourned here. King Philip was so much moved that he tried to throw himself into the tomb with him and had to be forcibly restrained. The Countess Marie of Champagne, your half-sister, was there, too, the only member of your family to attend, as Lord John is in England with the King and Duke Richard is in Aquitaine. She has established a mass for the repose of his soul. It has been a great shock to everyone and will be to you, too, I know. In Normandy everyone is concerned about what will happen to Brittany, left in the rule of Countess Constance. If her child is a boy, he will become Count, of course, but someone will have to rule for him."

Joanna's first thought was relief that it was not Richard. She had never been close to Geoffrey and could not now remember him clearly. She was grieved, though, for Constance, left with one young child and another on the way, and for her parents, who had now lost three of their five sons.

Constance's child was born at Easter the next year. It was a son and she named him Arthur. Adèle, in her letter, said that Queen Eleanor was angered by this choice of name and she and Constance were on very bad terms. There were rumors that King Henry was talking of marrying Alice, still held in Winchester, to his son John and making him his heir.

ଔ ✿ ๛

It was the year 1187, a year which everyone was to remember for a lifetime. The conflicts of King Henry of England and King Philip of France, of the Emperor and the Pope, of William and the Emperor of Cyprus, were suddenly ended. King Henry and King Philip were meeting under the elm at Gisors to discuss their grievances when the Archbishop of Tyre brought them the news, which caused the two rival Kings to sink their differences in the Truce of God, with the kiss of peace. Pope Urban had the Bull of Excommunication for Emperor Frederick lying on his table ready for signature when a Genoese mission brought him the news. And in Sicily, William and Joanna had been out hawking on a clear autumn day.

Years afterward, people would ask each other, "What were you doing when you heard the news?" and everyone remembered. William and Joanna had not even returned to the palace. They had taken the birds back to the mews and were walking along one of the crunching gravel paths. William was in a good mood, slapping his heavy leather hawking glove in his hand and turning to talk and laugh with the courtiers following them. It was late October and the gardeners were burning dead leaves in a bonfire somewhere nearby. Always afterward the smell of burning leaves would bring this moment back to Joanna. The news was so urgent that the messenger had not waited in the palace. He came to meet them and flung himself at their feet.

"Sire, Sire, Jerusalem is fallen!"

CHAPTER THIRTY

William stood like a statue, his glove held before him in both hands, one foot slightly forward, staring down at the kneeling messenger.

"Jerusalem ..." he said at last, on a long exhaled breath.

Behind them, the courtiers shuffled silently forward and spread out into a semi-circle, peering over each other's shoulders.

"My lord, Saladin has taken it. Balian has surrendered. The Saracen army is in the Holy City, the citizens have been massacred and the Cross, Sire, the True Cross is in the hands of the infidels."

William bowed his head. He had not wept at Queen Margaret's burial nor when his army was defeated in Greece, but he wept now. Joanna saw the tears spill from his eyes and trickle down his cheeks. Stiffly, like an old man, he knelt on the gravel path and they all knelt with him. The gravel pricked her knees through the thin stuff of her gown. She could hear sobs and groans from the group behind them.

William cleared his throat. "Let us all pray for the Holy City, that all Christians will come to her rescue, that she may not remain long in the hands of infidels."

A murmur arose immediately, some praying in French, saying whatever came to them, and others in Latin, turning to the familiar words for support. *"Miserere nobis, Deus"*, she heard and *"De profundis"* and "Merciful God, let me live long enough to fight Your enemies and free Your Holy City." Beside her, William held his glove clasped to his heart as though he were swearing an oath. He was murmuring in Latin. Joanna, overwhelmed, could not think of a prayer to utter. They remained on their knees until William rose again.

"We will go inside," he said.

They walked in silence. The smell of burning leaves was heavy on the air and Joanna could see a plume of blue smoke off to her left, rising above a wall. Somehow, the rumor of important news had spread. The Great Hall was lined with servants, crowding silent and tense along the walls.

William took his seat on the dais and Joanna sat beside him. In the body of the Hall, the courtiers stood, still holding their hats and gloves and whips. In silence they all listened to the messenger. The last news they had heard from the Holy Land had been of King Guy's defeat beneath the little double-summited hill called the Horns of Hattin. There, in July, Saladin had surrounded the heat-dazed, thirsty, exhausted army and had taken King Guy prisoner. Now they heard the rest of the terrible tale. Tiberias had fallen the day after the battle of Hattin and, after that, Acre. The other Christian citadels had been taken one by one, in quick succession, Nablus, Jaffa, Sidon, Beirut, and Ascalon. The last, Gaza, had surrendered without a struggle. The Holy City had held out under siege for twelve days under the leadership of Balian of Ibelin, but on Friday, October 2 the walls had been breached by Saracen sappers and Balian had surrendered.

William listened to the account without interrupting. He gave only one order, to recall the fleet from Cyprus, then he withdrew to his apartments. No one except his personal servants saw him for four days. Joanna heard that he had dressed himself in sackcloth and was fasting and praying.

He emerged for the special Mass held in the Palatine Chapel. He looked pale and drawn, all his jewels laid by, his forehead daubed with ashes like everyone else there and the rough sackcloth hanging on his slender frame. After that, he reverted to his normal dress and set himself to writing letters to all the Kings of Christendom.

There was no doubt it would be another Crusade. William spoke of nothing else. He planned to devote all his considerable resources to the cause and to go himself to deliver Jerusalem and he urged his fellow monarchs to do the same, encouraging them to take the sea route and break their journey in Sicily.

"What a sight that will be!" he said enthusiastically. "They will all come. How could they not? Your father, Joanna, and Philip Augustus of France and Emperor Frederick and all the lesser kings, their ships filling all the harbors of Sicily, such a fleet as the world has never seen! And I shall sail with them, from here to the Holy Land!"

"Oh, if only I could go, too!" Joanna cried. "I wish I were a man! To see the Holy City and free it from the Saracens—I would give anything to be able to do that!"

Envoys came and went every day. Pope Urban had died on October 20 of a broken heart, from the shock of hearing the news. The new Pope, Gregory, was calling on all Christendom to take the Cross, and everywhere men were coming forward in response. King Henry and King Philip exchanged the kiss of peace, and Philip and Richard, and even King Henry himself, took the Cross on their shoulders. King Henry would not go to Jerusalem himself but he promised to back the Crusade with all his resources. Archbishop Baldwin of Canterbury issued a writ of automatic excommunication against anyone who broke the peace of God in the next seven years.

In the Hall at Panorme, there was little talk of anything else these days.

"Margaritus has done well, my lord King," Matthew said. "It was an excellent move of yours to send him so fast."

"And the *only* move anyone has made so far," Count Roger grumbled.

William had had the fleet refitted and sent to Palestine under the command of Margaritus.

"Yes," he said now with satisfaction, "I am very pleased with him. He has forestalled the Saracens at several ports."

"Margab and Latakia and Tyre," Matthew said, "and now his arrival off Tripoli has made Saladin raise his siege of the great Krak des Chevaliers."

"And God willing, next year we'll drive that heartless infidel dog out of the Holy Land altogether," Count Roger gloated.

"Not so heartless after all, it seems," Tancred said smoothly. "The first news was exaggerated. In fact, I would say Saladin behaved rather better than our fellow Christians a hundred years ago in Jerusalem."

"Do you dare defend that—that cursed ..." Count Roger shouted, turning red.

"He's right, though," William interposed. "Saladin has shown remarkable magnanimity. Every Christian in the city allowed to ransom himself, and of those who are too poor to do so, he has already liberated half, as well as all the old and widows and children. No bloodshed, no looting. I'm afraid we cannot say as much for the Franks, who murdered all the Moslems and burnt all the Jews alive in their synagogues. Saladin is a chivalrous opponent. But he is an infidel and the True Cross must be rescued from his hands."

Joanna watched him fondly. He had recovered his optimism and enthusiasm, and she was happy to see it. Also she was glad to have news regularly of her brother Richard, with whom William was corresponding, though she could have wished for more personal news. Richard wrote only of plans for the Crusade, choice of routes, numbers of men, and so on. He did not even write of his problems in Aquitaine. It was from other sources that Joanna and William learned of the war in France.

"God's ribs," William shouted, striding into her ante-chamber with a letter in his hand. "Your father has declared war on Philip! At a time like this!"

Joanna dropped her needlework in astonishment and stared at him. She had never seen him angry. He strode the length of the chamber and swung about.

"In the face of such a desperate challenge to Christendom as the fall of Jerusalem, there they are wrangling like boys over insults and castles and selfish demands!"

"But why, William? What of the Truce of God? How can they be at war?"

He came over and sat opposite her, thrusting his head toward her. There were lines on his neck and deeper lines where his brows were drawn together in a frown.

"Your brother Richard invaded Toulouse and took eighteen castles and the town of Cahors. He claims it was in reprisal for Toulousain attacks on merchants and pilgrims from Poitou who were passing through their county. Count Raymond of Toulouse appealed to Philip and Philip struck back by taking Chateauroux and other castles. Your father said this was a violation of the Truce of God so he declared war on Philip. And that's not all yet!"

He glared at her. "That was in July. Last month, it seems, they met under the elm at Gisors and one of your father's Welshmen thought the Franks were making fun of them, so he loosed an arrow at the Franks. *They* charged the English. The English took shelter in the castle of Gisors, so the Franks, deprived of their prey, fell on the elm tree and cut it down. King Henry was so angry about it that he renounced his allegiance to Philip and has been ravaging the countryside around Mantes. By the wrath of God! Here we are, planning the most important campaign of the century and they are quarrelling over a tree that one of them chopped down!"

He got up to go and added, as he left the room, "Your mother is confined in Salisbury again."

Joanna, remembering her father's fiery temper, understood it more easily than William did. But the conflicting reports that followed made her wonder if they were hearing everything right. First, Philip was retaliating against Richard's incursions into Toulouse and then, it seemed, they were the best of friends. Messengers reported that Richard was in Paris with Philip and they were so close that they ate from the same dish and slept in the same bed. In November they met with King Henry, this time at Bonmoulins, away from the stump at Gisors, and Philip as

325

usual demanded the return of the Vexin, which had been Marguerite's dowry, and the immediate marriage of his sister Alice to Richard. On top of this, Philip demanded that all the vassals of Normandy, Touraine, Maine, and Anjou should do homage to Richard as the heir of England. King Henry refused and Richard at once, kneeling before Philip, did homage to him for all the lands he claimed.

It was hard for Joanna at this distance to understand Richard's motives. She sat silent when William and others criticized him. She knew it was wrong for him to defy their father, but in her heart of hearts, she was on his side. Perhaps it was because of their mother. She believed that Richard had come to hate him because of that.

In Sicily, Christmas was celebrated with the usual splendor, but William was distracted and impatient. He was raising an army and planning to receive the crusading Kings, but while the conflict continued in France, everything was held up. In Paris, Philip and Richard held a joint Christmas court, and in Saumur, King Henry held a depressed and depleted court with only John, of all his family, with him.

In the spring, Philip and Richard invaded Maine and by June they were before the city of Le Mans.

"Not Le Mans!" Joanna exclaimed. "It's my father's native city, the one he loves the best, and his own father is buried there. Richard knows it!"

"My lady, Le Mans was set afire and King Henry was forced to flee," the messenger said.

Joanna was appalled. "My father lay sick of an old wound in Le Mans, you said. Did my brother deliberately set fire to the city?"

"No, my lady. It was King Henry's own seneschal. He set fire to the eastern suburbs to destroy cover for the besiegers, but the wind carried the flames along the city walls and the thatch roof caught on fire."

"He has never fled before," she said, "never in a whole lifetime of warfare."

The messenger looked at her. "They say, my lady, that when he looked back at Le Mans in flames, the King cursed heaven and swore to rob God of the thing He most prized in him, his soul!"

Joanna crossed herself. To blaspheme like that and at his age and in bad health too! She felt pity for him. He must have been bitterly hurt by Richard's defection and by the loss of Le Mans. She wondered again what kind of man her brother had become. They said he was hard and arrogant, but she could not forget the smiling boy who had taught her to ride.

The summer of 1189 was a hot one, more than usually so, or so it seemed to Joanna, but perhaps that was only because they had stayed in Panorme instead of going up into the hills. William, impatient to pursue his plans for the Crusade, wanted to be where he could hear the news from France as soon as possible. He had advised Joanna to go to the Parco or Mimnermo, but she was as anxious as he to know what was happening. It was, after all, her family, her father and brother, who were fighting.

She was lying down on her bed when the rider came. It was the hot time of the afternoon when even the crickets seemed to be silenced. In the town, it was siesta time. There was no sound in the streets but an occasional dog barking. She heard the rider come galloping down the dry dusty street to the palace and recognized the urgency in his pace. The shutters of her chamber were closed. One of her women was sprinkling rose water around the room and a clerk was reading to her from the lives of the saints. Joanna was not listening. She was waiting for the sound of footsteps outside her door and presently it came. The reader broke off and looked up.

Countess Sibylla knelt by Joanna's bed. "My lady Queen, the King desires your presence at once in the audience chamber."

Joanna swung her legs over the edge of the bed. She had been resting in her chemise; already two of her women were going to the wardrobe for her gown.

"Not that one, no." She stood up slowly. "It's something important, I know. Bring me the white one. Yes, yes, that. And my coronet, the one my lord King gave me at our marriage."

She was impatient to go down and hear the news but she made them dress her hair formally and bring her jewels. At the last moment, she crossed the room and knelt briefly at her prie-Dieu.

"Now I am ready," she said.

The door was held open for her and she went on out into the dark hallway, her white silk gown trailing on the cool marble floor. The guards on either side of the entrance to the audience chamber opened the doors for her. She saw their eyes flicker sideways for a moment to look at her and knew she had done well to dress royally. She held her head up and went into the chamber. Her women filed in behind her. William came to meet her, his hands outstretched to take hers. He looked grave.

"My dear, I have sad news for you."

His hands, grasping hers, felt damp with sweat. She noticed for the first time the little vertical lines between his brows and other fine lines at the corners of his eyes. He had always had such a boyish face that it was hard to remember he was no longer young. How old was he now, she wondered irrelevantly. His natal day was this month. Would he be 35 or 36?

"The King your father is dead."

She felt cool and dry and very controlled. "God rest his soul," she said, crossing herself.

"Amen to that." He released her hands to sign himself. "Come and sit. The messenger will tell us how it happened. Would you like some wine?"

"No, nothing, I thank you." She mounted the steps to the throne and sat down.

The room was not large and it was very crowded. They stood in serried ranks along the walls, courtiers, advisers, clerics and staff. Joanna saw none of them. She was looking at the messenger who knelt at the foot of the royal dais.

"My lord King, my lady," he began, raising his voice so that all could hear him, "the great King of the English is dead. The King who united the Angevin lands and the great Duchy of Aquitaine to the throne of England and of the Dukes of Normandy to form a kingdom stretching from the borders of the wild Scots to the foothills of the Pyrénées ..."

William raised his hand. "The oration comes later and not from you. Give us the facts. We heard that King Henry had fled Le Mans and that the city was burned. That was the last news we had. Where did he go? Did King Philip and Richard pursue him?"

"Sire," the messenger spoke in a more subdued voice, "King Henry lay that night at Fresnay, some ten miles from Le Mans, and from there he made his way to Chinon. The King was in poor health, suffering from an old sore that had been reopened by the ride from Le Mans, and distressed by the news that King Philip had taken Tours. King Philip summoned King Henry to meet him near Tours, but King Henry sent word that he was too ill to come. Duke Richard, it seems, advised King Philip that this was a ruse."

His eyes rose briefly to Joanna's face. Joanna wondered whether Richard had really believed that or whether he had not cared.

"When was this?" William asked.

"King Philip's soldiers took Tours on the Monday, Sire, the third of July. On Tuesday, he summoned King Henry to meet him. When King Henry arrived at the place, he looked so ill that even King Philip pitied him. He ordered a cloak to be folded and put on the ground so that King Henry might sit on it. King Henry refused. He remained on his horse as was his custom at a parley. It was not a conference but a laying-down of terms. After they read the terms to him, there was silence and then two loud claps of thunder. Everyone wondered what it presaged but now it is made clear. King Henry would have fallen from his horse but his men supported him. He accepted the terms and asked for a written list of all those men who had deserted him. They had to carry him back to Chinon in a litter."

William sucked at his teeth and the courtiers stirred and murmured. Memories of her father flitted through Joanna's mind. She saw him striding down the Great Hall at dinner, a tankard in one hand and a hunk of meat in the other, moving lightly and swiftly for such a heavy man, his red hair ruffled, his pale blue eyes keen, his mouth stretched in a loud laugh. She saw him on horseback, his gauntleted hand reaching out to pat his horse's neck, his cloak askew. It was hard for her to imagine this vigorous, impatient man grown old and tired, his rufous hair gone grey and his high-colored cheeks ashen with ill health, abdicating his power—for that was what it amounted to—and riding in a litter.

"He was taken to Chinon," the messenger went on, "where he confessed, was absolved, and received communion. The next day one of his men, one Roger Malchael, who had stayed behind for the list of deserters, brought it to him." He paused dramatically. "The first name written there was the name of the Lord John, the King's son."

"John!" Joanna exclaimed sharply.

They looked at her in surprise. She folded her lips in anger. John had always been a self-seeking little toad but her father had loved him and favored him. How could he have deserted their father on his deathbed? She calmed herself with an effort and asked, "Who remained with him?"

"William Marshal, my lady, and the King's son Geoffrey."

Faithful William Marshal! Joanna felt the back of her throat go tense. Of all his sons, only the bastard son Geoffrey had been faithful to him.

"King Henry would not hear the rest of the list. He said, 'Let the rest go as it will. I care no more for myself nor for anything in this world.' Then he turned his face to the wall. He was delirious, sometimes sleeping, for two days. The last thing anyone heard him say was, 'Shame, shame on a conquered King.' He gave his Plantagenet signet ring to Geoffrey, the Chancellor, who was with him at the end. He died on Thursday the sixth of July and his household kept his wake in Chinon that night."

"And he is buried in Chinon?" William asked.

"Sire, they have taken him to the abbey of nuns at Fontevrault. William Marshal rides with the body."

The tears rose suddenly in Joanna's eyes and she wept, clasping her hands in her lap and bowing her head. William reached over and laid a hand over hers.

"And Duke Richard? Where is he?"

"Sire, William Marshal sent word to King Richard, that his father was to be entombed in Fontevrault. I left before any news was heard of him."

Joanna's head jerked up. King Richard! She wiped her eyes with a lace handkerchief. In all the account of her father's death, she had quite forgotten one thing: Richard was King of England!

CHAPTER THIRTY-ONE

Not that I am saying anything against your father, God rest his soul, but I do feel that it is for the best. Richard is, no doubt of it, more ardent for the Crusade. I know your father promised to support it with money and men, but in the past he made such promises—to Heraclius, do you remember?—and nothing much ever came of it. Richard now will lead his men himself and *that* makes all the difference. Also, he is on friendly terms with Philip. At least, he was. Now that he is King of England, who knows? Still, at least there is no war to hold things up." William rolled over on his elbow and reached out for another grape, then drew his hand back. "No, I think I won't. I feel a trifle queasy today. Something I have eaten, perhaps."

"My lord, should you be out here if you are unwell?" Count Roger of Andria was instantly solicitous.

William waved a hand dismissively. "It's nothing. It will pass. Just an uneasy feeling in the belly. A day's fast will cure it. Or it's the heat perhaps. It's unusually hot for this time of year, isn't it?"

They had gone up to the Parco after a month's mourning for King Henry. William's preparations were as complete as they could be at this stage; now he had to wait for his fellow monarchs, and he decided to wait in the comforts of his summer palace. They had been here for two months; it was almost November and the leaves were changing color, but the past week had been as hot as summer again.

"There's going to be a storm," Joanna said, fanning herself. "Can't you feel it?"

"The Queen is right. We'll have rain before tomorrow." Count Tancred squinted up at the sky "Of course, the Queen is always right," he added, with the hint of a bow and a smile.

She had grown used to him now and could see him without hating him, but he still irritated her. She folded her lips and looked up through the jagged, layered branches at the sky. There were clouds to the north.

"Do you remember, my lord," she asked lazily, "when you first brought me here? It was the year of our marriage. We had a picnic here. Adèle and I cooled our feet in the lake, there where that dog is lying."

William looked across. One of the hounds had waded into the cool water and lay there, with his tongue out, panting. Mud rose in the water round him. He saw them looking at him and jumped to his feet expectantly and shook himself. A lady-in-waiting nearby shrieked as the muddy water spattered her gown.

"It was a bad day to choose," William said abruptly. He shook his head. "September 3. A bad day for his coronation. All my astrologers said so. Egyptian day."

So they were back to Richard.

"And then that story of blood flowing from King Henry's mouth and nose when Richard knelt at his bier. As though he were cursing his son from beyond the grave. A bad omen."

"If it is true, my lord," Tancred said.

"True? We heard it from two different messengers, didn't we?"

"Yes. But that doesn't prove it. And one of them said that King Richard showed no emotion at the sight while the other said he wept and denounced himself as the cause of his father's death. So what is one to believe?"

"Your mother must be an amazing woman," William said, changing the subject. "She is old and has been confined for years, but no sooner released than she's riding all over the country, convening assemblies, taking oaths of allegiance for Richard and even expelled a papal legate for setting foot in England without her warrant! And she must be almost seventy by now!"

"She was already at liberty when William Marshal came to release her," Joanna said proudly. "They did not dare hold her one day in captivity after they heard of my father's death."

"Is it true, Joanna, that Richard speaks no English?" William asked.

"Yes, it's true. He never expected to be King of England, you see."

"Yes. He will have much to learn." William was proud of the fact that he spoke all his subjects' languages, French, Italian, Greek, Arabic, and Hebrew. "Your mother is obviously trying to buy popularity for him by such measures as freeing all the prisoners. A doubtful move, I should think. It hardly redounds to his credit to have thieves and murderers singing his praises."

"Except the Lady Alice," Tancred said. They looked at him and he added, "She did not free the Lady Alice."

There was an awkward silence and one or two of them glanced at Joanna. Everyone knew why, when all the jailbirds in England had been released, only Alice was in confinement.

"She is perhaps merely in custody still," William said, smoothing over the awkwardness. "Richard will marry her when he returns from the Crusade. I'm delighted that he has abandoned the overland route to Palestine and will come by sea. It was what I advised in the first place, but King Henry wanted them to go overland and had already got their safe conducts from Hungary and Byzantium. And Richard is raising plenty of money, too, I hear."

"They are saying he said he would sell London itself if he could find a buyer," someone commented with a laugh.

William frowned. He did not like the idea of a king taking his obligations so lightly. "He should recognize an heir before he leaves. It should be his nephew Arthur of Brittany, who is next in line. But of course he is only an infant. He obviously doesn't mean it to be Geoffrey the Chancellor since he is trying to push him into the See of York, though I hear he is quite unsuited for it, but of course if he were Archbishop, then he couldn't be King."

"Anyway, he's a bastard," Roger said, with a sidelong look at Tancred.

"So was the Conqueror," Tancred countered swiftly.

"That leaves John," William went on.

"Oh, not John! I hope he won't name John," Joanna cried.

"And who is this fellow Longchamp that King Richard has made his Chancellor and chief Justiciar? I hear he's a little misshapen dwarf of a man!"

There was an awkward pause and no one looked at Tancred, who had recently been appointed Master Justiciar of Apulia.

William had not spoken for several minutes. Now he laid his hand on his stomach and grimaced. "I think I shall go back. I have a belly ache."

He walked slowly over to where the flat-bottomed boats were pulled up on the island's shore. The boatmen scrambled to their feet, stopping up their leather wine flasks and wiping their mouths with the backs of their hands. Joanna watched as they rowed away. It was the heat, she thought. They all felt listless and under the weather. A good night's rest would put him right.

The storm broke during the night. Joanna was woken by thunder and almost immediately the rain began, a heavy downpour that drummed steadily on the tiled roofs and flagged courtyards. In the distance the horses neighed in the stables and a rooster crowed. With the rain came a welcome cooling of the air. Joanna had been sleeping with the covers pushed back; now she pulled them over her and lay in the dark listening to the steady pounding of the rain.

It rained for two days. William kept to his apartment. Joanna sent enquiries and was told that the King's stomach was still paining him, but it was nothing serious. On the third day it cleared. There was no sun; the sky was overcast with pale grey clouds. Birds splashed noisily in the puddles standing in the courtyards and water dripped from the eaves and sills.

They left the same day, accompanied by the court, leaving the servants behind to pack their things and follow them. William rode in a curtained litter with his attendants around him and they made frequent stops. Joanna, riding sidesaddle, arrived at the palace an hour before him. By the next day, he was worse. When Joanna went to see him, she was shocked by his appearance. His face was pale with spots of high color on his cheekbones and great dark circles round his eyes. He looked thinner and lay like one exhausted.

"My lord," she murmured, sitting on the edge of the bed. "William ..." She took one of his hands. It felt hot and dry.

"The journey—it tired me somewhat. That is all," he said in a husky voice. "Water. Give me some water." He turned his head sideways and sipped from the cup one of his men held for him. "Jesus! My belly is on fire. Cursed sickness. I hope it doesn't last long. There is news from your brother Richard; he is in Normandy now and his ships are being laden already. His men will muster in Tours in the spring. Not long now and we shall be sailing for the Holy Land! Emperor Frederick has elected to go overland, you know. Well, that is his decision, but at least the English and the Franks and the Flemings will be coming here. Oh God, I have such a griping pain! Tell them to send Matthew to me, will you? What do you do today? Is it too hot for hawking?"

"It's not hot today, William."

"Isn't it? It seems so to me."

When she left the chamber, she signalled to Ahmed, the King's physician, to follow her. As soon as the door was closed and they stood in the ante-chamber, she turned to him.

"What is the matter with him? Is it serious?"

He surveyed her gravely. "It is the flux, Your Majesty. It is always serious. But the King is in his prime, he is strong and has always been a vigorous man. I have every hope he will pull through. He has a fever now. That is why he looks so ill, but that will burn itself out."

"Has he been bled?"

"Of course, my lady. We bled him last night and I administered a purge to clear his bowels of the poisons in them."

"Are there no medicines you can give him?"

"Useless, my lady. They would run right through him."

When Nurse heard this, she snorted in her usual way. "What that black Ahmed should do is send for the hangman to bring him the boiled-down fat of a dead felon. *That* does the trick almost every time. There's nothing like it. Or wrap a wolf's tooth in a bay leaf and put it under his pillow."

Joanna sighed. There was no convincing Nurse that Arab physicians knew anything compared to the tried and trusted methods of the Angevin countryside. They were a mealy-mouthed, soft-headed lot who would sooner put a poultice on an abscess than cut it out, and preferred to keep their patients happy with soothing syrups instead of giving them potions that would really do them good: with bats' blood and the powder of vipers' flesh and ground ivy and dung and boar's fat and burnt worms and moss from the skull of a hanged man, the latter to be collected at moonrise, of course.

"Ahmed is not black, Nounou," was all she said. "He's an Arab."

"Black, Saracen, what's the difference? They're all heathens. I wouldn't fancy having one of them come near me if I were sick and *that* I can tell you! And I don't know why a Christian King should surround himself with them."

"William says the Arab doctors are a hundred years ahead of the Christians, though the new school in Salerno is a good one."

"Why, I call that blasphemy!" Nurse exploded. "Do you think God wouldn't guide His own to do the right thing? You mark my words, if that Ahmed doesn't make him worse rather than better, with all that nonsense of doing nothing but put cold cloths on his brow and give him boiled water to drink. At the very least, he could give him ale, which is more strengthening."

It was useless to argue with Nurse. Joanna herself preferred the Arab physicians but she knew that among the Normans there were many who felt as Nurse did. In fact, when she next went to visit William, she found Count Roger criticizing Ahmed in the ante-chamber.

"Plenty of good red meat, that's what he needs, to strengthen him, and bread for bulk and no drinks," Count Roger was shouting. He habitually spoke as though he were leading an army to war or at least following the hounds. "Stands to reason his bowels are still loose when you keep giving him all these damned liquids."

"My lord Count," Ahmed said coolly, "the King is losing fluids and that is dangerous. He needs to maintain the level of fluids in his body. That is why he is thirsty all the time and why I give him liquids. He is receiving nourishment, not solid meat, I grant you, but good meaty broth and whites of egg whipped with barley water and herbs and honey."

They faced each other, Ahmed's dark face impassive beneath his turban, Count Roger glaring down his long Norman nose.

Joanna advanced on them. "Count Roger, my lord King has every confidence in Ahmed. If you criticize Ahmed, you criticize the King's judgment."

Count Roger bowed and fell back unwillingly.

She turned to Ahmed. "How is my lord today?"

"The fever is running high, my lady. He is delirious but I expect it to break tonight."

William lay slackly against the pillows. The rose water sprinkled round the room could not hide the foul odor. She hesitated on the threshold, wrinkling her nose, then went over to him. He looked at her with dulled eyes but did not seem to recognize her and presently he looked away. His mouth hung open and he moaned and moved his head restlessly. One of Ahmed's assistants wiped the sweat from his face. He mumbled something that Joanna could not hear. His hands plucked at the bedcovers and he breathed harshly.

Ahmed took his wrist and felt his pulse. "It is fast. If the fever does not abate, we will bleed him again today."

"He must be bled from the groin, since we are in Scorpio." William's astrologer, also an Arab, was there. "The King is a Gemini, in the house of Mercury, which is hot and moist. It is dangerous for him to continue long in a fever. It creates an imbalance in the humors."

Joanna looked from one dark face to the other and was frightened for the first time. Was it possible that William could die of this? A week ago, less than that, he had been hunting with her. He was only thirty-five, which was not young, to be sure, but not yet old either. An evil smell rose from the bed.

"He has soiled himself again," Ahmed commented. "My lady …?"

She left the room, dazed and anxious. The ante-chamber was crowded. Count Roger was there, with a crowd of other Norman barons, and Count Tancred, off to one side with Chancellor Matthew.

Tancred came to walk beside her. She was too anxious and distracted to feel her old dislike for him.

"You are worried, dear cousin. Is the King worse?"

"I am afraid he may die," she said abruptly, surprising herself.

He shot a quick look at her. As if by mutual consent, they walked in silence to the window overlooking the front of the palace. There was a crowd gathered below, waiting for news of William, no doubt. They stood and looked down at it.

"Should I send for Constance?" she asked at last.

Again that quick look. "Has the King asked you to send for her?"

"No. He is delirious."

"I see. No, I should not send for her yet. It would take her two months to get here and by then, God willing, the King will be his old self again." He studied her. "But if not, have you thought, dear cousin, what you would do?"

"Do?" She had not thought. She had never considered her future if she were widowed. "I would stay here, I suppose, until—unless—Constance would be Queen and she would treat me well."

"That's where you're wrong, dear cousin. Constance would not be Queen. Oh, in name, yes. But in reality, Henry would be King. Do you think the people will like having Henry of Hohenstaufen as their King?" He nodded out of the window at the crowd.

"No, they won't like it. Perhaps there will be riots, but Henry will know how to handle them. What choice have they, after all?"

"There are always choices." Tancred was at his smoothest and she always distrusted him in this vein. "Between you and me, dear cousin, there are those who would not hesitate to offer them a choice. If I mentioned Count Roger of Andria as one who would not be averse to taking William's place …"

"Count Roger?" She was horrified. "You think he would try to make himself King? But he swore an oath of fealty to Constance."

Tancred clicked his teeth. "Your naiveté is always charming, if I may say so, my dear. We have had our—difficult moments in the past, but I want you to know I am quite sincere when I say I have always admired you and you can always rely on me to help you."

Joanna did not answer. The crowd had caught sight of them standing together in the window and people were pointing them out excitedly to each other. They were shouting now, acclaiming her. She inclined her head automatically and raised a hand. Tancred was staring down into the street. He raised his hand too and his eyes gleamed with satisfaction as he turned to look at her. Startled, she heard the shouts properly. "Regina!" they were shouting, but over and above that, almost drowning it out, came the cries of "Tancred! Tancred! Tancred!"

"You!" she said, wondering. "They like you!"

"Yes." He drew himself to his full height, which was still less than hers. "I am an Hauteville. The only other Hauteville besides William."

CHAPTER THIRTY-TWO

For a moment Joanna regretted that she had not studied Sicilian politics more attentively. She had followed William's lead and for twelve long, peaceful, sunny years they had played while others had ordered and perhaps laid devious plans. Was it conceivable that Tancred harbored thoughts of power for himself? Tancred was smiling obsequiously again. She had refined too much on the crowd's acclamation of him. It could only be because he was the King's cousin and even if, unbelievably, he was popular on his own account, it would do him little good to have the common people on his side. For a successful coup, he would need leaders.

William's fever had lessened by the next day. He was in pain but calm and able to talk rationally to her. From the feeling of relief that swept over her at the sight of him, she realized how great her anxiety had been.

"Can you not give him something for the pain?" she asked Ahmed.

He spread his hands. "My lady, I have tried, but he will not let me. He says that if it is God's will for him to suffer, then it would be impious for him not to accept it."

"Well, it will not last long, I hope. He is on the mend now, isn't he?"

Ahmed hesitated. "My lady, I would be deceiving you if I did not say I think his condition very grave. He is passing blood and mucous now and his strength is very low."

"But what are you doing for him? Has he been bled today?"

"No, not today. It would only weaken him. Do you see how pale he is?"

She looked back from the door where they stood and she was afraid again. William looked shrunken and frail in the great bed.

"Is there nothing you can do?"

Ahmed shrugged and spread his hands again. "It is in Allah's hands now, my lady."

In the Palatine chapel, Joanna prayed and wept. She wept for William and for the wasted years in which they had never been really close despite the many shared nights, and for their childlessness, and for her uncertain future if he died. They were all the same grief, she saw. She had failed as a Queen and as a wife because of her barrenness. She wept again for little Bohemund, now seven years in the tomb. A son would have been a bond between them and a guarantee of her position here. Being a Queen in itself was nothing. She remembered her mother's words, "Sons are a woman's best weapons." She prayed urgently that it was not too late, that William would recover and they might yet have a son.

William was worse when she saw him again. He was sleeping or unconscious. She sat for two hours by his bed before his eyelids fluttered and he opened his eyes. She leaned over him and took his hand.

"William …"

She saw the pain come back onto his eyes. He bit his lip and sweat stood out on his pale face and his nostrils flared. He breathed gustily.

"William … Let Ahmed give you a draught of poppy syrup. You are in pain."

He answered her with an effort. "No, no, my dear. I am in great pain but by the will of the Lord Jesus there will soon be an end to this agony."

Her throat constricted and she said nothing, but gripped his hand more tightly. After a while, he seemed to relax. Ahmed himself wiped the sweat from his face.

"There! I am more comfortable now. It comes and goes in waves. Joanna, you must send for Constance. Do not delay. I shall not live until she comes, but Matthew will govern until then, Matthew is efficient and you can trust him to do what is best for the country. But there may be trouble. I know Constance's German marriage was not liked. So send for her without delay. Once they are here, she and Henry ..." He gave a long sigh and turned his head to the side. "Henry ..."

She knew what he was thinking and felt reproached for her failure to bear him a son. She bowed her head. William reached out his hand to cover hers.

"Joanna. It's not important now. All things are as God wills them and we must not repine. I could have wished for your sake ... But Constance and Henry will take care of you. You will have the dowry I settled on you when we married and the estates in Monte San Angelo. You can live there if you do not want to stay here."

There was a disturbance behind them. Joanna lifted her head and wiped her eyes with a kerchief. Mistily, she saw William's confessor, in a purple chasuble, coming into the chamber and through the open door behind him, clerics bringing the oil for extreme unction.

Away from William, Joanna could believe at times that he would recover, that in another week or two they would be laughing over all this as they rode to the mews. When she was with him, she knew he was dying. His skin had a strange, pale, greyish-green cast; his flesh seemed shrivelled on his bones, his slender form skeletal, his cheeks hollow, and his eyes staring from deep shadowed pits.

At his request, they carried him on a litter into the chapel and laid him on a couch facing the altar. He seemed barely conscious. Occasionally his eyelids lifted and he looked dully round him.

Ahmed held his wrist and a page stood by his head, fanning him. His astrologer was there, too, and the courtiers stood around in silent groups in the transepts. Candles flickered on the columns and on the high altar. They had brought a seat for Joanna and she sat near the altar steps, with her women clustered around her. The only sound was the soft murmuring of the litany for the dying. Without consciously listening to it, the Latin syllables infiltrated her mind through their constant repetition: O God the Father, have mercy upon the soul of your servant. O God the Son, have mercy upon the soul of your servant. O God the Holy Ghost, have mercy upon the soul of your servant.

When this sound suddenly broke off, Joanna looked up and then stumbled to her feet. Ahmed had laid William's hand on his breast and was closing his eyes. Archbishop Walter stood on the other side, his hand lifted in blessing. *"In manibus tuis ...* Into your hands, O merciful Savior, we commend the soul of your servant, William, now departed from the body. *Requiem aeternam dona ei, Domine, et lux perpetua luceat ei."*

It could not be true. Joanna stood frozen, staring at William's still form. They were looking at her, waiting for her. As if in a dream, she went forward, supported by her women. She felt as though she were standing apart, a small, cold spirit, watching herself bend and kiss William's forehead. Even as she knelt weeping beside his couch, this other Joanna had objectively registered that his skin was still warm, that the lines of his face had relaxed and he looked younger.

This sense of unreality, of being split into two persons, persisted for days. Part of her mind kept repeating to her the scene in the chapel: William was still alive, she sat waiting on the chancel steps, Ahmed had laid William's hand down and was signalling to her, she went forward, William's eyes were open and he was smiling at her, he had recovered ... Then she saw again Ahmed closing his eyes, the Archbishop lifting his hand in benediction and that still, pale face on the couch, and she wept again, painfully, hopelessly.

They buried him on the third day. It was the 21st of November, just a month past Joanna's 24th birthday. The coffin was sealed. Joanna guessed but did not ask the reason: his flesh was already becoming putrid from the workings of the disease in him.

Quarrels had broken out almost immediately. Joanna had been in seclusion for the three days before his funeral and was amazed to find she was following his bier to Archbishop Walter's new cathedral of Panorme, which was almost completed. William had said quite clearly that he wished to be buried in Montroyal, so she sent for the Archbishop. A message was brought back to her that he would see her at the cathedral when she arrived there. It brought home to her forcibly for the first time the reality of William's death. If she had ever had any power in Sicily, she had none now. She bit her lip and lifted her head and paced behind the coffin on its great hearse pulled by black horses. The streets were lined with the citizens of Panorme, dressed in black, weeping and calling out as they passed. She was surprised at the extent of their grief for a King who had done little enough for them. The Saracen women in particular were noticeable, dressed in sackcloth, with their hair undone and hanging down, wailing loudly.

Joanna's head was aching by the time she reached the cathedral, with the noise of the crowd's lamentations and the constant thumping of the tambourines that accompanied the procession. The Archbishop was at the altar. She saw that he did not mean to let her speak to him until after the funeral.

She sat enthroned, listening grimly to the oration delivered by the Archbishop of Reggio. He spoke of William's piety and his dedication to the Christian cause, of the grief that not only all his loyal subjects must feel at his loss, but also men all over Christendom, and especially those Franks of Outremer deprived of his support in their struggle against the Saracens. He praised the peace and tranquillity of the kingdom during William's reign, of the justice and harmony that had prevailed for a quarter of a century.

"In this land a man might lay down his head under the trees or under the open sky as safely as if he were home in his own bed; in this land the forests and rivers and the sunlit meadows were as hospitable as the walled cities; and the King's bounty was spread over all, ever-generous and inexhaustible."

William's body was laid in his sarcophagus. Archbishop Walter came down to speak to Joanna. He was an old man now, his hair white, his red face deeply lined. He moved slowly, his hands folded over his paunch, and was wheezing when he reached her.

"Allow me to offer you all the condolences ..."

She interrupted him brusquely. "My lord Archbishop, it was the King's desire to be buried in Montroyal, his own foundation. Surely you knew this?"

"Your Majesty, we thought it more fitting for the King to be buried here in his capital than ..."

"We? Who are we who decided this?"

He gestured vaguely. "His council. Myself. The Chancellor. The citizens of Panorme would not wish to see their King buried in a distant abbey where they could not pay their respects to him."

"You had no right, and you know it, to overturn the wishes of your King!"

She could rage as she liked but she knew there was nothing she could do. When Constance came ... She set all her hopes on that. She had sent for Constance when William told her to. It would take perhaps a month; she should be here by Christmas. After that, William's body would be removed to Montroyal and peace would be restored. The Archbishop of Montroyal, she knew, was openly quarrelling with Archbishop Walter over William's burial place. Nor was theirs the only quarrel: there were many who were bitterly opposed to Constance, knowing that this would mean ceding Sicily to her husband Henry. But William had made all his chief vassals swear fealty to Constance as his heir before she left to marry, so Joanna was not seriously concerned. Once Constance arrived, all these differences would be ended.

She was still hoping for Constance's arrival when messengers battered on the door of her chamber one day. The lady-in-waiting who had opened the door stood aside helplessly as they pushed past her. Joanna closed the book she was reading, the verses that Tancred had given her years before, and rose to her feet. She was still in deep mourning.

"What is the meaning of this intrusion?"

"My lady, we are sent to tell you that other apartments have been prepared for you. You are to move into them immediately."

"On whose orders?"

"Count Tancred's, my lady."

"Count Tancred?" She stared from one face to the other, aghast. "By what right?"

"My lady, Count Tancred is in command in the palace."

"And if I refuse?"

The men looked embarrassed. They glanced back at the door. She followed their glance and saw the armed men standing there.

"He would not dare! I am the Queen!"

"Those are our orders, my lady," the first man said stubbornly. "It will be easier for all of us …"

"I will not go!" she shouted in a sudden fury, flinging down the book she had been holding. "He has no right to order me. Tell Tancred to come *here* to speak to me in person and I will tell him what I think of his orders!"

She crossed the room and sat down with a thump on her tiring-chair and folded her arms. The men hesitated momentarily, then they came in and picked up her chair. She made to rise but subsided. It was clear that they would move her by force if necessary. Her face grim, she sat where she was and let them carry her.

Her new apartments gave onto an inner courtyard and she understood the move at once: she was to be allowed no chance to stir up the sympathy of the people for herself or Constance. Like her mother before her, she was a virtual prisoner. Tancred did not visit her. She was left with five of her women, including her Nurse, and the doors were guarded by armed men night and day. Her meals were brought to her in her apartments and any requests were promptly met. Even things she had not asked for were brought to her, cushions, wine, books. She realized that Tancred was doing his best to make her prison comfortable but for all that it was still a prison.

She had been there for a month when Tancred came to see her, shortly before Christmas. Not wishing to show him any sign of respect, she remained where she was, seated by the window. Tancred appeared unperturbed. He crossed the room, pulled up a chair for himself and sat down to face her.

"I have nothing to say to you, Tancred, unless you have come to tell me that this disgraceful and inexcusable confinement in which you are holding me is ended."

"I wish I could. Believe me, it distresses me as much as it does you to keep you here, but if you were to swear to renounce your support of Constance's claim to the throne ..."

"*Queen* Constance's *right* to the throne," she interrupted angrily. "You swore allegiance to her, too, Tancred."

"I know I did. That is precisely why I was going to say: that if you were to swear to renounce your support of Constance's claim, I still could not trust you enough to set you free while my position is not yet secure. Also, it is for your own protection. There has been fighting this past month, as you may know."

"In the streets. Hardly an excuse for keeping me shut up here. I think you must be mad, Tancred. When Henry and Constance come, you are a dead man."

"If Henry comes. Meanwhile Henry has other fish to fry. By the time Henry comes, I shall be King, Joanna, and I shall have the whole of Sicily behind me to resist him. No, at present, it is not Henry, but Roger of Andria who is my rival, but I have the edge over him." This was no longer the obsequious Tancred she had known and she noticed she was Joanna now, not his dear cousin. Tancred's little eyes gleamed beneath his thick brows and his chin jutted out.

"You are a fool if you think you can make yourself King, an upstart little bastard like you."

"Bastard I may be, but not a fool. It was my precious true-born cousin William who was the fool. He should have known the people of Sicily would never accept Henry of Hohenstaufen as their King. But then he knew nothing of the people. All he was interested in was his harem and his game parks. You know it as well as I. I care nothing for either, but I do care for the kingdom, its people and its laws. I shall be King. He never ruled this kingdom; it was Matthew who ruled it and Matthew is on my side."

"Matthew?"

"Yes. Does that surprise you? He is a true Sicilian patriot and will never hand Sicily tamely over to the German barbarians. The people are for me and I have the army behind me and what's more, Pope Clement. Matthew handled *him* for me, but of course the Pope doesn't want to see Sicily and Germany united on either side of him."

Joanna stared at him, fascinated and horrified. It was almost inconceivable that this ugly, treacherous, little man could make himself King, but it seemed it was possible.

"And Count Roger?" she asked.

"Roger has the nobles on his side, though he has not my claim to royal blood. But I think we have him now." He smiled wetly. "Matthew has discovered certain—irregularities, shall we say?—in Roger's private life and I think we can use this information to turn quite a few of his followers against him. So you see, it's almost a *fait accompli*. Now, if you will throw in your lot on my side and make a public stand against Henry and Constance ..."

"I won't do it! Is there no one for Constance?"

He shrugged. "Archbishop Walter. And a few others who think it better to let Henry come in peace rather than shed blood. But these cowards are few and the Archbishop is old. Most Sicilians will fight with me to keep the Germans out. If you will not be for me, will you at least agree not to be against me?"

"I promise you nothing. You are a usurper, a traitor, forsworn ..."

He interrupted her coolly, pushing his chair back and standing up. "I had hoped you might join us on Christmas Day. Now I see I should be unwise to allow it. I wish you as joyous a Christmas as may be, in the circumstances." He bowed ironically and left her.

Joanna spent Christmas in her apartments with her women. One afternoon in the first weeks of the New Year, they heard shouts from the city, which carried over the roofs of the palace to their inner windows. The noise went on for several hours and they could tell a crowd of some size had gathered in front of the palace. At first they thought it was another riot but they could hear bells and cheering.

When her supper was brought, Joanna went to the door herself.

349

"What news is there? What is all the cheering?" she asked, hoping against hope that Constance had come.

"Why, my lady, King Tancred was crowned today! Crowned by Archbishop Walter in the cathedral and the people are cheering for him and Queen Sibylla."

Behind her, she heard Nurse gasp. "What? That ape is crowned?"

CHAPTER THIRTY-THREE

Once Tancred was crowned, Joanna was given the freedom of the palace, though it was a limited freedom. Wherever she went, she was followed; she was allowed to walk outside only in the enclosed gardens; her letters were censored and she had no private talk with any of the messengers who came and went from the court.

Most of all, she missed being able to ride. She longed to spring onto Cigale's back, nudge her with her heels, and feel her lift forward, surging into that light, even gallop of hers. Tancred had told her that Cigale was being exercised but Cigale was hers and no one knew her as Joanna did. She hoped that whoever rode her had a light hand and would not ruin her sensitive mouth. Cigale was quick and needed only the lightest of touches.

Tancred was always courteous to her, but she treated him with as much contempt as she dared. Dining in the Hall again was a mixed blessing: it meant she had to see Tancred in the place of honor at the High Table and Sibylla taking the seat that used to be hers, and, more painful still, their son Roger beside them. Their other son, William, was still too young to eat in Hall.

In the spring, Archbishop Walter died and Tancred yielded to Joanna's requests to have William's body transferred to Montroyal. Encouraged by this and by the fact that Tancred was distracted by fighting in the city between Christians and Moslems, Joanna asked his leave to retire to her estates in the County of Monte San Angelo.

"Out of the question, Joanna. I'm sorry. Besides, you would not deprive us of the pleasure of your company here at court, would you?"

Tancred looked as though he took little enough pleasure in that or anything else these days. She knew that he had a full-scale insurrection to deal with in Panorme and that on the mainland, Roger of Andria was gathering forces against him.

"Monte San Angelo is mine. William left it to me. If I can retire there, I promise not to conspire against you."

"William, unfortunately, died intestate. Who knows what he meant to leave you?"

"It was in my marriage settlement," she said, stung. "You cannot deny it!"

"I don't deny it. But I can't let you go there, right on the frontier, with the Germans gathering to march into Apulia. Joanna, I can offer you something better than a life in retirement in Monte San Angelo. That would never be enough for one who has been Queen."

"I *am* Queen of Sicily," she said, lifting her head.

"Dowager Queen." His eyes were fixed on her. "How would you like to be Queen again?"

"Queen?" She held her breath, staring at him.

"Joanna, marry me and you will be Queen of Sicily. Your life here was a good one, wasn't it? You need never leave. I offer you position, wealth, the life of ease you are used to. I need you, Joanna. With you as my Queen, I could get the barons on my side as well as the people ..."

"And an alliance with the King of England! You are despicable, Tancred! Do you think I would ever help you strengthen your hold on the throne you have stolen from my husband's rightful heir? And if that were not all, even if you were the last man in the world, I would not marry you. You disgust me! You have always been a scheming, contriving, vile ..." She spluttered, raging, at a loss for words. "How *dare* you make me such an offer?"

"You Plantagenets are such a passionate breed. Well, I don't think the less of you for it. I like a woman with spirit. But can you not for a moment set aside your violent feelings and consider dispassionately the advantages of a match between us?"

"Then—dispassionately—I tell you, Tancred, that I am surprised at you. What of Sibylla? Oh, no doubt you have some idea of putting her away, and I'm sure you would do that if it suited you, but Sibylla's brother leads your army on the mainland. Do you think he would still be for you if you forced his sister into a convent? Or could it be that you are wicked enough to cause Sibylla to die a natural and opportune death? If so, I would denounce you publicly to everyone, even to the Pope himself!"

"My dear Joanna, you are hardly being dispassionate! No such thing. I am fond of Sibylla and she of me and I shall be sorry to see her enter a convent, but personal feelings must yield to political advantage. She is devoted to our sons, and for their sakes I am sure I can convince her that this is the best thing to do. Yes, I need her brother and am likely to need him more when the Germans invade, so he must see that Sibylla is willing. So what do you say?"

"Never! I would rather enter a convent myself! I would rather die! I will write to my brother Richard. He will know how to deal with you."

"You will not write to your brother. You will not write to anyone. I have been too generous with you. Dowager Queen or not, there is such a thing as treason. I am sorry for it, Joanna, but I shall have to order you confined again."

Joanna was back in her apartments, with the same view of the inner courtyard, the same guards at her door. She was allowed out only to go to the royal balcony of the chapel to watch the Mass.

The Germans invaded in May, coming down the Adriatic coast into Apulia, but Sibylla's brother, Count Richard of Acerra, prevented them from joining up with Count Roger's forces and the rebels of Campania. Joanna knew this and she knew too that, in July, at Vézelay in France, Richard's crusading army had met with Philip's, to start the journey south. Richard was embarking his troops at Marseilles and Philip, who was afraid of the sea, was marching overland through Italy.

It was a hot summer. Joanna fretted and paced in her apartments, finding her confinement intolerable. She thought often of her mother, who had endured sixteen years of captivity and her admiration for her grew. She resolved that she too would emerge from this with her spirit unbroken and her head high. But at times, listless and sweating in the still hot air of her chamber, she fell into a depression and feared that she would never emerge. Tancred was overcoming all his enemies. The Moslem insurrection, though still sputtering on in outlying areas, was virtually over. Henry had his hands full in Germany: his father, Emperor Frederick Barbarossa, had drowned in June in a little river on the plains of Anatolia on his way to the Holy Land and Henry was too occupied with securing his succession to the Empire to worry about the kingdom of Sicily. On the mainland, the German army had withdrawn to northern Italy and Count Richard of Acerra had taken Count Roger prisoner.

Joanna's only hope lay in her brother Richard. She had been prevented from contacting him before he left France and now he was on the sea, on his way to Messina. She was afraid that he would stop only to meet up with Philip and replenish his stores and then they would sail to the Holy Land, leaving her still held prisoner in Panorme.

Joanna paced up and down her ante-chamber. It was three days before Michaelmas, a golden beautiful day. She could see the blue sky from the window, above the tiled roof of the palace. As she watched, a seagull swooped down, coasting above the courtyard, and then lifted again toward the sea.

The door opened abruptly and a messenger came in, a young man she had not seen before. He looked round the room and came over to kneel before her. "My lady, you are summoned to Messina."

"To Messina?" A pulse beat suddenly in her throat.

"Yes, my lady. The King your brother is waiting for you there."

"My brother? I am to join him? And Tancred lets me go?"

"King Tancred himself sent me to you. You are at liberty to leave as soon as you wish."

"At liberty! Do you hear that, I am at liberty! All of us. We can go." Careless of its value, she threw the book she held high in the air above her head. It spun and fell half-open, its pages bent. Joanna whirled on her women. "Blanche, Agnes, Nounou, do you hear? We are free!"

She embraced them all, crying and laughing at the same time. "Pack my things at once. And bring some wine for this fellow here. Get up and come and sit by me. I want to hear everything you know about my brother. What is your name?"

"Richard, my lady."

"Richard? The same name as my brother! That is a good omen. Oh, I am so happy! When did he come? Is King Philip in Messina? How did he persuade Tancred—I *will* not call him King Tancred—to let me go? Have they met?"

"My lady ..." He spread his hands helplessly.

"Yes, well, drink some wine first. Take your time and then tell me everything from the beginning."

She watched as he sipped from the cup. He seemed a very ordinary young man, of medium height and build, with thick brown hair and a short gingery beard, but she had seen no one she liked as well all year.

He wiped his mouth on the back of his hand and set the cup down. "Thank you, my lady. I was in Messina. I saw them both arrive. Yes, King Philip is there, too. He arrived on—let me see," he counted on his fingers, "it was the fourteenth of this month. When we heard his ships had been sighted, everyone rushed to the port to see him. I should think every citizen of Messina, man and woman, was there, all eager to see the King of the Franks. The other ships stood off and just one came into the port. We were all craning to see but there were many men on deck and no way of telling which was the King, so although we cheered, we all felt disappointed. Still, we thought we'd get a good sight of him when he stepped ashore. But not even that—they disembarked privately, in a group. The crowd was held back and we could not see at that distance and he and his men left the port at once, so we never did see him. There was a lot of grumbling and people

355

wondered why he shrank from letting himself be seen."

"And King Richard?" she urged.

"Ah, my lady, *that* was another matter, I can tell you! *There* is a man made to be King, and no mistake! Well, we'd heard that King Philip was a lamb and King Richard a lion, but what we'd heard fell short of the truth. Everyone rushed down to the beach again to see him come in. It was nine days after King Philip landed, so that must have been the 23rd."

"Just three days ago?"

"That's right, my lady. We were all jostling and pushing to get a better view. Well, the first thing we saw was this great line of ships with colored sails coming in and the water all churned up with their oars. And we could hear trumpets and horns clear across the water. As they came closer, we could see the galleys all rowing in order, and the pennons on every masthead and the knights on deck with their banners on their spears and all the prows of the ships painted with coats of arms—it was a brave sight indeed! The crowd was wild, what with the noise of the trumpets that kept on all the while and the sea positively boiling with so many oars. There was one ship that stood out before the others and *he* stood on its prow, where we could all see him clearly."

"Richard ... Yes, that is like him. I remember."

"He seemed larger than any of the others on board. Perhaps it was just that he was standing up there on the prow. But he was magnificent! Dressed in scarlet and wearing a crown—the sun flashed on the gold—he stood there with his arm raised as the ship came in. We all shouted ourselves hoarse. They were saying around me, and I felt it myself, 'There is a man rightly made King!'"

Unconsciously, Joanna sat straighter. "I would give you gold, Richard, but I have none here with me. I will not forget you. So now the King my brother is lodged in Messina?"

"Thank you, my lady. No, I think there has been some quarrel over that. King Philip, you see, arriving first, took up residence in the royal palace in Messina and so King Richard was directed to take up quarters outside the city walls, and I gather he did not take kindly to that. This is hearsay, you understand, but we were told by some of those in his service that he was furious. And I don't know what passed between him and King Tancred, but I do know that I was sent off that same day with orders to give you your liberty as soon as possible."

In the excitement of being free to leave at last and about to see Richard again after so many years, Joanna quite forgot about her dowry. She was already on board the ship that had been prepared for her when the Treasurer brought her the sum of one million taris, by order of King Tancred. Her bed and its furnishings had also been loaded but when she asked about the revenues of the County of Monte San Angelo, to which she was entitled, the Treasurer knew nothing. He only knew that King Richard had written to King Tancred, saying that he would not leave Sicily until his sister was set free and demanding also the golden throne that was her traditional right as a Norman Queen. Whether she was to be given that, he did not know either.

Joanna, at that moment, did not care. It was enough to feel the sea air on her face and watch the gulls flapping and shrieking over the masthead and look back at the somber Pisan Tower of the Royal Palace, thrusting up from among the palm trees. She would have preferred to go overland, riding astride and galloping all the way, but both Richard and Tancred had ordered the sea route, fearing perhaps for her safety more than her comfort.

At the end of September, she sailed into Messina. Richard himself came out to sea to meet her. She saw the ship with his pennon flying from it and went forward to get a better look. Richard was standing on the forecastle. She could not see his features. All she could see was a tall man with a thick mane of hair that shone tawny-gold in the sunlight and she knew it was her brother. She clutched the wooden rail and stared at him as the gap between their ships narrowed.

Close up, she saw how he had changed and aged. He had been a young man of nineteen when she had left him at the port of Saint-Gilles to sail to Sicily, slender though muscular, with a skimpy beard and unlined face. The man she saw now was in his thirties, powerfully built with heavy shoulders and chest and long arms and legs. His full reddish beard merged into his golden hair, framing a face burnt a dark red-brown from years in the sun and there were deep lines around his eyes. He looked magnificent, she thought, just as the messenger had said.

The ships came alongside and grappled and a gangway was thrown across. Richard sprang onto it. For all his size, he was agile and he jumped lightly down onto the deck of her ship. The sailors, moving about the deck on bare feet as they took in the sails, watched him round-eyed. The women who were on board with her sank into curtseys and stayed there, their bright skirts fluttering around them in the sea breeze. She wondered if she should curtsey, too, but Richard had come swiftly over to her and they clasped arms, hands to elbows.

"Joanna! My dear!"

He bent and kissed her on both cheeks. She felt his warmth and strength and felt suddenly safe, as though morning had come at last after a long, dark, terrifying night.

"Richard! You don't know how glad I am to see you! You look magnificent."

He smiled, pleased, and released her. Her women rose to their feet again, whispering together, eyeing him.

"Let me look at you, Joanna. I don't think I'd have known you. Yes, perhaps I would. By your eyes, those green eyes. Well, well! We always thought Eleanor the pretty one, but you have grown into a beauty. You were just a skinny little slip of a thing, all hair and eyes. I used to call you squirrel, do you remember?"

"Of course I remember!" She laughed happily. It was so easy, as though they had never been apart. "And you were a lion. You look more like one than ever. I can see why they call you Lionheart."

He took her elbow. "Come and talk with me. We won't be landing for fifteen minutes. So much to talk about. You were always my favorite, you know. Matilda was too bossy—you knew Matilda died last year, did you?"

"Yes, I heard. I never really knew her."

"And that John is married? Did you get news of us far off here in this island of yours?"

"Of course I did. And Sicily is not far off, I'd have you know, it's the center of trade routes and learning."

358

He laughed easily. "Very well. I see you have become quite a Sicilian. I won't dispute with you. It is at least a rich kingdom and I have a bone to pick with Tancred. William promised Father a large legacy, part of it several more ships, fully provisioned, for the Crusade. As Father's heir, I am entitled to that legacy and I mean to get it."

"Tancred! God's teeth, Richard, I don't even want to think of him. I hate the man! You knew he was holding me prisoner in the palace?"

"I heard, yes. We wondered why we had heard nothing from you after William's death. Once I heard, even before I got here, I sent him a message from Salerno saying he should free you and give you your marriage settlement. Yes, I am angry with him, too. To think he would dare to use *my* sister so!"

"He wanted me to marry him. *That* you didn't know, I'm sure."

"Did he? Well, I can see his reasoning. It might even be a good solution. Queen of Sicily again? Hm. If he paid a good enough price, I might give my consent to that."

"Well, *I* would not give mine! He is despicable! He has no right to the throne, he is a bastard, he is an ugly little man ..."

He raised his hand. "Pax, pax! But Kings are not so easy to come by. We'd have to go far afield to find you another."

"I am in no hurry to marry again."

He looked at her curiously. "Why, what else can you do? It's either marriage or the convent for women."

Her fingers tightened on the rail. "Not true. I shall ..."

She thought swiftly. What could she do? "I shall go back to France. I can live with Mother. I shall visit my friend Adèle. And *you* seem to be in no hurry to marry either."

His face hardened. Momentarily she was afraid of him. "I shall marry," he said at last, "for the sake of an heir."

"You will marry Alice at last?"

"I didn't say that." He looked directly at her. "I shall never marry Alice, Joanna. That little whore." He spat over the rail into the sea.

"Where is she now?"

"Alice is in Rouen. Shall I tell you something, Joanna?" He smiled again and leaned toward her. "I have chosen my bride."

"You have?" She took her hands from the rail and the boat lurched, making her grab for it again. "Richard, tell me who. Come, you can't tell me that and then not tell me who she is."

"For your ears only. You will not spread this?"

"Cross my heart and hope to die," she said as they had said when they were children, and she signed herself.

"Very well. She is Berengaria of Navarre."

Joanna's mouth fell open, her eyes widened. "Berengaria? Navarre?"

"Her brother is a good friend. I saw her once at a tournament in Navarre."

"But Richard," she protested in amazement, "you could have any woman in the world! Why Navarre? Surely that's a tiny unimportant kingdom? Ah!" her face split into a delighted smile, "I see what it is! You fell in love with her, Richard! Why, that's beautiful—you saw her only once at a tournament and no other woman would do."

Richard looked disgusted. "Sweet Jesus, Joanna, what do you take me for? No, I did not fall in love with her."

"Then why?"

He shrugged. "I told you. Her brother Sancho's a friend of mine. He's a good man. We've fought in many tournaments together."

"Seriously, Richard. You can't be marrying her just because you like her brother."

"Can't I? Well, then, it's because she pleases me as well as another and, I judge, will not cause any trouble." He glanced sideways at her. "You heard about Henry and Marguerite?"

"Yes, I heard."

They stared in silence at the wharf now drawing close. Lines of men stood waiting to receive them and the beaches on either side were thick with crowds of people pressing to see the King of England and his sister the widowed Queen of Sicily.

"How is Mother?" she asked.

"Mother," he said warmly, "is well. An incredible woman, Joanna. I have never known another like her, with her dignity or her energy. And still beautiful, even at her age!"

Behind them, the trumpets blared suddenly and she jumped. Cheers went up from the crowd on the beach. Joanna saw someone stumble and fall at the water's edge. They were very close now. Beside her, Richard stood very straight, the slightest of smiles on his lips. The sun shone on the golden leopards on his chest. Smoothly, the ship came into the port. There were shouts behind them and the flapping of sails as the sailors furled them. The ship bumped once against the wharf, moved on, bumped again more gently and then slowed as hawsers tightened round the bollards. Behind the men lined up on the quayside, trumpeters sounded a fanfare and were answered by trumpets and horns from the ship.

Richard took Joanna by the hand and together they walked to the head of the gangway. The cheers and shouts of the crowd rose above the trumpets. Richard paused and lifted his free hand in a salute. The wild cheering shifted into a rhythmic chant. Joanna could hear the words clearly as the trumpets stopped.

"Coeur de Lion! Coeur de Lion!"

They stepped out onto the gangway hand in hand.

CHAPTER THIRTY-FOUR

My lady, my lady, the King of the Franks is coming!"

"Here?" Joanna asked, whirling round from the window. "Is he coming to see me?"

"I'm sure he is, my lady, and he's coming in state, with all his lords, his cousin the Bishop of Beauvais, and the Duke of Burgundy."

Joanna and her attendants were lodged in a hospice in Messina. It was a simple place but they had tried to make it fit for her by hanging the walls with rich tapestries and covering the bare wooden floors, in the Arabian style, with brightly patterned carpets. Her bed was set up in the largest chamber; her followers filled all the other chambers.

From the windows of the hospice parlor, she could see the walls of Messina, and beyond them, the tents of the English with Richard's flag flying above them, and beyond them again, the sea. It was the day after her arrival in Messina and she had been standing looking out at this.

"Quick!" Joanna ordered one of her women. "Fetch me my coronet from the chamber! And the emerald necklace. My hair," she said to those around her, "will my hair do? How do I look?"

Hastily, her women rearranged her hair and settled the coronet on it and fastened the emeralds round her neck. She was thankful that this day, in celebration of her first full day of liberty in Sicily all year, she had put on her favorite gown, of white silk embroidered in green and thread of gold. She stood in front of the window so that the sunlight streaming through it would turn her Arabian muslin veil to a halo of gold around her head, and pinched her cheeks to bring the color to them.

There was a murmur of men's voices at the door. Joanna's pulse beat faster with anticipation. She was curious to see the French King at last, and for a year she had been deprived of company and court ceremony.

They filed in, the taller ones ducking their heads under the parlor's low lintel, and all of them looking curiously at her. Their leather boots thumped on the wooden threshold and then sank silently into the carpets. Motes of sun-flecked dust danced in the shaft of light that fell around her shoulders and across the room. The small room seemed suddenly full of men, of their bulky presence, of their smell, compounded of horses and leather and perfume and sweat and ale. She was looking along the line of men for the King and to her dismay all she could think of was that a full year had passed since she had lain with a man. Her nostrils flared and she felt the hot blood rising to her cheeks. That one there now, richly dressed, standing arrogantly with his legs spread and his hands on his hips ... No, too old. Too old to be the King or too old for bed?

She tried to concentrate. Next to him was a greybeard; she passed over him quickly and went on to the next, a handsome, dark-haired man in his early thirties, dressed in blue and yellow. Her gaze flickered to the next man, hesitated and came back; there was something familiar about that face. She could not place him but knew she had seen him before. What had he looked like fourteen years ago? The blue eyes beneath the straight dark brows met hers and he smiled slightly. She felt sweat prickle on the back of her neck and her muscles tightened. Yes, of them all, she would choose him. But oh God, she was forgetting about the King. She looked further along the line, to where a man was stepping forward, a rather ugly young man with only one good eye. She would certainly not choose him. Jesu! Her color rose, she bowed her head and sank into a curtsey. She remembered now that Philip Augustus was blind in one eye. Had she stared at it? She hoped not.

"No, no, I pray you, rise. You are a Queen and my sister, are you not?" His French sounded formal and precious to her. With Richard she had gone back to the langue d'oc, a little rusty at first but sweet to her ears. With her women she spoke the Norman dialect.

She rose gracefully, aware of all the eyes on her, and shaped her mouth for the best langue d'oïl she could muster. "Sire, you do me too much honor. I am ashamed to receive you in this humble setting."

He raised an eyebrow, opening wide his milky, opaque blind eye. She tried not to shudder and looked at his good eye.

"It is I who should apologize to you for occupying the royal palace here while a Queen—and such a young and beautiful Queen—is lodged in a simple hospice. I am glad to meet you at last, my lady." He leaned forward and kissed her on both cheeks. His mouth was wet. "Will you do me the honor of letting me present my lords to you? My cousin the Lord Bishop of Beauvais ..."

One by one they stepped forward and bent to kiss her hand. She had herself well in control now and had a courteous word for each. With his face turned away from her so that she could not see his blind eye, Philip Augustus was not, after all, so very ugly. He had a thick unruly thatch of brown hair, a long narrow face, and lantern jaw. His one good eye was cold and shrewd and in profile his Adam's apple jutted from his thin neck.

"... Raymond de Saint-Gilles, heir to the Count of Toulouse," Philip said and the man with the dark hair and the disturbingly familiar face moved forward.

"We have met before, my lady, in France, with your brother the King," he said, looking up at her over her hand.

"Yes. I remember," she said, more shortly than she meant because her breathing had suddenly tightened and uncomfortable heat pricked her shoulders and ribs and groin. She hoped he could not feel how the palms of her hands were sweating.

"I asked a favor from you once at a tournament in Poitiers, wasn't it? You were a child and I did it at your brother's request. With a bad enough grace too, I am afraid." He smiled a slow smile that curved his lips and traveled up to touch the corners of his eyes. Then the smile was gone and his eyes narrowed infinitesimally. "I should not need to be asked to do it now. You would outshine any ladies anywhere. Not even a king could keep me from seeking your favor."

She stared at him, angry at his audacity, flattered by the compliment, and violently attracted to him. Philip had turned to her. His eye was cold.

"These Southerners can never let pass an opportunity for courtesy, even with their superiors. Their ways are easier than ours—but I was forgetting, you are partly a Southerner yourself, I suppose, like your brother Richard."

Raymond was the last. The French lords stood back by the door. Philip looked around him. Servants brought chairs for them and they sat by the window, their knees almost touching. The light spilled over her skirt and turned the thread of gold embroidery to liquid glinting rivulets meandering over her lap. Philip was dressed more simply than most of his lords, in brown and black. His face was pale except around the jaw line which was dark though closely shaven. Mother of God, why did he not wear an eye patch? She focused on his good eye.

"I feel I know you well already," Philip said. "Your brothers have all been good friends of mine. Henry used to come often to Paris and of course through him we are brother and sister, are we not? And soon to be linked by another marriage, I hope, when Richard makes up his mind to marry my sister Alice." He smiled but his gaze was shrewd.

She schooled herself to show nothing on her face. "Indeed, my lord, I have fond memories of the lady Alice. She was a friend to me in Poitiers and in Winchester, when I was a child." Alice came to her mind's eye, a pert pretty face with pouting lips and large eyes, smiling that sly smile of hers. With a sudden shock, she realized that Alice would be thirty in a few days.

"I was devoted to your brother Geoffrey, too. His death was a great loss to me, may God rest his soul." Philip crossed himself, not taking his steady gaze from her. "And of course Richard and I have long been friends and, I believed, close friends at times, though since he succeeded to your father he has not always used me as a friend should, let alone a vassal."

Joanna said nothing.

"Forgive me. I did not mean to come here to complain of your brother. Believe me, I would rather charm you than antagonize you." He smiled again. "Unfortunately, not being a Southerner, I am less practiced in the art of charming a beautiful lady. We have so much in common, you and I. Born the same year, though I must say," he added hastily, "that no one would think it. You have the freshness of a girl. With the elegance of a great lady." He thought a moment and added, "And the dignity of a Queen. A potent combination."

Joanna felt a sudden nervous desire to giggle at these lumbering compliments, but she murmured, "You are too gracious, my lord." Privately, she reflected that he was quite right: no one would take them for the same age. Philip looked much older.

"And both of us recently widowed," he went on. "Allow me to offer you my condolences on the loss of your husband King William. I greatly admired him and regret that I will not now ever meet him. His death is a loss to all of us, to the cause of the Crusade, to Christendom itself, but must be felt most deeply by yourself."

"Thank you, my lord. And I, too, am sorry for your bereavement, more recent than my own. It is especially sad as Queen Isabella was so young."

"It is not good to be alone," he said reflectively. "You, of course, dear lady—may I call you Joanna?—will not long be alone, I am sure. I do not speak even of your birth and rank and dowry, which would in themselves assure you of and entitle you to a splendid marriage, but you are still young and to crown it all, beautiful. Yes, indeed, you are worthy in all ways to be matched with the greatest Kings in Christendom." He smiled again.

Joanna stared at him, holding her breath. Thoughts raced through her head. There could be little doubt that Philip was considering offering for her in marriage. Queen of the Franks! She could be Queen of the Franks like her mother. Her newfound liberty and Richard's arrival had not made her forget the uncertainty of her future. Richard would soon leave for the Holy Land and she would be here in Sicily, widowed, landless, and at the mercy of a king she hated. To go to France as the betrothed bride of its King would certainly solve the problem and would realize, too, her childhood ambition. She could aim no higher. Niggling objections raised themselves. Philip was one-eyed and unattractive, he could not ride a horse, he was a cold-blooded schemer and her brother's rival, and almost certainly a graceless lover. But to be Queen of France! She suppressed her distaste and smiled back at him.

"My lord, flattery from so great a King as yourself ..."

"No, no," he interrupted her, "let us not stand on ceremony with each other. We do not yet know each other well, but I hope to know you much better. I shall be offended if you call me anything but Philip, in that charming accent of yours."

It was absurd. Philip could never hope to charm her with his person, only with his throne. He would do better, she thought, simply to go to Richard and say "I offer your sister rank and riches" instead of leering at her like this. She continued to play the game however and dropped her gaze coyly.

"Philip, then. I am so overwhelmed by your kindness to me that I hardly know how to express myself." She looked directly at him with her most alluring smile. "You, too, I suppose, will soon be looking to marry again. France needs a Queen and your little son needs a mother. How old is Louis now?"

There was some warmth in that cold grey eye at last. "Louis is three and the bravest little knight you can imagine."

He talked at some length about his son while Joanna encouraged him, smiling and asking questions and even expressing the hope that she would one day meet such a promising and endearing child, though even as she said it, she reviled herself for her hypocrisy.

At last he rose to go. He kissed her hand and then held it in both his. "Joanna, this meeting has been a greater pleasure than I anticipated even. We shall meet again soon, I trust."

The French lords followed him out. Joanna, watching them go, caught an enigmatic and slightly sardonic smile from Raymond de Saint-Gilles. She stared coldly back at him.

When they had gone, she ran to the window to watch them ride down the street. Her heart was beating fast. Queen of France! She knew that she could be Philip's Queen if she wanted. But did she want it? And if not, what should she do? She turned the options over in her mind. To remain in Sicily was impossible, to join her mother in England unattractive. Poitiers then? She no longer knew anyone there. She saw herself living out her life without rank, without a purpose, in a succession of empty days, the ex-Queen of Sicily, dependent on her brother's charity. She thought again of Philip, ugly, cold, one-eyed, and suddenly remembered William. She had not thought of him for days. His face rose before her, his beautiful impassive face, and his great dark liquid eyes turned to her. If only he had not died, she would not be faced with these frightening decisions. Could she put Philip in William's place, even for the throne of France?

She did not see Philip again. Two days later Richard came to tell her that he had occupied the town of Le Bagniare on the Calabrian coast and she was to settle there until he had dealt with Tancred.

"It's only temporary, but I want you out because I think there's trouble brewing here. These damned Greeks are stirring up fights with my men. There's been trouble over some of the local women, it seems. They know I am against it but some of these damn fools can't keep their hands off them. They will be punished for it but I won't have these goddamn arrogant Greeks attacking my men. I've a good mind to teach them a lesson for that and for lodging the King of England outside their walls."

Messengers came and went regularly between Le Bagniare and Messina. Joanna knew that Richard had seized the monastery of the Savior, on the promontory across the harbor from the town, had evicted the monks and moved his army into it. She was not surprised to hear of rioting a few days later. A crowd of Messinans gathered outside the monastery insulting and cursing

Richard and the English. Richard's men attacked them and within hours they had entered the city and Messina was in flames. The Sicilians fled and the English plundered the city and raised Richard's ensigns and standards above its walls. Richard was building a huge wooden castle on a hill outside the city, which he had named Mategrifon, Death to the Greeks. Joanna knew this was doubly insulting, as calling the local Greek shopkeepers griffons implied that they were rapacious thieves.

Not until later did Joanna learn from Richard himself of the negotiations he had undertaken with Tancred on her behalf. Tancred seemed to vacillate between Richard and Philip. He sent Philip handsome gifts but, as Richard said, had offered him not so much as an egg. Then he invited Richard on a pilgrimage to Mt. Etna and showed him confidential letters from Philip offering to help Tancred if he would refuse Richard's demands, and painting Richard as an oath-breaker who could not be trusted.

"But why would Tancred show you those letters?" Joanna asked.

It was Christmas. She had returned to Messina and they were in Mategrifon, Richard's new wooden castle. Richard was eating figs. He leaned back sideways in his chair with one leg slung over the arm of it and dropped the figs, one at a time, into his mouth.

"I thought it showed a fine openness on his part," he said.

"Tancred? Don't believe it, Richard. He is a schemer. Don't trust him."

"I'd trust him before Philip any day. No, you've let your feelings sway you, Joanna. Tancred is not so bad. In fact, I think he'll make a good King. Ugly little devil, of course, and I suppose, being a woman, that's all you thought of."

"All ...? Richard, he held me prisoner, he tried to force me to marry him, he ... the man is despicable."

"Quite reasonable, you know. He explained it all to me and was most apologetic. No, he will do. I have no desire to see Henry of Hohenstaufen on the throne of Sicily."

"So you signed a treaty with Tancred," she said bitterly. "And you didn't even get me the County of Monte San Angelo."

Richard spat a stem out on the floor. "Strategic position for him," he said through a mouthful of fruit. "I could understand that, speaking as one soldier to another. But he gives you another twenty thousand ounces of gold over and above the million taris, and twenty thousand to me, in place of the legacy which William promised Father. And I got you your furniture and plate, so you have nothing to complain about, that I can see."

"You recognized him! Constance is the rightful heir."

"Constance? You mean her husband Henry. You know there's no love lost between our family and the Germans. No, it's better this way. I've promised to support Tancred and we have agreed to betroth young Arthur and Tancred's daughter."

"Geoffrey's son? Is he your heir?"

"For the time being."

"How does Philip feel about all this?"

"Philip?" Richard shrugged. "I imagine he resents it, but what can he do?"

"Don't underrate him, Richard. I think he's shrewd and he could do you a lot of harm."

"Philip? I'd like to see him try. The man can't even sit a horse unless it's standing still."

"He's King of France and close to the Hohenstaufens."

"God's teeth, Joanna, are you trying to teach me my business? As for Philip, I don't care *this* for him!" and he tossed another fig into his mouth.

The great Christmas banquet of the year 1190 was held in Mategrifon. Philip had accepted Richard's invitation and so had many Sicilian nobles. Joanna was aware of the tensions. The Sicilians bowed stiffly to Richard and were overly formal and courteous. Philip looked sullen. She was glad to see he was wearing an eye patch this time. The Franks clustered together at one of the long tables down the left of the room and the Sicilians sat as far from the High Table as they could. Richard was using the twelve-foot golden table that he had wrested from Tancred, and the gold plate. It glittered in the light of innumerable wax candles. Down the center of the room the English were boisterously shouting and flinging pieces of bread at each other, half-drunk already.

At the High Table, Joanna sat between King Philip and his highest vassal, Count Philip of Flanders. On Philip's other side, at the center of the table, was Richard, resplendent in scarlet and ermine, with a gold coronet on his head. He appeared untroubled by the rancor he must have sensed in so many of those present, so Joanna decided to ignore it too and enjoy the first feast she had attended in well over a year.

The diners were applauding the pantomime that had just ended, representing the Crusaders' capture of Jerusalem in 1099. The actors bowed, hands on hearts, and then turned and saluted the descendants of the men they were portraying: Count Robert of Flanders, the French King's brother Count Hugh of Vermandois, Godfrey of Bouillon, Duke Robert of Normandy, and Count Raymond of Toulouse. Off to the left with the French, Joanna saw Raymond de Saint-Gilles acknowledge the latter with a smile and a tossed coin. The actors dragged away their elaborate set, which included a rigged ship and a turreted castle with scaling ladders. Behind the High Table, a choir accompanied by viols began to sing. The next course was brought in, peacock resplendent in its feathers, and rabbits, birds, and roasts. Joanna took a little venison in frumenty and a roast lark.

Count Philip was speaking to her. "... very cleverly done. And most appropriate. Let us hope that our success will be as ..."

She saw his eyes go beyond her and his voice trailed away. Behind her, King Philip was speaking angrily and rapidly. His voice was low but she could hear the tightness in it. She turned in her chair. Philip's back was to her. His attitude was rigid and the hand that lay on the table was clenched into a fist. Beyond him, Richard sat back in his chair, his eyes narrowed, listening warily.

"... you take every opportunity you can to belittle me. Those letters were a forgery, but of course you would not take *my* word. I believe you and Tancred were in collusion. You rejected my attempts to mediate between you. You raised your flags over Messina. By what right? Without consulting me and, no doubt, such is your arrogance, without consulting Tancred, though you have recognized him as King here. Pride goes before destruction, Richard, and a haughty spirit before a fall. And believe me, there are times when I should not be sorry to see your pride brought low. Because of your greed in getting your legacy from Tancred, we have all been forced to waste the winter here and use up our treasure. You assume direction of our councils though we have sworn to share and share alike, though if either of us were to lead, it should be I, your liege lord. I treated you as a brother, we shared bed and board and I took your side against your father, but you have shamefully repaid me for my friendship. The Vexin, which was Marguerite's dowry, has never been returned to me and it has been seven years now."

Philip's voice had risen to an alarming shrillness. Down the Hall, the clatter of knives and booming of voices was dying down and heads turned to the High Table. Richard sat very still, leaning forward now, his eyes fixed on Philip.

"You have never been trustworthy. All the same, you Plantagenets. Your father was just such another. He humiliated my father, his overlord, time and again. I tell you, I'll not stand for it, Richard. You attacked Toulouse, though it is in my vassalage, in contravention of your oath of fealty. But oaths mean nothing to you, do they?"

Joanna saw how he was trembling and she could smell his sweat. He had risen to his feet and spittle sprayed out from his mouth as he shouted at Richard.

"You are an oathbreaker, Richard! My sister Alice … No more prevarication. First your father, now you, with one excuse after another, but I'll accept no more! I insist you marry her. You swore to once, God knows how many years ago. Swear to it again before this company!"

Richard rose to face him. He stood half a head taller than Philip and dwarfed him with his bulk. His head jutted forward like a beast about to spring. The musicians had stopped playing and down the long tables, the company sat motionless, riveted on the dais. The only sound that broke the silence in the Hall was the crunching of a bone in a dog's jaws somewhere under a table. Off to the side, the panter stood frozen with his knife in one hand and the bread in the other, and the surveyor stood half turned away from the aumbry, where the flagons of wine were set out.

"No, I'll not swear it," Richard said quietly. "I'll rather swear that I will never marry her. And since you bring it up here, then by God, you shall hear the reason why and so shall all this company." His anger burst suddenly. In his battleground voice he bellowed, "I will not marry your sister because she is a whore! She was my father's whore for years. Everyone knew it. It was the talk of the court. And what's more, she had a child by him."

"A child?" Philip's voice sounded thin and breathless. "Where is the child? You have no proof."

"Dead. Who knows? That's not the point. The point is, this is the reason I have forborne to marry her and the reason you have now forced me to acknowledge publicly. If she had been another man's mistress all these years, I would still not marry her, but my own father ... Never, Philip!"

"And I tell you this, Richard, King of the English," Philip thrust his face close to Richard and fairly hissed the words, "if you put aside my sister Alice and marry another woman, I will be the enemy of you and yours as long as I live!"

He thrust back his chair and stood confronting Richard, breathing deeply, for a moment before he swung away. In silence, the company watched his lean figure striding down the length of the Hall. With a scraping of benches and the thump of tankards being set down on the table, the Franks picked up their knives and followed him.

Richard sat down heavily. He scowled before him, watching the last French knights file out of the room. Then he flicked his fingers to his cup and a little dry smile curled his lips. The cupbearer knelt before the table and filled his cup with wine.

"Well, sister," Richard said, still smiling, "I think that settles the question of Alice once and for all!"

Joanna realized she was holding her breath and let it out in a long sigh. "He will never forgive you."

"Underneath, I dare say not. But publicly he will have to. I only told him the truth, after all, and God knows it's a good enough reason to cry off the marriage."

"But publicly like that ... To humiliate him before his own men."

"Huh! Philip humiliates himself every time he mounts a horse before his men. Besides, he was in the wrong to bring it up when he was a guest at my board and on Our Lord's birthday, too." His brows drew together. "Do you take his side, Joanna?"

"Of course not," she said hastily. "You could not marry Alice now. But I was thinking of the Crusade, with its two leaders fighting between themselves. That is more important than Alice."

"Yes, by far. And that is why Philip will have to be reconciled. Besides, it is high time we settled the question of Alice. Mother is on her way here with Berengaria." He shot her a quizzical look. "You see how restrained I was! At least I did not tell Philip that!"

Joanna leaned toward him, excitedly. "Mother? She's coming here? When will she arrive? Where is she now? Oh Richard, it's been so long ... What is she like now?"

"My God, Joanna, which question do you want me to answer first? Yes, she's coming here. I told you so. She went to Navarre to fetch Berengaria and must have left there by now, but I don't know how far she's come."

"Across the Pyrénées and the Alps in winter? At her age? Jesus, Richard, Mother must be almost seventy."

His smile flashed. "And that answers your last question. What Mother is *not* like is an old woman of seventy, so don't expect it. Ten to one, she's riding horseback the whole way and won't use a litter. She has more energy than plenty of young knights I could name."

"So, if they arrive before Lent, you will marry Berengaria here?"

"Where else? With any luck, she will produce a son for me while I am away on the Crusade."

"You won't take her with you to Jerusalem?"

"Take her with me?" Richard was startled. "Of course not. Women are forbidden to accompany the Crusade." He laughed suddenly and raised his cup. "Well, Joanna, I'm sorry if I spoiled your hopes of becoming Queen of France. I don't think Philip is very well-disposed to our family any more!"

CHAPTER THIRTY-FIVE

oanna sat and stared at her mother. After two days in her company, she still could not keep her eyes off her. Queen Eleanor had aged, of course, but she still sat upright in her chair and her eyes were clear. There were fine lines set like little stitches round her mouth and a deeper line between her brows. Her cheekbones seemed more prominent and the skin below them soft and flaccid. Her eyes were set in deep shadowed hollows, giving her a tragic noble look that ill accorded with the briskness of her speech and manner. She wore a wimple that hid her hair and neck, and over the wimple, a light floating veil held in place by a gold circlet. It was her hands that betrayed her age, long slender hands with swollen veins and knuckles that bulged below her heavy rings.

"I dare say they were just thinking of their own comfort, but they swore the passes were snowed under, so there was little enough I could do," she said sharply. "Would you have had me toil up there to see for myself and then turn back if the scouts were right?"

"No, no, Mother, of course not. It's just unfortunate that you did not arrive sooner. I don't blame you." Richard set down the hanap he had been drinking from and slumped in his chair, his long legs thrust out before him.

"Yes, it is a pity, but there's no use regretting it now. The question is, what's to be done? I had hoped to see you married before I left. You were not always so nice about the Church's requirements."

"True, but I have taken the Cross and am under oath. No, I cannot marry until Lent is over and I want to sail. Philip will be in Acre before me and God only knows what kind of a mess he will make of things."

"You mean," said his mother with a wry smile, "you are afraid he may steal some of the glory before you arrive. Well, I can't say I blame you. And you are needed there. I can't imagine how Guy de Lusignan ever came to be King of Jerusalem. He tried to take me in an ambush once. Failed, of course. And now the softheaded fellow thinks he can besiege Acre. I suppose he's preferable to Conrad of Montferrat. At least he's a Poitevin. But that's not the point. We are discussing your marriage. You cannot marry during Lent and you will not wait here until after Lent, so what's to be done?"

"Can you not take her back to England with you?" Richard suggested. "Keep her there and I will marry her on my return."

"No, I cannot," his mother said tartly. "I didn't drag her all the way down here, across the Alps and the whole length of Italy as far as Sicily, for nothing. Besides, your life is not charmed, though you sometimes act as though it were. If you fall in the Crusade, I want you to leave a son behind you. You have a duty to your country to ensure the succession. *You* don't remember the civil war when your father fought Stephen for the throne. I don't want to see that happen again."

"Arthur is my heir."

"Arthur? Pooh! I'd rather see the throne go to John than to Constance and those power-hungry Bretons of hers and God knows John is a fool and a scoundrel, though he *is* my own son. Your father spoiled him, of course. No, I want to see you with a son before I die."

"Don't talk of dying, Mother. You have many years ahead of you, I hope."

"Many years ahead of me when I've almost had my threescore and ten? Don't talk rubbish. I don't want to die, not at all, but I hope I have the courage to look the facts in the face. You must take her with you on Crusade, Richard, and marry her when you can."

They looked at her, startled. Richard sat forward and leaned on the arm of his chair. In the corner of the room, the object of their conversation lifted her head and looked almost pleadingly at Queen Eleanor.

They had arrived two days earlier, sailing in from Brindisi where Richard had gone to meet them, on a bright sunny spring afternoon. Philip and the Franks had sailed out of Messina that very morning, unwilling to meet them. Joanna, waiting in the harbor, saw only her mother at first, standing tall in the forecastle with Richard. It was only after they had landed, after the embraces, the exclamations, the laughter and tears, that her mother turned and said, "Oh, and this is Berengaria, Joanna, Richard's bride."

Berengaria had been standing patiently to one side, waiting. She came forward then and dipped her head to Joanna. At first Joanna was startled, almost shocked. Richard could have had any woman in Christendom and he had chosen this one! She was no longer in her first youth nor did she have the assurance and bearing that might have compensated. Berengaria was small and dark haired. Her upper lip was wider than the lower one and jutted over it. The faint shadow of a moustache lay on it. She was neither beautiful nor ugly, but rather, plain and certainly unimposing. Her hair was parted in the center and drawn back sleekly on either side, an unbecoming style and one which revealed ears that stood out from her small head. She raised her eyes to Joanna and gave a little smile and suddenly Joanna saw a sweetness and a strength in her face. She looked timid and yielding but also intelligent and had understood Joanna's surprised hesitation. Embarrassed, Joanna moved swiftly forward to embrace her.

Joanna thought of that scene now, sitting in the chamber at Mategrifon. The windows were open and the bright spring sunshine streamed through them, making sharp shadows of the angles of chairs and tables. The room smelled of sun-warmed wood and polish and from the windows came the typical Sicilian smells of lemon and thyme and sea air. She could hear the sea, the gentle lapping of waves and the splash of oars and boats. The sound of hoofs and men's shouts came from the monastery of the Savior where Richard's army was quartered.

She smiled reassuringly at Berengaria, feeling guilty about her earlier neglect of her.

"Yes, Richard, why don't you take Berengaria with you?"

"I can't do that!" he protested. "I have made a ruling against women on this Crusade!"

"That's good enough for the others, of course, but you are the King," Queen Eleanor said. "You made the rule. Surely you can unmake it for yourself."

Richard stirred uneasily. "I don't like it. Women would be a distraction. She would have to have ladies-in-waiting and servants and baggage and where would she stay? She wouldn't want to sleep in a tent, you know."

"My dear Richard, I *do* know, at least as much about it as you do. You forget I went on a Crusade before *you* were even born and I see no reason why she should not sleep in a tent, if need be. Her people will take her furniture, of course. Anyway, I have to go back to England. I have brought her here to you and now she is your charge. My part of it is done."

She pursed her lips firmly and tapped her foot on the floor. "The sooner I get back to England, the better. John, you know, is trying to get all the power for himself that he can. You should have ordered him, like Geoffrey, to stay out of the kingdom while you are away. It's my belief that John will be more of a problem to you than Geoffrey would have been."

"God's body, what more can he want? I gave him six earldoms and eight castles, he has the estates in Cornwall and a royal revenue."

"Power! He wants power. Doesn't everyone? And William de Longchamp, that you made Bishop of Ely and Regent for you—did you know he has put his own family in every post he can and is signing writs with his own signet ring instead of the Great Seal?"

"I know, I know. I've sent Walter of Rouen back to England with authority to take whatever steps are necessary. And when you get there, you will bring them all under control. I have the greatest faith in you, Mother."

"Hm! I'll see the Pope on the way back and get his approval of Geoffrey to the See of York. I plan to leave tomorrow."

"So soon? You have only been here two days. You should rest after your long journey."

"Nonsense! There's no time for rest and I don't need it anyway. I only came to bring you Berengaria and it took longer than I intended. You will have to find a married woman of rank to accompany her, you know."

"I haven't yet agreed …"

The idea came to Joanna in a flash, whole and perfect. She leaned forward eagerly and caught Richard's arm.

"Richard! Take Berengaria with you and I will come as her chaperone! It's the perfect solution." She jumped to her feet and swirled about the room. "Oh, I've always wanted to see the Holy Land! To travel anywhere, in fact, but especially there. Jerusalem! I'd give anything to see it. And it solves everything, don't you see? I can't, and won't, stay in Sicily after you leave and I've nowhere to go in France and I *don't* want to go back to dreary rainy England with Mother. *Please*, Richard, say that we can come with you."

Richard hesitated. He turned to Berengaria. "Berengaria, you have said nothing all this time and this concerns you. What would you choose to do?"

Berengaria said quietly, "I will do whatever pleases you, my lord."

"*That's* not much help," Richard muttered but then Berengaria raised her dark eyes and looked at Joanna.

"But, if you would not object, my lord, I think the lady Joanna is right and I should be most glad to have her company on the voyage."

"You'd have to have a special ship, a transport ship," Richard mused. "I know you women will want to take enormous loads of baggage with you. It will be a slower sailing ship but that's just as well perhaps. I may have taken Acre by the time you arrive and then you can be lodged there."

"So you agree?" Joanna exclaimed. "We are to go?"

Richard sighed, then smiled at her. "You always were a headstrong and persuasive little chit! Yes, I agree. But no delays, mind! We sail within days."

℞ ✿ ℟

Joanna lifted her skirts to run up the steps to the aftercastle, with Berengaria following more decorously behind her. From there, leaning against the thigh-high crenelated wooden walls, they could look out over the harbor of Messina. Richard had already left the ship and was standing on the quay, shading his eyes from the sun. Joanna could see his swift galley, the *Trenche-la-Mer*, Sea Cleaver, tied up further down the harbor. More than 150 vessels rocked gently side by side in the harbor, their ropes creaking and relaxing in turn. Joanna and Berengaria were embarked on a large dromond, less swift than a galley but with more room for all their baggage and attendants. There were other dromonds among the galleys, which would carry soldiers and horses and fodder. Some were already loaded with engines and sling stones and mangonels.

"Did King Philip have this many ships?" Berengaria asked, looking out at the forest of masts.

"I think not, though I didn't see him leave. Of course, many of his men left before him, before Christmas, even. And Philip slunk off so suddenly, with hardly any warning to anyone. He couldn't bear to meet you!"

"But they are reconciled, aren't they? King Philip and your brother, I mean."

"Oh yes. Count Philip of Flanders finally arbitrated between them. It was agreed that Richard could not be expected to marry Alice in the circumstances. But I don't think Philip has forgiven it, for all that."

"Poor Alice," Berengaria said. "I can't help feeling sorry for her. She is over thirty now and quite unmarriageable."

They watched the last chests being carried on board.

"I heard that Alice is in Rouen, under close guard," Berengaria said. "Queen Eleanor freed all the prisoners but her mercy didn't extend to Alice. Alice will be held there until the

Crusade is over, and then, who knows?"

"Poor Alice indeed!" Joanna put her head back, feeling the sun on her face and breathing in the salt air. "Berengaria, I don't think I would change places with anyone in the world at this moment! To be going on an adventure like this is marvelous! Thank you for backing me up."

Down in the waist of the ship the oarsmen had settled on their benches. Their oars were still shipped. Out beyond them, Joanna could see the boat that would tow them out of the line at the quayside. The ropes were thrown on board. The master stood on the forecastle. On either side of him, the royal flags of Navarre and Sicily fluttered in the breeze, and at the head of the tall mast, Richard's standard, with its three golden leopards on a scarlet background, flapped steadily.

There was a sudden jerk. Joanna turned and held the rail. The ship was moving slowly from the quay. Richard raised his hand and waved to her.

"I'll see you in Acre!" He shouted. "I'll be there before you in *Trenche-la-Mer.*"

It had been only two days since she had suggested accompanying Berengaria, back in that little sun-filled chamber in Mategrifon. She could see the fortress now, its wooden turrets and battlements rearing up against the long grey line of the walls of Messina. Her mother had left on the following day, anxious to be back in England to straighten out the confusion there, and Joanna's old nurse and those of her attendants who were not going to the Holy Land with her, had gone with the Queen. Nurse had fretted and fussed over this sudden departure, but she dared not miss this chance of a safe escort and somehow she had been ready, though still complaining. Tears ran down her face as she kissed Joanna goodbye.

"You take care of yourself, my lamb, in those heathen lands. Don't drink the water and don't go out in the sun."

"I'll be all right, Nounou. *You* take care of *yourself.* You'll be glad to be back in Anjou, won't you?"

"There's no one there now," Nurse said, sniffing. "My sister is dead ..."

"Well, your nephew will welcome you, I'm sure. And I shall only be gone a year or so, perhaps only six months. I promise I'll come and see you first thing when we get back." Joanna did not want her happiness marred by the slightest disappointments anywhere. She assured herself that Nurse would cheer up as soon as she was really on her way home to Anjou and she bid her farewell dry-eyed.

The dromond was slipping smoothly across the harbor waters. As they pulled away, she could see the walls of Messina spreading out and above them, the tower of the royal palace, no longer flying Philip's standard, but Tancred's. She folded her lips and stared at it.

"Tancred will be in trouble soon," she said. "Henry of Hohenstaufen is in Italy and it can't be long now before he invades."

"*Emperor* Henry, you mean," Berengaria corrected her. "Your mother said she had met him south of Milan. He was on his way to Rome for his coronation. With Empress Constance."

"I can't believe Constance is the Holy Roman Empress now. When I first arrived in Sicily, I thought her a dowdy frumpish old thing. She used to lecture me on," she pursed up her lips, "*frivolous and worldly pursuits.*' I would never have thought to see her Empress. But then I wouldn't have imagined that horrid little Tancred King of Sicily either."

"But Richard has recognized him?"

"Yes, yes, Richard and Tancred swore friendship and exchanged gifts and so on. Tancred gave Richard some ships and Richard gave *him* King Arthur's sword, Excalibur."

"What! The sword they just unearthed in Glastonbury? *That* was a handsome gift! If Tancred believes it really is King Arthur's sword." And Berengaria looked at her with a little smile. Once again, Joanna saw her quick intelligence.

"I don't believe he does. Tancred is shrewd, if nothing else. But of course he didn't say so to Richard. I'm sure he was all oily flattery and disgusting deference. But Excalibur or not, it won't be much help to him against the Empire when they attack."

She put her face back and felt the breeze tug at her hair. The ship was rocking more as they neared the harbor mouth.

"Oh Lord, I'm so happy! I just hope to God the journey won't be anything like the terrible crossing of the Mediterranean when I first came to Sicily. I was horribly sick all the way. But this ship is large and stable and I'm older now. I was only eleven then. God, it was ages ago! I think I was sick with nervousness as much as anything else. Going to an unknown country and an unknown husband, for all I knew for the rest of my life. This is different."

"Yes, you were very young. I was lucky that my father, and then my brother, allowed me to stay single until I agreed to a marriage. I know my aunt Margaret was very homesick when she went to Sicily to marry your William's father."

"Of course, I had forgotten that Queen Margaret was your aunt." Joanna shot a quick look at Berengaria. "So you refused all earlier matches, but were willing to marry Richard?"

"How could I ever hope for anyone better? And besides, I had met him with my brother Sancho."

She said no more, but the two women smiled at each other. *Of course*, thought Joanna, *how could she not have been impressed by Richard, handsome and energetic and always the cynosure of all eyes.*

From the deck below came a rattle as oars slid through the openings. The ship seemed to hesitate for a moment and then there was a *thump* as the keel hit the first wave outside the harbor walls. The galley master was walking up and down, chanting rhythmically as the oarsmen leaned forward to pull.

Up on the forecastle, the master squinted at the sky and held up a finger to test the wind. She saw him turn and shout orders to the men on deck. A dozen of them, barefoot, suntanned in sleeveless leather jerkins, leapt to the single great mast and swarmed up it, crawling out at the top along the yardarm like monkeys. Below them, others sprang to the sheets. The halyards were untied and the great sail billowed down, showing the Plantagenet leopards. The wind filled it and the ship slewed to starboard. Below her feet, Joanna heard a little shriek and then giggles as someone presumably fell or staggered.

From here they could see the hills around Messina, still green and flecked with yellow spring flowers. Soon the sun would burn the hillsides to a golden-brown, but she would not be there to see it. Joanna felt the ties that bound her to Sicily snap, one by one, irrevocably, as the ship drew further away.

She thought of William as she stared back at his kingdom. They were already calling him William the Good. It had been a good marriage for her, all things considered, but she felt no pain now that it was over. She had realized her childhood ambition, to be a Queen. It had not, after all, been as satisfying as she had thought. At last she felt free to stop trying to be her mother and to be herself. No longer King Henry's youngest daughter, no longer King William's wife. She was Joanna, herself. As she watched the coast of Sicily spread out before her, she felt not loss, but liberation. For better or worse, that chapter of her life was closed.

The rowers banked their oars; the wind was strong enough for sail alone. It was a good omen, she thought. She turned her face away from the retreating coast of Sicily and looked ahead, past her own Sicilian standard flying bravely at the bow, across the choppy, sun-flecked waves, toward the Holy Land. Three weeks and they would be there! She breathed a deep breath of pure exultation. She was young, she was beautiful, she was a Queen, and rich, and above all, she was free! Everything lay before her: the adventure of a lifetime, travel ... Again the thought of that handsome knight Raymond de Saint-Gilles slid into her mind. He would be in Acre before her, she would see him again. She thought he would not be averse to a little harmless flirtation, at least. Firmly, she pushed the thought from her mind. They were on a Crusade, a holy endeavor, and she should not sully it, even with her thoughts. At the end of the journey lay Jerusalem, the Eternal City, itself.

She flung her arms out in joy and the ship hit a wave and knocked her, staggering sideways, into Berengaria's arms. Spray flew up and splashed them. They giggled and then, helplessly, began to laugh until tears ran to mingle with the salt spray on their cheeks.

The sun stood high above the mast and the ship pulled strongly toward the golden East.

AUTHOR'S NOTE

All the characters in this book are historically accurate, as far as I can ascertain, with the exception of Nounou, Joanna's nurse; Adèle, Joanna's lady-in-waiting; and Master Hubert, the pastry cook in Poitiers. However, she must have had a nurse, ladies-in-waiting, and cooks, so I have only invented the names, not the positions. Similarly, for the events: I invented the incident of Raymond asking Joanna for a favor at the tournament, but otherwise it all happened as described. The questions posed at the famous (or infamous) Courts of Love are actual questions they discussed; Chrétien de Troyes was in fact patronized by Marie de Champagne and the quotations from his work are actual.

I have anglicized some names for simplification: Henry of Hohenstaufen was in reality Heinrich, Philip was Philippe and Alice was Alys, though medieval spellings varied a good deal. I have made no attempt to reproduce medieval speech as no one would understand it. To them, of course, they sounded completely contemporaneous, so I have used standard English and tried to avoid anachronisms. In some instances, the speeches are historical, but I have modernized them.

In later years, Eleanor, Joanna's younger sister, wife of King Alfonso of Castile, had 13 children, of whom 9 survived. Two of her daughters became nuns and one, Blanca (Blanche) became the mother of a saint. I had this in mind when I wrote the conversation between Eleanor and Joanna before the former's departure for Castile.

Marguerite, wife of Young Henry, married for a second time to King Bela of Hungary in 1186. She was widowed a second time in 1196 and died on pilgrimage to the Holy Land in 1197, just days after her arrival there. She was 39.

Alice was betrothed to Richard from 1169 until 1191, when Richard married Berengaria. Her brother, King Philip of France, then suggested she should marry Richard's younger brother John, but Queen Eleanor prevented this match. She finally married the Count of Ponthieu in 1195, when she was 35. Her daughter Marie was the grandmother of Edward I of England, so Alice did eventually become ancestor of the English royal family.

Tancred remained King of Sicily until his death in 1194 when the throne passed to his young son William. Henry, the Holy Roman Emperor, invaded Sicily the same year and took the island as part of his province.

GLOSSARY OF MEDIEVAL TERMS USED

Aftercastle: structure at the stern of a sailing ship, usually housing the captain's cabin and perhaps other cabins. Forward on the ship was the forecastle, or fo'c's'le, with the sailors' living quarters.

Almoner: religious functionary whose duty was to distribute alms to the poor. Kings, bishops, and nobles had an almoner in their employ.

Aumbry: small cupboard

Baldaquin: a ceremonial canopy, usually of fabric, over a throne or procession or dais

Bliaut: woman's over-garment with a voluminous skirt and fitted bodice, usually with sleeves fitted to the elbow and then draping to the floor

Brancher: a young bird (such as a fledgling hawk) that has left the nest and taken to the branches. A falconing term; see also eyases, seeled, jesses, merling, tiercel, creance

Buttery: not, as you might think, a place for butter, but a storeroom for wine and liquor (from butt, or wine cask)

Chapmen: merchants

Creance: a line used to leash a hawk during training

Crupper: leather strap fastened to the saddle of a harness and looping under the tail of a horse to prevent the harness from slipping forward

Dalmatic: long wide-sleeved tunic worn by bishops and monarchs

Destrier: a knight's warhorse; see also palfrey

Dromon: large medieval ship

Ewerer: this one is easy to guess; he was the servant who brought water to the nobles at table and poured from his ewer

Eyases: an unfledged bird, a nestling hawk

Fibula: in this context, not a bone, but a brooch

Free lance: an expression that has survived to modern times; originally a mercenary soldier or knight who fought for himself, not under the colors of an overlord

Frumenty: a popular dish made primarily from cracked wheat, with milk and eggs added, or almonds, currants, saffron, honey, etc.

Gambesons: a quilted jacket worn under armor or on its own

Garderobe: obviously meant wardrobe originally, and was still used for that, but in Joanna's age had become the euphemism for the latrine set into the outer castle wall directly above the moat usually

Hanap: rich goblet

Hauberk: a shirt of mail

Jesses: a short strap fastened around the leg of a hawk

Langue d'oc: language of Southern France. When the Romans colonized Gaul, they brought with them the Latin language. There was, curiously, no word for "yes" in Latin; they used the phrase *"hoc ille"* or, roughly, "this is it". In the South, they shortened this to "hoc", then to just "oc". In the North they used the second word, "ille", which became elided in time to "oïl". So the two languages, in Joanna's time, were known as langue d'oc (language of oc) and langue d'oïl (language of oïl). The latter is the ancestor of modern French as "oïl" in time became "oui". Langue d'oc is still spoken, or understood, as Provençal in France and Catalan in Spain. Joanna spoke both forms of French.

Lists: the enclosed field of combat at a tournament

Mangonel: military machine for hurling stones and other missiles

Merling: a small falcon

Mesnie: military personnel of a castle household; more loosely, a group of knights attached to a feudal lord

Miniver: a white or light gray fur

Necromancer: a sorcerer or magician

Outremer: literally, overseas; referred to the Holy Land

Palfrey: a lighter-weight riding horse, popular with noble ladies

Pallet: a simple bed or mattress, filled with straw or hay, usually for servants to sleep on

Panter: keeper of the pantry, but specifically in charge of bread ("pan")

Pleasance: a place laid out as a pleasure garden or promenade

Quintain: an object mounted on a post used as a target in jousting exercises

Seeled: not a typo for "sealed". They used to sew closed the eyes of young falcons during parts of their training; this was called "seeling".

Seneschal: an important post, the seneschal was in charge of all domestic arrangements in a medieval household

Sexfoil: sixfold

Sirventes: a medieval poem or song of satirical character

Sixte/ Nones/ Vespers/ Prime/ Matins: In a time without clocks or watches, time was governed by church bells ringing at set hours. Sexte was midday, Nones 3 PM, Vespers 6 PM, Compline 9 PM, Matins midnight, Lauds 3 AM, Prime 6 AM, Tierce 9 AM. The origins of the words from Latin is pretty clear: Prime was the first hour of the day (time to go to work), Tierce the third hour, Sexte the sixth, Nones the ninth, Vespers (end of the working day). The monks measured time with water clocks or sundials, none of them very reliable.

Solar: the solar was a room, generally on an upper floor, for the private use of the lord and especially the noble ladies of the family. The Great Hall on the ground floor was where everyone, noble or servant, ate, lived, and often slept. The family's quarters were upstairs away from all this in the solar. Perhaps called a solar because it let more sun in? (entirely hypothetical)

Steward: in charge of the whole household, basically a deputy to the lord himself, often of noble family

Subtlety: elaborate form of dish often for entertainment as much as for consumption

Sumpter: a pack animal

Tansy: an herb

Tiercel: a mala hawk

Trencher: originally, a trencher was a slice of bread (French "tranche") used to serve food; our expression "a good trencherman" would be someone with a hearty appetite who would consume the trencher or plate after eating all the food on it! Later it came to mean a simple wooden plate. It was only at grand banquets that they would have used anything else. Typically, one trencher was shared by two people. They brought their own knives to the table. Forks were virtually unknown except in Byzantium. People ate with their hands.

Triclinium: a dining couch along three sides of a table

Vavassor: a vassal or tenant of a baron

Vielle: a medieval stringed instrument similar to a modern violin

RECOMMENDED READING

Eleanor of Aquitaine and the Four Kings, by Amy Kelly, 1950. This was the book that first got me interested in Joanna and her story.

Eleanor of Aquitaine, by Marion Meade, 1977.

The Kingdom in the Sun, by John Julius Norwich, 1970.

I used many reference volumes but, on the lighter side, also enjoyed a series of murder mysteries set in the age of Henry II by Ariana Franklin. The first in this series was *Mistress of the Art of Death*, 2007. One of these books features Joanna on her way to Palermo: *A Murderous Procession*, by Ariana Franklin, 2010.

I was looking forward to more of these, but sadly, the author died in 2011.

ABOUT THE AUTHOR

Hilary Foister Benford grew up in England. As a child, she experienced the blitz bombings of World War II around London. She has a degree in French literature from the University of London and also studied in Cambridge, Strasbourg, and Paris. As a student, she worked various jobs in France as a waitress, hotel receptionist, chambermaid, and switchboard operator. She taught English at a French high school for a year and then taught French in both England and California. She married an American physicist and they have two children.

She co-authored *Timescape* with her brother-in-law Gregory Benford in 1980.

She has traveled extensively in 40 countries and still loves to travel. She has made a point of visiting all the sites where Joanna, sister of Richard Lionheart, lived, from Fontevrault to the Holy Land, from Sicily to Toulouse. She has a lifelong interest in history, languages, the Middle Ages, and her hobbies include genealogy, cooking, crosswords, and reading mysteries.

She currently lives with her husband in the San Francisco Bay Area.

IF YOU LIKED ...

If you liked *Sister of the Lionheart*, you might also enjoy:

Clockwork Angels
Beasts of Tabat
City of the Saints

OTHER WORDFIRE PRESS TITLES

Our list of other WordFire Press authors and titles is always growing.
To find out more and to see our selection of titles, visit us at:

wordfirepress.com

Made in the USA
Charleston, SC
28 August 2016